A SILENCE OF SHADOWS

THE WHISPERBOUND SERIES

1

ANNIE ANDERSON

A SILENCE OF SHADOWS
Whisperbound Book One
Annie Anderson
Published by Annie Anderson
Copyright © 2025 Annie Anderson

Edited by: Angela Sanders
Cover Art by: Tattered Quill Designs
All rights reserved.
Paperback ISBN: 978-1-960315-90-8
Hardcover ISBN: 978-1-960315-91-5

For the girls who keep their secrets behind scars and smirks, and for the boys stupid enough to fall for them anyway.

We are all broken, that's how the light gets in.

— ERNEST HEMINGWAY

WHISPERBOUND

A word once banned from royal records. A bond not spoken aloud, not marked, not claimed—only felt. It was said to exist between two souls when the tether between them becomes more powerful than any vow.

It is whispered that when Evara, the Goddess of the Dead, lays her hand on two souls, declaring that they will be each other's ruin, and Tharos, the God of Chaos and Will, dares them to choose each other anyway, the result is a bond stronger than death.

The Whisperbound are not chosen by Fate. They are forged in blood.

One taste.

One drop.

That is all it takes.

When blood is shared between two souls meant to

be bound, the magic answers. And once it answers, it never releases its hold.

The bond does not scream—it whispers. Quietly. Eternally. Through blood, through bone, through silence.

Those bound this way can sense each other across cities. Hear what isn't said. Feel what the other bleeds.

To drink from your Whisperbound mate is to seal the tie.

To deny it... is to suffer until madness takes root.

One drop is instinct.

Two is truth.

Three is forever.

I caught the glass before it hit the ground, the thick-cut crystal still cold from the spelled liquor. The amber liquid sloshed up the side of the glass, but nary a drop spilled.

This little feat wasn't magic—not really—simply instinct, muscle memory. Well, that, and the shriek of alarm blaring in the thoughts of the witch who nearly elbowed it off the bar.

My eye twitched, a spike of pain blooming in my temples at the sheer volume of her mind.

Shit, not again.

The screech of her consciousness signaled that it was time to pay Sable a visit, and much sooner than I'd like. It had only been three weeks since she'd whipped up the last suppression elixir instead of the usual six. At this rate, I'd be broke long before I found a way to stop the constant barrage of other people's minds invading mine.

One would think I'd be used to the incessant buzzing filling my head, but as I aged, the thoughts only got louder, more painful, more debilitating. If I didn't want to drink myself into an early grave or throw myself off a cliff, suppression was the only way to go. Plus, if anyone ever found out about my little talent, I'd be six feet under before I could even blink.

Telepathy was forbidden. Not frowned upon, not illegal. Banned. There was no trial, no mercy. If anyone ever found out what I could do, I wouldn't just disappear—I'd be erased along with everyone I'd ever cared about.

Without a word, I slid the glass back in front of her, all too eager to get away from the witch. She didn't so much as look at me, too deep in conversation with her companion—something about cursed heirlooms—her thoughts screaming about a grandmother who wouldn't die fast enough.

Charming.

The Lock & Key thrummed—not from music, but from life. Magic hummed under the floorboards, tangled in the laughter, the deals, the lies my patrons thought were safe to tell here. They weren't—especially not when I was behind the bar. What was said and left unsaid had never been safe from me.

I'd built this place brick by brick, claiming a little slice of the Divide for myself.

The Divide was supposed to be neutral ground—sacred, lawless, and inconvenient enough for the Crown to ignore unless it became useful. But neutrality didn't mean safety, and it sure as hell didn't mean peace.

When I first arrived, this corner of it had been left in complete ruin. Half a roof, rotting floorboards, and the kind of stench that kept even the desperate away. Everyone said I was wasting my time, but I saw the bones of something better. Something mine. With no family and no memory of my past before I'd woken up on the steps of an orphanage when I was just a child, it had been perfect for someone like me—a forgotten piece of land that no one cared about, just aching to be taken care of.

So I carved it out. Fortified it. Ward by ward, brick by brick, blood offering by blood offering. I'd scrimped and saved, stolen when I needed to, and done jobs I wasn't proud of, but the bar was mine.

Now the Lock & Key stood like an anchor in the chaos. A haven for people who didn't belong anywhere else. A place where magic pulsed through the woodwork, the liquor was spelled, and secrets spilled faster than the drinks.

Some came here for sanctuary. Some came for vice. All of them came thinking this place wouldn't judge them. They were wrong. I judged everyone. But I let them stay, anyway—so long as they played by the rules.

Moving on with a fresh drink in hand, I weaved through the crowd of regulars and sketchy newcomers to deliver the concoction to Jex before swiping away his empty. He tipped his horns to me, his gray skin shimmering in the dim light. Most people assumed he was just another patron—big, brooding, covered in jagged ink that crawled up his throat and down both arms. But Jex wasn't here to drink. He was here to keep the peace.

And by peace, I meant bones intact and blood off my floors.

I gave him a nod and turned toward the bar, only to find Rhett already in my way, leaning against the counter like he hadn't a care in the world.

"You spoil him, you know," he signed, his fingers quick and teasing. Rhett signed smoothly, one of maybe a dozen people in this room who knew how.

He hadn't always. But working with me meant adapting—or leaving. Most regulars picked it up fast. The ones who didn't either got tired of guessing or learned the hard way that I didn't do repeats. Letting them believe I was deaf just made everything easier.

No expectations. No small talk. No slipups.

The truth was, however, harder. I wasn't deaf, I just couldn't speak. And if I pretended I couldn't hear anything at all, I wouldn't react to every errant thought that sliced like a pickax through my brain.

Still, I didn't dignify his teasing with a response. Instead, I snagged the pricey bottle of Amoranthe he'd failed to recork and bumped it into his chest. Spilling that particular brew wouldn't just cost us the spelled liquid. It would turn my bar into a giant orgy.

No, thank you.

He caught it one-handed, grinning. "Admit it. You'd miss me if I died."

I rolled my eyes and kept walking, but he was right. I would miss him—even if he drove me to drink most nights.

Rhett was infuriating—too pretty, too smug, and entirely too good at reading people without needing mind magic. If anyone in this place suspected the truth about me, it was him. And yet he stayed, working beside me like this bar was his, too.

It wasn't, but I let him pretend.

I kept moving, the regulars giving me a nod or a lift of the chin. The newcomers looked twice—first out of curiosity, and then because they realized I hadn't said a word. The smarter ones didn't ask questions. The cocky ones usually didn't last the night.

Moving from patron to patron, I refilled drinks, anticipating needs before they were spoken. Most didn't bother ordering. They'd learned. If I handed you something, it was what you wanted. Or what you needed. Those weren't always the same.

But the night seemed to be holding its breath, and it didn't know why yet.

Jex leaned against the far wall, arms crossed, observing the room with that bored, violent expression he wore right before someone lost teeth. A pair of rowdy wolf boys near the back caught his golden eyes and immediately remembered how to behave.

Rhett tossed a bar towel at me as he passed, grinning like he hadn't just left Amoranthe uncorked ten minutes ago.

"You missed one," he signed, jerking his chin toward a goblin waving a chipped mug.

I raised a brow, flipped him off, and topped off the mug, anyway. The goblin beamed like I'd handed him gold, his green skin wrinkling in delight.

Rhett laughed and moved on, dragging purple smoke through a glass with practiced ease. It condensed into a vibrant fuchsia liquid that shimmered in the light. Most people needed a spell or a chant for that kind of flair. Rhett did it with a flick of his fingers and a wink.

This was the rhythm, the pulse of the Lock & Key. It was organized chaos on sacred ground, and I loved every square inch of the place. The night buzzed around me—magic, memory, lust, and longing—all of it wrapped in whispers, soaked into the wood and the walls.

Then the door opened, and the whole place inhaled.

His mind brushed against mine—thick, cold, impenetrable—like falling into a frozen lake and realizing too late that there was no way back to the surface. I could barely catch a flicker of his thoughts, even though his mind pressed in on me as if it were seeking me out.

But one thought still slipped through.

She's not what I expected.

I looked up, finding him through the crowd as if he'd whispered right in my ear.

Kieran Veyne. Second-born prince. The king's favorite. And the one handed the Crown Province while his older brother got pushed to the edge of the map.

He waltzed into my bar like he owned the gods-be-damned foundation. Maybe his family had at one point, but he didn't own it now, and he sure as shit shouldn't have stepped one toe in a place like this.

The Divide was neutral territory, and the Lock & Key doubly so. Even royals obeyed the rules if they knew what was good for them.

But he walked in anyway, carved from shadow and arrogance. His coat caught the light as if it were stitched from midnight. Dark hair. Sharp cheekbones. Icy eyes that scanned the room, then landed on me and didn't move.

Every conversation nearby faltered.

A vampire girl at the bar went pale, like she'd just seen her worst nightmare in the flesh.

She wasn't wrong.

He approached with deliberate ease without so much as an ounce of posturing or flair, just quiet confidence, and something dangerous curled beneath his skin.

Before he approached the bar, I was already pouring his drink.

He hadn't said a word, but the edges of his mind—intent, recognition, interest—were enough. They were blurry and far too slippery to hang onto, but they were there. He studied me for a moment and then pursed his lips as he examined the glass.

"Impressive trick. But I haven't ordered anything yet."

His voice was smooth like honeyed steel, low and deliberate—the kind of sound that could slice without ever raising in volume. I both cursed and rejoiced that I wasn't *really* deaf. A voice like that was meant to be heard.

Just not by me.

I slid the glass toward him. Dark liquor, neat and laced with a bitter tincture meant for clarity and caution, something he needed if he thought waltzing through the Divide was a good idea.

Meeting his gaze, I signed slowly and deliberately, "Drink it or don't. Doesn't matter to me either way. But you'll need it if you want to stay."

His brow ticked up just slightly, like he was trying to decide whether I'd just insulted him or read him for filth, but either way, he'd understood me. This meant one of two things—he'd either studied sign language for Court, or someone had warned him about the "deaf" bartender long before he'd ever stepped into my bar.

I was betting on the latter and that did not give me the warm and fuzzies.

He lifted the glass, sniffed the concoction like a food critic, and sipped as if he expected disappointment. Surprise flickered across his face—quick, but there—before he wiped it clean. The soft *clink* of glass on wood followed, and I fought the urge to flinch.

"Not bad."

Rhett leaned in beside me, eyebrow cocked as his shoulder bumped mine. "Was that supposed to be a compliment? You've got to do better than that, man."

Kieran didn't look at him at first, just kept his eyes on me. Those icy blues were measuring, sizing me up in a way that left me unsettled. Normally, if someone were staring at me like that, I'd be privy to every thought in their brain, but not Kieran. He was just as enigmatic then as he was since he'd set foot in my bar.

And I didn't like it one bit.

Then, slowly, he turned his head, eyeing the spot where Rhett touched me.

Rhett held his gaze with a lazy smile as he held up his hands in surrender. "Right. Your funeral," he muttered, and slipped back down the bar.

I reached for the nearest glass, wiping it with a cloth

I didn't need. Kieran didn't move, didn't speak. He just watched me, and somewhere in that stillness, my control slipped—just for a second. It was long enough to feel something cold and sharp skimming the edge of the room.

Not thought. Not spell. Just... *intent*. And it wasn't his.

The moment I recognized that cold, quiet threat that had just slithered into my bar wasn't coming from Kieran Veyne, the first attack hit.

The front window shattered inward in a burst of glass and smoke. Screams tore through the room. Magic surged—raw and uncontrolled—as a wardstone detonated above the door in a flash of acidic green light.

A hexbomb—the kind that didn't warn, it confused, it maimed, it *killed*. And it sure as Vireth wasn't one of mine. A cloaked figure stepped through the acrid haze, blade in hand, eyes locked on the bar, on *him*. He didn't speak, but his mind screamed with purpose.

Strike fast. Kill the prince. No witnesses.

I moved before the thought finished forming. My hand closed around the small, silver-edged paring knife Rhett had left by the fruit tray: a lifeline I hadn't known I'd needed until just that moment.

And then I threw.

In the midst of the chaos and frightened patrons, the blade caught the attacker right under his collarbone just as he lunged. He roared in pain before his scream cut off in a gurgle as he crumbled to the ground. And then all seven hells broke loose.

Another looming figure appeared near the back—taller, faster. Magic danced along their fingertips, bright and crackling. They raised a hand to cast, cloudy-blue mist coating his fingers before Jex *moved*.

One moment he was against the wall, and the next he had the caster by the throat, slamming them into a support pillar hard enough to splinter the wood. His golden eyes gleamed as a demonic smile curled his lips in delight.

To my left, another attacker darted toward the goblin booth. I vaulted the bar, heart pounding as I grabbed the nearest bottle—heavy in my hand, cold, familiar—then hurled it with every ounce of fury I had. The glass shattered across his face, and the freezing enchantment inside burst into a cloud of frost. He stumbled back, cursing, clawing at his withering skin as it blackened and cracked.

Kieran hadn't moved, not at first, but now he was a blur of motion and death.

He disarmed the fourth one in a single, fluid motion—twisting the weapon from his hand, driving his elbow into their throat, and sinking the attacker's own wicked dagger into his ribs before he hit the floor.

It wasn't flashy or panicked. Kieran's movements were simply a level of precision that was out of most people's reach. Then again, being a centuries-old vampire had its perks.

By the time the smoke cleared, three attackers were dead, their blood staining the wood floor bad enough that it would take years to kill the smell. One moaned on the ground, clutching his ruined face.

Spelled mist curled toward the ceiling as I surveyed the damage to my one and only livelihood. Tables and chairs were overturned, some broken in half. Bottles of spelled liquor and glass littered the bar and floor, smashed into a million pieces as their contents burned through the rough-hewed planks. Someone was crying softly behind the counter, their frightened, almost child-like thoughts nearly bringing tears to my eyes.

Rhett was already herding patrons toward the cellar door. Jex dragged the surviving attacker toward the back, blood streaking the floor behind him.

Yanking my knife from the corpse at my feet, I straightened slowly, my heartbeat thundering in my ears. Everything I'd built, everything I'd worked for, felt like it was slipping away, my tenuous hold on my life falling like sand through my fingertips. My bar was in shambles, and there was no way to pay to fix it. The prince of Morathen watched me use my ability, and now there were dead bodies littering my floor.

The room had gone silent. Not quiet—silent. Like even the magic was holding its breath. In that hush, I stood over the body, weapon dripping, heart pounding, no longer invisible. I wasn't just the mute bartender anymore—not after this. Not with blood on my hands and a corpse at my feet.

I'd just made myself a target.

Not because I killed him, but because of how I knew to do it. The weight of every secret I'd ever kept settled on my shoulders, and still, I didn't move. Couldn't.

Because the moment I did, I'd have to face what came next.

Then I lifted my gaze to his.

Kieran looked at me, really looked.

His gaze drifted to the velvet choker at my throat like he knew what was behind it. Then to the attacker at his feet. Then to the blood staining my palm.

"Who the hell are you?" he murmured.

Not curious. Not impressed.

Just... *interested*.

And I still had no way to answer.

CHAPTER 2
KIERAN

Blood smelled the same no matter where you spilled it. Fresh or old, royal or gutter-born—it clung to wood and stone with a stubbornness that no soap or spell could erase.

The Lock & Key would reek of it for weeks until time finally stole it like it did all things.

And still, despite the blood and bile, despite the threat still clinging to the air, I couldn't take my eyes off her.

She stood over the corpse with a paring knife dripping red, her chest rising too fast as defiance burned in her gaze. She was the sort of woman who should've been trembling, screaming, running, and yet she hadn't flinched when the first strike came. She'd moved like she'd seen it before anyone else. Like she'd *known*.

Which was precisely why I was here.

My intel had painted her as an oddity. A bartender who never spoke. One who never asked for orders but always delivered the right drink. "Deaf," they'd said. Mute. Broken. A curiosity in a world where true psychics were rarer than godsdamned miracles.

From afar, I'd had her watched by one of the few allies I still trusted, but the moment the attacks on my Court grew too precise, too well-timed, I knew curiosity wasn't enough. I needed certainty—needed my eyes on her, and proof she was everything I thought she was. Because I was running out of time.

Servants I'd relied on had wound up dead. Alliances —once concrete—frayed overnight. Poison slipped past tasters, spells snuck past wards. It wasn't chance. It was someone inside my own walls, moving pieces I couldn't see.

And if I were to root out a traitor in my own Court, I needed more than a blade or a spy. I needed foresight. I needed the one thing even the oldest of us couldn't beg, borrow, or steal—someone who could see the strike before it fell. Tonight had just proven what the whispers suggested: Merrit Locke wasn't just guessing. She'd thrown that knife before even *I* could react. She'd known it was going to happen.

Most psychics were rare—my father saw to that. Precogs were rarer still. And if she truly was one…

I stood over the body, but it wasn't the corpse that held my attention. It was her.

The little paring knife she'd yanked from the assassin's chest was still clutched in her hand, blood slicking her fingers where it had slipped against the hilt. Silent. Watchful. Defiant. Secrets wrapped in silk.

Not just a bartender.

Not just a survivor.

Maybe exactly what I needed.

A low groan pulled my attention to the far side of the room. The horned brute who'd been leaning against the wall earlier now dragged the last surviving attacker toward the cellar, golden eyes alight with something that looked far too much like pleasure, blood streaking the floor in his wake.

"I want him alive," I growled, though my order was mostly ignored.

The brute—Jex, I'd heard him called—didn't so much as acknowledge me. His golden eyes flicked to Merrit, waiting for her approval. It was only when she gave him a simple tilt of her chin did he shift course, dragging the half-dead would-be assassin back toward us. Without ceremony, the demon snatched up a fallen chair and planted the man on it, slamming his clawed hands down on the bleeding man's shoulders.

"You stay," Jex said, wordless grit in the set of his jaw. He waited for Merrit's nod before he eased away.

Interesting. It had been a long time since I'd been defied so openly, but somehow, I couldn't seem to fault him. I respected loyalty—even if it wasn't to me.

The other one—the bartender with the smug grin—had already started hustling patrons toward the door, but too many lingered, eyes wide, stupidly rooted in place. Their fear stank, sour and acrid, their heartbeats too loud, their murmurs grating.

"Out," I snapped, voice carrying with the steel of command. "Unless you want your blood staining these floors next."

That did it. Chairs scraped. Bottles toppled. A rush of bodies pushed for the door.

But Merrit didn't move. Instead, she threw her knife down—steel tip biting into wood with a *crack* that made even the last cowards flinch. Her hands cut the air, sharp and furious. "Who the fuck do you think you are, walking into my bar and giving orders?"

A challenge. Direct. Reckless. The kind of fury that should have driven me back but instead lodged under my skin, hot and consuming. Gods, she fascinated me —and that was dangerous. It led to weakness. And weakness had no place in my Court. Yet here I was, already counting the beats of her pulse like they mattered.

She turned—not to me, but to her own men. Her fingers moved with clipped authority. "Rhett. Jex. Out."

The smug bartender froze mid-step, mouth opening like he'd argue. Jex didn't budge at all, his golden eyes slicing to her, waiting for the smallest shake of her head to countermand her order.

"Now," she signed again, harder, stabbing her hand toward the cellar door.

Rhett muttered something under his breath but obeyed. Jex lingered, muscles tight, until she gave him a look that brooked no debate. Only then did he finally stalk toward the back, his gaze never leaving her until the last second.

And just like that, the Lock & Key emptied around us.

The assassin tried to laugh, wet and bubbling. "Prince doesn't own the Divide," he spat, hatred carried in every syllable.

I didn't bother answering him. He wasn't walking out of here anyway.

No—the only one who mattered was the woman standing in front of me, silent but blazing, as if the whole damned bar still belonged to her alone.

"Who sent you?" I demanded, threading influence into the edges of my voice. The kind that loosened tongues, even when men thought they had nothing to lose.

"No one has to send me to kill a leech," he scoffed, spitting blood between red-stained teeth.

Not a professional's answer. No sigils etched into his skin, no handler's cant to hide behind. Just raw resent-ment, the kind that festered in the Divide until it curdled into violence. It meant the threat hadn't been organized, not in this man at least. Diffuse. Local. But no less dangerous, because hatred this common was harder to stamp out.

His eyes flicked sideways, shoulders coiling. I smelled the shift in him before he moved—adrenaline cold as steel, panic cutting through the musk of ale, soot, and old blood.

Another strike coming—I sensed it.

I reached for my dagger—too slow.

The assassin lurched to his feet, his wounded side tearing open with the effort, blood spattering the floor in thick arcs. He still managed to get his hand on the hilt at his hip—

And Merrit moved.

Quick as thought, she was at my side, her fingers closing over the dagger at my belt before I'd drawn it. One savage slash, clean as a soldier's drill, and the assassin's arm split open to the bone before his weapon cleared its sheath. His scream tore through the air, high and wet, before he collapsed back onto the chair, disarmed and useless.

My own blade was still warm in her hand. Not luck. Not instinct. She'd *known*. Again.

She didn't even look at me when she shoved the hilt into my palm, blood slicking our skin where it passed between us. Warmth and defiance, all pressed into me in a single heartbeat. Then she wiped the mess against my coat as though I were a servant boy instead of a prince. Audacity that should have enraged me—but instead, left her touch burning against my hand long after it was gone.

"You enjoy stealing from royalty?" I signed, sharp and mocking.

Her mouth curved—barely. A not-smile, all venom. Her fingers answered quick and biting. "Better than letting royalty get killed in my bar."

I barked a low laugh before I could stop it. Reckless woman.

The tavern was empty now—chairs overturned, glass glittering like stars across the floor. Only the three of us remained: her, the assassin bleeding into his own lap, and me. The silence felt thicker for it, the kind that pressed against the skin.

I stepped closer, the sound of my boots loud in the hush. The assassin groaned, but I barely spared him a glance. All my focus was on her. Closer, I caught the subtler notes under the stench of smoke and blood: leather worn smooth by years of use, potent herbs clinging to her clothes, something clean and citrus-bright beneath it all. No perfume. No polish. Just her.

And that velvet ribbon at her throat—high, deliberate, hiding what she didn't want the world to see. Scar or shame, it didn't matter. I wanted to tear it loose, to see what lay beneath, though I already knew whatever it was would cut me deeper than any blade.

"You're wasted here," I said aloud, low enough the words were almost a growl. Then I lifted my hands, precise, deliberate, each motion edged with command. "Come with me to Court. You'd have protection. Purpose. You'd be useful instead of squandered."

Her fingers curled into a fist before shaping her answer: "No."

No hesitation. No bargaining. Just flat refusal.

I smiled, sharp enough to bare a hint of fang. I signed as I said it, deliberate and cool: "Most people would leap at the chance to step out of this gutter and into power."

Her hands moved fast, furious: "And you wonder why no one likes royalty. Go ask those 'most people.' I'm not them."

Gods, she was maddening. Defiance where queens bowed. I should've been furious. Instead, fascination burned hotter.

"You know," I said, tilting my head, letting the weight of the words settle between us, "I could make you say yes." My gaze caught hers, held it steady and intense. "Compulsion works when someone insists on holding my eyes the way you do. One word, and you'd be following me by dawn."

Her pulse jumped—I heard it, bright and quick at the base of her throat, a rhythm meant to tempt teeth. But she didn't look away. Her fingers carved her answer, unflinching as Fate: "Try it. See what happens." A dare. A promise. A challenge that dragged me closer when I should have turned away.

For one maddening heartbeat, I almost did. But compulsion was blunt force, and I wanted more than obedience. *Obedience breaks. Leverage lasts.*

My smile curled darker. I signed slow, deliberate: "No. Too easy. I prefer good, old-fashioned blackmail."

Her brows pinched—just the faintest fracture in that iron composure—before she caught it and masked it with steel.

I tapped the bar with one finger, slow, deliberate, letting the sound echo in the silence. "Word on the street is you owe the pack a tithe for this land. The Divide isn't as free as you all like to pretend. Your sanctuary—this bar—stands because they allow it. They could come tomorrow and burn this place to the ground, and no magistrate would stop them."

Her hands froze mid-motion, then tore through the air, furious. "How do you know about that?"

"Because it's my job to know what people owe. And because debt makes for useful leverage." I leaned closer, my voice lowering into something cold as my fingers sliced through the bitter tension coiling in the air. "You think tonight was chance? That knife you threw? You and I both know you didn't just get lucky. You saw it before it happened."

Her fingers clenched against the wood as she took a stuttered step backward, but she didn't deny it.

"That's what I need," I said, signing the words as I spoke them aloud. "Someone who can see before the strike falls. I have traitors in my Court, moving pieces I can't catch. If you are what the whispers claim, you'll help me root them out."

Her jaw tightened, eyes like glass catching light. "And if I say no?"

"Then the pack remembers their tithe," I said smoothly, signing methodically. "They decide your debt isn't worth the trouble of collecting, and when that happens, the Lock & Key burns." I let the pause stretch, then added, "But if you serve me until the traitors are gone, the pack never comes. Your bar stands. And when my enemies fall, you walk away. Debt cleared. Free."

Her throat bobbed once against the velvet ribbon. Her hands slashed the air, clear and precise. "That's extortion."

"Semantics," I said, signing, lips curving in a humorless smile. "I could compel you, take your will with a word. But compulsion breaks people. I prefer bargains. Blackmail, if you like the uglier word. Trust me, it lasts longer."

She stared at me, jaw tight. Her hands moved, fast and sharp enough to sting the air. "You threaten my home. You threaten my people. I won't be bartered or sold." The signs were clipped, practical—anger with a seam of calculation beneath it.

She stepped forward until the space between us was a knife-blade. Close up, I could see the way her throat worked against velvet, the flare of her nostrils, the steady thump of a pulse that had no intention of quitting. She did not reel, did not shout. She signed again, the motion hard and clear: "I won't go with you."

Defiant. Bare. Useful.

I let the silence sit a breath, then forced the civility I needed. I rested my hands on the counter for a moment to steady myself and then signed, "There is a cancer in my Court. Men who move like shadows. My life"—The word caught on something I didn't soften—"is at risk."

I did not dress it as mercy. It was simply the truth, and I had learned the Court respected that more than pleading. She watched me. No pity showed in the planes of her face, only calculation.

The thing I wanted was not ownership of her person. It was sight. It was the one advantage I no longer possessed: the ability to know a strike before it hit. "You saw tonight. Twice." I kept my voice spare. "Saved my life. Twice. If you are what the whispers claim, you can help me find the ones who send steel into my rooms and poison my tables. I need someone who sees before it happens. I need an advisor who can anticipate a move I cannot."

Before Merrit could move again, I flipped the dagger in my grip. One clean thrust under the assassin's ribs, angled to the heart. His body jolted once, then slumped. Final. The kind of death that couldn't be undone.

Wiping the blade on his cloak, I let him fall into silence. Only then did I look back at her. She hadn't flinched, hadn't looked away. She'd watched me kill a man in her bar as though it bound us in blood. That same unyielding fire in her eyes didn't dim—it burned hotter. Gods, she intrigued me. A lure I knew would ruin me, but one I couldn't stop feeding on.

I let the dagger rest between us, hilt toward me, steel toward her, a promise and a threat in one. My hands shaped the words slow, deliberate: "This is what waits in my Court. Shadows with knives. Poisoners in my hall. I can't see them coming. But you can."

Her fingers flexed, sharp and incredulous. "You want me as your spy."

"Advisor," I corrected, sliding the blade back into its sheath. "My eyes where mine cannot reach. You tell me what you see before it strikes. You stand at my side until the traitors are found. Then you're free. Done."

She tilted her chin, unimpressed, but there was the smallest pause before her next sign. "No chains?"

I shook my head. "No chains. No leash. Just survival —for both of us."

Silence stretched. Her gaze flicked to the ruined bar, then back to me. Finally, she signed one word, clipped and brutal: "Fine."

The word was enough. More than enough.

I inclined my head, satisfaction curling low. "Dawn," I signed, precise as a contract. "You come with me. You advise. You stay until the work is finished. Then you walk."

She echoed the sign back—"Dawn"—expression unreadable.

The bargain was struck. Temporary, yes. Necessary, absolutely. And when the sun rose, Merrit Locke would step into my world not as a curiosity in a gutter bar, but as my newest—and most dangerous—advocate.

The rest I'd worry about later.

If there was a later.

CHAPTER 3
MERRIT

The Lock & Key had never been this quiet.

No laughter. No music. No clatter of glasses. Just overturned chairs and the copper stink of blood drying into the floorboards. I should've been scrubbing, trying to salvage what was left of my bar before the stain set in. Instead, I was shoving clothes into a satchel with hands that wouldn't stop shaking.

Not from fear. From fury.

Kieran Veyne thought he could walk in here, spill blood on my floor, and shackle me with a bargain I couldn't refuse. By dawn, I'd be in his Court—his "advisor," his leverage, his tether.

I should have left it alone. I should have let those men attack him. I should have let him die.

The satchel strap creaked under my grip as I tightened it, ready to run straight to Sable before the prince returned to collect his due. If I was going to survive Court, I needed more elixirs, more tricks to keep my secret buried where no vampire could dig it out.

The back door groaned, and I froze.

Rhett's voice carried first, low and tight, and I fought off the urge to flinch. "What the hell do you think you're doing?" Rhett signed, worry sharpened in his hands.

His mind was louder, panic in jagged shards. *Don't leave us. Don't do this.* Fear and anger tangled together until it scraped across my ribs. He was framed in the doorway, arms crossed, expression caught between concern and fury.

Behind him, Jex ducked through the frame, golden eyes already narrowing at the sight of my half-packed bag.

Shit.

"You planning a midnight vacation?" Rhett asked, his tone too light, the kind he used when he wanted to pick a fight. "Or were you gonna leave us a nice little note on the bar before you vanished?"

I didn't answer. My fingers just kept moving, deliberate, stuffing another shirt into the satchel. None of my clothes would be fit for Court but cramming them in a bag felt better than standing still.

Jex stepped closer, shoulders tense as he signed, his motions blunt as stone: "He made you a deal."

Not a question. A fact carved in granite. My hands

stilled on the buckle. A demon would know plenty about deals, and I'd just made one with the devil himself.

They hadn't heard what bargain had been struck, but they weren't stupid. They'd seen the way Kieran looked at me, the way the entire bar emptied around us, and now here I was, packing like the hounds of Tharos were already nipping at my heels.

Rhett swore under his breath. "Godsdammit, Merrit." He raked a hand through his hair, pacing a step before snapping back toward me. "Tell me I'm wrong," he demanded, his fingers shaking with fear or worry or maybe both. "Tell me you didn't just agree to walk into his gilded cage."

My hands moved before I thought better of it, rough and clipped. "I didn't have a choice."

"You always have a choice," Rhett shot back, reading me clean as ever, hands moving furiously. His voice cracked at the edges, like he was trying not to shout. His thoughts cracked harder—images of me chained in marble halls, a knife at my throat, blood blooming too fast to stop. "You could've told him to shove his bargain. You could've—"

"She saved his ass," Jex interjected, low and rumbling, golden eyes hard on me. "Twice." His jaw flexed as though the admission cost him. He signed almost mechanically, as if each word hurt his very soul.

Jex's thoughts were quieter, pressing like stone: *That's why he won't let go.*

My chest tightened. He wasn't wrong. But that didn't make it easier to hear.

Rhett swore again, softer this time. "You think men like him let go once they've got their claws in? He's not just gonna let you stroll back here when he's done sniffing around. Court eats people alive, Merrit. And you—" He broke off, shaking his head. "You don't belong to him."

"I know that." My fingers slashed the air. "That's why I'll survive it. Because I'll never belong to him."

The satchel snapped shut, buckle biting down with finality. I hoisted it over my shoulder, even as Rhett's mouth flattened into a line of protest and Jex's growl vibrated the walls.

"Then at least let us come," Rhett said finally, fingers moving as desperation edged past his anger. "If you're walking into that viper's nest, you're not doing it alone."

I slammed the satchel onto the bar so hard the bottles on the shelves rattled. My hands carved the air, sharper than any blade. "Do you think I want this? Do you think I planned for tonight?"

Rhett flinched at the force of it, but I wasn't done. My fingers moved fast, furious. "Look around. Broken chairs. Shattered glass. Stock ruined. Windows gone. I can't pay the tithe now—not this month, maybe not next. The pack will come calling, and when they do, they'll take more than money. They'll take this place. Everything I've bled for."

Rhett's mind spat curses—*We'll fight them. We'll fight everyone if we have to.* Jex's golden gaze burned, his thoughts little more than a vow carved in iron.

"So no," I signed, stabbing the air with each word, "I don't want him. I don't want his Court. I don't want to walk into his damned trap. But it's the only way to keep the Lock & Key alive."

Rhett opened his mouth, shut it, then scrubbed both hands over his face like he wanted to tear his own hair out. "You think he'll protect this place? You think he gives a shit about your bar?"

"No," I signed, my chest heaving. "But I do. And if I have to walk beside the devil himself to keep it standing, I will."

The silence stretched, heavy as stone, until Rhett exhaled hard and let his hands fall. "Then we'll hold it for you," he said, voice rough, his signs rougher. "Then let us watch it while you're gone."

My head snapped up.

He spread his arms, a crooked smile tugging at his mouth. "What? You think we'll just let the Lock & Key rot while you're off playing advisor to a prince? Not a chance. We'll keep the doors open, keep the lights on. Hell, we'll even keep the bar fights to a minimum. Maybe."

Jex grunted in agreement, golden eyes steady on

mine. "This place will still be standing when you come back."

Something hot pricked behind my eyes, and I had to look away before they saw too much. My fingers shaped the words slower this time, softer. "It's not fair to ask you to do that."

Rhett barked a laugh, signing, "Please. You think we're doing it for you? I like free whiskey. And Jex likes breaking skulls too much to give it up."

The demon's mouth twitched—his version of a smile.

Rhett shrugged, a little helpless pull to his brow that twisted that shriveled thing in my chest I called a heart. "You don't owe us the 'why,' Merrit. But we're not letting some drunk with a grudge torch the place while you're off doing whatever it is he thinks you can do. This is your bar. Always will be. We'll just... stand guard until you come back."

Jex rumbled low in his chest, nodding once, his hands moving like a gentle hum in the air. "Yours," he said simply. "We'll keep it yours."

I hesitated, throat tight, then slipped the little brass key from my pocket—the one that had lived under my palm every night as I locked the front door—and set it on the bar between us. My fingers lingered for a heart-beat before I pushed it toward them.

"Don't lose it," I signed, sharper than I meant.

Rhett reached for it carefully, like it weighed more

than iron. He tucked it into his shirt, patting it once over his chest. "We won't."

He was already moving when I slung the satchel over my shoulder, muttering something about broken chairs and "more blood than whiskey on these floors." He fetched a bucket, already scrubbing at the worst of the stains like muscle memory had kicked in.

Jex didn't bother with water. He bent, hauled one limp body over his shoulder as though it weighed nothing, and carried it toward the back. The sound of the door opening and shutting again was solid, final. One by one, he took them where they needed to go, no complaint in his stride.

"You'll come back to it clean," Rhett said, his voice too even to be casual, even though his signs were rough as broken glass. "No trace of tonight. Just your bar again."

"Yours," Jex added when he returned for the next body. His golden eyes caught mine for a breath before he turned away again, dragging silence with him.

The ache in my throat burned hot and raw. If I stayed another second, I'd crack. So I didn't.

I pulled the satchel strap tight and slipped out the back door.

The Divide met me in shadow.

Shops were shuttered, stalls covered, lamps burned low, but the streets were far from empty. This place never slept. Too many eyes gleamed from doorways, from upper windows, from the mouths of alleys where smoke curled lazy and sweet. Some shimmered faintly in the dark—Fae pupils catching lamplight, a wolf's gaze gone gold for half a blink before vanishing.

No one spoke. No one needed to. The quiet was its own kind of noise, thick and watchful, a hundred strangers measuring me as I passed.

A witch cradled a charm that pulsed green in her palm, muttering under her breath. A pair of shifters played dice against a wall, bones rattling in claws instead of hands. A vampire leaned too far out of shadow, smiling with too many teeth before melting back again.

Every step felt marked, cataloged, like the Divide itself had turned its head to watch me go.

And somewhere in that watchful maze waited Sable and the elixirs I needed to keep my secret buried.

The bell above Sable's door didn't jingle. It shrieked. A piercing, metallic cry that scraped the back of my teeth and announced me to every charm stitched into the walls.

Inside was warmer, thick with the smell of incense and spice, burnt sage, dried lavender, and something bitter, metallic under the tongue. Candles guttered in sconces, their flames bent at unnatural angles, casting shadows where there should have been light and light where there should have been shadow.

Sable looked up from behind the counter, her dark

hair braided tight against her scalp, sleeves rolled to her arms as though she'd been elbow-deep in spellwork before I arrived. Her gaze cut across me, keen and evaluating, then softened—slightly.

"You're late," she said, though the clock hadn't even struck midnight, her voice smooth with a rasp underneath. "And you're bleeding on my floor."

I glanced down. A smear of red still streaked my knuckles where I'd gripped the dagger. Not mine.

My hands moved before I thought better of it. "Not important."

Her mouth curved—not into a smile, but something knowing. "When it drips, it matters. But you never did like hearing that, did you?"

I didn't answer. Instead, I pulled the satchel tighter over my shoulder and stepped closer. My fingers shaped the words, sharp and clipped. "I need more elixirs. Stronger. Enough to last at Court."

Sable stilled. Just for a breath. Then she leaned her weight against the counter, studying me like I was a spell she hadn't quite decided to cast. "So it's true," Sable murmured. "The prince came for you."

Her words landed heavier than they should have, stirring the charms strung across the ceiling until they chimed like restless bones.

Before I could sign a reply, a streak of rust-colored fur leapt onto the counter. His paws skidded across the wood, scattering a stack of runes and sending a jar of dried yarrow clattering to the floor.

"Damn it, Trouble." Sable scooped her familiar up before he could nose at my satchel. His tail swished like he knew exactly how close she was to smacking him.

The little beast twisted in her arms, bright eyes locking on me. He yipped once, sharp and accusing.

"She doesn't owe you anything," Sable said to him— or maybe to me. Her gaze followed the blood at my knuckles, then climbed to meet my eyes again. "Especially not her life."

I set the satchel down on the counter harder than I meant to. The bottles inside clinked against one another, and Sable's jaw tightened like she wanted to scold me for it. My fingers moved before she could. "I don't have a choice."

"You always say that." She set Trouble down, and he darted across the counter, curling against the jars as though he owned them. "Like you don't have a mind of your own. Like he didn't walk in here and bleed all over my floor, and you—" Her mouth snapped shut, but the heat in her glare finished the sentence for her.

I crossed my arms, my signs clipped and angry: "The tithe is due. The bar's wrecked. I can't pay."

Sable's lips thinned. She understood exactly what that meant. "So you made a deal with a Veyne," she said at last. "Gods, Merrit."

Trouble yawned, pointed little teeth flashing in the candlelight.

"I need elixirs," I signed, fingers biting the air. "Before dawn."

Sable's laugh cut like glass. "Of course you do. Not tonight, not tomorrow, but before dawn. You think I've got shelves of miracles just waiting for you to stroll in and demand them?"

Trouble gave a little huff, curling tighter against the jars as though he agreed with her.

I didn't rise to the bait, only pulled the satchel open and laid the few empty vials I had left on the counter. The faint scent of bitter herbs still clung to them. My hands shaped the words: "You're the only one I trust to brew them right."

That made her pause. Not soften, but pause.

Sable dragged a hand over her face, muttering something about reckless bartenders and suicidal princes. Then, quieter, almost to herself: "Like I don't have enough of my own debts."

My head snapped up.

Her eyes were already back on the vials, shoulders stiff. "What? You think you're the only one chained to someone else's terms? The pack bleeds you, sure—but me?" She gave a bitter laugh that didn't reach her eyes. "I made a bargain I didn't want. Now I owe someone who doesn't let go."

Trouble's ears flicked, his amber gaze darting

between us as if even he didn't like the taste of that truth.

I signed slower this time, careful, "You never said."

"And you never asked." Sable's mouth quirked, humorless. "Not that it would've mattered. You don't lie to me, Merrit. You can't. I taste it." Her tongue flicked against her teeth, pointed and deliberate. "And gods help you if you ever try."

Her glare burned, but her thoughts were worse— bitter chords of debts unpaid and bargains she wished she'd never struck. *Don't end up like me,* hummed beneath every thought.

She pulled the vials closer, inspecting them one by one. "Fine. I'll mix what you need. But don't think I'm happy about it. Brewing in the middle of the night isn't easy, Merrit. Some ingredients don't like to be rushed. Neither do I."

Trouble hopped down from the counter, his tail brushing across my wrist like punctuation.

I tapped the wood once, steadying myself. "I wouldn't ask if it wasn't life or death."

Sable's gaze flicked to me, hard and assessing. Then she sighed, the fight bleeding out of her as she swept toward the shelves. "Life or death. Always life or death with you. Gods help me, one of these nights I'll let you walk in here and bleed out on the floor, just so you learn."

But she was already pulling jars down, setting her mortar out with brisk, efficient movements.

Sable swept a clay jar toward her, the stopper coming loose with a *hiss* like it resented being opened. The air filled with something acrid and bitter, metallic as blood and sweet as rot all at once.

"Hold this," she muttered, shoving a mortar into my hands before I could sign refusal. The stone throbbed faintly, warm as though it had a pulse.

Trouble hopped back onto the counter, tail twitching as he watched her measure out a pinch of ash-black powder and a sliver of dried root that oozed sap even after death. Each ingredient sparked faintly against the air, the candlelight bending around them.

Sable ground them together, muttering under her breath—not words I recognized, not even ones meant for untrained ears. The sound tasted bitter on my tongue, like glass scraped over bone.

The mixture smoked in the bowl, gray tendrils curling into shapes I almost recognized before they vanished. Faces, maybe. Shadows. Futures I wasn't ready to claim.

She caught me watching. "Don't," she said flatly. "Elixirs don't like being stared at. They start thinking you want answers, and then all you get are lies."

I set the mortar down carefully.

Trouble sneezed, spraying a little puff of smoke.

The air smelled thicker now—mint, iron, crushed roots bleeding their secrets into the mix.

She poured the first elixir into a vial with a practiced hand, corking it tight before sliding it across the counter toward me. Then another. And another. Each soft *clink* felt like a verdict.

"Don't waste them," she muttered. "I'm not brewing more if you burn through these in a week."

I gathered the vials carefully, tucking them into the satchel like fragile bones. My fingers moved once more, slower this time. "Thank you."

Her mouth curved—wry, reluctant. "You'll owe me for this, Merrit. And don't think I won't collect."

Trouble yipped from his nest of jars as if to second the threat.

I shouldered the satchel and stepped back. The bell shrieked overhead when I pulled the door open, charms sparking once more as if they disliked letting me leave.

Sable's voice followed me out, softer than I expected. "Come back breathing, Locke."

The wards snapped shut behind me, and the Divide swallowed me whole. The vials *clinked* softly in my satchel, each one heavy as a chain. The street stretched ahead—crooked, restless, alive with too many eyes watching from shadowed corners.

Whispers brushed against my skull, stray thoughts seeping past the cracks of my fading elixir: hunger gnawing like bone on stone, suspicion cold as steel, envy curling like smoke. *Easy prey,* one mind hissed. Another flashed an image—coins spilling from a broken purse, a knife flashing in an alley. Too many voices I didn't want, each one a reminder that I couldn't keep this secret buried forever.

I pulled my cloak tighter and kept walking, the Lock & Key only a few turns away. By dawn, the prince would come to collect his due. And I would step into Court with nothing but a satchel of elixirs, a scar at my throat, and a secret sharp enough to cut us both.

The Divide breathed even at midnight—shutters drawn, lamps guttering low, but its veins still pulsed hot. Alleyways hummed with dice and low spells, doors wore stitched wards like teeth, and every head that turned carried an assessment. Here, titles meant nothing. Here, a prince was just meat with a price.

And still I walked, shadow to Merrit Locke's flame.

She minced quickly through the crooked streets, her satchel bumping her hip, cloak pulled close. Not running but not strolling, either. Merrit was a woman who knew exactly how many eyes followed her and didn't give that first fuck. Gods, I wanted to know what that silence cost her—that blade-keen calm after she'd split a man's arm open without blinking.

"You're an idiot," Solis muttered at my shoulder. My

enforcer. My weapon when I needed blood drawn, my shield when I needed someone else to bleed for me. He'd been at my side longer than anyone still breathing.

I didn't so much as glance at him, not once peeling my gaze off my prey. "For coming here?"

"For thinking you could sneak into the Divide without me," he said, voice pitched low. "Half these bastards would've gutted you before you reached the corner. And the other half would've sold your boots with you still in them."

"I had it handled." I, in fact, did not, but he didn't need to know that.

"You almost never have it handled." His teeth flashed in a grin that was all bite. "Besides, someone's gotta keep you pretty. Nadia would skin you if you came back missing an ear."

I snorted, eyes still on Merrit. "You told me she was special. I came to see it for myself."

"I did," Solis said easily. "Didn't think you'd actually listen to me this time."

She disappeared into a crooked shopfront ahead, the bell's shriek carrying even out into the street. Wards snapped across the threshold, the kind that hummed against the skin if you strayed too close. Witchwork, old and bitter—the kind of work that kept polite people polite and thieves careful.

Solis leaned against a lamppost, arms crossed. "You're really doing this."

"Already did," I murmured, gaze fixed on the door she'd vanished through. "She agreed."

"Agreed, or you boxed her in so tight she had no way out?" His tone was teasing, but his eyes weren't—sharp edges gleamed beneath the calm. "Blackmail's a short leash, Kieran. Leashes snap. Knives don't."

I ignored the barb, though the words cut deeper than I liked. I hadn't wanted to blackmail Merrit, but I couldn't take it back now. There was too much at stake. My top advisor was in the infirmary, pale and sweating from a poison meant for me. Tobias had lifted the cup without hesitation, taken the swallow I hadn't, and dropped within breaths. If Solis hadn't shoved the healer into the room, he'd be dead.

Loyalty like that demanded repayment. It also meant my enemies were closer than I'd thought. If they could reach him, they could reach me. Merrit was the only chance I had at staying one step ahead.

The Divide shifted restlessly around us, shadows prowling. Somewhere, a fight broke out, metal on bone, quickly silenced by a burst of magic that lit the rooftops green before winking out. No one paid much attention. Just another night.

A part of me respected this slice of the continent— the way it seemed to survive no matter what was thrown at it. The other part of me knew everything balanced on the razor's edge, and I didn't want that for my people. But my mind wasn't on the street. It was behind that door, where Merrit Locke bartered secrets with a witch.

Solis tilted his head, studying me like he studied battlefields. "What do you think she's buying in there?"

"Insurance, protection. Maybe both," I muttered.

"Against you?" His grin widened.

"If she's smart? Against everyone."

And gods help me, I respected her for it. I would've done the same after Tobias hit the floor with my cup still in his hand.

Solis fell into step beside me, his long stride loose and deceptively casual. Most guards bristled when I left them behind—Solis only smirked, as though watching my back was a game he'd already won.

"You know," he drawled, "most princes prefer courtiers for their advisors. The kind who bow and scrape instead of throwing knives across the room."

I gave him a withering look. "And most princes end up dead because they trusted them to watch their backs."

His grin widened, but his eyes stayed hard. "She's fire, Kieran. Pretty to look at, dangerous to touch, and she'll burn you down if you're not careful."

I disregarded the warning, though the words stuck anyway. "Twice tonight she moved before anyone else could. I need that."

"What you need," Solis said, voice dipping into something almost serious, "is to stop collecting strays and start thinking about who's sharpening blades in your own hall."

The words dug deeper than I let him see. Servants gone. Food soured. My own allies were bleeding out before I could name their killers. It wasn't chance. It wasn't luck.

And Merrit Locke wasn't chance, either.

"She's a risk," Solis pressed, shoulders brushing mine as though daring me to argue. "One that'll either save your neck or put it on the block."

I let a thin smile curve my mouth. "Then it seems we're well matched."

Solis snorted, the sound rough as gravel. "Well matched my ass. You're not dragging her to Court just to sit at your elbow. You'll dress it up. Wrap it in silk and teeth. Make it look like something no one will dare question."

I arched a brow. "And what would that be?"

His grin curved sharp. "Your consort. That's the game, isn't it? Court won't blink if you chain yourself to a pretty throat. But tie yourself to a bartender with knives in her boots? They'll smell blood in the water. A mistress is gossip; a consort is spectacle. People respect spectacle."

I didn't answer. Couldn't. Because he wasn't wrong. This had been my plan all along: to pass her off as my latest fling to keep her throat intact and me breathing free.

Solis leaned in, lowering his voice until it brushed like a whisper. "Just remember—pretend long enough, and the Court won't be the only ones who believe it."

My jaw tightened, but I let the silence stretch. Better that than admit how close his words hit.

The moment Merrit Locke stepped back into the Divide, she'd belong to me—whether she liked it or not.

After what seemed like eons, the wards shivered once before releasing, and the shop door groaned open. Merrit slipped back into the street, satchel heavier now, the stink of witch-smoke clinging to her cloak. She didn't pause, didn't look around—just pulled her hood lower and walked like she could outpace every eye in the Divide.

She couldn't outpace mine.

I tracked her through the crooked streets, Solis a quiet shadow at my shoulder. Dice clattered in alleys, shutters rattled in the breeze, someone laughed harsh and ugly in the dark. None of it touched me. All I saw was her—silent, quick, carrying secrets like thorns under her skin.

Dawn bruised the horizon by the time she reached the edge of the Divide, where cobbles gave way to dirt and the air smelled less of wild magic. That was where I stepped out of the dark.

"Merrit Locke," I said, her name curling like smoke between us.

She stopped hard, the satchel swinging against her

hip. Her hands came up fast. "You shouldn't be here," she signed—short, clear.

I smiled without warmth, signing, "And yet, here I am."

Solis hung back, broad arms folded, his gaze sweeping over her like he was measuring a threat. Merrit's eyes flicked to him, wary, then locked back on me with a look that said she'd rather see me in the dirt.

"Dawn waits for no one," I told her, inclining my head toward the paling horizon. "And I don't linger where I'm not welcome."

Her fingers signed hard and defiant: "Then leave."

I almost laughed. "You agreed, Locke. You walk into Court as my advisor or my leverage. Either way, you walk beside me."

Her jaw flexed, anger sparking in those piercing green eyes, but she didn't deny it.

The horses waited tethered nearby, black hide gleaming even in weak light. I untied the reins and offered them to her. She looked at the beast, then at me, suspicion carved into every line of her face.

"You ride with me," I said simply.

She hesitated, then swung up smooth as a born rider, settling onto the saddle without so much as a wobble. I mounted behind her, the leather creaking as I slid close, my chest brushing her back, her hips pressed snug to mine, her ass settling firm against my groin. Every shift of the horse made the contact unavoidable, a slow drag of heat and pressure that sent my focus scattering places it shouldn't.

Too close. Gods, far too close.

Her hair smelled faintly of lavender and something wild, a copper strand catching on my jaw. Heat curled through me, intense and dangerous, the kind that made men ruin themselves. I set one hand on the reins beside hers, the other at her hip, light enough to feign balance. Gods help me, even pretending restraint burned.

I didn't bother with words she couldn't hear. My fingers flicked against the air, sharp and deliberate where she could see them. "Don't fall."

She glanced back just enough to meet my eyes, defiance sparking in hers. Her spine stayed stiff, every line of her body daring me to try and hold her tighter.

The satchel bumped against my thigh with each stride as the horse carried us toward the road to Morathen.

Beside us, Solis fell into an easy pace, his laughter low and needling. "Most princes take courtiers to Court. You bring a woman who looks like she wants to kill you in your sleep. Bold choice, Prince."

I ignored him, my mouth curving anyway as Merrit's shoulders tightened. She didn't belong at Court. She didn't belong to me. And still, here she was.

And I'd be damned if I let anyone else take her.

We rode in a line of breaths and hoofbeats, the Divide shrinking to the long, raw road between it and the Crown Province. Dawn washed the world in a weak, gray light that softened nothing. The air tasted of damp earth and old smoke.

Solis snorted, the sound like gravel rolled in a jar. He fell quiet for a breath, then struck with the sort of fact that landed like a thrown knife. "While you were hiding out," he said, "a minor merchant turned up at the west gate with a poisoned parcel. Not meant for you—yet—but meant for someone who eats at the same table as you. It was a test run. Someone's practicing."

The words sliced through the pretense of strategy.

"Anyone notice?" I asked, my chest tightening.

"A guardsman with an honest face. He fumbled the parcel as he checked it, and the thing hissed when it split. A crate of wine caught the spill. No one died. Yet." Solis' jaw ticked, eyes narrowed. "But the work was sloppy—mundane wards, clumsy runes. That means there are at least two hands in play: one to strike, one to distract."

My jaw set hard enough to taste copper. Tests scared me more than strikes—they meant someone knew my patterns, and that teeth were coming where I'd thought myself safe.

"When?" I asked.

"Tonight. Just before you cast your shadow over the Divide. The guard sent word, and I put a tail on the courier. The trail went cold in the market outside the river bridge." He spat to the side. "Someone's practicing reach."

I stared past Merrit's hooded shoulders at the road ahead. Small frame, steady seat, every line of her posture carried its own kind of defiance. The risk wasn't theoretical anymore. A poisoned parcel could cut down my steward, my taster—hell, even me if timing went wrong. Gossip and spectacle wouldn't cover that.

Solis eased closer, voice low. "A pretty dress and fake love story will buy you a month, maybe two. But you walk her into the lion's den, they'll claw at her to see if she bleeds. Keep her close. Keep your exits cleaner than your lies."

I nodded, though my thoughts had already shifted from costumes and cover stories to maps and sentries. "We'll parade, yes," I murmured. "But I won't hand her to the wolves just to amuse the Court."

Solis let out a single, barking laugh. "That's the first decent answer I've heard tonight."

We rode on. Hooves beat a steady rhythm, but my mind kept circling the poisoned parcel, the hiss of runes splitting, the notion of sloppy hands testing for weakness. Tests meant timing. Tests meant patience. Whoever was behind it wasn't ready to strike—yet. Which only made me wonder how long it would be until they were.

The horizon peeled open ahead, the spires of Mora-then catching the first light of dawn. Gates loomed, stone etched with sigils that hummed faintly against the skin, the air shifting from wild to Court-marked in a breath. A pair of sleepy guards blinked at the sight of us —a prince pressed too close to a cloaked woman, Solis shadowing at our flank—then straightened fast, dipping into shallow bows at my sigil.

Their obedience should have settled me. Instead, it only reinforced the reminder that danger was already in my house.

I slid from the horse as the gate opened, the world narrowing to Merrit's keen eyes as she dismounted. Even here, with guards watching and dawn burning the shadows away, she looked like a knife someone had forgotten to sheath.

And gods help me, I needed that knife sharp.

CHAPTER 5
MERRIT

The world beyond the Divide was too bright, too neat.

Fields rolled out in ordered lines; each one bound by low stone walls carved with wards so deep they hummed in my bones. Villages clung to the hillsides, chimneys coughing smoke, while banners—the Veyntheir raven clutching a coiled serpent—whipped against the pale dawn. Everything felt sharpened, disciplined. Even the magic in the air marched in rhythm, drilled into step instead of pulsing wild and unbound like it did in the Divide.

And the voices—gods, the voices were worse.

At the province gates, the guards straightened fast when they saw Kieran, dipping into bows that didn't reach their eyes. Their thoughts slashed clean through me:

Not his usual type.

Another bed-warmer, then. She doesn't look frightened enough.

Pretty throat, though. Bet she doesn't last the week.

The words sliced, leaving raw edges I couldn't cover. I bit the inside of my cheek until I tasted copper, fighting not to flinch. They weren't speaking to me, not really. Just careless thoughts leaking out of closed mouths. But they pressed against my skin all the same, seeping into places I couldn't shield.

Kieran didn't so much as glance at me. His warmth stayed steady at my back, his hand easy on the reins as though none of it mattered.

But it mattered to me.

The guards' thoughts clung to me long after we passed, sticky as cobwebs.

Pretty enough, but what's she hiding?

He'll tire of her fast. He always does.

My throat ached with the effort it took not to react. Not to flinch. Usually the elixir dulled it, smoothed the edges until the world was only a background hum. But I hadn't had a drop since the ambush, and now every stray suspicion, every careless cruelty, bit into my skull.

And worse? I had no fucking clue what I was supposed to be doing.

Kieran thought I was a seer. A prophet. Someone who could point to the shadows and name which one would strike first. I was none of that. I was just a bar owner who knew how to pour drinks without flinching, how to read the thoughts of men too drunk to guard them. That wasn't a gift—it was a curse. One I'd hidden my whole life.

But now Kieran Veyne, a prince with too many knives at his back, thought I was the answer. That I could stand at his side and keep him breathing. As if I wouldn't fold under the first real test. As if I wouldn't shatter under the weight of their whispers, their eyes, their thoughts.

How long before he realized what I really was?

How long before the lie I'd agreed to got me killed?

I shifted in the saddle, just enough to ease the ache between my temples. Kieran's hand tightened briefly at my hip, steadying me as though he thought I wavered from the ride, not from the panic rattling my ribs. His chest was a wall of heat at my back, too close, too steady, and for one fragile breath, it held the rest of it out.

Then the road bent, and I saw it.

The castle of Morathen didn't just rise from the city, it consumed it.

Black spires bit into the sky, walls etched with runes that shimmered faint as veins of silver in the stone. Wards crawled over the outer ring, prickling my skin worse than the guards' thoughts. The air thickened the closer we came, every stone humming with old magic. It pressed in on my skull, louder than tavern noise at its worst, every stray thought around me swelling until I could barely separate mine from theirs. This was no ramshackle Divide, rough and half-forgotten. This was control laid in mortar, centuries of power pressed into stone.

And it loomed like a predator waiting for blood.

The road funneled us straight into the castle's shadow where a young woman stood waiting in the archway, her skirts brushing stone.

Her gown was deep violet trimmed in silver, her hair braided into a crown that gleamed bronze when the sun caught it. Too polished for this early hour, too alive for a place built on blood and silence. Most vampires were nocturnal creatures, but this woman seemed ready to take the day by storm.

Her thoughts reached me before her words did, quick and bright as sparks: *She's tiny. Beautiful, though. Wilder than the last one. Maybe trouble enough to survive this place.*

When her gaze landed fully on me, her smile curved like a secret. "So it's true. You've dragged something interesting home, cousin."

Kieran signed and spoke at once, his hand flicks clipped and precise: "Serenya."

She swept into a bow meant more for show than

deference, her skirts sighing across the stones. Then she stepped close, bold as brass, and gave me a once-over that wasn't cruel—just curious. Like she was taking inventory.

"Well, aren't you a surprise." Her grin tilted sideways, almost conspiratorial as she signed. "You don't bow like the courtiers. You don't simper. You're either brave or stupid, and either way, I like it."

I should have flushed, should have shrunk. Instead, I lifted my chin a notch, meeting her gaze like I'd done a hundred drunkards in the Lock & Key. I'd been stared down before. Survived worse than that.

Solis snorted as he dismounted his horse. "She's more trouble than both of us combined. Don't encourage her."

"Oh, I plan to," Serenya said, her tone low and delighted, like mischief was a language she spoke fluently. She circled me once, skirts swishing, braid bouncing, eyes dancing as though she wanted to laugh. "The Court won't like her. But then, they never liked me, either. That's what makes it fun."

Something in my chest loosened at her words. No pity. No judgment. Just kinship, sharp-edged and a little wild. Kinship was dangerous. I knew better than to want it. But gods, for the first time since leaving the Lock & Key, I almost let myself.

Her thoughts brushed mine again, warmer this time:

She looks steady. Good. He needs steady. Vireth knows the rest of us aren't.

I swallowed hard, her kindness almost unbearable.

Then another voice carved across the courtyard, cool, clipped, and irritated.

"Is this some kind of joke?"

A tall man strode from the archway, every line of him pressed and perfect. Hair like spun gold bound at the nape, his doublet black as midnight and stiff with embroidery. His bow to Kieran was shallow, perfunctory. His eyes, when they slid to me, were hard as flint.

His thoughts hit harder than his words: *Saints save us. He's barely kept Tobias breathing, and now he brings a stray through the gates?*

Kieran's hand shifted against my hip, steadying me as he said, voice cool, "This is Merrit Locke. She'll be standing at my side until the Crown's safety is assured." His fingers moved, too, signing so I could follow: "She sees what others miss. I'll have no more blades at my back."

The man's mouth tightened into a thin line, his jaw clenching hard enough to break teeth. "You mean to tell me after Tobias nearly bled out on your floors last night, you think this"—His gaze struck to me again, voice dripping disdain—"this ragged girl from the gutter is your solution?"

The words flayed, but his thoughts were worse: *She smells of horse. No silks, no jewels, not even a trunk to her name, and he waltzes into the castle with her? Does he mean to parade her like this? I've met drowned rats with a better chance of surviving.*

Solis straightened from the wall, his grin all bite. "Careful, Elias. You forget yourself."

"Do I?" Elias snapped, eyes hard on Kieran. "Because I remember nearly losing your right hand, and instead of shoring your defenses, you ride out to fetch—what? A silent girl with no pedigree? And at any point is she going to speak up for herself? Are you playing charades or are you just stupid?"

The courtyard went taut as I fought off the urge to rip Kieran's blade from his belt and play pincushion.

Kieran's hand slid from my hip as he dropped from the saddle, boots cracking against the stones. He closed the space between us and Elias, not loud, but lethal.

"Enough." The word sliced the courtyard in half. "You forget yourself, Elias. You advise me like you advised my father, but unlike him, you do not command me. And you will not insult the woman who has already saved my life twice while you were still catching your breath."

Elias stiffened, but Kieran pressed harder, his voice cool as frost.

"You pride yourself on diplomacy, then practice it. Because if you cannot keep a civil tongue in your head, you will find yourself very quickly shut out of every conversation that matters. And when the Court asks why, I'll tell them my advisor thought it wise to spit on the one weapon keeping me alive."

His gaze flicked toward me, then back to Elias, sharp enough to draw blood. "She stands at my side because I chose her. That makes her untouchable. Remember that."

Untouchable. He made it sound like fact, but I'd lived too long to believe in safety and had a scar across my throat that reminded me when I forgot.

Elias tensed, his thoughts burning hotter than his words. *Reckless. Foolish. She'll break and drag us all down with her.*

Elias' sneer lingered, that taunt about charades still hanging like smoke.

Sliding from the saddle, my boots found stone. I closed the distance until Elias couldn't look away with showing cowardice. I lifted my hands, then stilled—not in hesitation, but in decision. Slow, deliberate, I pushed my cloak back from my hair, fingers sliding to the velvet ribbon at my throat. His gaze tracked the movement, curious, faintly scornful.

But if he wanted a game, I'd play.

One tug, and the fabric slipped loose, sliding down my chest as I bared the skin I never showed in the light. A single scar cut clean across the base of my throat— one cruel line, pale against my skin, the mark of a blade that had stolen my voice forever. One I couldn't remember and didn't want to.

The courtyard held its breath, even Serenya's bright expression fading to shock.

I let the silence stretch, let him see it, let them *all* see it. Then I raised my hands.

"As it turns out," I signed, each stroke of my fingers measured, "I'm very good at charades. Better than most."

Kieran's mouth curved in something that wasn't a smile—more like the shadow of a weapon unsheathed. Serenya let out a breath that trembled into laughter, edged with disbelief. Solis went still—not the lazy stillness he'd worn in the saddle, but something harder, fiercer. His eyes locked on my throat, then snapped away too fast, jaw tightening like he'd bitten down on something that made him bleed. Recognition. Fear. Both flickered across his face before he caught them, dragged that easy grin back into place like a mask that didn't quite fit anymore.

Elias went rigid, the blood draining from his face before fury crashed back in. His jaw ticked hard enough to crack teeth, and his thoughts beat against me like fists.

Insolent. Dangerous. What has he brought into our house?

I tugged the cloak back across my shoulders, the velvet ribbon still dangling useless from my fingers. Their eyes felt like claws on my skin—too many, too sharp. I'd bared the truth, and it hadn't made me stronger. It had just given them another wound to aim for.

Untouchable, Kieran had said. But every heartbeat screamed the opposite. If this was what it meant to stand at his side, then I was already bleeding.

Then Serenya clapped her hands once, bright and mocking as a bell. "Well," she drawled, grin tilting wicked, "that was more fun than breakfast. Come inside before the servants start wagering who bleeds first."

Her eyes flicked to me, softer in the wake of the jest, carrying something that felt dangerously close to comfort.

The courtyard exhaled. Guards shifted, Solis grinned, Serenya swept toward the archway like she was tugging the tension with her. For a fragile breath, I almost let myself believe the hard edges had dulled.

But Elias lingered. His bow was shallow, his smile thinner than glass.

"If she is to stand at your side until this crisis is resolved—as you say—then surely, she'll attend tonight. A proper introduction, before every watching eye. By all means, Your Majesty"—His gaze slid back to me, acerbic as frost—"do bring her. The Hunt begins tonight."

The courtyard shifted, unease rippling like wind over water. Serenya's grin faltered, Solis' easy smirk thinned, even the guards' minds went brittle with sudden hunger as the words clung to my skin like iron shackles. My stomach dropped, though I kept my spine straight, my hands steady at my sides. I didn't know what "the Hunt" was, not exactly, but the weight in the air told me enough.

Whatever it meant, it sure as shit wasn't survival.

Especially not mine.

CHAPTER 6
MERRIT

The castle swallowed us whole.

Stone consumed sound differently here, catching every footfall and spitting it back hollow. The air was cooler than outside, laced with smoke and iron as incense burned to veil the copper tang beneath. Wards stitched into the walls hummed low enough to make my teeth ache, and every step seemed to drive them deeper.

Balconies climbed the walls like ribs of a great beast, torchlight catching wards that shimmered as faint as constellations. The ceilings arched so high they disappeared into shadow, every stone a reminder that this place had been built to last longer than bloodlines, longer than kingdoms. It wasn't just a castle—it was a cage grand enough to worship.

Servants lined the halls, heads bowed, eyes quick. Their thoughts pressed harder than the stones themselves.

Another one. Pretty, but rough.

No jewels, no silks, no chest of things—what is she doing here?

She looks like she came from the stables.

I bit down until copper bloomed again on my tongue, steadying myself against the urge to flinch. Kieran took my hand before I could draw breath. His fingers threaded through mine, sure as a man staking a claim.

The gasp caught in my chest before I could stop it. He didn't look at me, didn't sign. He just kept walking, dark head high, my satchel tucked casually in his other hand like it weighed nothing. On the outside, he wore the look of a smitten protector, a man ushering his newest obsession into his den. But every muscle in his body was taut, precise, warding me like a shield.

Serenya fell into step on my other side, skirts whispering along the stones. She flicked quick, easy signs as she spoke aloud, "Ignore them. They'll choke on their tongues later. Better to let them talk now."

Her grin was sly, but her thoughts hummed sharper. *Please don't let her crumble. If he's chosen you, they'll cut deep to see you bleed.*

Solis trailed a step behind, his bulk a shadow

stretching down the corridor. He didn't bother to sign, but his grin carried just enough teeth to look mocking. His thoughts betrayed him, anyway. *Vireth help us, she'll gut him before the week is out.*

The hallways narrowed, staircases climbing and curling, until finally the doors changed. No longer plain wood or stone—these were carved, lacquered, their handles wrought-iron in the shape of coiled serpents. Guards flanked them, eyes hard, thoughts harder.

Another ornament for his collection.

He brings them close, but never this close.

Why her?

Kieran squeezed my hand once before letting go to push the doors open.

His chambers weren't what I expected. They weren't velvet decadence, nor the damp crypt I half-feared. They were both—somehow. A long chamber stretched wide enough to hold a hunting lodge, beams of black-wood arcing overhead. Tapestries covered the walls, dark with age, scenes stitched in threads of silver that caught the torchlight like blood. A fire burned in a stone hearth big enough to stand in, its smoke carried away by unseen wards. One side of the room opened into a smaller parlor with chairs and a heavy table. Beyond, tall doors led to what must have been a balcony.

It should have felt domestic, even comfortable: the fire crackling, the table set for wine, the balcony doors cracked for air. But the wards etched into the beams hummed like veins carrying power, and the bed loomed like a predator crouched in the dark. Home and hunger stitched together until the whole chamber felt less like a sanctuary and more like a trap dressed in velvet.

And the bed—gods, the bed was a thing built for conquest. Four posts carved into spears, the canopy heavy with drapes of midnight cloth. The sight of it made the back of my neck prickle, though it wasn't the bed itself that threatened me. It was the thought of being anywhere near it.

Kieran dropped my satchel on the table, casual as if this had always been its place. The fragile bottles *clinked* together, and I fought off the urge to wince at any of them being damaged. His gaze swept the room once, assessing, before flicking back to me. That single look was enough to pin me where I stood as he dismissed Serenya with a curt nod. She obeyed with a smirk, skirts swishing as she vanished through a side door.

Solis lingered longer, gaze flicking between us before he signed clumsily but clear, "Don't kill each other."

His grin stayed plastered on his face, but his eyes went raw—more worry than mockery. His thoughts, though, snapped against my skull. *He's too close already. Saints, don't let her gut him.*

Then he was gone, too, and the silence left behind felt dangerous.

The door's echo hadn't fully died before the air shifted. It wasn't silence anymore—it was waiting. Kieran's waiting. And I realized too late that whatever came next, I was already cornered.

For a handful of seconds, the suite held only the small noises of a lived-in room: the fire unhurriedly popping, the wards humming like distant bees, the faint scuff of a curtain. The absence of others made the air tighter, as though the castle itself was drawing breath and watching. I was suddenly aware of every detail—how the tapestry's silver thread caught flame, how the ash on the hearth settled in impatient puffs, how the satchel on the table looked absurdly mundane against the carved wood.

Kieran didn't move right away. He let the door's weight shut behind Solis, then took two slow steps toward the table, removed his coat, and hung it on the back of a tall-back chair. The motion was casual and practiced, but it carved the space between us the way a blade cuts cloth: clean, inevitable.

He watched me while he moved—as if he were measuring, not with eyes but with the piece of something inside him. When he finally lifted his head, our gazes met, and the air shifted.

I edged back a half-step, instinct tugging me toward distance, toward air. But there was nowhere to go—the wall was too close, and his presence filled the chamber like smoke. I lifted my chin anyway, a tiny rebellion, even as my spine screamed to flee.

He saw it. The corner of his mouth curved, faint, as though my retreat—and my resistance—were both expected and claimed.

When he came toward me, it was slow, unhurried, but there was no mistaking the intent. One step, then another, until my shoulders brushed cold stone. He caged the space deliberately, not with noise or force but with steadiness, the way a predator lets its prey realize there's no way out.

My hand twitched at my side, the urge to shove him back coiling tight. He noticed that, too—his gaze flicked to the movement, then back to my eyes with cool amusement, like he dared me to try.

His hand rose, brushing a copper strand from my cheek, knuckles grazing the pale seam at my throat. The contact lingered, deliberate, his thumb pressing lightly against the mark I never showed to anyone.

"You're not deaf," he said softly, the words too low for anyone else to catch but bright enough to land on my skin.

My heart slammed against my ribs, betraying me. His eyes flashed as the faintest curve of his lips pulled at his mouth as though he'd been waiting for it.

"This scar robs you of your voice, but you hear me just fine," he continued, thumb stroking the puckered flesh. "Your heart gives you away, did you know that?

Every time I don't sign, it flutters like a bird." His gaze dragged down my throat, lingered there, then lifted to catch my eyes again. "I like it—knowing I can reach you without moving a finger. That no matter how steady you keep your face, your body answers me."

The words slid clean as an executioner's axe and just as deadly. My skin prickled, and something darker than desire trailed it. He let his hand rest against my sternum for a beat, feeling the bird-quick beat beneath.

"Let them think you're deaf," he murmured, softer now, though the steel in his tone didn't falter. "Let them talk carelessly in your presence, never dreaming you can hear every word. That's where your worth doubles —you'll spy for me in silence, as the seer I know you to be, and as the mute girl they'll instantly dismiss. Two weapons, one blade. And all of it mine."

The room shrank with every word that fell from his mouth, tightening like a noose around my neck.

"Every vampire here will hear your heart," he said, his voice a low rasp, thumb still circling that scar. "They'll scent desire if you feel it. Disdain, too. Fear. You think you can hide behind silence, but your body will betray you if you let it. And they'll tear you apart for the weakness."

His words crawled under my skin, threading with my pulse until I swore he could feel every wild beat.

I forced my hands into stillness, fingers curling at my sides. *Show nothing. Flinch for no one.*

"What part," I signed tightly, "am I supposed to play?"

Kieran's smile wasn't kind. He stalked forward a step, herding me back until the carved panel of the wall pressed between my shoulders. His hand braced beside my head, the other still at my throat, pinning me with nothing but presence. His gaze devoured mine, blue and merciless.

"The part I give you." His mouth dipped, the barest breath brushing my jaw, close enough to smell the iron on his skin. "Tonight, you are my consort. Mine before every watching eye. They'll see you at my side and think me smitten, and they will not question why I keep you close."

The word slammed into me, harder than his body did. *Consort.* Lover. Pretend or not, it was a cage dressed in silk.

"And if I refuse?" I shaped the words like a threat.

His mouth curved, dark amusement ghosting across his features. "Then you won't live long enough to regret it." His hand slid down my throat, over my racing heart. "Because the Hunt begins tonight, and every eye will be on you."

The words hit like a bell in a quiet room. I had expected threats, fears, curses—but not that. Not some courtly sport wrapped up in fangs and silk.

"Explain," I signed before I could stop myself. My fingers were clumsy with the tremor under my skin.

He laughed, a sound without humor. "You'd already heard the name."

"I've heard nothing" I signed, my panic rising by the second. "You didn't even give me the where, the when, or the how."

Kieran's thumb pressed once more at the scar, light enough to be tender, heavy enough to be ownership. He let his hand fall from my chest and stepped back, giving the room a breath. "The Hunt is as old as my bloodline," he said. "A provincial rite and a Court spectacle. Nobles pair with companions—gifts, displays, sometimes wagers. Tonight, the hunters are not hunting beasts in the wood. They hunt the ones who stand beside them, to see who will falter and who will hold. It's a test of nerve, sometimes a test of flesh. Tonight, you won't be hiding in silk in my chambers. You'll be on the field, visible to all. You'll be watched, prodded, invited to fail. If you fail—if you look weak—this place will devour you."

So that's what Elias had meant. Not a feast. Not a dance. A spectacle of predators and prey, and I would be shoved to the center of it. A game for them, a death sentence for me.

My throat closed. "So you bring me to a hunt where I'm the quarry," I signed through shaking fingers. "And you think that's protection?"

"I think it's the only thing that will keep the daggers from hitting the right places," he said it softly, like a confession. "You standing with me is a statement. A stranger no one in Court knows, an outsider, an oddity. But if I parade you as mine—as my consort, my companion—then they have to account for you. A man who lays a hand on my consort answers to me and will pay in blood. That will slow them down. It won't fix everything, but it buys us space. And tonight, I'll buy us as much as I can."

The warning settled into me cold and absolute. He expected me to perform. He expected me to wear seduction so convincingly that it looked like belonging. He expected me to make people believe I wanted him.

I had never been taught to perform desire for survival. Time had taught me to stand steady. To listen. To keep secrets. Now I had to become a lie made flesh—practiced, polished, and deadly. And Kieran stood so close I could count every fleck of red as it bled into his irises. He expected me to learn fast.

He loosened his grip once, just a breath, and for a moment—the briefest flash—the man who'd scooped me from blood and bargaining looked almost human. Protective. Fractured. Dangerous in ways that had nothing to do with courtcraft.

"Tonight," he said quieter, as if offering me a choice that was not a choice at all, "you do this for me. For my life. For yours."

Kieran's thumb lingered at my throat, stroking the scar like it was a tether he meant to use.

"You've lived your whole life hiding reactions to cruelty, I'd bet," he murmured, his breath brushing my cheek. "If the Divide is anything like the Court, any slight, any handicap, is a liability, a weakness. I don't doubt you can keep your face stone when they spit at you. That's not what I'm worried about."

His hand slid lower, flattening over my chest where my pulse beat wildly against his palm. "This," he murmured, his voice dangerously close to a growl. "When I put my hand on your waist in front of them, when I bend close, when I kiss your hand, your neck—*this* is what will betray you. Every vampire in the room will hear the way your heart flutters. They'll scent the truth of your nerves. If you look like prey in my arms, they will know it."

He moved in until his chest was a hard wall against me, his scent drowning my lungs—iron and smoke, old leather, and something darker, the faint metallic tang of blood. For a second, the world narrowed to that smell and the heat of him; the air seemed to shrink around us. His eyes slid down, blue at the edge and liquid red at the center, a flash of fang-sharp hunger that set my teeth on edge.

He leaned in until they grazed the skin just beneath my jaw. The contact was almost nothing—a whisper of lips, a ghost of breath, but my body betrayed me almost instantly.

My skin prickled as a tremor skimmed down my

arms. Heat pooled low in my belly, an unwelcome curiosity tangling with the primal, more urgent need to stay alive. He was a vampire for Evara's sake. A predator built to smell weakness and taste fear, a beast, and yet, I couldn't make myself move from that spot. My breath came shorter as an ache uncoiled in all the wrong places.

Half of me wanted nothing to do with him, to shove him away, to take his blade and run him through no matter what it cost me just to prove I could. The other half burned to know what his bite would feel like. Frozen, my pulse hammered, loud and accusing.

Kieran's lips curved against my throat, lingering at the hollow beneath my jaw. "There," he said, voice low, satisfied. "You've failed already. Your heart gave you away. But your *scent...*"

He let the word drip, tasting me like prey. His tongue darted once, sampling the rapid beat in my throat before he pulled back enough to meet my gaze. His eyes flashed red as his mouth curved in something close to cruel delight. "It means you'll at least be convincing, even when you lie."

Heat scorched my face. Shame tangled with the rush of something darker. My hands flew in clipped signs. "I'm here to save your ass, not play games."

He laughed, a rough sound threaded with hunger as he braced me tighter against the wall. "Games are the only way anyone survives this Court," he murmured, thumb still circling my scar. "Every word, every touch, every stolen breath is a piece on the board. And tonight, little liar, you're mine to play."

My pulse faltered under the weight of it, and for the first time since leaving the Divide, I didn't know which of us would devour the other first.

CHAPTER 7
KIERAN

Merrit's blush burned hotter than the firelight, and gods help me, I felt it in my teeth. The distinct ache of fangs pressing to drop, the coil of hunger tightening low and insistent. One step closer and I'd taste her blood, find out if the heat in her pulse was fear or something darker.

It was a siren call, threaded through the silence she carried like armor. Her heart thundered; the scent of her desire sweetened. Not submission, not exactly, but something that dragged at every instinct I had. I wanted to push her further, to see if she'd break—or to see what she'd become if she didn't.

My hand lingered at her throat a moment too long. I should have stepped back already, but the heat of her pulse beat against my palm like a drum, and every instinct in me ached to sink fang to skin.

I pulled in a breath that did nothing to steady me. "Serenya will see you dressed," I murmured, my voice rougher than I meant it to be. "Solis will show you the exits and the faces worth remembering."

The words came out clipped, too harsh, as if the hunger in my teeth had eaten their polish. I let my hand fall away and forced myself to turn before I did something reckless. "They'll make you look the part," I added, each word ground past the ache, "but no one here can teach you how to stop your body from betraying you. That's on you."

The silence stretched, thick with firelight and her scent. I couldn't stay in it. Couldn't stand the thought of hearing her heart trip one more beat for me.

I tore my coat from the chair, swung it over my shoulders, and strode for the door. The wood shut heavy at my back, sealing her in with the fire while I bled into the cooler hush of the corridor, every muscle wound tight against the pull to turn around.

My chest felt too tight, my body wound like a bowstring. The wards in the stone thrummed against me as I dragged in a breath, but it didn't clear her scent. Smoke and copper and that elusive warmth—hers—still clung, crawling under my skin as if she'd followed me out.

Gods damn her.

She should have shattered under my hands, but she hadn't. She had stood there, a spine of steel, those glittering green eyes keen as her heart pounded so loud I could feel it in my teeth. That sound haunted me as much as her silence.

I'd told her someone would come to prepare her for tonight, and they would. My household knew their roles —Serenya would see her dressed and schooled in the bare minimum of etiquette. But none of them could coach her in what really mattered. How to walk into a pit of vipers and make every bastard believe she wanted to be there.

I strode through the castle corridors, restless. My thoughts circled her—the pulse beneath my palm, the way she froze when I leaned close, the scent of her body betraying her, even as she lifted her chin. *Useful*, I told myself. That kind of reaction would make her convincing. A consort who didn't blush at her prince's touch would be nothing but another prop. She could play the game. I could *make her* play it.

But underneath that logic, hunger gnawed. What would she taste like? Who had carved that scar into her throat? Why hadn't she told me? Questions with no answers, and the need to press closer to her, to wring them out of her, clawed at me until I forced my mind elsewhere.

Elias' words at the castle steps scraped back next. He hadn't ordered Merrit into the Hunt, not outright—but he'd left no room for refusal. A maneuver dressed as suggestion, backed by enough eyes to make defiance look like weakness. That son of a bitch knew exactly what he was doing—testing me, testing her. Elias never moved without an angle. Once, he'd advised my father with that same smooth tongue, and I'd learned young that nothing he gave came without a hook. Tonight, he'd be watching for cracks, hoping to see me stumble.

And I couldn't stumble. Not with enemies circling closer every day. Not with Tobias still recovering in the infirmary.

The thought drove me down the servants' staircase and across the keep to the healing wing. The air here was crisper, cleaner, heavy with sage and salt. Wards thrummed low and steady, muffling sound so no one outside these halls would hear what happened within.

I found him where I knew he'd be: on a narrow bed, tunic gaping at the throat, face pale from the poison's burn. The toxin had unstitched his body—he'd bled where no blade touched—through mouth, nose, eyes— until the healers had purged it and feeding began to knit him back together. Feeding was the only thing that would restore him.

A donor sat beside him, neck arched, eyes glassy as Tobias drank. Not hungrily—never hungrily—but with measured care, each swallow deliberate. His hand cupped the man's jaw, thumb brushing slow and absent, as if to remind him he was safe even with fangs at his throat.

I waited until Tobias drew back, licking the punctures closed with a neatness that almost looked tender. The donor sagged, pale but steady, and Tobias murmured, "Thanks" before sending him away. Only then did his gaze lift to me.

Tobias looked young, as we all did—smooth skin, lean muscle, fangs gleaming white in the firelight. But the centuries showed in quieter ways: silver threaded through the dark at his temples, pale-gray eyes that missed nothing, a patience honed sharp as steel. Next to him I always felt reckless, a match struck too close to kindling.

"You shouldn't be walking the halls without a guard," he said, voice roughened by thirst. His faint smile didn't quite reach his eyes. "But then again, you never listen when I tell you things like that."

I caught myself watching the trace of red at the corner of his mouth, the precision of his restraint. It should have calmed me. Instead, it made the memory of Merrit's pulse slam back into my teeth. Tobias had fed like a priest at an altar—gentle, reverent. And I? Gods help me, I wanted to drag her head back and drink until her heart stuttered.

"You'd think you'd stop wasting your breath by now," I muttered, dragging a chair beside his bed.

"I've had centuries to practice," Tobias said, dry as dust.

I should have laughed. Instead, guilt coiled tighter. "I'm sorry," I said before I could stop myself.

His brows rose faintly. "For what? For being attacked? For dragging me into the middle of your mess? Or for the fact you think you can carry this little rebellion on your back and never bleed for it?"

The words struck, but not cruelly. They landed the way his counsel always did: honest, tempered, steady.

"I should have seen it coming," I ground out. "Whoever planted that poison—"

"—wants you dead." Tobias leaned back, pale-gray eyes sharp, even as he closed them briefly. "Yes. And they nearly had me instead. That's not your sin, Kieran. That's theirs."

He opened his eyes again, gaze steady. "But you need to ask yourself who stands to gain. Your father would rather see you stumble than shine, and you know it. And your brothers..." He let the words hang, deceptively mild. "Proximity is power. The nearer provinces have much to gain if Morathen is weakened. Lorenzo especially—too rigid for his own good. He'd rather inherit ashes than see you take root."

He shook his head, voice softening again, all concern and no malice. "I don't say this to drive you against them. But if you don't start asking yourself the hard questions, you'll miss the answer standing right in front of you."

I scrubbed a hand over my face, suspicion coiling like smoke. Tobias' words slid too neatly into place, feeding fears I didn't want to name. But no. Not

Lorenzo. My brother was stubborn, disciplined to a fault, but treachery? That wasn't in his marrow. He'd bleed for the Crown before he'd betray it.

"You're chasing shadows," I muttered, voice flat, though the unease Tobias had planted stayed lodged beneath my ribs.

He only watched me, calm as ever, as though he knew I'd come around to his point in time.

"I've got an ace in the hole," I said at last, low, as much to convince myself as him.

His brow arched slightly. "Do you now?"

I let the silence carry, offering him nothing. No mention of Merrit. Not yet. Not until I knew the truth of what she could do—and whether I could trust her with it.

Tobias smirked, though the faint tightness at his mouth betrayed lingering strain. "Keep your secrets, then," Tobias murmured, settling back against the pillows. His voice was calm, steady, almost indulgent. "But don't let your brothers scent weakness. Lorenzo least of all."

His eyes closed again, the picture of exhaustion, and the words might have been nothing more than counsel from a wounded friend. But they clung sharp as burrs as I left him, lodging under my ribs where doubt already lived.

His words lingered long after I left him, sinking hooks I couldn't shake. The halls swallowed me again, ward-lines humming steady in the stone. My stone. My wards. My power. Yet every turn of the keep felt tighter, every rune another bar on a cage I'd built with my own hands. Morathen bowed to me, yes—but it watched me, too, every servant's thought a whisper of judgment, every courtier's glance another test.

And tonight, with Merrit at my side, that cage would close a little tighter.

Their laughter reached me before their faces did. Two courtiers, all lace and polish, lounged against the stone arch as if the corridor itself were their stage. They straightened when they saw me, but the bows they offered were shallow enough to sting.

"Your Highness," one crooned, voice sticky with false deference. "Whispers run wild already. A new consort from the Divide, is it? Bold." His gaze slid toward me like a predator testing for weakness. "One might think Morathen's noble daughters no longer hold your attention."

The other's smile was thinner, crueler. "The Divide breeds gutter rats and tavern trash, not consorts. Best keep her leashed before she mistakes your bed for your throat."

The words landed like steel driven into old bone. For a heartbeat, all I saw was Merrit's scar—raw, puckered, the proof of someone else's knife. My jaw locked, fangs biting the inside of my lip until I tasted blood.

I smiled anyway but it was all fang. "Careful. Say

one more word about my consort's throat, and I'll rip yours from your pathetic little body and watch you bleed out on this stone."

The air thickened, heavy with the promise of violence. Their grins faltered, but pride made one of them push anyway. "Perhaps you'll parade her tonight, then? Let the Hunt see what prize you've dragged home. We do so love a spectacle."

"*Perhaps* I will." I stepped forward, close enough that torchlight carved harsh shadows in the folds of their masks. "So you and your ilk can all see who I claim as mine."

Their smiles turned simpering, the fake upturn to their mouths eating at me just like every single stone in this gods-forsaken fucking cage. I wanted to wipe it all away.

"Remember, your lands, your titles, your pretty little privileges exist only because I allow them. Step out of line again, and I'll rip it all away: your power, your wealth, everything down to your fucking names. I'll watch you claw at empty air while everything you used to own rots with you alongside it."

A hiss of movement answered me from the dark. Solis stepped forward from the shadows like a priest of Tharos. "Because what I see," he said, voice flat and amused, "is two pampered fops loitering where they're not wanted. Unless you'd like me to teach you the polite way out, I suggest you find somewhere else to wag your tongues."

The courtiers blanched, their bows suddenly deep enough to scrape the floor. "Of course, my lord," one stammered, tugging the other back. They slithered down the corridor, whispers trailing like shadows.

Solis spat after them, contempt thick in his voice. "Vermin."

My hands still itched for their throats. I exhaled once, a slow drag of air through clenched teeth. "They'll spread their filth anyway," I muttered.

His grin widened, teeth flashing. "Let them. I hope they choke on it."

I watched the two courtiers slither away and the corridor settle like a beast that had been prodded. Solis lingered, arms folded, waiting. A pageboy in house colors hovered at the far end, wide-eyed, and trying not to breathe too loud.

"Bring Serenya to my chambers," I said, voice flat. "Four trunks. No nonsense—one for day-to-day garments, one for formal court attire, one for practical riding and travel, and one for jewels." The words were a promise and a threat stitched into one.

The boy blinked, then bowed, already calculating which trunks would fit where. "From the vault?" he asked, his shoulders nearly vibrating.

"Yes. From my vault." I let the sentence land. My house had more than enough glitter to drown a rumor before it started. She'd be dressed properly, and if the gossips wanted to sneer, let them choke on silk instead.

The boy nearly tripped over his bow before bolting. Good.

Then I turned to Solis. "Double the watch on the south lane. Shift the mounts and put eyes on the gates. No one I don't know comes within sniffing distance of my chambers. And find a woman who can school her in the posture and smiles this snake pit feeds on."

Solis' grin was the kind that warned other men to breathe carefully. "On it."

When he disappeared into the dark, the corridor finally fell quiet. The smell of her didn't need to follow; the thought of it had already braided into the muscle memory of my hands. It stayed with me in the small, private places—the press of my palm against stone, the drag of boots on flagging—and no ward in the keep could scrub it out.

I had dragged a woman from the Divide into the center of a beast's feast. Now I meant to make sure she looked like the prize I'd claimed.

Tonight, the Court would watch.

Tonight, the Hunt would begin.

And gods help me, I wanted their eyes on her when I sank my fangs in.

CHAPTER 8
MERRIT

Wood met stone with a hollow *crack*, the sound stealing through me. My heart picked it up, battering my ribs as if trying to escape the imprint of Kieran's hand. Every nerve sang, my throat burning with the ghost of his thumb.

I hated that I felt it. Hated the heat clawing through me more than I hated his threats. Because he'd read me —so easily. A heartbeat, a tremor, a blush, and he'd laid me bare. And he was right: every vampire in this gods-forsaken Court would do the same.

The room pressed close, heavy with the scent of amber and woodsmoke, the taste of him still lingering in the air. I needed to scrub it off me, burn it away before it rooted deeper.

The adjoining chamber gleamed like something stolen from a dream. Black marble underfoot, copper fixtures curved like serpents, a basin deep enough to drown in. Runes glowed faintly along the pipes, waiting.

At Lock & Key, I had a shower hacked together from charms and half-rotted plumbing, the pressure wheezing worse than an old drunk. Here, a brush of my fingers over the sigils stirred the wards awake, water humming through hidden veins in the stone until steam curled heavy in the air.

I stripped fast, dropping Divide-stained clothes in a heap. Horse, sweat, the scent of the road clung to them —proof of safety already lost. The heat rose, bright and scented with herbs I didn't know. Luxury surrounded me, thick enough to choke.

But I slid into the basin, anyway. Because in the Divide, you didn't waste what you were given. Comfort was rare, fleeting, meant to be taken when it appeared. If tomorrow brought ruin, then tonight I'd bank this moment against it.

The water hit like absolution. Hot enough to sting, hotter still as I sank beneath the surface. It pulled the tightness from my muscles but not the memory of him. I could still feel the press of his chest, the brush of his mouth on my throat. A shiver broke over me, heat colliding with cold, shame with something I didn't want to name.

I ducked under, scrubbing until my skin burned and every freckle felt raw. Soap stung my eyes as I worked it through my hair, suds tangling with strands until the water foamed pale around me. Glass vials lined the ledge, their contents shimmering faintly: herbal tonics, potions bottled in jewel tones.

I uncorked one. The scent burst bright and sweet, something like crushed roses over embers. Another smelled of mint and rain, bright enough to sting my nose. At home, I made do with rinses from witch brews traded for coin or favors, whatever kept my hair clean and manageable. This—this was indulgence dressed in glass and silk ribbon.

I let the rose-smoke tonic spill over my scalp, fingers massaging until my hair grew heavy with silk instead of grit. For a moment, I let myself savor it—the way the strands slipped clean through my fingers, the way the steam carried unfamiliar scents into my lungs.

But the thought rose anyway, insistent as a bruise: tonight, I had to stand at his side and make the Court believe the lie. His consort. His lover. His prize.

And saints help me, I didn't know if I feared failing him... or myself.

Steam blurred the edges of the room as I sank deeper into the water, until only my face broke the surface. For a blessed moment, silence pressed in—no thoughts, no whispers—only the hollow beat of my own heart. Heat stole the tightness from my muscles, the weight on my shoulders lifting until I felt almost human again. Almost free.

But silence was never mine to keep.

I surfaced, pushing hair from my eyes, and forced myself out of the basin before I grew too comfortable. Plush towels waited, thick enough to consume me. I buried myself in one, the fabric greedily drinking away water until my skin tingled. Beside it hung a dressing gown—silk, rich and heavy, with a crest stitched into the breast. A raven clutching a serpent. His mark.

The robe smelled faintly of him—cedar, steel, and something darker underneath. I hated how easily it settled over my shoulders, how the fabric skimmed my skin as though it belonged there.

My satchel sat across the chamber where he'd dropped it, sagging against the carved table, ordinary as any pack—except for the weight inside.

I padded toward it, bare feet silent on stone. My fingers found the strap, then the glass edge beneath worn leather. The elixir. A mouthful of bitter herbs, enough to dull the roar of thoughts to a manageable hum. Enough to quiet the Court's venom before they slid too deep.

One mouthful, and the edges would soften. My breath steadied just thinking of it. But the memory rose sudden and sour—one night in the Divide, a tavern brimming with thoughts like hornets, my skull buzzing so loud I'd taken the elixir too fast. Sluggish, unbalanced, I hadn't noticed the man at my back until his hand found my shoulder.

Jex had peeled him off me with the same calm efficiency he used to throw drunks into the street. His silence had been its own warning: Next time, he might not be there. Rhett always said I spoiled Jex, letting him skim coin from the tables and drink whatever he pleased. But I knew his quick hands and quicker temper were the only reason I was still breathing.

I gripped the vial tighter, the cork biting my palm. The temptation was always the same: drink, breathe, survive. But surviving with my senses dulled was just another kind of risk. Here in Morathen, I couldn't afford to stumble.

With a hiss, I shoved the satchel closed. The cork would stay sealed. Not drunk but not forgotten, either. I tucked the vial into an inner pocket, close enough to reach if the noise became unbearable. My throat ached with the wanting, but my spine straightened with refusal.

I cinched the robe tighter, pulling my hair into a knot. Tonight, I would face the Court unclouded. And if the silence broke me, I'd have my absolution close at hand.

The satchel shut with a hollow *snap*, the vial heavy against my ribs. I drew the robe tighter and turned— just as the door banged open.

"Finally," Serenya announced, sweeping in like she owned the place, her fingers following her words in broad, theatrical signs. "If you'd soaked any longer, I'd have sent someone in after you with a net."

Attendants hustled in behind her, staggering under the weight of trunks and velvet-wrapped bundles. The scent of cedar oil and lavender burst into the chamber as they set their burdens down, clasps snapping, lids creaking open to reveal a small mountain of silk, satin, and glittering jewels.

Serenya grinned wide enough to show a hint of fang, her hands flashing as fast as her tongue. "Don't look so grim," she teased. "This is the fun part. Clothes, jewels, paint—everything a girl needs to make a room full of bloodsuckers choke on their envy."

I blinked at the pile of finery as though it might sprout teeth. "Fun" wasn't the word I would've chosen.

She clucked her tongue at me, already striding over to paw through a heap of gowns with all the delicacy of a wolf in a henhouse. "Kieran was right—you're a disaster. But don't worry, cousin Serenya's here to fix you." She tossed a gown at one of the attendants without looking. "Not that one. Though green will set off her eyes. And the silver combs. Gods, do we have time for braids?"

The attendants exchanged nervous glances, but Serenya was already elbow-deep in another trunk, muttering happily about hems and décolletage.

I stood rooted, robe heavy on my shoulders, while the tide of color and silk rose around me. Divide pragmatism whispered that all this was excess. But Serenya's grin was infectious, the room brighter just for having her in it—and for the first time since stepping into Morathen, the weight pressing down on me eased, if only by a thread.

Serenya darted to the largest trunk, flung it open, and gave a triumphant, "Ha!" She held up a gown blacker than midnight, the fabric alive with embroidery that caught the light like scattered stars. She spun it once, sheer sleeves and high collar glinting wickedly.

"Perfect," she declared, thrusting it at an attendant for safekeeping. "The Hunt is half-bloodsport, half-theater. This will make them wonder if she's come to play or to kill."

The attendants exchanged glances, just as she meant them to, before bustling me toward a chair. Hands descended—combs tugging through damp strands, brushes dusting powder across my skin.

Saints, her hair is thicker than it looks.

The prince's taste, though...

We'll never finish in time.

Their thoughts pressed in, a constant buzz beneath the tug of pins and the sweep of paint. I sat motionless, spine stiff, forcing my breath to slow.

Serenya lounged nearby, grinning like a cat with cream. "Eyes open, darling. Chin up. You're about to be made lethal." She signed as she spoke, exaggerated flourishes that drew giggles from the attendants.

One muttered as she painted salve across my lips, "Plaything or not, she'll turn heads tonight."

Another's thought snagged—*If the rumors are true, she won't last long in his bed.*

I slammed a wall tight, refusing to flinch. Pettiness wasn't what I was hunting for. I needed whispers of treachery, of daggers aimed at Kieran's back. So far— nothing.

At last, my hair was twisted into an elegant knot, silver combs catching the light. Powder gleamed across my cheeks, blurring my freckles to a suggestion beneath the shimmer. I hardly recognized the stranger in the mirror propped against the trunk.

Serenya clapped once, triumphant. "Now. The dress."

The attendants brought the gown forward like an offering, black silk spilling between them in a shimmer of embroidery and heavy beadwork.

Cold fabric kissed my skin as they slid it over my head, tugging and fastening, adjusting and smoothing until the full weight of the garment settled over me. Heavier than it looked, it was as if I were wearing a night sky stitched with stars.

The high collar rose snug around my throat, concealing the scar I usually hid beneath ribbons and necklaces. A mercy, though the fabric's weight made it harder to breathe. The back plunged low to the small of my back, beads tracing my spine in cool rivulets, a deliberate contrast of beautiful cage and carnal invitation.

It clung where I wanted freedom, the beaded bodice pressing close, but when the attendants spread the skirts wide, slits parted up the sides like shadows.

"See?" Serenya grinned, flicking the fabric aside to bare the opening. "Court fashion with common sense. You'll be able to run if you have to. Or kick someone, which is almost as important."

She gave the bodice a sharp tap with her knuckles, beads clattering like tiny stones. "And this? Weapons-grade glamour. Anyone gets too close, you just lean in and let them catch an elbow."

Then she winked, slipping her fingers into the folds of the skirt. "And before you thank me—yes, I had them sew in a pocket. Don't look so shocked. A prince's consort needs somewhere to hide a dagger. Or, I don't know, a flask."

The attendants tittered, but my hand slid down instinctively, brushing the hidden seam until I felt the faint outline waiting for me. Relief loosened something in my chest. The vial would not be left behind.

One attendant's thought sparked bright with admiration—*She looks like a queen already.*

Another's curled with envy—*Like prey trussed for slaughter.*

I forced my spine straight, chin high, though the gown felt equal parts armor and cage. If I had to wear his mark, then I'd wear it like a blade. Let them choke on it.

Serenya straightened, her grin bright enough to dazzle the room as her hands signed the words: "Don't worry, darling. In this dress, they'll never know whether you're meant to be kissed or feared."

The attendants laughed as if it were a joke, but the weight of it settled under my skin, heavy as the gown itself.

Silk whispered when I shifted, beads dragging cool along my spine. The mirror propped against the trunk showed a stranger staring back—her freckles blurred, her hair gleaming in intricate knots, her throat hidden behind a collar that belonged to someone braver. Someone willing to play consort in a Court of wolves.

But it was still me beneath it. Still, the girl from the Divide who kept a bar running on grit and half-truths. A liar in borrowed silk, carrying poison in her pocket.

I drew a slow breath, forcing my shoulders square. If this was the part Kieran needed me to play, then I would play it without mercy.

The door opened again.

And there he was.

For a heartbeat, he simply stood, framed in the doorway, his gaze locking on me. Then his pupils blew wide, the ice of his irises bleeding red, his fangs lengthening in the lamplight.

A ripple ran through the attendants' thoughts— envy, shock, giddy speculation—as Kieran crossed the room in three long strides. His hands caught me at the waist, and he lifted me clean off the floor, hauling me flush against him, chest to chest.

The beads of my gown pressed hard into the muscle of his shoulders, the high collar digging as my breath hitched between us. His body was solid, unyielding, his hunger written in the tension of every line. Heat seared across the small of my back where his hand met bare skin, the touch so startling it felt like fire catching on silk.

For a breath, I thought he might lower his mouth to mine. The world seemed to hold still—steam, silk, even the buzzing in my head faded to silence.

Then, just as suddenly, he stilled. A blink, a breath, the brutal edge of control snapping back into place.

"Leave us," he said, voice low and edged with command, while I was still held against him.

The attendants scattered like startled birds, skirts and whispers rushing for the door. Even Serenya lingered just long enough to flash a grin, her fingers signing a cheeky "Good luck" before she swept out.

Only when the latch clicked shut did he finally lower me. Slowly, deliberately, as though releasing something he hadn't meant to steal. His hands lingered at my waist a heartbeat too long, heat searing through the silk.

I didn't know if the display had been for them... or for me.

Kieran turned away before I could steady my breath.

His fingers went to the clasp at his throat, tugging it loose with a practiced flick. The jacket slipped from his shoulders, the heavy fabric folding in his hands before he tossed it carelessly across a chair.

"You'll need to keep close tonight," he said, as though we hadn't just been pressed chest to chest. His voice was calm, even, while the lines of his body tightened in the lamplight.

He pulled at the cuffs of his shirt, buttons sliding open one by one until tan skin and the sweep of black ink came into view. Tattoos curled over his chest and down his arms, an older language etched across muscle built for both violence and control.

I swallowed hard, pulse thudding in my ears. It wasn't fair, the way he could look like a predator stripping down for the kill and a man simply shedding his layers in the same breath.

His hands—broad, veined, strong—braced against the table for a moment as he finally shrugged free of the shirt. Then he looked up. Pale, icy eyes locked on mine, so stark against the warmth of his skin that the strike of them stole my breath.

A smirk curved his mouth, faint and deliberate, as if he'd caught my stare and meant to keep it. Then he turned back to his task.

"The Hunt is theater," he murmured. "They'll be watching us as closely as the quarry. You'll smile when I do. You'll let me touch you, and you won't flinch. And you'll remember—companions are the quarry. Some nobles protect theirs, others don't. Either way, weakness is blood in the water."

His eyes stayed on me as the lamplight carved shadows across his chest, ink shifting with every breath, curling dark over muscle that looked built for war.

I held myself still, refusing to shrink beneath the weight of his stare. But inside, my pulse thundered. Because I wasn't sure which was worse—being caught in the Hunt... or being caught by *him*.

CHAPTER 9

KIERAN

I should never have touched her.

Her heat still clung to my hands, her bare back branded into my palms like I'd held fire. I'd meant only to play the part, to make the attendants believe what they were supposed to believe. But then I'd lifted her against me and—Vireth save me—I hadn't wanted to put her down.

Now I stood half-naked, shirt discarded, her eyes on me like a physical weight. She stared as though she wanted to sink her teeth into me, though she had none to bare. As though she wanted to claim.

And I wanted her to.

My cock ached, straining against trousers I hadn't yet shed, and all I could think of was the way her pulse had thundered against my chest, the scent of her desire slick in the air. She wanted me and hated that she did. I could taste it, salt and sweet, fury and hunger, all tangled together.

One more breath and I would have kissed her. Bitten her. Driven myself into her until she forgot every reason she had to hate me.

Instead, I forced a smirk, stripped the rest of the shirt from my shoulders, and turned away before I did something I couldn't take back. She could never know how close I'd come.

I had to bathe. Dress. Focus. The Hunt wasn't a game I could afford to lose and dragging her into it was already a gamble. She was clever enough to play her part, but the Court would test her, probe for weakness, and every eye would be looking for the moment I slipped.

And if I caught her—

My jaw clenched. Best not to think of that.

This was meant to be simple: a role she would play for a night, then return to her bar in the Divide, to her surly guard and quick-handed bartender, to the safety of her small life. Not mine. Never mine.

So why did the scent of her still cling to me like a promise? Why did every breath remind me she already was?

The water should have been a reprieve. Scalding heat to strip her from me, to bleed the tension out of my muscles before the Hunt.

But the steam carried her with it. Embers and rose-water, the faint bite of Divide dust clinging to her clothes, the raw tang of fear threaded through with something sweeter. Hunger. Need. It coated the chamber, soaked into the very stones, until I breathed nothing else.

My cock throbbed beneath the water, swollen, heavy, demanding, and I gave in—wrapping my fist around myself, slick heat sliding as I stroked once, twice, harder. Not because I wanted her—*gods, I couldn't afford to want her*—but because I needed my head clear. A quick release. A purge.

But the moment I closed my eyes, she was there. Pressed chest to chest against me, her back bare under my hands, skin hot silk beneath my palms. Her scar hidden like it belonged to me alone. Her lips parted on a breath I'd almost taken. The fire in her eyes when she looked at me—like she wanted to sink her teeth into me, claim me, even without fangs.

My grip tightened, hips jerking up into my palm. The echo, the scent of her clung to me, dragging me down, winding me tighter. My breath stuttered, cock leaking as release hovered, violent and consuming—

—and then vanished. Gone, ripped out from under me because it wasn't nameless. It wasn't simple. It was *her.*

With a snarl, I let go, water slapping hard against stone as I shoved back, chest heaving. My head was worse for it—aching, empty, and I was harder than before.

No amount of heat or discipline would burn her out of me. Not tonight. Not ever, if I wasn't careful.

I scrubbed myself down fast, as though soap and water could scour her out of me. They couldn't. Not when her scent was baked into my skin, into the marrow of my bones. By the time I hauled myself out of the basin, my cock was aching, the attempt at release only making it worse.

A towel waited, thick and soft, and I wrapped it low around my hips. The robe that should have hung beside it was gone. *My* robe.

Silk against her bare skin—that thought landed like a blow. I imagined it clinging to her damp curves, wrapping her in something that smelled of me. My cock jumped at the thought, straining tighter against the towel. She'd stolen it, whether on purpose or not, and the thought of her wrapped in my robe made me want to drag her out of it and fuck her into the stone.

Growling, I pushed open the bathing chamber door. Steam rolled out with me, curling into the wider room where she waited.

Her gaze snapped up and caught. She froze, eyes widening as they dragged over me, taking in the water dripping down my chest, the ink curling over my arms, the towel hiding nothing at all. She flushed and tried to look away. Gods, she even managed it for half a breath. Then her eyes slid back, helpless, hungry.

I let her stare as I crossed the chamber, slow enough for every step to weigh on her. I didn't bother with shame; I'd never had use for it. Nudity was just another weapon.

At the chair, I tugged the towel loose and reached for my trousers. Her want hit me like another hand around my cock, searing and relentless and impossible to ignore. She didn't even realize she was staring, not until my voice cut the silence.

"If you don't want to get fucked right out of that pretty dress," I murmured, fisting the fabric in my fingers, "I suggest you stop staring at my cock."

Her breath caught, sharp and furious, her flush spilling down her throat. But she didn't move, didn't blink, didn't even try to deny it.

And gods help me; I wanted her all the more for it.

Her teeth sank into her lower lip hard enough to bruise. The sight made my cock jerk, straining heavy and bare between us. She turned then, too fast, her back stiff, shoulders locked like a soldier bracing for a blow. A refusal. A retreat. But gods, the heat rolling off her told the truth her body wouldn't admit.

The line of her spine drew my eyes down, beads glinting as they traced the curve of her hip. My hand twitched, half a breath from following that path, from testing the heat where silk gave way to skin.

I tore my gaze away, gripping the trousers like they were a lifeline, rough and impatient as I shoved into them. Leather scraped against damp skin, my cock too thick to settle comfortably as I fastened the ties.

And all the while, it was her silence that gave her away—the quick hitch of breath at the sound of buckles, the audible swallow when I bent to lace my boots. She didn't look at first. But she couldn't help herself.

The weight of her gaze slid back over me, hot as a touch I could feel on every inch of my body.

Good. Let her stare. Let her know she'd stripped me raw without lifting a finger.

I pulled the laces tight, every motion deliberate as I tried to bind myself back into some semblance of sanity. The ache in my cock throbbed with every tug, every scrape of leather against skin.

A tunic followed, then the hardened leather cuirass, the straps biting into my shoulders as I buckled them down. Layer by layer, I rebuilt myself: boots laced tight, belt drawn snug, blades slipped into their sheaths until I felt less like a man and more like the weapon I was born to be.

And still, I sensed her watching.

Her breath hitched when steel whispered from its scabbard as I checked the edge of a dagger. Her pulse fluttered when I bent to cinch the last strap across my waist. She thought herself subtle, but gods, I could *feel* her eyes dragging over me, her body betraying her at every turn.

I straightened, the last piece of armor snug across my chest, and finally turned to face her. The gown clung like sin, beads glinting at her throat and down the curve of her spine, silk shifting with every shallow breath she took. For tonight, she would stand at my side—not because she belonged to me, but because I needed her.

"The Hunt isn't just bloodsport," I murmured. "It's politics wrapped in silk. Half the knives are aimed at the quarry. The rest are aimed at me." My hand stayed steady, palm open, inviting. "That's why you're here. To see what I can't. To sense the danger before it strikes."

Her fingers hesitated before brushing my sleeve, lighter than a whisper.

"You'll hate them all just as much as I do," I added, leaning closer, the words meant for her alone. "But if your sight gives us even one step ahead... it matters. And for that—" I let the corner of my mouth turn, a rare, fleeting curve. "For that, I'm grateful."

I held her gaze as I closed my fingers over hers. "One more thing," I said, keeping my voice low. "They'll all be watching. Every glance, every smile, every word. They'll think you can't hear them, so they'll be reading me. Don't assume your signing is private, either. Everyone here will understand you. Evara's temples demand silence, so half the kingdom grew up fluent.

And nobles love it—discreet enough for passing threats across a banquet table."

Her brow furrowed, just slightly. "So even if they don't care about their god, they care about gossip."

"Exactly. Faith makes hypocrites fluent." I stepped closer, lowering my voice further. "I'll sign names, nothing more. Harmless things they expect me to tell you. What matters is how I touch you. That's what you'll watch."

Her throat worked as she swallowed, but she didn't look away.

"If I kiss you here"—I brushed my thumb along the underside of her jaw, heat flaring at the contact—"it means they're dangerous. If I hold your hand, it means I believe they might be useful. If I don't touch you at all..." I let the corner of my mouth curve. "Forget them. They're nothing."

Her pulse jumped at my touch, faster than she'd likely wanted it to, but she gave me a tight nod, and that was enough.

The door waited, carved and heavy. Beyond it lay theater, blood, and vipers testing for weaknesses. But in here, in this single breath, all I felt was her heat against my arm and the gnawing ache of knowing that if I caught her tonight, I might not let her go.

The door to my chambers opened into shadow and flame.

Lanterns guttered in their sconces, washing the

marble in bands of gold and black. The air outside the chamber was cooler, but it carried the low thrum of the Court gathering in the hunting grounds—laughter pitched too high, music tuned taut, the hum of a crowd fattened on wine and hunger.

Every step forward tightened the mask I wore. Crown Prince. The one they watched. The one they feared. Tonight, every movement would be judged, every whisper twisted into rumor. That was the Hunt as much as the blood and the chase.

Merrit's hand rested on my arm, feather-light, her posture stiff as steel. She looked the part Serenya had dressed her for—dark silk, jeweled collar, skin pale against the beads trailing her spine. But I felt the tremor in her fingers, the half-second lag in her breath. She knew, as I did, that this was a performance we could not afford to fail.

We stepped into the courtyard, into firelight and spectacle.

Torches flared in iron braziers, their smoke thick with resin. The air was alive with the scents of horse-flesh, honed steel, and too-sweet bloodwine. Music curled through it all, strings and drums hammering a rhythm that made the gathered nobles sway like wolves waiting to feed.

Every gaze found me.

Heads bowed, some deep and reverent, others shallow with practiced insolence. They respected me because they had to. They whispered anyway, because they couldn't help themselves.

"The Crown Prince's companion?"

"Divide-born," they said. "A tavern girl dressed like a queen."

"Look at her hands—too rough for silk."

"He'll tire of her by dawn."

Merrit's smile came a heartbeat late, tight around the edges. Her fingers flexed once against my sleeve before stilling. I signed in broad, deliberate strokes—"Lord Caziel"—then bent to press my lips to the hollow beneath her jaw. Her pulse jumped under my kiss. To the Court, it was possession. To her, it was warning.

We moved on. Another bow, another name. "Lady Thane." My hand slid to cover hers where it rested on my arm, a courtly gesture that drew a ripple of indulgent laughter. Useful.

"Duke Renvar," I signed, making no move to touch her. Nothing. Irrelevant. She tilted her chin higher, catching the look I gave her, and played her part with stubborn poise.

Behind us, the whispers spread like wildfire.

"He's shameless. In front of everyone."

"No—look at him. Besotted."

"Divide-born or not, she'll burn fast in his bed."

Good. Let them talk. The more they choked on their envy, the less they'd question why she stood at my side.

The Hunt spread before us like a stage—servants

passing goblets of bloodwine, hunters flexing gloved hands, companions shifting uneasily in their finery, knowing they were as much quarry as prize. Respect crackled in the air, but beneath it all lay the truth: pageantry, sex, blood, and daggers hidden in laughter.

I bent again, pressing another kiss to Merrit's jaw, letting the Court see it, letting her feel the heat and the warning beneath.

They thought they were watching me claim her.

Only she knew I was arming her.

A long feast table dominated the center, draped in black silk and heaped with food more suited to decadence than sustenance—roasted game glistening with fat, wheels of cheese carved into crowns, jeweled fruits split to display their bleeding hearts. Silver goblets overran the boards, some filled with wine dark as ink, others with thicker, richer fare that clung to the rim in crimson streaks. The air was thick with rosemary, char, and iron.

Merrit's fingers tightened on my arm, just once, before she stilled. Her gaze caught on the table, lingered a heartbeat too long. Pride kept her face smooth, but hunger always found a way to show itself.

I plucked a slice of pheasant from a nearby platter as if it were mine by right, lifting it to her lips with the indulgent air of a prince flaunting his consort. She hesitated, eyes flashing, but she took the bite, jaw tight, chewing like she wanted to fight me even as she ate.

Whispers rustled at our backs:

"Besotted."

"Hand-feeding her like a pet."

"Divide-born and already eating from his hand."

The goblets had already begun their circuit, deep red in silver stems, thick as the veins they'd been drawn from. I caught one, its weight familiar, and lifted it high enough for the nearest cluster of courtiers to see. A Crown Prince feeding his consort. A performance.

Merrit's stomach had betrayed her earlier when I pressed food to her lips, but this was different. She couldn't drink this, not without exposing herself.

So I leaned close, pressing the rim to her mouth, letting the dark sheen stain her lips. My thumb tilted her chin as though coaxing indulgence. "Don't drink," I whispered against her skin, voice low enough to vanish beneath the din.

She obeyed—of course she did. The crimson gleamed against her mouth, obscene and perfect. Saints, it looked like she'd fed, like she belonged among us. My cock throbbed hard, hunger and want tangling until I couldn't tell one from the other.

Before I could stop myself, I leaned in and dragged my tongue across her lower lip, slow and deliberate, licking the blood into my own mouth. She jolted, breath catching, but she didn't pull away. Couldn't.

The taste slammed through me—copper, sweetness, and her warm skin beneath it. My restraint cracked. I nipped her lip, sharp enough to draw a gasp, soft enough to pass for theater.

And then I saw it. The heat in her eyes, sudden and naked. Not performance. Not pretense. Hunger as real as mine.

She wasn't acting anymore.

Whispers swelled around us, delight and shock, envy bitter as poison:

"Obsessed."

"Mad for her already."

Only I knew the truth of what had flickered between us.

And gods help me, it was the last thing I could afford.

My lips still burned where his tongue had been. Where his teeth had grazed but not pierced.

That was the worst part—that he'd stopped. One breath closer and he would have kissed me for real, would have bitten deep, and saints help me, I would have let him.

Every step beside him was a battle. My pulse thrashed like a trapped bird, my skin fevered where his hands had pressed. I hated it, hated him more for it. Because he wasn't mine to want—he was the Crown Prince of Morathen, the man draped in silks and plenty while the Divide starved on scraps. He hadn't bled us dry, no—but he'd never spared us, either.

And yet... gods, my body still ached with the ghost of him.

The head table rose at the far end of the courtyard, draped in black silk, standing above the feast like a throne carved for wolves. We climbed to it under a hundred watching eyes, torchlight painting the marble gold and blood-dark. Courtiers bowed as we passed— some deep, some shallow enough to sting—but every one of them whispered.

"Divide-born."

"Tavern filth."

"Too rough for silk."

I let my mask curl into something like a smile, even as my gut twisted.

Kieran pulled out my chair with infuriating ease, a performance of gallantry, and I lowered myself onto the seat. Silk and beads whispered against carved wood, and then there was a brush of cold under my palm. But it wasn't his hand. No, this was metal, slim, balanced, deadly.

My fingers closed around the dagger before I'd even given myself permission, the leather hilt biting into my palm, familiar, grounding. My breath caught, but I didn't look down. Didn't dare.

Instead, I eased it into the hidden pocket Serenya had insisted on, silk whispering as the weight settled against my hip. Her joke about stashing a flask echoed in my mind, but saints, this was better.

"Don't hesitate," he murmured, voice low enough to vanish beneath the swell of music. "If they corner you."

The feast was a cacophony of noise, perfume, and rot. Torches spat resin, smoke sweet as sickness. Meat glistened on silver platters, fat dripping into the fire below until it hissed. Goblets bled over the table's edge, dark wine and darker still, the iron bite of blood carried on the steam.

And beneath it all, the thoughts. Too many, pressing hard and unrelenting against my skull.

Tonight. His blood will paint the stones. The Crown Prince won't see the blade until it splits his ribs.

Cold slid down my spine. I couldn't just sit here, painted and silent, while knives were drawn in the dark. But how could I warn him without giving myself away?

My free hand found his beneath the table. Strong, steady fingers met mine. I traced a line into his palm— the kind of shorthand you used in the Divide when words weren't safe. Then, pulse hammering, I spelled it out against his skin.

D-A-N-G-E-R.

He didn't so much as look at me. To the Court, he lounged like sin made flesh, lazy smirk in place, lifting his goblet as if the whole feast existed for his pleasure. But the muscle in his arm went taut, a flash of truth beneath the act.

His thumb pressed once against my knuckles. A promise. Then another stroke, deliberate against my skin.

U-N-D-E-R-S-T-O-O-D.

Relief loosened my chest—but only for a breath. Because even as I tried to steady myself, another thought pierced through the crowd's murmur:

Tonight, we'll gut the prince while he chases his whore.

Ice slid down my spine. I lifted two fingers, brushing them across the silk hiding my scar. A second warning. A plea.

Please gods, let him understand the rest.

Kieran rose from the head table, goblet in hand, and the courtyard fell quiet. Not silent—never silent—but the hum of laughter and music dipped low, anticipation crackling through the air.

His voice carried easily, smooth and commanding, steeped in the kind of confidence only centuries could breed. "Tonight, Morathen remembers what it is to hunt. To chase. To claim. To test ourselves against the dark."

The nobles leaned forward, eager, restless. My stomach clenched at the way their eyes slid toward the companions seated at their sides, each dressed in finery that looked more like bait than celebration.

"Some of you will protect what is yours," Kieran continued, letting the words drip like blood into a river. "Some of you will not. But all of you will be seen."

Laughter rippled cruel as broken glass, the sound skittering down my spine. My fingers twitched beneath the table, itching for the hilt of the dagger I'd hidden in my skirts.

Kieran lifted his goblet higher, gaze sweeping the crowd. The torchlight turned his eyes to chips of ice, his fangs catching the firelight when his mouth curved.

"Run well. Feed well. Make them remember why this Court is feared."

The horn's echo rattled through my bones, low and brutal, vibrating up from the stones beneath my feet. Around us, the companions stiffened, their silks whispering like leaves in a storm. The nobles smiled, lips curving around fangs and hunger, the gleam of anticipation brighter than the steel at their belts.

Kieran set his goblet down, the sound final as a gavel, and reached for my hand. His grip was firm, claiming, but the pressure of his thumb told another story: *stay close.*

The head table emptied, chairs scraping back as courtiers surged toward the open gates of the courtyard. Beyond them stretched the Hunt grounds—an expanse of tangled woods lit only by torches at the edge, their shadows swallowing everything past the tree line. The air shifted, cooler, carrying the musk of earth and pine, undercut by iron and smoke.

Beside me, Kieran was all cold poise, his stride long, purposeful, every movement calculated to remind the Court that Morathen's prince led the way. But I felt the coil of tension in his body, the careful edge in every step. He'd read my warning. He knew the knives weren't only waiting in the dark—they were already in the hands of those walking at our sides.

We passed beneath the torchlit arch and into shadow. The trees closed in fast, thick with mist, branches clawing overhead until the night swallowed the feast's light and music whole.

A ripple of thought rasped against my skull. *Run her down first. Break her. Make the prince watch.*

My chest squeezed. I couldn't tell where it came from, whose hunger had painted it in my head—but it was close. Too close.

I shifted, fingers brushing the dagger hidden in my skirts. Cold steel met my skin, grounding me, even as my pulse thrashed against the beaded collar at my throat.

Kieran's hand tightened on mine, anchoring, steady. But his pace never faltered. He walked as if the woods belonged to him, as if the predators in the dark were nothing but audience.

And maybe they were.

The second horn split the night, higher than the first. It shivered through my bones, and then the courtyard erupted.

Companions bolted, skirts and cloaks flashing dark as they scattered into the trees. Nobles followed with the slow, deliberate grace of predators who already knew their prey couldn't escape. Laughter speared through the smoke, fangs gleaming in torchlight before the shadows swallowed them whole.

Kieran's hand left mine. The loss of it jarred me more than the horn. He moved like the ground belonged to him, slow and certain, as though the Hunt itself bent to his command. Every step drew eyes, even in chaos. Even mine.

I forced myself to break away, skirts rustling as I slipped into the tree line with the others. The forest clamped down quick, damp earth and pinesap smothering the reek of the feast. The music faded behind me, replaced by breath and branches snapping as bodies crashed through the dark.

Something shifted to my right—a flash of silk between trees, a companion running blind. Her thoughts were white noise, panicked and scrambled. Behind her, the tread of boots, steady, hungry. My chest tightened.

Then another ripple, closer, meant for me. *Divide-born. Soft target. She'll scream pretty when we bring her down.*

My pulse spiked. Not if I put steel in their ribs first.

I sank low, skirts catching on bramble, and forced my breathing quiet. The shadows pressed close, thick enough to choke, but I welcomed them. I'd grown up in darker places than this. Let them think I was prey.

They'd learn the hard way that the Divide didn't breed weakness.

It stomped it out, starved it, but it sure as fuck didn't feed it.

The woods swallowed the last of the torchlight quick, shadows thick and wet with mist. My breath clouded in the cold air, loud in my ears. I forced myself still—knees bent, weight on the balls of my feet, dagger slick in my palm.

Too many thoughts flooded in, ragged and greedy. *Catch her first. Break her. Make him watch.*

I pushed past them, searching for the real threats, the ones barbed with intent. Somewhere in this mess was the strike meant for Kieran's ribs. If I could just—

He hit me before I even saw him move. A blur of silk and fangs, a fist cracking across my jaw so hard my teeth clacked together. My head snapped sideways, stars bursting across my vision. I staggered, caught a root with my heel, and went down hard enough that my breath ripped out of me.

Leaves stuck to my cheek. Cold earth filled my mouth. By the time I rolled, he was already there— dagger arcing down.

I twisted, the steel skimming my ribs, hot and vicious. Silk tore, skin split, blood wet and slick down my side.

"Pathetic," he hissed, looming over me, breath iron-thick. "Divide gutter rat."

I slashed upward with my weapon, wild, desperate.

He caught my wrist mid-swing, grip crushing, bones grinding. Pain shot white-hot through my arm as he slammed my hand into the dirt. My blade jarred loose.

His laugh was low and smug, his fangs bared. "You'll scream for me."

Rage roared hotter than fear. I drove up my knee. It caught, but he twisted, taking the brunt on his thigh instead of his balls. He snarled and backhanded me. My head cracked against bark, sparks blotting out the world for a heartbeat. Warm blood flooded my mouth, copper and salt.

No. Not like this.

My fingers scrabbled through dirt and roots until they hit steel. I clenched, yanked Kieran's dagger free again just as he lunged to pin me. His weight crushed down, suffocating, every inch of him stronger, faster, built to tear me apart.

I jammed my forehead into his nose. Cartilage gave with a sickening *crunch*. He reeled back, blood pouring.

I didn't think. I *moved*.

My arm screamed as I rammed the dagger up under his ribs. The resistance was awful—grating bone, tearing flesh—before the steel punched through. His breath hitched, wet against my cheek. His hands clawed my shoulders, raking furrows that burned like fire, but I shoved harder, twisting, grinding steel into heart muscle.

Blood filled my mouth, spilling past my gritted teeth as I shoved the blade deeper, close enough for him to see the fury in my eyes.

His body jerked once. Twice. Then went slack, weight collapsing heavily across me. For a heartbeat, I thought he'd rise again. Thought I'd botched it. Then the light bled from his eyes, and the forest went too quiet.

I heaved him off, gasping, chest burning, dress shredded and sticky with blood—his and mine. My arms trembled with exhaustion. My side throbbed where his dagger had sliced deep. My jaw ached, my mouth full of blood and dirt.

But I was still breathing. He wasn't.

For a moment, all I could do was kneel in the dirt, the world tilting around me. My hands shook as I wiped the dagger clean on what was left of his coat, smearing red across already-ruined silk. His weight lingered like a bruise, phantom fingers crushing my throat, phantom teeth ready to rend flesh.

A scream split the trees—not mine. Too far away, but close enough to rattle my skull. It cut off with a wet sound that made my stomach lurch. Laughter followed, low and pleased, predators closing in on their quarry.

I staggered to my feet, dagger clutched tight, and spat blood into the leaves. My ribs shrieked when I straightened, every breath a fresh agony of its own, but I forced my spine upward.

The woods pressed in—mist curling thick, branches snagging at my torn skirts, the night alive with pursuit and pain. Every direction hummed with danger, voices in my head all hunger and cruelty.

This was only the beginning.

CHAPTER II
MERRIT

The forest wouldn't stop tilting.

Every step jarred my ribs; every breath rasped like bark in my lungs. My jaw throbbed where his fist had landed. Blood slicked the side of my dress, hot at first, then clammy in the cold. I kept moving anyway, dagger glued to my palm, thoughts slashing through my skull in a riot that made the trees blur until I wanted to claw my own head open and let them pour out.

Not prey, I told myself. *Not tonight.*

A twig snapped above me, and the cold dread of reality skimmed my spine.

I looked up and they were already falling—two shapes peeling from the branches like the night had shrugged them loose. No rustle, no warning, just weight and hands and the reek of blood and death.

A strong fist slammed into my chest, knocking me flat. The other caught my wrists and pinned them high, his knee grinding into my hip. Cold fingers fisted in my hair and jerked my head back so hard my vision burst white. Air stabbed my throat. A laugh rasped across my cheek.

"Divide-born trash," the one at my wrists crooned. His breath was sweet with rot, with death. "But I bet your blood is warm enough."

The other leaned in and dragged his tongue along the line of scarlet under my ribs. The sting made me buck so hard my teeth clicked together. He hummed like he'd tasted sugar. "She'll sing sweeter when she bleeds."

I bared my teeth and tried to spit in his face. He laughed and slapped me, open-palmed, a sting that lit my cheek on fire. Fingers tightened in my hair, wrenching harder, opening my throat. Fangs grazed skin. Not biting—yet—just a promise.

The thoughts in their heads were thorns in my skull. *Split her open. Make him watch her bleed.*

I went feral.

Slamming my knee up, I caught the one at my hip on the inner thigh hard enough to make him grunt. I twisted and sank my teeth into the wrist holding mine. Copper burst over my tongue. He swore, jerked, and I tore free: one arm long enough to drive down the dagger I'd managed to hang onto.

It hit muscle and skidded across bone, burying deep in his thigh. I smiled as he howled, but my victory was cut short. My blood-slick fingers slipped from the hilt when his companion brought his elbow down across my forearm, the shock making my hand go numb, and the dagger clattered off into the leaves.

"Little rat," he hissed, knocking me off-balance and slamming me into the dirt. His weight crushed my ribs as his fangs scraped my throat—a cold promise that made the world tilt.

No. The thought slammed through me with brutal clarity, but no sound left my throat. My fingers twitched against the bracken, useless for the signs they wanted to make.

I was going to die. Right here in the forest with my throat open and their laughter in my ears. Not in a Court's velvet cage and not in a bar where the rules made sense—here, like a rabbit whose legs had finally given out.

Then the weight on me vanished.

It didn't feel like a choice so much as a natural disaster. One heartbeat, I was pinned and failing; the next, the world ripped sideways, and the vampire at my wrists went airborne. He slammed into a birch so hard the bark cracked. The other reared back, fangs bared, and then a blur tore across my vision and dragged him off me like he weighed nothing.

Kieran.

Not the man from the head table, draped in finery and jewels. This was a monster unmasked, all civility scraped away to reveal the animal underneath. His eyes were wrong—no, not wrong, exactly. No, they were honest. Pure. This was the truth buried under layers of politics and polish.

All the icy blue was long gone, replaced with pure scarlet malice.

Blood streaked his temple. His coat hung shredded off one shoulder. His mouth split into a snarl that revealed fangs meant for rending flesh.

He didn't posture. He didn't speak.

Kieran hit the vampire who'd held my wrists with his whole body, and bone gave with a sound I felt in my own ribs. The man gurgled as Kieran's hand locked in his hair, yanked his head back, and tore into his exposed throat.

The sound he made when he snuffed out the man's life wasn't civilized, either. It was wet and obscene and full of a hunger that had nothing to do with wine and everything to do with survival. Blood arced, spraying hot across my cheek and the leaves and the torn front of my dress. The vampire kicked twice, heels plowing weak furrows in the earth.

I felt him in my head. *Not like this. Saints, no. He said it would be easy.* The thought cut off as his body went slack.

The second one lunged for Kieran's back. I threw a

rock, heard the crack of bone as it struck his jaw, but it barely slowed him. It didn't matter.

Kieran spun, snarling, and let the sword fall. His hands hit the vampire's chest with a crack of ribs. Fingers dug in like claws, forcing past bone and sinew until they closed on what beat beneath. The man screamed, high and animalistic, as Kieran tore his heart out in a spray of gore, the muscle still twitching in his fist.

His dying thoughts hit harder than the blood. *Promised—easy kill. Wrong. Wrong—*

The words broke apart into static, collapsing in on themselves as Kieran crushed the heart to pulp in his palm and dropped the body like trash.

He bared his fangs in a smile that was nothing like human.

Silence thundered, vibrating through my pulsing temples.

I lay there panting in the dirt, dress shredded open at the side, ribs leaking warmth into the cold night. Fangs had scraped my throat without piercing, and the ghost of it was worse than the sting. My hands shook so hard I could hear my bones chatter. The torches at the tree line guttered and spat resin. Somewhere distant, the horn for the Hunt sounded again, a hollow note that made the birds shudder from their roost.

Kieran stood over me, chest heaving. Blood slicked his mouth, painted the notch of his collarbone, ran in a dark ribbon down his wrist, coating his fingers. He looked at me as if I were the only thing in the forest, and also as if the forest had to go through him to get to me. The wild edge in his eyes hadn't faded. If anything, it focused.

He dropped to a knee in front of me, sudden enough that my breath caught. Up close, he smelled like the cold edge of winter. His fangs gleamed. His hand lifted—and before I could flinch, he brought his thumb to his own mouth, pierced it on one long fang, and pressed the bead of blood to the worst of the wounds at my ribs.

The heat of it burned through me like fire, bright and searing, until I thought I might arch away from the touch. Then it shifted, a molten rush beneath my skin, the edges of the wound knitting even as it throbbed. Pain dulled, twisted into something that wasn't quite agony and not quite relief—too raw, too consuming to name. My breath dragged in like I'd been drowning and only just remembered air.

My hands shook, but I forced them into signs, jerky and uneven. "I killed one. Before you came. That dagger saved my life."

His gaze snapped to mine. Shock flared in the red of his eyes, then burned away, leaving only something darker—pride, jagged and brutal. His mouth curled, blood streaking his teeth.

"Good," he said, his voice low. "Better they rot by your hand than you by theirs."

His gaze raked over me, from blood-slicked fingers to the ragged edge of my torn dress. The snarl on his lips didn't fade; it deepened, pride tangled with fury. He looked every inch the predator he was—one who might just devour me next.

Kieran's hand lifted again, thumb streaked with his own blood. He dragged it across the gouge at my ribs once more, pressing harder this time, forcing more of that fiery heat into the wound as if sheer force of will could erase every mark they'd left on me. My breath hissed through my teeth. He didn't stop.

"I'm fine," I signed, jerky, trying to push his wrist away.

He caught my hand instead, pinning it flat against my stomach as if daring me to argue. His eyes burned scarlet, jaw flexing like he was holding back words—or fangs. "They marked you," he growled, low and savage. "A single bruise is too much. I did not bring you here to suffer at the hands of my Court."

His gaze slid higher, to my throat. The scrape where fangs had kissed my skin without piercing. The muscle in his jaw jumped, and before I could stop him, he reached, fingers brushing the edge of the wound. My pulse leapt against his touch.

The blood on his mouth was close enough to taste in the air.

I signed with my free hand, clumsily, "I wasn't bitten. It's fine."

He leaned in anyway, close enough that the heat of his breath swept the line of my scar. His thumb lingered under my jaw, tilting my face up into the cage of his shadow. His mouth was still painted red, his chest heaving with leftover rage, and for a single, shattering moment I couldn't tell if he meant to seal his lips to mine—or sink those teeth into my throat.

The world narrowed to him. To the iron heat of his hand, to the furious rasp of his breath, to the throb of my pulse hammering against his thumb.

Mine.

The word wasn't his voice, not really—it was something I wasn't even sure I heard, more a spark that burned across the raw edges of my mind. A glimpse. A slip. Then it was gone, the rest of him sealed away again like always.

My breath hitched, chest burning, and still, I couldn't move. His thumb traced the line of my jaw, slow and dangerous, until it hovered just below my lip. Blood smeared from his hand onto my skin, hot and sticky. The copper tang filled the air between us, making me dizzy.

I couldn't read him. Not the way I read the others. Only shards ever bled through, never enough to tell if the wild in his eyes meant danger or something else entirely.

I should have pulled back. Should have told him to

stop. Instead, I tilted my chin higher, defying him, even as I gave him more of my throat.

A sound rumbled in his chest, low and rough. His thumb swept higher, brushing the corner of my mouth. He froze there, scarlet eyes burning, his lips parting just enough to bare fangs still wet with blood.

My hands trembled. I signed against his chest, small, broken, "Don't."

The snarl that ghosted across his mouth didn't seem meant for me—almost like it was for the memory of hands on my body that weren't his. His grip on my jaw tightened, not cruel but certain, as if he were anchoring me to him for fear I would slip away.

He leaned closer, his breath scalding my cheek, and for one long moment, the whole world balanced on the edge of those fangs. His mouth lowered—slow, inexorable—and every nerve in my body screamed to brace, to surrender, to run.

The forest held its breath with me.

And then the spell shattered with the snap of branches. Torchlight swelled through the mist as laughter spilled harsh and ugly between the trees.

Kieran's head whipped toward the sound, every line of him going taut. His blood still burned through me, hot and electric where it had touched my wound, but before I could drag in enough breath to sign again, he moved.

One moment, he was crouched before me, the next,

his arms scooped me off the ground. My legs dangled uselessly, my body light in his grip. He pressed me hard into the rough bark of the nearest tree, caging me there with the solid weight of his body.

My breath caught. My fingers clutched instinctively at his shoulders as my heart hammered, panic and something hotter colliding in my chest.

"I'm sorry," he whispered, voice so low and ragged I almost thought I'd imagined it. "Saints forgive me."

Sorry? For what? For lifting me, for pinning me here, for the wild hunger burning in his eyes? I didn't have time to understand.

Then his mouth dropped to my throat. Fangs split my skin, and fire tore through me. Pain landed first—sudden and shocking as it wrenched a gasp from my chest. Then a flood of white-hot pleasure followed, molten and unbearable, coursing through my veins until every nerve ending burned alive.

My head hit the tree with a *thud.* My hands fisted in his shredded coat, clutching like I could anchor myself against the dizzying rush. Every pull of his mouth sent another surge through me, vicious and searing, until I thought it dissolved itself into the ether.

The world collapsed down to him—his mouth at my throat, the scrape of fangs, the relentless heat curling low in my belly. My body shook with it, caught between terror and something hotter, impossible to deny.

At the edges of reality, torchlight flickered. Voices

cracked through the dark, muffled and faint. A ripple of thought scraped past, but it barely touched me. None of it mattered. Not when Kieran's mouth was on me. Not when I was unraveling in his arms.

I was so close—shaking, strung too tight, my body spiraling toward something that terrified me as much as it consumed me—

And then he wrenched away, leaving my throat cold and wet, my body trembling on the edge of something that never came. The rush shattered, leaving me raw and aching. My chest hollowed out, brutal as a stab between the ribs. He'd given me fire, dragged me to the brink—then left me in the ashes.

"Enough," he rasped, voice rough and cruel in the quiet.

The word burned hotter than his fangs had. "Enough." As if I were a mistake. Like I hadn't wanted every brutal second. Saints help me, for that breath, I almost hated him for it.

My knees buckled, useless beneath me. I would have slid down the bark if his hand hadn't caught my arm, steadying me just long enough to make the rejection worse. His grip was merciless, impersonal, the touch of someone restraining, not someone holding.

My fingers twitched, jerky, trying to form the signs that crowded in my skull, but they came out broken, useless shapes, my hands shaking too hard to make sense of anything. He didn't look. He didn't let me finish.

The wild glow in his eyes dimmed to something colder, harder.

He bent, snatched my fallen dagger from the leaves, wiped the hilt once on his shredded coat, and pressed it into my palm, curling my fingers around the hilt. Not a gift. Not a comfort. A reminder.

Then his arms swept me up again, like steel around my back and knees. My body curled into his chest whether I wanted it to or not, too weak to fight the hold. His jaw was tight, his gaze fixed ahead, every line of him carved from fury.

Through clenched teeth, he rasped, "I should never have touched you."

The words cut deeper than the puncture wounds still throbbing at my throat. My hands twitched against his chest, wanting to strike, to do *something*—but nothing came. It was as if every single second I'd been in his arms had been a mistake he couldn't wait to wash away.

And still he carried me, my stiff body in his arms as if I were his trophy, his jaw set, his stride unbroken, returning me to that den of vipers he called a Court.

CHAPTER 12
KIERAN

Her blood was wildfire.

I hadn't meant to take so much, hadn't meant to take any at all, but the second her pulse broke against my tongue, I was lost. It wasn't just the taste of her. It was heat, blinding and endless, searing down my throat until my veins felt too small to hold it. I could have drowned in her and called it mercy.

Pulling away was like tearing flesh from bone. Every instinct in me screamed to stay, to sink deeper, to drink until Merrit was mine in every way that mattered. The way her body arched, trembling, the way her hands fisted in my coat—saints, I wanted her.

And I'd almost taken her right there. Against the bark, in front of whatever vipers still prowled the Hunt, like some feral beast that didn't know better.

My jaw clenched until my fangs ground against each other. Her taste lingered, copper-sweet and electric, a brand stamped into me from the inside out. I couldn't spit it out, couldn't forget it. I'd never wanted to keep anything the way I wanted to keep this.

Which meant I had to let her go.

The thought curdled in my gut, acid-hot. My hands were still shaking with the urge to drag her back against me, to sink my teeth into that scarred throat until she understood what she was doing to me. But her eyes—wide, dazed, confused—made something ugly inside me snarl.

I couldn't let her see how undone I was. Couldn't let her know that one taste had me half-mad.

So I straightened, forced my arms to cage her instead of clutch her. Forced my mouth to twist into something cruel instead of desperate. Forced my voice into gravel when it wanted to beg.

"Enough."

The word hit harder than any fist. For me as much as for her. Because nothing in me believed it. Nothing in me wanted to stop.

And yet I had.

For now.

I carried her because I couldn't make myself let go.

Her weight against my chest was nothing—less than nothing. But the heat of her blood still sang through me, every step another reminder that I should have kept drinking, that stopping had cost me more than I wanted to admit.

The mark of my teeth stood bright against her throat, her dress torn open where my mouth had been. And worse—far worse—was the scent clinging to her skin. Not just fear, not just blood. Want. Her desire twined with mine until it made my fangs ache all over again. I'd bitten hundreds of women, fed thousands of times, but never once had their blood burned like this, never once had their bodies answered me the way hers had. Not once had I ached for them the way I ached for her.

Those long pulls of her blood should have been enough to sate me. Instead, I was like a man trapped in the driest of deserts, aching for another sip.

The trees thinned, torchlight swelling ahead, and with it, came the Court. Their laughter, their hunger, their endless watching. They would smell the blood. They would see her trembling, hear her pulse, feel the echo of what had just happened between us.

And I would make them believe it was because of me.

Let them whisper "Claimed." Let them swallow their defeat. Better that than let them scent weakness. Better that than let them guess how close I'd come to losing her—to them, to myself.

So I shifted her in my arms, cradling her as though she were glass, as though the whole damned Hunt had been staged, only so I could find her and keep her. My jaw ached from holding back the snarl, but I let my mouth curl instead into the prince's smile.

The courtyard stilled when we stepped into the firelight. Then the whispers started, hissing as fast as the torches spat resin:

"Blood at her throat."

"Divide-born trash, and yet—"

"He looks like he'd kill us all if we touched her."

I let the smirk stay, slow and lazy, the kind that made them grind their teeth. They could call her trash, witch, plaything—I didn't give a fuck. As long as they believed she was mine, none of them would dare lay a hand on her.

But the hunger in their eyes was a tide pressing close, thick as quicksand and twice as deadly. A baron's wife near the steps let her gaze slide over Merrit's torn dress, then licked her lips like she was imagining how she'd taste. My grip tightened until Merrit stirred faintly in my arms, and I had to unclench my jaw before I snapped.

Solis waited at the arch, torchlight catching on the scar across his mouth. His eyes flicked to the blood on my lips, to the mark at Merrit's throat, then back to mine. No judgment, no surprise—just the faint twitch of a grin, as if he approved. I didn't slow, didn't give him the satisfaction.

Another cluster of courtiers leaned together, their

laughter too thin, too eager, eyes gleaming like wolves scenting blood. They would have torn her apart if she'd been left alone. Now they only dared to stare at what was mine like they had any right.

I adjusted Merrit higher in my arms, ignoring the gasp it drew from those closest. She looked broken open and blood-slick, her throat marked where my fangs had been. Every inch of her screamed possession. And Evara forgive me, I let them believe it.

Because if they thought she was mine, then at least for tonight, she was untouchable.

I didn't stop until the doors of my chambers slammed behind us—leaving them, leaving Solis, Serenya, and everyone else behind.

The Court's whispers clung like smoke, but in here it was only her heartbeat I heard—fast, uneven, hammering against my chest. I should have taken her to a healer. Should have handed her to Serenya and walked away. Instead, I'd brought her here, to my rooms, because the thought of anyone else laying hands on her made my fangs ache, made my heart hammer in my chest, made me lose what little hold I had on sanity.

I set her on her feet, but I was far too rough. She staggered, caught herself on the wall, and before I could even string a word of apology together, her palm cracked across my jaw.

The sting snapped my head half a step sideways. Not enough to hurt, but enough to shock. The slap should have sparked rage. Should have had me snarling, fangs bared, reminding her what I was. Instead, the fire in her gaze struck harder than her palm, stopping me cold.

Her hands flew, harsh and trembling. "Don't ever use me like that again. Don't ever parade me like I'm yours."

Heat burned up the back of my throat, bitter with fury and something darker. "Better they think you're mine than think you're prey."

"I've survived worse than your Court," she signed, her breaths heaving. "You don't get to decide how I look in front of them."

"You'd rather look weak? Broken?"

Her chin lifted, defiance carved into every ragged line of her. "I'd rather look like that than your trophy."

The word hit harder than the slap. "Trophy." Like I'd won her. Like parading her through the courtyard, blood on her throat and mine, had been a prize to show off. Saints, wasn't that exactly how it looked?

Her fingers slashed the air, shaky but sure. "From the Divide, you've taken. Dragged me from my bar, shoved me into your Court, and stole every choice I had. I am here doing you a favor—and all you've done is take."

Her hands didn't stop, even though her chest heaved. "You carried me in there like a prize. You said 'sorry,' but what you should have done was ask."

I flinched at that, her words hitting harder than the

slap. Saints, she was right. But I couldn't let her see it—not when the memory of her blood was still burning in me, not when every step through the courtyard had been teeth in my throat.

"You think I wanted that?" My voice cracked harsher than I meant. "You think I wanted to parade you in front of them? I had to control what they saw, or they would have shredded you where you stood."

Her eyes sparked, her hands rising again. "I could have handled it."

A laugh tore out of me, ragged, furious. "No, you couldn't. You were bleeding, shaking, half-broken—and I won't let them lay another finger on you. Do you understand? I couldn't stomach it. Not one hand. Not one look. Not one thought of them touching you. I *forbid* it."

Her chin lifted, defiant as steel. "Then admit it wasn't about protecting me at all. It was about you not being able to stand your own mistake."

The truth of it ripped me open. And still I stepped closer, caging her against the wall, my restraint cracking. "I should never have touched you," I repeated, voice low and wrecked.

She flinched—barely—but she didn't look away. Her hands rose again, trembling but merciless. "Then why did you?"

I could have lied. Could have made something up. Could have schooled my reaction like I'd been taught my whole fucking life. But instead, the truth poured from my lips in a bitter whisper: "Because I can't stop."

The words detonated between us, hot as wildfire. Her breath caught, her eyes blazing, and for one long, trembling heartbeat, neither of us moved.

Then, my mouth crashed down on hers, rough, punishing, tasting of fury and blood. She stiffened, then snapped back at me, biting hard enough to split my lip. Copper filled my mouth. Saints, it only made me hungrier.

I pressed her against the wall, caging her there, my body pinning hers. But her eyes met mine, daring, dark with need, and when her fingers clutched my coat and pulled me closer, every shred of restraint burned to ash. I tore at her ruined dress—fabric ripping, beads scattering over stone—because I couldn't stand the stink of them on her any longer.

"Not theirs," I snarled against her mouth. "Never theirs."

I spun her, dropping her back onto the oak table. Glass shattered against the floor, jagged and glittering, but she didn't flinch. She arched into me, lips parted, breath coming fast, and saints, I was undone.

The insides of her thighs were slick already—wet heat smeared against my knuckles before I even found her cunt. When I did, it was molten—soaked, dripping, like she'd been waiting, aching, starving for me. I spread the wetness across her flesh, dragging it up over her clit just to feel her jolt under my hand.

My vision went red at the thought of anyone else ever touching her there. *Never.* She was mine. Every wet, trembling inch of her was mine. She just didn't know it yet. Her whimper broke like a prayer, small and wrecked, and my cock jerked so hard I nearly came in my pants before I'd even gotten a taste of her.

"So fucking wet for me," I rasped, forehead pressed to hers, needing to see her break apart. "Saints, you're—*fuck*—" The words strangled in my throat, burning out in a growl.

I shoved two fingers inside her, rough and greedy for the feel of her. Her cunt was scorching, clenching around me so tight it felt like she was dragging me under, slick walls gripping and fluttering as I curled deep to find what would break her. The second I hit it, her gasp tore high and breathless, her hips grinding down hard on my hand. The muted moans spilling out of her—broken, desperate, almost soundless—lit me up like fire catching dry kindling.

Her nails raked my shoulders, sharp enough to sting, then fumbled lower. And then she wasn't fumbling at all—she was tearing at my belt, ripping at the fastenings with shaking hands.

"Saints—fuck, Merrit—" I snarled between my teeth as she dragged me bare, her trembling fingers closing over my cock, the head already slick with pre-come. The sight of her drenched around my fingers, desperate enough to rip me open herself, snapped the last of my control.

I pulled my hand from her cunt, spread the slick up over her clit once more just to hear her choke on a moan, then lined myself up and slammed into her in one brutal thrust.

Her cry broke, desperate and breathless, a muted moan that still tore through the chamber like a scream. *Fuck.* Her cunt clutched me so hard I saw stars, choking me in that wet heat, gripping like she'd never let me go.

"Look at me," I snarled, dragging almost all the way out just to feel her flutter, then slamming back into her so hard the table shuddered under us. "Don't close your eyes. I want every fucking sound you make when I'm inside you."

Her gaze stayed locked on mine, glassy with want, her lips parting around those tiny, wrecked whimpers that owned me completely. Every desperate roll of her hips dragged me deeper, squeezing, milking me. Every broken moan vibrated against my mouth until I thought I'd lose my godsdamned mind. Her cunt was a vise, wet and greedy, and every second inside her was another chain around my throat I didn't want to break.

I fucked her harder, faster, frantic like I was trying to drive myself through the table and into her all at once. Wood groaned, glass cracked and skittered to the floor, but I didn't stop—couldn't. Her back scraped the surface with every thrust, her nails clawing at me hard enough to sting, her hips rolling up wild to meet me, slick and desperate.

My hand tore up her body, palming her breast, squeezing rough until she gasped. My thumb dragged over her nipple, circling, flicking, until her breath hitched and she moaned louder—choked, broken, beautiful. I wanted every sound. Needed them. My mouth devoured her throat, teeth scraping, biting everything but the vein I'd already claimed, marking her everywhere else I could reach.

Her cunt clamped down harder with every thrust, wet heat choking me, milking me, driving me insane. The lewd slap of our bodies filled the room, her wetness running down my thighs as she squeezed around me, tighter, wetter, so fucking perfect.

And then she shattered.

Her body seized under me, legs snapping tight around my waist, heels digging in, her cunt clenching so hard around my cock I nearly blacked out. Her muted whimper tore through me, raw and trembling, dragging me with her.

"Fuck—fuck—fuck—" I hissed through my teeth as I roared against her skin, snarling as release ripped me open. It tore through me, spilling in violent surges as her cunt clamped down, milking me until I was shaking, until every thrust sounded like sin made flesh. I fucked her through it, thrust after thrust, until the table

rattled and we were both shaking, ruined and breath-less, nothing left but sweat, blood, and the raw scrape of need finally given shape.

For a single moment, I stayed buried inside her, fore-head pressed to hers, dragging in her breath like I'd drown without it. Her cunt still clutched at me, milking every twitch, every aftershock, until I didn't know where her shudder ended and mine began. Her scent—desire, blood, *me*—wrapped around my skull like chains, pulling tighter with every gasp. My venom still burned through her, as her blood through me, but it had never hit like this. Never been so intense, so potent. It felt like it was binding us together vein by vein.

Wrong. Impossible. Too much.

I should have pulled free. Should have let go. Instead, I lingered, buried in her, staring into wide, dazed eyes that held nothing but trust and ruin. Saints, she was perfect. Saints, she was *mine*.

And that was the problem.

The thought was a blade across my heart. I tore myself back anyway, even as it felt like ripping my own heart out to leave her empty. Her lips were swollen, her chest still heaving, her body wrecked and trembling underneath mine—wrecked because of me.

For half a heartbeat, I almost told her the truth. That I'd never felt anything like this. That I couldn't stop.

Instead, the words came out jagged, almost cruel. "We shouldn't have done this."

Her eyes flickered, flashing with hurt, but she masked it fast. I watched the light die there, a shutter slamming down until nothing but cold remained. Her hands stilled, steady now where they'd trembled before.

"You're right," she signed, stiff and deliberate. Her throat worked like she was swallowing glass. "It meant nothing."

The lie gutted me, but I forced myself to nod, as if agreeing could make it true. Better she hated me than know the truth—better her fury, her coldness than the bond between us that was burning me alive.

CHAPTER 13
MERRIT

My lungs heaved against the silence, every sound in the chamber drowned beneath the hollow thud of my pulse as his touch finally dragged from my skin.

Somewhere between the dirt and his arms, I'd lost my shoes. I couldn't remember when, only that they were gone now. Bare toes curled against nothing, the ground too far below. Glass glittered across the stone like spilled stars, sharp enough to carve me open the moment I touched down.

But it wasn't the shards I feared—it was the warmth still slicking my neck and the echo of his words hollowing me out from the inside. *I should never have touched you.* That cut deeper than any glass ever could.

Kieran's shadow loomed. He didn't speak. Didn't apologize. Just lifted his hand and bit into his own thumb, a bead of crimson welling at the tip. His fingers caught my chin, tilting my face until my throat stretched bare, and then he pressed that blood against the punctures he'd left there.

The sting was instant, brutal as fire. His blood burned as it sealed my flesh, sinking under my skin until it felt less like healing and more like being branded. My jaw locked, nails biting crescents into my palms to keep from flinching away.

Mercy shouldn't have felt like cruelty. His touch shouldn't have felt like chains.

When the last of the heat faded, he released me. His hands shifted lower—one at my waist, the other braced at my thigh—and he lifted me down from the wreckage of the table. My bare feet touched stone just shy of the shards, his grip the only thing keeping me upright when my knees buckled.

And then he let go.

He turned without a word, the sweep of his coat cutting through the air like a backhand I never saw coming. The sound of the latch catching was louder than the shatter of glass, sharper than his teeth had ever been.

The door shut behind him, final as a blade, and I was left shaking in the ruin he'd made of me—blood cooling on my throat, glass at my feet, and nothing inside me but the ache of what he'd taken away.

I stood there, bare, bloodied, the tatters of my dress

shredded beyond use. His blood slicked my throat, warm where it had sealed the punctures, a brand I couldn't scrub off. The heat of him still clung between my thighs, sliding down my legs with every tremble, proof of what he'd taken and left.

The chamber was silent but for the uneven drag of my breath. I forced myself toward the arch leading into the washroom, each step unsteady, my skin prickling cold in the vast silence.

Inside, brass taps waited, carved with runes that glowed faintly as I twisted them. Water surged into the stone basin, steam curling up, hot and clean, threaded with the mineral tang of magic.

I lowered myself into the heat and hissed when it lapped against bruises, when it found the cuts his blood hadn't touched. My scar tugged tight at the heat, my chest rising, tightening with the burn.

I slid deeper until the water covered me, until steam blurred the world, until my skin prickled raw.

The sob rose fast, vicious, lodging in the back of my throat. I clenched my teeth until my jaw ached, refusing to let it free. Not for him. Not for anyone.

Never again.

I scrubbed. Hard. Nails dragging over my throat, my chest, my thighs—anywhere he'd touched, anywhere his blood lingered, anywhere I still felt him. I scraped until my skin burned, until the water turned cloudy, until I felt hollow and scraped thin inside.

But the more I tried to wash him away, the deeper he sank in.

When the water cooled and my skin was rubbed raw, I climbed out, dripping, bruises blooming purple against pale flesh. Steam ghosted off me as I wrapped myself in a towel, but it did nothing for the cold squatting inside my chest.

The chamber beyond was still. The glass had been swept away, the oak table scrubbed clean as if nothing had happened. A tray waited in its place, silver domes hiding food that smelled rich and spiced, meant to tempt, to soothe, to bind me tighter.

I wanted to spit on it. To shove it away untouched.

But survival was a louder voice than pride. My stomach knotted and growled, and I'd bled too much already. Refusing food wasn't defiance—it was suicide.

I sat, pulled the tray close, and forced myself to eat. Bite after bite went down like stone, no matter how tender the meat or sweet the bread. It filled the hollow in my gut, but not the one he'd carved in my chest.

When the worst of the hunger dulled, I dug through my satchel until my fingers closed on the thin vial Sable had pressed into my palm before I left the Divide. Elixir. Harsh, bitter, necessary.

I pulled the cork with my teeth and tipped it back. The liquid burned like acid, biting all the way down, but I swallowed it anyway.

A choice.

My choice.

When the last of the elixir burned down my throat, I set the empty vial on the table, its tiny *clink* against the wood a reminder to myself that I hadn't let him take everything.

The food and potion dulled the edge of my hunger and steadied my hands, but the ache inside me only grew heavier. Every muscle trembled with it. Even my scar felt tight, like a seam ready to split.

I wrapped the towel tighter and glanced toward the door leading out of his chambers. For one heartbeat, I thought about walking. About finding another room. About sleeping on the cold floor before I'd let myself crawl into anything that smelled like him. Hell, I considered strapping on my boots and hiking back to the Divide.

Then a wave of dizziness hit, black creeping at the edges of my vision, and my knees gave just enough to remind me how much blood I'd lost.

Survival over pride. Always.

I stripped the towel, slid between the sheets of his bed, and sank into the dark. The linens smelled of cedar smoke and cold iron and him—every breath another needle stitching his ghost deeper into my skin. The mattress was warm, but my chest stayed cold. My eyes stung, but I clenched my jaw until my teeth ached, refusing to give the sob an inch.

The betrayal sitting in my chest wasn't his. It was

mine. Because as much as I didn't want it to, it had meant something. Every single second, every scrape of teeth and clutch of hands—I'd trusted him. I'd let myself believe, and he'd proved me a fool.

And the worst of it all? I knew better. I knew better than to trust him, knew better than to ache for someone that would never be mine. This was a business transaction, nothing more, and I'd let it spiral away from me, hanging my heart on hopes and dreams instead of hard, cold reality.

I wouldn't let him play me again. Not ever.

I curled tighter, tucking my knees up until the world narrowed to the scent of him and the weight of the sheets. The elixir's warmth dulled my limbs, pulling me under, even as my mind spun. The ghost of his mouth still throbbed at my throat, a brand I couldn't scrub off.

And in the silence, alone in his bed, I finally slept.

THE SHEETS WERE COLD WHEN I WOKE.

Not all of them—just the hollow on the other side of the mattress, indented deep where a body had lain. His body.

Kieran had come back. After walking out, after tearing me open with those words, he'd returned long enough to leave his weight pressed into the linens. The dip in the mattress mocked me, bitter as the memory of his mouth. Proof he hadn't stayed, not really. Proof I'd been foolish enough to hope for more.

My chest tightened, stupid and traitorous. He'd gone before I woke, left without a word, without a trace. I shouldn't have cared. Saints help me, I shouldn't have cared. But hope and loss both squatted in my chest, fighting for space—I didn't want to give either.

I rolled onto my back and froze.

I wasn't alone.

The shadows in the far corner were wrong. Too thick. Too still. They shifted when I blinked, stretched like they had shape of their own, and then a woman stepped from them, leather whispering against leather.

"You're finally awake," she drawled, flipping a knife lazily in her hand. "Good. Saves me the trouble of poking you with something sharp."

My stomach dropped. My gaze flicked to the table where my dagger should have been, but the wood was bare. She noticed, her mouth curling like she'd read the thought right out of me.

"If I wanted you dead," she said, casual as smoke, "you wouldn't have woken up at all."

She tossed something at me, the heavy black fabric settling across my stomach—a robe.

"Put that on," she said, quirking a brow. "Might make you feel better. Or not. But strutting around naked in the Crown Prince's chambers is a bold move when half this Court already wants you gutted."

My jaw clenched, but I shoved my arms through the sleeves, anyway. The robe was thick, smelling faintly of cedar and the subtle citrus oil from the trunks Serenya had brought in yesterday.

She paced while I covered myself, the shadows of the room drawn to her, twitching at her heels like obedient dogs. She twirled the knife once, then caught it by the hilt with a bored flick.

"Name's Nadia," she said, dropping onto Kieran's chair like she owned it, one boot hooked on the edge of the table. "I keep to the dark corners. Makes me good at hearing things people would rather I didn't. And before you wonder—I've been watching you for weeks. I know you hear just fine, so let's skip the signing and save us both time."

I lifted my hands, precise and deliberate. "And what exactly do you want with me?"

Her grin sharpened. "Relax, Divide-girl. I'm not here to kill you. I'm here to keep you alive—whether you like it or not. Funny thing about staying alive…" She leaned closer. "Someone put a hit out on you before the Hunt even started."

My brows rose, my signs clipped with frustration. "No shit."

I'd already tasted it in the chaos of their dying thoughts, the splintered fragments that told me I was never meant to walk out of those woods. Nadia wasn't telling me anything new. She was just putting words to the rot I'd already felt pressing in, the truth I'd pieced together in blood and silence.

Nadia barked a laugh. "Oh, I like you. No wide-eyed 'why me,' no pathetic handwringing. Just straight to the meat of it. You're already more fun than half this Court."

"Tell me something I don't know," I signed, slower this time.

"Yeah?" She leaned forward, closer this time, shadows twitching with the motion. "Then here's what you didn't figure. The order didn't come from outside the walls. It started inside them. The kind of rot that doesn't creep in from the edges, but blooms at the center from the ones you're supposed to trust most."

The room shrank around me. I tugged the robe tighter, cold settling in my chest like a stone.

She saw it but didn't soften. Just flipped her knife end over end, shadows curling up her wrist. "I was there, you know. In the forest. Watching his back. Sorry I didn't get to you sooner, but between him and you, I'm betting on the man who can pay my rate. You? I don't know. Him? He's got coin, reputation, and a way of surviving impossible odds. It's basic math."

Her gaze slid back to me, sharp as her tongue. "Don't take it personal."

My hands rose, still sluggish from the elixir's weight.

"Business is never personal. And no offense, but I don't trust the barkeep who pours my ale half the time. Why the fuck would I trust you?"

It was the truth. In the Divide, I'd dealt with enough men and women who talked like friends, who smiled while they thrust the dagger in your back. Nadia didn't bother with a smile, but that didn't make her any safer. It just made her honest about the blade in her hand.

Her laugh came low, amused. "You shouldn't. You don't owe me trust. You owe yourself caution. Remember that."

She pushed to her feet, pacing again, dagger flashing with each turn. "But since I'm feeling generous, there are two things you should know." She counted them off with the blade.

"One: that elixir? Not exactly street stock. Too rare, too pricey, and too fucking noticeable when someone's using it. Maybe your supplier's loyal, maybe they'd never sell you out—I don't care. Doesn't matter. Because word about who even *has* access to it travels fast. You drink it too often, and the wrong people start asking questions. Like maybe why some backwoods barkeep even needs something that powerful. I'd bet you don't want your name anywhere near those conversations."

My stomach clenched, but I kept my face smooth. Of course she'd dig where it hurt—that's what people like her did. No point proving her right. I'd survived the

Divide by keeping my secrets close, not by handing them to the first shadow who came sniffing.

The knife twitched, point lowering toward me like a warning. "Two: the king's already asking questions. Quiet ones. That's worse than the loud ones. He likes having a file on everyone, likes pulling it out when it's useful. If he doesn't like the story attached to your name, he'll make you into an example. Considering there's nothing about you before the age of ten when you showed up bloody on the steps of a Divide orphanage, I'd be concerned."

She let that hang before tucking the dagger away, shadows licking higher up her arms like restless pets. "So, around these vultures, keep your answers short. Keep a blade close enough to draw blind. And when you leave a room, watch your back. People move in patterns. Learn them or bleed for it."

She tilted her head, eyeing me with a glint of something I couldn't name. "Then again, you're from the Divide. I figure you know how to watch your own back already, don't you?"

A flush of something hot rose in me—gratitude or anger, I couldn't tell. My hands flexed, forming the signs anyway. "Nice to know who you picked to save. I suppose I should be grateful you gave me anything at all."

Nadia's smile flickered. "Yeah, well. He pays better.

But you're alive, aren't you? Play it smart and you might even stay that way."

A knock rattled at the chamber doors. Serenya's voice followed, dry with impatience. "Kieran, open up."

Instinctively, I turned toward the sound. And when I looked back, Nadia was gone. Not a sound. Not a whisper. Only shadows trembling in the corner, settling back into nothing, like she'd stepped through them into some private dark that belonged only to her.

Saints, I should've stayed in the Divide. Better the wolves I knew than the shadows in this place.

CHAPTER 14

KIERAN

Her taste was still in my mouth.

Copper, heat, want. A poison that didn't weaken me but set fire in every vein. Her blood coiled inside me, wild and alive, a brand I couldn't spit out. I'd left her because I had to—because staying would have burned us both to ash—but the memory of her curled in my bed, scar bare, wrapped in nothing but sheets haunted every step I took.

I hadn't slept. Not really.

After the table had been cleared, after the shards were swept from the stone, after I'd set food on the table like some pathetic offering—I still couldn't leave it there. While she bathed, I made myself useful. While she ate, I stayed away. But when the chamber quieted and the steam had faded, I came back.

I lay beside her long enough to hear her breathing

slow, to see the tension bleed from her brow. Long enough to pretend she was safe because I was near. But I didn't close my eyes. I couldn't. Every time the scar at her throat caught the lamplight, every time her silence hummed like a tether, I knew staying was a cruelty. So when her sleep deepened, I rose.

The couch in the corner held me for the rest of the night but not sleep. Only fits. Half-dozes shattered with every sound, every imagined falter in her breath. My body begged for rest, but the taste of her blood burned too hot in my veins. It was a drum in my chest, steady, merciless, daring me to forget her for even a moment.

And now the lack of rest amplified everything—the ledger's words, the stink of ink and bloodwine, the hollow cadence of names read like debts. It made me dangerous in ways linen and titles couldn't soften.

The chamber smelled of bodies and worry. Long oak tables stacked like pews, faces set like stone, each pair of eyes a small tribunal. The Hunt's ledger lay open where the clerk had left it, a thin river of names and short, bureaucratic notes: who'd come, who'd bled, who'd lost their lives to the game.

Solis had been right: they loved lists. They loved the cadence of accounting for death as if it were a tidy debt. The clerk in the center of the room read with a precise, almost bored cadence that made the whole thing feel like a mundane business meeting rather than the tallying of lives.

"House Daren—Lord Mavren, pierced through the throat by his companion's hand. House Hollen—two men, snapped necks, possibly a misstep near the bramble line. The Baron of Gesset—fall from a bank: shattered skull." The clerk's voice flattened the horror, reducing deaths to inked lines.

They swallowed the names of the fallen like a Sunday roast, with practiced ease, lacking even a hint of guilt.

I kept the prince's mask in place, but each entry was a pin struck into the map I'd thought I knew. Mavren—dismissed as a drunk, never a threat. Hollen's boys—green hands who thought the Hunt a boast. Gesset—soft and careless. All of them dead by design.

The ledger did not say how many of the killed had been used as pawns. It did not say "compelled." It did not say hands turned on companions under orders. It never wrote the inside work. Nadia's warning thudded in my skull: inside. At the center.

A line in the clerk's list caught my eye and tightened something in my gut: "Ravik—mutilated, throat and side." "Jolan—mutilated, crushed sternum."

They'd been cataloged like any other casualty, but I remembered them clearly. Ravik had lunged for me at the tree line, a knife, bright and greedy; I'd ended him with a clean twist that left blood and nothing poetic. Jolan had come for Merrit—he'd meant to tear her throat open—and I'd snapped his neck between a trunk and my elbow before he could scream her name.

Those two were not innocent. They were the tools who'd been shaped and sent. I had put an end to them before they completed what they'd been paid to do. I had not been the passive spectator the ledger implied; I had been the executioner's axe.

The clerk went on: "Companion Hest—throat torn, probable ambush. Solnik—blunt force to skull, accidental fall indicated." He flipped pages like a surgeon turning charts. The glib cadence made violence an administrative task. A man in the gallery laughed, too loud, brittle as bone.

Tobias lifted a finger to point at a map. "Most casualties fell in the Southeast grove. That suggests—"

"—a failed pincer," Solis finished, grin wolfish but the steel under it real. "Or someone meant to leave a message."

"The message," I said, and the chamber stilled because a prince's voice had weight whether I wanted it to or not. I kept my eyes on the ledger as if it were the only thing I cared for, then raised them until the room could only meet my gaze. "Whoever did this knows how to reach into places we thought safe. They corroded the inside. That changes the game."

They looked away from the ledger then and toward me, hungry for the ritual of vows and investigations. They wanted show. They wanted a prince who performed grief and promised retribution in tidy phrases. Fine. I would give them performance.

I'd give them teeth, too.

A lord at the back, fat with certainty and the stink of bloodwine, let his words drop like stones into still water. "You drag a Divide whore into the Hunt and wonder why the forest bleeds? Standards rot when princes scrape the gutter for their playthings."

It wasn't the first insult, not the worst, but it chose to wear its venom loud in my presence.

I rose slowly and closed the distance in three silent strides. My hand came up, and the man's jaw folded under the force. A mouthful of blood erupted, hot and sudden as teeth clattered across the marble, one popping free like a rotten stone. He slid to the floor, dazed, eyes blown wide in a stunned, insipid question he already knew the answer to.

And I didn't stop. My fists fell, hard and precise at first, then with a growing, controlled fury that refused to let me go. Bone gave, cartilage collapsed, his nose crumpled into a wet smear. I kept going until his face was a ruin—cheeks mashed, mouth a ragged hole, a grotesque, pulpy shape on the floor that barely passed for a man. The chamber went deathly quiet, every eye fixed on the wreckage at my feet.

That, for some, should have been the end. A private lesson against public mockery.

But other mouths opened. A baron, heftier from

long dinners and the luxury of arrogance, leaned forward and spoke with the confidence of someone who'd never had a hand come down in anger. "A bold performance, Prince. If you break men for a word about your whore, how long before you break a house?"

He had the wrong sort of bravado for the moment.

I moved with cold precision. My dagger slid free from my belt with a whisper, and I stepped in. The blade found the curve of his gut as if it were a path I'd walked a hundred times; steel sank home to the hilt. He made a sound like a struck animal, eyes bulging, color draining from his face in a quick tide.

For the briefest second, he stared at me as if the world had split and I was its new, terrible truth. Then he crumpled to one knee, hands clawing at the hilt at his middle. Blood wetted his palm, hot and bright, and he teetered—a man astonished to discover his own mortality.

The chamber folded inward, somewhere between outrage and relieved curiosity—the way crowds reacted when a performance became real.

"Remember this," I thundered, loud enough to echo off the walls. "You want to whisper about me, fine. But you put her name in your mouth again, and I'll carve it out with your tongue still attached."

Silence crashed through them all, solid and absolute.

Solis let out a short, savage chuckle that cut the

tension like a knife. "Well done, Your Majesty. I've always liked carnage with purpose." His grin was a scar splitting wider, the kind that promised he'd savor every drop of the fallout.

Tobias' hand fell on my arm, steady and blunt. "Don't make this a show, Kieran. Contain it; don't let it feed the wolves." He met my eyes with that curt appraisal he always gave when a thing needed wrapping in usefulness, not spectacle.

I shrugged him off. "It stopped being a show the second they spat her name like rot." My voice carried, deliberate, meant for every ear in the chamber. "This isn't theater. This is consequences. And I stopped being a frightened boy in this Court a long fucking time ago."

Silence rippled, taut as a drawn bowstring. I let it hang a breath, then severed it with steel.

"Station men at the south wall. Double the roving patrols. Lock the eastern gate until dawn. The two you're dragging out will live—but they'll live with the scars they've earned. Let the rest of the Court see them crawl and let it serve as a reminder: my patience has a limit, and they just reached it."

The guards obeyed without hesitation, hauling the groaning lords out in a trail of blood and silk.

Across the chamber, Solis leaned back in his chair, a grin tugging crooked at his scar. "Patience with teeth is more accurate," he hooted, amused. "Saints save us, the prince finally grew his fangs."

Tobias' hand still hovered near my arm, but I shrugged him off and met his gaze. His expression didn't crack, but the ledger in his grip went still. Not disapproval—just the quiet pause of a man who was used to steering the current, only to find the river had its own course.

The silence that followed wasn't shock anymore. It was caution.

For the first time in years, the chamber weighed me not as ornament, but as danger.

But the ache for Merrit—left to stitch herself together without me—was a cold ache at the center of it. I would burn the rot from my Court. I would make sure no one ever called her prey in my presence again.

My list had already begun to form, names slipping into place like knives on a belt. Who had access to the Hunt routes? Who could slip a note into a huntsman's hand? Which of the men I'd smiled at and dismissed had fingers already greased with other people's blood? There would be a ledger for them, too, and I would inscribe it in fire. Find the routes. Check the suppliers. Watch the servants who exchanged favors for coin. Ask about the late-night visitors to the northern lodges. Keep the men who knew too much awake until they told me what they'd been paid to do.

The chamber was still vibrating with the echo of my threat when Tobias finally broke the silence, his ledger shut tight in his hands.

"Enough blood for one morning," he said evenly, though his eyes flicked to the lords still groaning as the guards dragged them out. "There's the matter of tonight's gathering. The barons expect their supper, their toasts, their theater. Apologies, but you'll need to bring your Divide guest."

The word "guest" was measured, calculated like a surgeon deciding where to cut, and I fought off the urge to bury my fist in one of my oldest friend's faces.

I didn't answer, only flexed my hand where the baron's blood still clung to my knuckles. Merrit in that room, ringed by the same mouths that had dared spit her name—saints, it would be carnage before the first toast.

Solis leaned back, scarred grin wide, unhelpfully amused. "Oh, I do hope you bring her. Court hasn't had proper entertainment in years."

Their eyes were on me, waiting. I let the silence stretch, then let the fake princely smile curl slow and sharp.

"If they're hungry for a spectacle, they'll have one," I promised. "She'll be at my side."

Serenya's brisk knock vibrated through Kieran's chambers, yanking my gaze from the spot where Nadia had just vanished. Still reeling, I hesitated to move at all, worried the odd woman would step from the shadows just to scare me.

After a few long moments of watching and waiting, I pushed to my feet, cinching the robe tighter at my waist. The movement tore the stillness apart, and pain flared in its place. Yesterday's violence came rushing back—deep aches flaring where adrenaline had once kept them quiet.

Not the surface sting of cuts—those were long gone, sealed under Kieran's blood—but the deep, slow throb of battered flesh left behind. Bruises I hadn't yet seen but could feel blooming beneath the skin were hot and heavy as coals. My ribs ached when I drew breath. My shoulder pulled like it had been wrenched from its socket. Even my jaw complained, tight when I clenched it, tender where a blow had landed.

The adrenaline that had carried me through the Hunt had burned away, leaving nothing but the wreckage it buried. Every step was a ledger of impact: stone against bone, fist against face, ground against spine. Pain uncoiled through me, familiar and unwanted, reminding me I was still mortal beneath all the masks.

The door opened before I could reach it. Serenya swept in with her usual rush of perfume and silk, words on the tip of her tongue for Kieran.

They died on her lips when she saw me instead.

Her eyes flicked quick as a whisper, taking me in head to toe. Mischief tugged at her mouth, but there was no mistaking the edge underneath. "Saints, girl," she signed. "You look like a bruised peach."

Worry pinched my brow. I glanced down, tugging the robe aside—and froze. Shadows bloomed across my ribs, violet and yellow. My arm was mottled dark from shoulder to wrist. I caught my reflection in the sideboard mirror and stifled a gasp. Even my cheek had gone purple at the edge of the bone, reaching up to my temple where I'd been struck.

I supposed Kieran's blood could only do so much.

Serenya clucked her tongue, already digging in her satchel. "Of course he didn't bother to take you to a healer. Typical." She tossed me a small vial, the glass clinking against my palm. "Drink. It'll kill the ache and make you look less like roadkill. Not as good as another mouthful of your prince, but unless you're keen for round two of that"—Her grin went sly—"this'll have to do."

I pulled the cork with my teeth. The tonic was bitter, metallic, searing down my throat like firewater. Warmth unfurled in its wake, dulling the ache, washing shadows from my skin as if they'd never been there.

Serenya leaned back in Kieran's chair, satisfied. "Better. You'll need it. There's a supper tonight—formal, grand, and stuffed with barons who'd chew you up just for sport. Congratulations, you get to be arm candy."

I signed tersely, "His itinerary is not my problem."

She only shrugged, eyes gleaming. "It is now."

I pressed my lips together, fingers curling tight at my side. *It is now.* The words grated, burrowing deep in my chest like the edge of a razor.

I could leave. The thought rose sudden and vicious. Walk out of this castle, down the long roads, back to the Divide where no one dressed bruises in silk or paraded women like trophies. It would be simple. Quiet. One bag, two steps, and I'd vanish like I'd never been here at all.

The bar would still be there—the cracked counter-top, the familiar noise, promises poured cheap into chipped mugs. The only place that had ever been mine. If I went now, maybe it would still feel like home.

Serenya tilted her head, keen eyes narrowing. "You look about two breaths from bolting."

I signed, slow but firm, "Better that than playing his pet at supper, watching barons bloated on too much bloodwine insult me to my face."

Her grin flickered, half-amusement, half-sympathy. "Can't say I blame you. But unless you want the whole Court whispering 'coward' behind their wine cups, running's the worse look."

The word burned. "Coward." It would follow me all the way to the Divide. I absolutely loathed that she wasn't wrong.

If I couldn't run, and I couldn't hide, then I would just have to fulfill my duties a hell of a lot faster than originally planned. That meant not staying in this stuffy, gilded cage for one more second than I had to.

My hands stilled, then moved again, sharper this time. "The sooner I find the assholes trying to kill him, the sooner I can leave."

Serenya considered that, lips quirking. "So. Brooding in here or prowling the halls, pretending you're not watching everyone too closely? Tough decision."

The robe pulled heavy on my shoulders, suffocating in its softness. After last night, the thought of facing him again—of being paraded at his side like a bauble— made me want to gargle glass. But walking, listening, searching... *that* I could do. At least it gave me a sliver of choice.

"I think I'll take a walk. See the sights," I signed.

"Fine." Serenya swept a hand toward the wardrobe. "But at least get dressed first. Unless you plan on scandalizing half the Court clad only in a robe."

Heat prickled my neck. Once again, she wasn't wrong. Sighing, I crossed to the chest, dragging out leather pants and a dark tunic, cut simple and practical: clothes meant for moving, not parading. I felt halfway back to myself as soon as they slid into place, and even better once the heavy-soled boots were laced up. A jacket with weight enough to feel like armor settled on my shoulders, and though the clothes were higher quality than anything else I'd ever worn, they were Divide through and through.

"Fine, but if you're set on roaming, at least don't make it boring. Come on, I'll show you where the vultures circle." She slipped past me into the corridor, skirts brushing the stone, and tipped her head for me to follow.

I fell into step beside her, boots striking steady against the polished floor.

"That way's kitchens," she said with a casual flick of her fingers. "If you don't mind smelling like onions, you'll catch the best gossip there. Over there—guards' barracks. They strut like roosters, but half of them can't keep their mouths shut. Watch their faces when they drink."

Her gaze slanted to me, mischief sparking. "You've got keen eyes. Use them. People will forget a mute little seer is watching, even when they should know better."

"And here I thought you liked keeping secrets," I signed, lips twitching despite myself.

She grinned. "Oh, I do. But what's the point of knowing things if I can't show off a little?"

Serenya stopped, skirts swishing around her ankles, and leaned close enough that her perfume curled warm at my throat. "Every noble here wears their mask like a second skin," she murmured. "Learn which cracks are painted on, and which ones bleed when you press."

We reached a landing where two staircases curved in opposite arcs, shadows pooling thick between them. Serenya slowed, skirts whispering against stone, casting me a sidelong glance.

"This is as far as I'll walk you," she said, her grin sharp. "I've got other fish to fry before supper. Try not to look too obvious. You're supposed to be mysterious, remember?"

She winked, then swept down the left-hand stair, perfume trailing like mist in her wake.

I drew a long breath, leather creaking at my shoulders, and let the silence settle.

The castle unfolded before me, endless corridors stacked in stone and secrets. The air smelled faintly of beeswax and damp stone, threaded with the faint tang of smoke from unseen hearths. Gilt trim framed high-arched doorways, and windows climbed the walls so tall they seemed meant for giants, each one spilling pale light across polished floors.

The walls carried voices—whispers, laughter, the clink of goblets—and every sound echoed longer than it should, bouncing off marble and velvet. Servants flitted past like startled birds, heads bent low, their arms piled with linens and trays. Guards leaned against spears at every other doorway, armor catching the light in quick flashes. Courtiers drifted in clusters, jeweled and perfumed, their movements choreographed like a dance they'd been practicing all their lives.

It was dazzling, suffocating. Too much silk, too much shine.

Dulled as it was by the elixir, my ability still made itself known. While only fragments bled through—half-formed thoughts, flashes of intent—they still drilled into my skull without warning.

...should've been quick. Too many eyes. Should've finished it before the Hunt started...

I blinked, gaze sliding toward a guard at the barracks door. He stood like carved stone, eyes forward, but his mind hissed with guilt. I made a note of his face before moving on.

Farther down, near the laundry: *...cloak still damp,*

blood won't scrub out—better burn it before the steward sees...

My pulse hitched, fighting the urge to round the corner and find who belonged to that whisper.

Out loud, a courtier muttered to another, "Divide trash, bedding the prince."

But the thought beneath curled darker: *...if the baron bought the Hunt, who else is already bought?*

The pieces were jagged, scattered, but they were not random.

I moved on, steps steady, breath shallow, waiting for the next shard to cut.

The corridor narrowed, tapestries swallowing the walls in velvet and gold thread. Scenes of hunts, battles, and coronations loomed above me, every woven figure staring with glassy, accusing eyes. My boots sank into a rug so thick it muffled the sound, until the hush of the place pressed too close.

A flash of silk broke the stillness. A noblewoman, jeweled to the throat, swept into my path as though she had been waiting for me all along.

She stopped, gaze raking me from head to boot, her lip curling in practiced disdain. "The prince does collect strays, doesn't he?"

The words were honeyed poison, but her mind was crueler still: *...but she shouldn't have survived. Someone failed their mark.*

The thought sliced deeper than her sneer. My spine

stiffened, pulse hammering, but I kept my hands steady as I signed, dry and cutting, "Better than sampling someone's old, rotten fruit, don't you think?"

Her painted mouth tightened, a flicker of anger breaking through her mask before she turned with a snap of silk and swept away. My chest ached with the effort of not grinning. Small victory, but it warmed me enough to keep moving. Good to know all of Kieran's Court understood me, even if they were back-biting dicks about it. Still, how many vipers were in Kieran's nest?

Too many to count. Too many for one woman to root out before the next blade found its mark. Was I going to die here digging through other people's lies?

I kept pushing along, but I didn't get far. Shadows bled thicker at the next turn, pooling like spilled ink. Before I could react, a hand shot out, catching my sleeve and yanking me into the dark.

Nadia.

She shoved me against the wall just as two courtiers rounded the corner, voices pitched low, their gowns brushing inches from where we stood. Her knife spun lazily between her fingers, glinting like a cat's eye in the dim.

"Careful, Divide-girl," she murmured, her grin all teeth. "Keep prowling like this, and someone's bound to notice you sniffing after their secrets."

Cursing that stupid elixir, I rolled my eyes, trying

not to show just how much she'd surprised me. "And yet you noticed first."

Her grin stretched across her lips. "Because I'm better at it, obviously. You should try harder."

I wrenched free, hands snapping quick. "Not your concern."

Nadia leaned closer, eyes glittering. "Maybe not. But if you're going to play prophet, at least learn when to get out of the way. This Court chews distractions for breakfast."

Her knife vanished as swiftly as it appeared. One heartbeat she was there, the next she was gone, the shadows swallowing her whole.

The corridor yawned empty again, but the weight of her warning clung as close as the stone.

By the time I found my way back to Kieran's chambers, my nerves hummed like bowstrings. The castle was too full of whispers, too many eyes flicking toward me and then away, as if they could smell blood on the air.

The door stood open. Inside, the room had been transformed—candles lit, gowns draped across the bed in shimmering rows like offerings. Serenya lounged in Kieran's chair as though it were her throne, one leg hooked over the armrest, expression bright with mischief.

"Didn't think you'd come back," she said cheerfully, her fingers following the quip, as if she hadn't just left me to the wolves. "Glad you did. Saves me the trouble of hunting you down."

I crossed to the bed, fingers brushing the silks. Soft. Fragile. Too much like a noose in disguise.

Serenya tipped her head, studying me. "You found trouble, didn't you?"

I kept my face smooth, my hands still.

She laughed softly. "Don't bother denying it. You've got that look. Like you've just bitten someone and liked it."

I said nothing, only turned my back to the gowns.

"Well," she went on, rising with a rustle of skirts, "the supper waits. He'll want you dressed before then. Better to walk into the wolves polished than dragged."

Her tone was light, but her eyes lingered on me, piercing beneath the humor.

I touched the nearest gown again, silk slipping between my fingers. Better to walk into the wolves than crawl home like prey.

If I was going to play their game, I'd play it sharp.

CHAPTER 16

MERRIT

Serenya had outdone herself.

The gown lay draped across the bed like a threat disguised as silk—long-sleeved, high-necked, black as ink, and heavy with beaded shimmer that caught the candlelight like scattered stars. The skirt fell soft and fluid until the slit ruined any pretense of restraint, slicing high along my thigh like a whispered dare.

"It's... a bit much," I signed.

Serenya, perched on Kieran's chair, with her feet propped on the table, arched a brow as she signed, "That's the point, love. Let them look. If they're going to whisper about you, make sure you give them something worth whispering about."

I stared down at the fabric, jaw tight. The thought of facing him again made my stomach knot. He'd left me naked on that table—no words, no backward glance, just gone. I told myself I didn't care. I told myself I'd stop remembering the heat of his hands, the weight of his body pressed into mine, the way his breath had broken against my throat.

Lies. My body still remembered.

And worse, some traitorous part of me worried. Nadia's words kept echoing—*Wolves bite when you stare too long.* The fragments I'd caught just hours ago tangled with them, ugly things that wouldn't quiet. *Should've been quick. Too many eyes. Blood won't scrub out. Someone failed their mark.*

Someone in this castle wanted Kieran dead.

And despite everything—despite his arrogance, his temper, the way he'd humiliated me—I couldn't quite stomach the thought of it. Brutal, yes. Arrogant, absolutely. But not heartless. Not deserving of whatever shadows were circling him.

"Get dressed," Serenya said, rising in a swish of skirts. "You've been glaring at it for ten minutes, and I'm starting to think you plan to kill it instead of wear it."

I glared harder, but stepped into the gown. The silk was cool against my skin, then warm, molding to me as though it recognized what it was made to contain. Serenya's deft fingers fastened the long sleeves, smoothed the seams, and finally closed the high collar at my throat.

"Perfect," she said, stepping back to admire her work. "Elegant, lethal, and only mildly terrifying. You're ready."

Her grin softened, and for a heartbeat, she almost looked kind. "You'll be fine, Merrit. Keep your chin up and your claws sharp."

The gown felt like armor, the high neck like a wall between me and his teeth. Maybe that was why I didn't feel naked walking toward the corridor.

The corridors pulsed with noise and candlelight as I made my way toward the great hall. Every step seemed to echo too loudly, the silk whispering around my legs like it knew a secret I didn't want to hear.

Guards lined the path, eyes forward, spears gleaming. None met my gaze. Either they'd been warned not to, or they simply knew better. The last time I'd seen their prince, his temper had been bleeding through his skin.

The scent of roasted meat and spiced wine grew stronger the closer I got. Laughter drifted from ahead—polished and brittle, the kind that could cut if you stood too close.

I wasn't afraid of them. Not exactly. I'd seen worse than noble vipers pretending to smile. But my palms were slick all the same. Because under the noise and perfume, I could still hear the ghosts of yesterday. The dying men on the field—their minds unraveling in flashes I hadn't meant to catch. The hiss of someone whispering, "Too many eyes." The wet sound of something breaking.

Someone was hunting him. I could feel it in the air. And saints help me, I didn't know which of us they'd reach first.

The doors to the great hall loomed ahead, carved with scenes of gods and battles long dead. Two attendants swung them open before I could reach for the handles. Light and sound spilled out in a wave.

The room was all glitter and gold—crystal chandeliers blazing, silverware shining like weaponry. Music thrummed low beneath the chatter. Every noble in Morathen must've been crammed inside, dripping jewels and smiles edged enough to draw blood.

And at the far end of it all, he stood.

Kieran.

He looked carved from the same marble as the hall: flawless, cold, impossible to ignore. His coat was deep blue, trimmed in black, his crown glinting faintly in the candlelight. He wasn't smiling, but people laughed around him, anyway.

The moment his gaze found mine, the air seemed to tilt.

He didn't move. Neither did I.

For a heartbeat, all I could see was him—the line of his throat, the cut of his mouth, the memory of his skin against mine. My body remembered too easily: the press, the heat, the sound he made when he lost control.

Then his eyes darkened—subtle, but I saw it. Recognition. Restraint. Something like hunger, buried but not gone.

My stomach twisted. I hated that I could still read him so easily, even across a room full of silks and serpents.

The nearest baron rose when I reached the dais, bowing low with the others. Kieran said something I didn't hear over the pounding of my pulse, and suddenly a chair was being pulled out beside him.

His hand brushed the back of it, a silent invitation—or a command.

I sat.

His scent reached me before his words did—cedar, smoke, the faintest trace of something wild. Kieran signed something polite to the room—a formal greeting—but when he turned to me, his gestures shifted, smaller and more precise, meant only for my eyes. "You came."

I managed to fight off the urge to kick him in the shin or kiss his stupid, beautiful mouth. "You summoned."

His mouth curved faintly, and in a voice pitched low enough that only I could hear, he murmured, "And you never disappoint."

I kept my gaze on the table. The silver goblet gleamed like a mirror, warping my reflection into something I barely recognized.

He turned then, eyes tracing the high neck of my gown before following the line down to where the slit revealed skin. The muscle in his jaw jumped once.

"New gown?" he asked lightly, his fingers following the movements.

"Serenya's idea."

"She has taste." His hands stilled, then he added under his breath, "And a sense of cruelty."

I refused to look at him. If I did, I wasn't sure which part of me would win—the one that wanted to slap him or the one that wanted to remember.

The supper was a blur of heat and candlelight, wine and whispers. The Court moved in practiced rhythm—laughter too polished to be real, smiles too calculated to be kind. Kieran sat beside me, playing his part to perfection. The prince again. No trace of the man who'd kissed me breathless and then left me naked on a cold table.

He hadn't spoken to me beyond what politeness demanded. Maybe that was for the best. The memory of his mouth on my skin still felt like a bruise I couldn't show.

One of his captains bent low to murmur something in his ear. Kieran's expression didn't change, but his shoulders went still. Whatever it was, it mattered. He rose, leaning in close enough that the Court saw a gesture that looked affectionate—a brush of lips against my cheek—but his breath was warm at my ear, the words for me alone.

"Stay here," he said softly. "I'll be right back. Hand on your dagger, just in case."

Then he was gone, crossing the hall toward the doors with his captain in tow.

My pulse was still thrumming when I realized how quiet it had become. The prince's chair sat empty, and eyes were turning toward me again—curious, assessing, half-hungry. I didn't look at them. I kept my hand where he'd told me, fingers brushing the hilt hidden under silk.

That was when the man in black rose.

He was tall, spare, the kind of handsome that came with a lifetime of power and no need to use it loudly. The chatter dimmed as he moved, like the sound itself bent to give him space. When he reached me, he bowed just enough to pass for courtesy.

"My lady," he said aloud, his voice smooth and rich. His hands shaped the same words as he spoke, precise and elegant. "Forgive me. I've yet to make your acquaintance."

He straightened with the ease of someone used to deference. "Lord Tobias. Advisor to His Highness."

He smiled dimly. "You caused quite the stir at the Hunt. I'm told you kept your head better than half the guard and all the companions. Bravo."

My hands moved before I could stop them. "I was trying not to lose it."

His lips quirked. "You succeeded beautifully."

He was too smooth, too calm, like a razor sheathed in velvet.

"You've given the Court something to gossip about," he went on. "The Divide girl who stood her ground beside the prince. They're still arguing whether it's bravery or luck."

"Neither," I signed, my hackles rising. "It was simply survival."

Tobias chuckled softly. "Then perhaps that's the difference. The rest of us have forgotten how."

His thoughts flickered faintly, teasing the edges of my mind. *Still reckless. Still thinks he's invincible.*

It could've been concern. Maybe it was.

"You must be special," he said, the words slow, deliberate, his fingers dutifully following them. "He guards you like his own personal ace in the hole."

The courtiers nearby tittered, but I kept my face still. "And you guard him?"

Tobias' smile turned slightly rueful. "When he lets me."

Another thought, colder this time: *He won't, not for long.*

I couldn't tell whether I'd imagined the edge to that thought or if it was my own anger at Kieran twisting it for me.

"You know," he said lightly, "I envy him. A woman like you could make even a doomed man look lucky."

That one hit like a spark—the kind meant to test to see if I'd burn. I met his gaze squarely and signed, measured and deliberate. "Careful."

He laughed, low and soft, genuine amusement flickering through his eyes. "Saints, you really are Divideborn. I'd have wagered the prince preferred his women gentler."

My fingers twitched with the urge to sign something that would make a courtier like him crawl into a hole. Instead, I smiled—small, cold, unamused. "Maybe you shouldn't wager on things you don't understand."

His head tilted, the motion lazy, appreciative. "Oh, I understand more than you think." His tone dropped a note lower, smooth enough that nearby courtiers leaned closer, pretending not to listen. "The prince's taste has always been... surprising. But then, a man learns best from his mistakes."

I lifted a brow, signing slowly, each movement deliberate. "And which am I—his upgraded taste or his continued mistake?"

He chuckled again, quiet enough that it felt private even in the crowded room. "Perhaps both. The line between them is thin, don't you think?"

Heat crept up my neck before I could stop it—irritation, not embarrassment. My pulse ticked in my throat. I signed fast, the movements cutting and deliberate.

"Are you trying to insult me, or is your head so far up your own perfectly powdered ass that you don't realize when you're being an asshole?"

For a heartbeat, he just stared. Then his laughter broke low and genuine, too quiet for the tables around us but bright in his eyes.

"Saints," he murmured, grin widening, "no wonder he's keeping you close. You might be the first person in this castle brave enough to talk to me like that."

"I'm not brave," I replied. "Just unimpressed."

His laughter deepened, smooth and pleased. "Then allow me to try something a little less polite."

The tone of his voice shifted—still soft, but darker, more deliberate. "You know, the Court's been buzzing since the Hunt. But not about you, for once."

My brows lifted before I could stop them, and I hated that he'd managed to catch me off guard.

Tobias' smile didn't change, but his eyes narrowed, observing me the way a cat contemplates a cornered mouse. "They say the prince lost his temper."

I froze.

He went on, almost gently, his fingers following his words. "Word is, he beat a man within an inch of his life and gutted another outright—simply for disparaging your good name." He sipped his wine like it was noth-ing. "I wish I could call it idle gossip, but I watched it with my own eyes. I imagine the servants are still mopping."

My throat went dry. The air around us seemed too thin.

"I hadn't realized you'd come to this little affair so soon after," he added, voice dropping low. "I suppose it's good for him to be seen smiling again, though the rest of us have learned to watch our tongues."

He glanced toward the wide double doors where Kieran had exited. "He's been... volatile, lately," Tobias murmured, eyes returning to mine. "Perhaps your presence steadies him."

It wasn't a compliment. It was a probe.

I forced a smile, shallow and cold. "Or maybe he just likes a challenge."

Tobias chuckled quietly, but his gaze lingered on me a moment too long. "Saints, he does love those."

That, at least, we have in common. The thought slithered through my head before I realized it wasn't mine. Tobias' mental voice was as smooth as his smile, and it chilled me to the bone.

His continuous laughter rolled quiet and low, the kind that drew curious glances from nearby tables. He didn't care who saw him. He was enjoying this—the sparring, the spectacle, me.

He was still smiling when the temperature in the room seemed to drop.

"Tobias."

The voice came from behind me, smooth and controlled, but the tone underneath it carried teeth.

Kieran.

He stood at my shoulder, posture loose, expression calm—but there was nothing calm about the tension coming off him. It rolled from him like heat off stone.

Tobias turned, all charm. "Your Highness."

"I see you've met my companion," Kieran said. His smile was polite; his eyes were not.

"Indeed," Tobias replied. "We were discussing Court manners. I seem to have lost mine."

"Easily done," Kieran said. "Some of us never find them again."

Tobias chuckled softly, unfazed, but I caught the warning beneath it. "You always did appreciate a woman with a sharp... tongue."

"Only when it's deserved." Kieran's voice stayed smooth, but the words carried weight.

Tobias raised his glass in mock salute. "Then I'll consider myself flattered."

Kieran's hand brushed my shoulder—light, but the contact set my pulse jumping. His smile never wavered. "You'll excuse us," he said. "She promised me the next dance."

Tobias inclined his head with a Court-perfect bow. "Then by all means. I'd hate to stand between the prince and his latest distraction."

The word "distraction" landed like the flick of a whip.

Kieran's hand tightened fractionally against my back. "Of course you would."

He didn't wait for a reply. His fingers slid down my arm, firm and insistent, and before I could think of an excuse—or a reason not to—he'd already taken my hand.

The musicians sensed it instantly, shifting into a slower melody. The crowd parted, eager to watch the show: the brooding prince and the silent girl from the Divide, stepping together into the light.

Kieran's hand settled at the small of my back, steady and hot through the thin silk. His other clasped mine, the contact burning in a way I hated to remember.

Tobias' words lingered in the back of my mind: *He beat a man within an inch of his life and gutted another outright—for you.*

It wasn't the killing that haunted me. I'd watched it happen before. I'd seen his blade flash and the blood follow. I'd felt his body shield mine while teeth and claws tore through the dark. We'd both killed for each other. That wasn't it.

What I couldn't stop thinking about was the "why."

Did he strike for survival—or because someone dared to touch what he'd claimed?

"Enjoying yourself?" he murmured, voice pitched low for me alone.

I kept my eyes fixed past his shoulder. If I could

have signed, I'd have asked if he always mistook fury for fun.

His thumb brushed the back of my hand, a barely there apology—or a warning. "You shouldn't have been alone with him," he said.

My answer stayed locked behind my teeth, but I didn't need words. I let my steps shift half a beat out of sync—enough to make him adjust. His hand tightened instantly, correcting me, drawing me closer.

Control, always control.

He bent his head slightly, his breath warm against my temple. "He's just as dangerous as the rest of us," he said quietly. "Flattery isn't always what it looks like."

I tilted my chin up, meeting his gaze at last. He didn't blink. Neither did I.

Then what was last night? I wanted to ask. *Protection —or possession?*

The music swelled, and Kieran's hand slid higher on my back, holding me there. To anyone watching, it looked graceful, effortless. Only we knew it was war.

The music slowed to a hush, the waltz winding around us like a trap. Kieran's hand fit against the small of my back, guiding every step, every breath. To the Court, we were perfect—graceful, poised. Inside, I was shaking.

He leaned in, his lips brushing the edge of my hair, the movement calculated for appearance's sake. "You're angry," he murmured, low enough that only I could hear.

I didn't answer. The rhythm carried us through a turn, skirts whispering, the hall spinning gold.

"I deserve it," he said after a beat, voice rougher. "For last night."

That startled me—not the admission, but the fact that he'd said it at all.

He drew me close again, his breath brushing my ear. "You think I left because it meant nothing. I didn't."

The words were quiet, fragile things, and I hated how badly I wanted to believe them.

He guided me into another step, the pressure of his hand steady, grounding. "I didn't trust myself to stay," he said quietly. "You were shaking. Bleeding. I didn't know how to touch you without..."

He stopped, breath catching, then steadied. "I cleaned the glass. Brought food. You were still in the bath."

The words tumbled out low, almost as if he hadn't meant to say them. "When you finally slept, I stayed for a while. You didn't wake." His hand shifted at my waist, a subtle, useless apology. "I didn't want you to."

The air felt heavier. Every word landed like the ghost of his hand on my skin—careful, aching, full of things neither of us should want to name.

He turned me once more, voice rough at the edges.

"I thought leaving would make it easier. For you. For me."

The corner of his mouth twitched—not quite a smile, not quite pain. "But you don't make anything simple."

The words landed like a weight against my chest.

He looked down at me then, his eyes impossibly dark. "You don't deserve how I've treated you. I'm sorry."

For a moment, everything in me wanted to thaw. But I couldn't. Not here. Not with Tobias' voice still whispering between us: *the prince lost his temper, all for you.*

I kept my face still, perfect for the crowd, even as my pulse roared in my ears.

He guided me through the last turn, his fingers tightening once, just once, before he let go.

The applause came like thunder, meaningless and loud.

Kieran bowed, the image of a prince again, and when he straightened, his voice was a whisper against my temple. "You deserve better than me."

Then he walked away.

And saints help me, I hated that I wanted to follow.

CHAPTER 17

KIERAN

She left before the applause ended.

Yes, I'd been the one to turn my back first, but the act of her fleeing felt like my ribs had been pulled from my chest and handed to a stranger. The music still lingered, high and hollow, but the world had already narrowed to the echo of her steps fading down the marble corridor. I could feel each one like a strike against stone.

For a moment, I couldn't move. My body didn't know how to stand without the shape of her beside me. Then Tobias laughed softly across the table—a sound full of wine and practiced falseness—and that was all it took.

I pushed away from the dais and went after her. The air in my lungs narrowed until I could taste copper. My heart pounded so loud I could hear it in my teeth. For once, leaving the hall didn't feel like command or convenience. It was a stab—hers—and I'd been the one to let her walk on the blade.

The corridors were dim and full of candle smoke. Perfume, bloodwine, and secrets—the whole place reeked of power and pretense. She walked quickly, her black silk dress moving like stormwater. Her shoulders were stiff, her head held high, but I could see the tension in her hands, the way her fingers clenched the skirt as she turned a corner.

"Merrit," I murmured, the sound still echoing off the stone, but she gave me nothing.

I tried again, louder this time. "Merrit."

She didn't slow, didn't even glance back. The silence she left behind her felt like judgment. When I caught up, I reached for her wrist, and she spun.

Her eyes were wet. That was the first thing I saw. Fury and tears, fighting for the same ground in those glittering green eyes. The second was the dagger, bright and firm between us. She raised it fast, single-handed, breath ragged, shoulders trembling.

Her signs came sharp, violent. "You left me. Again."

The motion of her fingers hit me harder than any insult.

I swallowed. "I had to."

"You always have to."

Her movements were wild—hand blurring almost

too quick to read, more emotion than words. Anger, disbelief, hurt. "You left me there like I was nothing."

It hit me harder than steel ever could. "I didn't want to."

"Then why did you?" Her fingers struck the air, hard enough to sting. "You didn't even look at me."

"I couldn't," I said. "If I had, I wouldn't have stopped."

She froze, tears streaking down her face. One slipped off her chin and hit the floor.

Then she lunged—not to strike, but to shove. The dagger's point pressed just below my collarbone, an inch from my throat. For a breath, I thought she'd cut me, and a part of me wanted her to. The jagged place inside me wanted to bleed the truth.

Her chest heaved; her lips pulled back into something that wasn't quite a snarl, wasn't quite a sob.

For a heartbeat, I thought she'd drive it in.

"Do it," I said quietly. "If it helps. Do it."

Her grip faltered. The blade wavered. Her eyes flooded again, too bright, and she looked at me like she hated that she couldn't hate me enough.

I reached out and closed my hand around hers. The dagger trembled between our palms, both of us shaking.

Together we lowered it an inch, the edge kissing my skin.

"If you want my blood," I whispered, "it's yours."

She stared at me, breathing hard. Then the dagger

slipped from her hand and clattered to the floor, spinning once before settling. The sound went through me like a strike. I bent and picked it up, the weight of it cold and familiar in my hand before I placed it back in the sheath at her thigh.

Her body sagged. She was still crying, silent but uncontained, and every tear felt like an accusation.

When I finally closed the distance between us, she didn't look up. Her lashes were wet, her breathing ragged and raw. It hollowed me out, left nothing but guilt and the need to fix what I'd broken.

I stood there, useless, while her tears soaked into the silk at her collar. The smell of her blood, faint and fading, mixed with the salt of her skin until I couldn't tell where remorse ended and hunger began.

She didn't back away, not meeting my eyes. The silence between us went on too long. I could hear her heartbeat—uneven, and harried, echoing against the walls—and beneath the thin fabric of her gown, her pulse stumbled.

As the candlelight shifted, I saw it: faint shadows crawling back under her skin, bruises reappearing like ghosts. The purple bloom at her jaw. The mottled dark along her collarbone. Her body was unraveling before my eyes.

She noticed it, too. Her hands went to her ribs, her breath catching with the pain she'd tried to hide.

"You took something," I said quietly, realization sinking in. "A healer's tonic."

She didn't answer, just pressed her lips together, trembling. I stepped forward and brushed my thumb just beneath her jaw—close enough to feel the fever in her skin, the bruise reforming beneath it.

"It's wearing off," I murmured, voice low. "You're hurting again."

Her lashes flicked up, glare bright through the tears as her hands shook. "Not your concern."

I almost laughed, but it came out as a breath instead. "Everything about you is my concern."

The corridor felt too narrow, too full of echoes that didn't belong to us. I noticed the bruise on her jaw darken by the heartbeat, and something in me gave way.

"You shouldn't be out here," I said, though I wasn't sure if I meant her or myself.

She swayed when she breathed too deeply, her hand catching the wall for balance. That was all it took. I stepped forward, catching her before pride could make her fight me.

She tried anyway—hands striking my chest, a flare of stubborn strength—but her knees nearly buckled.

"Enough," I muttered. "You're coming with me."

I scooped her up before she could argue, one arm under her knees, the other at her back. Her hair brushed my jaw, smelling of her pain and that gentle spice of her fire. She hit me once, twice, uselessly. The sound of it hurt worse than the impact. I carried her anyway, down the long corridor, past guards who pretended not to notice. The *thud* of my boots echoed too loud.

By the time we reached my chambers, she'd stopped fighting. The door slammed behind us, sealing the world out. What was left was her heartbeat against my throat, wild and breaking.

I set her down gently on her feet. For a moment, she swayed, fingers curling in the front of my coat before she realized and pushed me away. Her breathing was shallow, the anger still there, but under it, I caught a flicker of something else—pain. The kind that sank deeper than bruises.

Her legs shook when she tried to step back. I saw her wince, jaw tightening as color drained from her face. She was falling apart and still trying to stand proud. Saints, she'd rather collapse than let me see her hurt.

I reached for her again, slower this time. She didn't retreat, only lifted her chin in defiance.

I plucked her dagger from the strap at her thigh, the metal cold when it should have been warm from her skin. She watched me warily, trembling but not stepping back.

"Let me fix it," I said.

Her head snapped toward me, disbelief cutting through her tears. Before she could argue, I raised the blade and pressed it to my throat. The edge kissed my skin. A clean line of red welled up, bright as candle flame.

Her eyes went wide, hands flying, "Stop!"

But it was too late. Blood slid warm down my collar. She reached for me, but I caught her wrist before she could snatch the dagger away. "Easy," I murmured, gentler than I meant to be. "It's just a cut."

She struggled, silent and shaking, tears still wet on her cheeks. The fury had faded to something smaller, something wounded.

"Drink," I urged softly.

Her mouth parted, hesitant, confusion tightening her brow.

"My blood will heal you," I said. "No one's ever touched it. Not even my lovers."

The admission came out rougher than I meant it to, stripped bare by the thought of what I was offering. No lover, no enemy, no one had ever been this close.

I could feel the heat of the cut, the trickle sliding down my throat, and the way her gaze followed it: cautious, hungry, afraid.

I swallowed, voice fraying. "But you—"

Her eyes lifted, meeting mine through the shimmer of candlelight, wary and unsteady. The smell of blood hung between us, metallic and faintly sweet. My cock pulsed against the fabric of my trousers at the thought of her blunted teeth against my skin, of her tongue lapping the blood from my flesh. Something inside me craved it, needed it.

I sank down onto the edge of the bed so we were level. Even then, she had to tilt her chin up to meet my eyes.

"You can," I murmured, quieter now. The words came out like a confession and an invitation. This was more than an offering, it was a truce wrapped in a promise, and I had no idea what I was giving up.

The dagger clattered to the floor between us. The scent of blood thickened in the air—metallic, sharp, intimate.

Her lips hovered over the wound, trembling. I could feel the heat of her breath on my skin, every exhale brushing the cut like a promise she hadn't meant to make.

"Go on," I whispered. "It's all right."

She hesitated, shaking her head once, then inched closer. Her hands fisted in the front of my coat. When she finally closed the distance, her mouth met the wound in a touch so soft it nearly undid me.

The first pull sent heat through me so suddenly that I was lucky I'd decided to sit down. Her mouth was soft, cautious at first, then desperate as the taste hit her. The sensation wasn't pain—it was ignition. Fire racing through my veins, light blooming behind my eyes. Every heartbeat echoed hers. The world tilted, blurred, folded in on that single point of contact until I couldn't tell where I ended and she began.

I caught her shoulders, not to keep her still but because I couldn't bear the distance, dragging her into my lap until there was nowhere left for her to go but against me.

Her body went taut under my hands. A muffled sound escaped her—half-gasp, half-wonder—as the power took hold. I felt it more than saw it: the tremor in her muscles, the sudden steadiness of her pulse, the way the weakness drained from her as if the world itself remembered she was alive. Her breath hitched, quick and startled, and I knew it was working.

"Stay," I whispered, fighting off the urge to strip her bare and fuck her into the mattress. "Just a little more." This wasn't for me. This was for her.

She obeyed, shivering, her fingers clutching at my shirt as her scent sweetened with arousal. It was rain and wind and something wild and alive beneath the copper of my blood. It curled into my nose, lengthening my fangs as I imagined what fucking her while I fed on her blood would be like. Every part of me craved her, needed her, never wanted to let her go.

Her heartbeat fell in sync with mine as the room seemed to hum around us, a heartbeat shared between bodies that refused to stay separate.

Then it hit.

A resonance deep in my chest, a vibration that

wasn't sound but recognition. Her pulse beat through me; her breath moved inside my lungs. For a moment, we were the same rhythm.

The world didn't tilt—it sharpened. Every sound, every flicker of light snapped into painful clarity. The hum in my veins turned melodic, almost sentient. I drew in a breath that didn't feel like mine.

She pulled back before I could speak, eyes wide, lips red with my blood.

"Merrit—" I started, but the word splintered.

The air between us was vibrating, a faint, resonant pulse threading through the space she'd left. Not music. Not thought. Something older.

A whisper uncoiled in the back of my mind—*not* in my ears, but beneath them, in the marrow of me.

You remember me.

The voice was soft, feminine, yet threaded with something deeper—a sound like water over stone, wind through the trees. It didn't belong to any language I knew, and yet I understood it the way I understood my own name.

My pulse stuttered. The connection hadn't broken with her mouth—it had deepened. The air hummed with her heartbeat. The whisper threaded through every part of me, speaking again, clearer this time.

Bound and answered. Found and known.

The words rippled through me like something older than breath, as if the blood itself was remembering what it once was. I froze. The words weren't sound at all. They were blood. They were *hers*—woven through mine.

My chest ached. I couldn't breathe right; my body didn't know what to do with something this vast. The stories came back in fragments—old priestesses whispering of blood that heard, of bonds forged before language, before gods.

Superstition. Nonsense.

But her pulse still echoed through my veins, and the whisper was still there, patient and knowing. What I'd passed off as interest was obsession. What I'd once called fascination was nothing short of hunger. What I'd mistaken for curiosity had evolved into an all-consuming ache.

I looked at her, and the only thing I could manage to think was: *This is exactly what they'd meant.*

All the old myths. All the impossible things I'd sworn were fables. Everything I'd feared the second I'd tasted her blood. It was all true.

Whisperbound.

Saints help me, we were Whisperbound.

The silence after wasn't silence at all. It pulsed. Low, steady, rhythmic—an echo running just beneath my skin. Not my heartbeat. *Ours.*

Then I heard it.

Not aloud. Not even in my mind. It wasn't thought, and it wasn't sound.

It was *blood.* A single word unfurled inside me, soft as breath, inevitable as truth.

Whisperbound.

His voice—but not his voice. It moved through me like warmth remembered, like recognition buried too deep to name. It didn't echo in my ears; it bloomed in my marrow, coiling through every vein until I couldn't tell where I ended and he began.

This wasn't mind reading. I knew the feel of that— faint, cautious, a mind brushing against mine like fingers grazing glass. This was older. Wilder. It didn't ask permission. It *claimed.*

My knees weakened under the weight of it. My heart stuttered once, then fell into his rhythm, answering before my mind could catch up. When I looked at him, he was already watching me. His pupils were blown wide, his expression somewhere between awe and dread.

I lifted my hand, fingers trembling, and signed the word that still pulsed in my blood.

"Whisperbound."

Kieran's breath left him in a rush. His eyes darkened —not with fear, but with recognition of something he couldn't deny.

"You heard it," he said, voice rough, stripped of pretense. Not a question, a revelation.

I nodded once. "Clear as my own name."

He leaned forward slowly, each movement deliberate, as though the air between us had turned fragile enough to shatter. I didn't stop him. Couldn't.

When he spoke again, his tone was quieter than the candlelight. "This shouldn't be possible. Whisperbound mates are a myth. A fairytale. But…"

"It's true." I swallowed, my whole body trembling as reality set in. "One of my caretakers in the Divide used to tell us stories," I signed, the memory soft as breath. "Old things, half-prayer and half-warning. She said the gods still touched the world when no one was looking—

in the quiet between heartbeats, in the spaces where light and shadow blur."

I drew a slow breath. "She told us about Evara and Tharos."

The names felt strange after all these years, holy and dangerous at once. "Evara, Goddess of the Dead and the light that guides them—the merciful one, the keeper of endings. And Tharos, God of Chaos and Will—the defiant one, who gave mortals fire and never once asked forgiveness."

My hands moved, shaping the story the way my caretaker once had in the candlelight of the orphan hall. Mistress Samona had taught me to sign, taught me about the gods, and she'd taught me how to defend myself because we both knew no one else would. I'd loved her. I'd hated her. And after all this time, I should have known all her predictions would come to pass. Kieran thought me a seer, but I knew real ones.

Or at least I had once upon a time.

"She said that when Evara lays her hand on two souls, naming them each other's ruin, and Tharos dares them to choose each other anyway, something older than fate takes root. A bond forged in blood and defiance. A tether that doesn't scream, only whispers."

I met his eyes. "The Whisperbound."

"The bond runs both ways," I signed, the motions slower now, reverent. "When one of the Whisperbound dies, the other doesn't follow. Not right away. They live

—but half of them goes silent. The echo stays, whispering the way it did in life, until it fades into the shadows of their soul. Some say the survivors lose their minds trying to chase the sound."

I glanced at Kieran, heart hammering. "Others say they become something else. Touched by the gods. Carriers of the divine." I swallowed. "Either way, there are no secrets between them. The bond burns them out of you. What one hides, the other bleeds."

Kieran went still, every trace of movement narrowing to the quiet flicker of the candles between us. "You know the myths better than I do. It's been so long since I've heard the stories, I barely recall them. What happened to them? To the gods?" he asked almost like he knew the answer.

"They loved each other," I signed, the shape of it tasted like the stories I used to keep alive in silence. "They burned for each other. And in the end, it tore them apart."

My hands felt fragile, and the silence that followed stretched thin in the heavy air—like the story itself was afraid to be remembered. I could almost hear the caretaker's voice instead—low and certain, telling us that love borne of the gods was as beautiful as it was ruinous.

They were each other's ruin. How could we be any different?

"The stories say it's rare," I added. "Almost impossible. But very real."

When I looked up, his icy-blue gaze met mine and held. The pulse in my throat stumbled once, hard enough that I felt it against my tongue. "And I think we just proved it."

The silence between us took shape—like the moment before lightning strikes. Finally, he asked, rough and quiet, "What does that mean for us?"

I didn't know. But something in me did. The hum beneath my skin grew stronger, and for the first time, I felt what Samona must have meant. Every thought I tried to bury rose instead—heat behind my ribs, ache in my throat, truth beating at the edges of my mind.

It wasn't that I couldn't keep secrets. It was that the bond *wouldn't let me.*

If this was what it meant to be Whisperbound, there was no room left for lies. Only what was shared. Only what survived.

It took root under my skin, patient and knowing, curling through me like a vow I'd never spoken aloud. I leaned back a breath, enough to draw air that wasn't shared with his. "If this thing between us won't let us keep secrets..."

He nodded slowly, eyes never leaving mine. "Then we don't lie."

The vibration in my chest climbed higher, steady

and sure, until it felt like it was pressing against my ribs, my heart.

I hesitated. My fingers twitched, useless, before they found shape. "I need to tell you something." The signs came slow, reluctant, carved out of muscle memory instead of courage. "Before the bond drags it out of me."

Kieran didn't move. His eyes tracked every movement of my hands with absolute focus, refusing to let me hide even in the spaces between signs. The candlelight cut across the edge of his jaw, catching on restraint so tight it looked painful. He was still as stone, eyes steady, waiting for me to decide whether I was brave enough to ruin myself.

My throat burned. Tears stung, hot and sudden. Because I knew—once I said this, there would be no undoing it. No taking the truth back into the dark where it belonged.

My hands lifted. Fell. Lifted again.

I started to sign something else—anything else—but my fingers wouldn't form the shapes. They trembled in the air between us, caught between the lie I wanted to tell and the truth the bond demanded.

The hum underneath my skin grew louder, insistent, like the bond itself was pulling the words from my marrow.

My hands shook, but I forced them to move. "I'm not a seer."

The crease that formed between his brows was small, confused. He didn't understand yet. He couldn't.

"I never was." The signs came sharper now, clipped and fast, like I could outrun the weight of them if I moved quickly enough. "I let people think it because it's safer. Easier."

My fingers curled against my palms, nails biting into skin until it hurt. The next sign felt like pulling teeth—like carving the secret out of my own chest with dull blades.

"The truth is..." I stopped. Started again. My hands formed half the word before I jerked them back, pressing my fists against my thighs.

Kieran's hand covered one of mine—gentle, steady. Not forcing. Just... there.

I drew a shaking breath and made myself finish it. "I read minds."

Kieran blinked once, slow, as though the air had gone thin. His lips parted, but the words came rough and uncertain. "You're—"

"A telepath," I signed before he could finish. "Born that way."

He didn't flinch. Didn't move. Just breathed out once—hard—and I could see the muscles in his throat working, like he was trying to swallow the shape of this new truth.

But I wasn't done. The rest of it pressed against my ribs, hot and relentless, demanding to be said.

"I've heard you twice." I swallowed hard enough to make my chest ache. "Once—the first day we met. And now."

The air trembled between us. My pulse thundered so loud I could almost hear it.

"Whatever happened to me before the Divide... before I was ten... it left a mark I can't erase."

My hand rose, unsteady. I touched the scar at my throat—the raised, twisted skin that never stopped aching in the cold hidden behind the fabric of my gown.

"I don't remember how I got this," I signed, movements small, careful. "But I know it's tied to why I can't hear you. Everyone else, yes—loud, constant, too much sometimes. But you?"

My throat tightened, even though no sound came out. "You're quiet. Always have been. Like something carved the space between us and filled it with silence."

The last sign faltered. "Until now."

The air between us seemed to shiver, charged with something too alive to be still. Even the candles seemed to hold their breath.

Then he shifted beneath me, the movement subtle but enough to drag heat through every place we touched. The air shivered, warm against my skin. He was quiet for a long moment, eyes tracing my face like he was memorizing the confession he'd just pulled from me. Then his hand found mine—gentle, steady, anchoring.

"You could've lied," he murmured, the curl of those words soft as mercy, as though he was grateful I hadn't.

"I didn't want to."

His thumb brushed the back of my hand. "Everyone remembers the ruin," he murmured. "No one talks about what came before it—the part where they defied gods and fate just to choose each other. Maybe that's the point. Maybe it isn't about dying together. Maybe it's about living with something stronger than fear."

The words hit somewhere I didn't know was still raw. I wanted to believe him—to think this thing between us was a promise, not a prophecy. But I'd lived my life expecting the ruin to come. He was the first thing that made me hope it wouldn't.

He didn't kiss me right away. He only stayed there, letting me sit in the cradle of his lap, his arms loose around my waist as if afraid one wrong move would break the spell. The heat of him bled through the thin barrier of my dress, steady and grounding. Every breath I took brushed his collar, carrying the scent of him— cedar and spice and something darker underneath.

His pulse beat through my chest, matching the thrum that still pulsed under my skin. The air between us was charged, quiet, waiting. The bond sang between us, a sound just below hearing, threading the air like a living thing.

When his hand finally lifted, the motion was slow, uncertain. Fingers brushed my chin, the barest contact, and the hum surged. My pulse stuttered. Every inch of my body reacted before thought could catch up—skin tightening, breath catching, heat rising in places I hadn't meant to notice.

He hesitated there, thumb tracing the corner of my mouth as if testing whether the world would end if he crossed that last inch.

It didn't.

When his lips finally found mine, the world exhaled.

The kiss started careful, almost fragile—but I couldn't stand careful. Not with him. Not after everything we'd just confessed.

I bit his bottom lip hard enough to sting, and felt his growl rumble through my chest. His hands fisted in my dress, dragging me so tight against him I could feel every hard line of his body, could feel exactly how much he wanted this. Wanted me.

"Fuck," he breathed against my mouth, and the way he said it—reverent, wrecked—made something crack open inside me.

The kiss turned vicious—all heat and need and barely controlled desperation. He kissed me like he was trying to devour me, like he could swallow down every secret I'd ever kept. When his hand shot up to fist in my hair, yanking my head back to expose my throat, heat flooded between my legs so fast it made me dizzy.

"You've been in my head this whole time," he growled against my jaw, his other hand sliding up my thigh with almost bruising pressure. "Hearing every filthy thing I've thought about doing to you."

I hadn't—couldn't—but the accusation sent liquid heat pooling in my belly.

"When I fucked my fist thinking about you," he continued, voice gone rough, "imagining how tight you'd be, how you'd sound when I made you come on my cock. You heard all of it, didn't you?"

I shook my head frantically, but he wasn't looking at my signs. His mouth found that scar on my throat—the one he'd bitten before—and scraped his fangs across it hard enough to make me gasp.

"Liar," he whispered. Then bit down.

His fangs slid into my flesh and the venom hit like lightning. I nearly came apart, grinding down on the hard length of him as pleasure rippled through me. But it wasn't enough—not nearly fucking enough. I needed him inside me, needed to feel him break apart the way I was.

I yanked at his shirt until it ripped, buttons scattering. My nails raked down his chest, leaving red welts, and his hips jerked up hard against me.

"Vicious little thing," he hissed, pulling his fangs free and licking the wound closed. His eyes were black, pupils blown wide with hunger. "You want it rough? Want me to fuck you like I did against that table?"

Yes. Saints, yes. I reached between us and unbuttoned his trousers with shaking hands, shoving the fabric down until I could wrap my fingers around him. He was thick and hard, already slick at the tip, and when I stroked him, he made a sound between a groan and a snarl.

"Careful," he warned, but there was no threat in it. Only desperate need.

I pumped him once, twice, squeezing hard the way I imagined he liked it—the way I'd imagined him fucking his fist. His head fell back, tendons standing out in his neck, and saints, the sight of him losing control made me clench around nothing. Without thinking, I leaned forward and bit down on that corded muscle hard as I could with my blunted human teeth.

He made a sound I'd never heard before—somewhere between a groan and a snarl—and his hips jerked hard into my grip. "Fuck—Merrit—" His hand flew to the back of my head, not pushing me away but holding me there. "Do that again."

I bit him again, dragging my teeth along the tendon, and felt his cock throb in my hand.

"You like when I mark you?" I thought at him, even though I knew he couldn't hear.

But his response told me everything. "Yes," he hissed through his teeth. "Mark me. Want everyone to see what you do to me."

His hand slid between my legs, fingers finding soaked fabric. "Fuck, you're drenched already," he said, awe and hunger mixing in his voice. "All this for me?"

I nodded frantically, and he pushed my undergarments aside. When his fingers slid through slick heat, we both made broken sounds.

"You're dripping," he groaned, circling my entrance but not pushing in yet. "Absolutely soaking. Tell me what you need."

I couldn't sign with my hands on him, so I bit his shoulder—hard enough to leave a mark—and he laughed roughly.

"All right, vicious girl. I've got you."

He slid two fingers inside me, and the stretch made my eyes roll back. But he didn't give me time to adjust— just started fucking me with them, hard and deep, while his thumb found my clit.

"That's it," he growled against my temple. "Feel how wet you are? How you're clenching around my fingers? You're going to feel so good wrapped around my cock."

The filthy words combined with the devastating rhythm of his hand had me trembling. Every thrust of his fingers hit somewhere deep that made my thighs shake. I was close—already so close—but I didn't want to come like this.

I pulled back enough to meet his eyes, and whatever he saw in my face made him groan. Rising on my knees, I positioned him at my entrance. We were still mostly clothed—my dress shoved up around my waist, his trousers barely open, his shirt half off—too desperate to bother with anything else.

"Look at me," I mouthed, and his eyes snapped to mine.

I sank down on him in one brutal drop, taking him to the hilt. The stretch burned, too much too fast, but his venom turned the pain into something else entirely. We both froze, breathing hard, and I felt his cock twitch inside me.

"Fuck." The word broke from him. "You're so—saints—so fucking tight."

I lifted up and slammed back down, setting a punishing rhythm. No gentleness, no gradual build. Just raw and desperate. His hands gripped my hips hard enough to bruise, not guiding, just holding on as I rode him.

"That's it," he gritted out. "Take what you need. Use me."

The words shouldn't have affected me, but they did. I fucked him harder, chasing the building pressure, and when his hand slid between us to find my clit, I nearly screamed.

"You're dripping all over me," he said, voice wrecked. "Can feel you soaking my cock, making a mess. Such a good girl, taking me so deep."

I wasn't anyone's "good girl"—especially not his—but my body didn't seem to care. I clenched around him, inner walls fluttering, and he groaned.

His thumb circled my clit with perfect, maddening pressure while I rode him. Every downward thrust hit something inside me that made my vision blur. I was close—so close—but I needed more.

I grabbed his other hand and brought it to my throat, pressing his fingers against my pulse. His eyes went wide, then darker than I'd ever seen them.

"You want me to choke you while I fuck you?" His voice was pure gravel.

I nodded, desperate, and his fingers tightened just enough to make my head go light. The combination of his cock hitting that perfect spot, his thumb on my clit, and his hand around my throat sent me hurtling over the edge.

I came so hard I saw stars, clenching around him in waves that seemed endless. Distantly I heard myself making sounds—broken, desperate whimpers that I couldn't control.

"That's my girl. So beautiful when you come," he breathed. "So perfect."

He started to withdraw, and I made a sound of protest at the loss. But then he was moving, flipping us with surprising gentleness so I was on my back on the bed, him hovering over me. Still mostly clothed. Still tangled together.

For a heartbeat he just looked at me—eyes roaming over my flushed face, my heaving chest, the dress twisted and bunched around my body. Something shifted in his expression. Hunger, yes, but darker. More deliberate.

"My turn," he said quietly.

Then his hands fisted in the fabric of my gown at the neckline and he tore it open. Buttons exploded across the bed, pinging off the headboard, scattering across the floor. The fabric ripped clean down the front with a sound that sent another spike of heat through me.

"Been wanting to do that all fucking night," he growled, shoving the ruined cloth off my shoulders and down my arms until I was bare beneath him. His eyes raked over my exposed skin with raw hunger. "Want you in nothing but my marks."

He withdrew almost completely, then slammed back in hard enough to punch the air from my lungs. Then again. And again. Fucking me with brutal, deep thrusts that made the bed frame shake.

"You feel me?" he snarled. "Feel how deep I am? No one else gets to have this. No one else gets to be inside you like this."

Possessive bastard. But my body answered him anyway, still sensitive from my first orgasm, already building toward another.

His hand fisted in my hair, yanking my head to the side to expose my throat again. "Tell me you're mine," he demanded. "Tell me."

I couldn't—wouldn't—but my hands found his face, pulling him down into a kiss that tasted like blood and desperation and something tender, something worth keeping. He kissed me as if he were drowning and I was air, never breaking the rhythm of his hips.

The bond surged between us, humming so loud I thought my bones would shake apart. And then I heard him—actually heard his thoughts cutting through the pleasure-soaked haze.

Mine. Fuck, you're mine. Never letting you go. Kill anyone who tries to take you. Mine, mine, mine—

The possessive litany shattered me. I came again, harder than before, my whole body seizing as pleasure whited out everything else. He followed with a roar, hips stuttering as he spilled inside me, cock pulsing with each surge, my name on his lips like a prayer.

We collapsed together, both shaking, covered in sweat and bite marks and the evidence of what we'd done. His softening length was still inside me, and neither of us seemed inclined to move.

When I could finally think again, I became aware of his hand stroking my hair with unexpected gentleness. The contrast to how roughly he'd just fucked me should have been jarring, but somehow it wasn't.

"I'm yours, too," he breathed against the skin of my neck. "However this ends—whatever happens—I'm yours."

I couldn't answer him, not really. No one had ever been mine. Not like this. It was so big, so precious, I didn't know what to do with it.

"And no more secrets," he murmured against my

temple. Then his hand cupped my face, tilting it up so I had to meet his eyes. "And your secret?" His thumb traced my cheekbone. "It dies with me. Anyone who tries to touch you for it answers to me first. You're safe, Merrit. I swear it."

The vow settled something raw and aching in my chest. I signed against his skin: "No more secrets."

He caught my hand, pressed a kiss to my palm. "No more secrets."

We were bound now. Blood and fate and choice all twisted together. Each other's ruin, maybe.

But also each other's salvation.

MERRIT

I woke to warmth—not the oppressive heat of too many bodies in my bar, but the specific, deliberate warmth of *him*. Kieran's chest rose and fell against my back, his arm a heavy band across my waist, his breath stirring the hair at my nape.

For a moment, I didn't move. Couldn't. Because beneath the physical tangle of our bodies, something else hummed—a thread of awareness that wasn't quite thought, wasn't quite feeling. It pulsed between us, steady as a heartbeat, undeniable as breath.

The Whisperbound bond.

I could *feel* him. Not just his body pressed against mine, but something deeper. His contentment, warm and drowsy. A flicker of awareness as he began to wake. The ghost of concern threading through it all, worry he was trying to bury.

Mine, the bond whispered. Not possessive—just true.

His arm tightened fractionally, and I felt the shift in him as consciousness fully returned. Not panic, exactly, but a sudden awareness that cut through the drowsy peace.

"You're awake," he murmured against my shoulder, voice rough with sleep.

I turned in his arms, the sheets tangling around us. Morning light filtered through the heavy curtains, painting his face in soft gold. His hair was mussed, eyes still heavy-lidded, and there was something unbearably vulnerable about seeing him like this—unguarded, unpracticed.

"So are you," I signed, then hesitated. My hands hovered between us, uncertain. "I can feel you. Through the bond. Is it always like this?"

His expression shifted, something raw flickering across his features. "I don't know. I've never been Whisperbound before." His hand came up to cup my face, thumb tracing my cheekbone. "What do you feel?"

How could I explain it? It wasn't like reading minds—that was invasive, sharp, often unwanted. This was... softer. Like standing in the same room and knowing someone was there without seeing them. Feeling the warmth of another person's presence.

"You," I signed simply. "Your worry. Your..." I paused, heat creeping up my neck. "Your desire."

His pupils dilated, the bond between us suddenly thrumming with heat. "Can you feel this?" he asked, voice dropping lower.

The wave of want that rolled through him made my breath catch. It wasn't just his—it fed into mine, amplifying until I couldn't tell where his hunger ended and mine began.

"Yes," I mouthed, and then his mouth was on mine.

The kiss was different from last night's desperation. Slower, deeper, exploratory. Every slide of his tongue sent pleasure rippling through us both, doubling back until we were both gasping. When his hand slid down my side, I felt his satisfaction at my shiver *and* the shiver itself, sensation multiplied until it was almost too much.

"Saints," he groaned against my mouth. "I can feel what you feel. When I touch you here—" His palm cupped my breast, thumb circling my nipple through the thin fabric of the shift I'd apparently put on at some point. "I feel your pleasure and mine."

I arched into his touch, dizzy with the echoed loop of sensation. My hands found his chest, mapping the planes of muscle, and through the bond, his sharp intake of breath, the way his cock hardened against my thigh.

An impulse struck me—reckless, desperate. What if the bond could do more than just share feelings? What if...

I focused on the thread connecting us, that humming awareness, and pushed a thought along it. Not words, exactly, but meaning shaped into something he might understand.

"Good morning."

Kieran went rigid, eyes flying wide. "Did you just—" He stared at me, something like wonder crossing his features. "I heard you. Not out loud, but... in my head. Your voice."

My heart hammered against my ribs. *"You can hear me?"*

"Yes." His hand came up to cup my face, thumb tracing my cheekbone with something approaching reverence. "Saints, Merrit. I can hear you."

The magnitude of it crashed over me. For the first time since my throat had been cut, since I'd lost my voice—I could speak. Not to everyone, maybe not even to anyone else. But to him.

"Is it my voice?" I asked mentally, curious. *"Or just... thoughts?"*

"It's you," he breathed. "Your voice. I don't know how I know what you sound like, but I *know* it's you."

Something hot lodged in my throat. I had no memory of ever having a voice. That part of me had been stolen along with everything else before the orphanage.

"What do I sound like?"

His smile was soft, intimate. "Like smoke and honey.

Rough at the edges but sweet underneath." He pressed his forehead to mine. "Like you."

I had to blink back the sudden sting of tears. This bond—this impossible, mythical thing—had given me back something I thought I'd lost forever.

"Can I always do this? Talk to you like this?"

"I don't know." His thumb brushed away a tear that escaped. "But I hope so. I want to hear everything you have to say, every thought you've kept locked away."

"Be careful what you wish for," I projected, trying to lighten the moment, even as emotion threatened to overwhelm me. *"I have a lot of thoughts. Most of them inappropriate."*

His laugh was low, dangerous. "I'm counting on it."

I pushed him onto his back, reveling in his surprise rippling through me. The shift rode up as I straddled him, and his hands immediately went to my hips, fingers digging in.

"Merrit—" Whatever he'd been about to say died as I rolled my hips, grinding against the hard length of him. His pleasure spiked, the tight coil of his control slipping.

I did it again, slower this time, and his head fell back against the pillow. The feedback was intoxicating— every movement sent waves of pleasure bouncing between us until I couldn't tell whose sensation was whose.

His hands slid under the shift, shoving it up and

over my head until I was bare above him. For a moment he just stared, and through the bond, his awe, his hunger, the almost painful intensity of his want settled into my bones.

"You're so beautiful," he breathed. "Do you know what you do to me?"

I could feel it. The way his heart raced, the heat pooling low in his belly, the desperate need to touch, taste, claim. It should have been frightening—being so open, so vulnerable. Instead, it made me bold.

I leaned down, kissing along his jaw, down his throat, teeth scraping the spot where his pulse hammered. I felt the jolt of pleasure-pain, felt how close he was to losing control.

"Merrit." My name was a warning, a plea. "If you don't stop—"

I bit down, not hard enough to break skin but enough to mark. His hips bucked up, and the feedback loop of our shared arousal nearly shattered me.

"I don't want to stop." Then I took his hand and placed it between my legs so he could feel how wet I was, how much I needed this.

His control snapped.

In one fluid movement, he flipped us, pinning me beneath him. His eyes were wild, pupils blown wide, and I felt the leash he kept on himself fraying.

"You have no idea what you're asking for," he growled.

I wrapped my legs around his waist, pulling him closer. *"Then show me."*

And he did.

Afterward, we lay tangled together, both breathing hard, skin slick with sweat. The bond hummed between us, sated and warm, like a purring cat curled up in the sun.

Kieran's fingers traced lazy patterns on my shoulder, and his contentment mixed with mine, creating something that belonged to neither of us and both of us at once.

"We need to talk," he finally said, pressing a kiss to my temple. "About what happens next."

Reality crashed back in. The bond, the Court, the threat we still hadn't identified. I'd almost forgotten—lost in sensation, in *us*—that we were still in danger.

I sat up, immediately missing his warmth but needing the distance to think clearly. My hands moved, deliberate. "We keep the bond secret. For now."

"Though I wish we didn't have to," I added privately. *"This—being able to talk to you—it's everything."*

His eyes softened, and he reached up to cup my face. "I know. But if anyone knew we were Whisperbound..."

He didn't finish, but he didn't need to. His fear shot through me—not for himself, but for me. If the Court knew, I'd become an even bigger target. A way to control him, to hurt him.

"I understand," I projected, then signed: "I need to be more active in the investigation. I can't just stand at your side and look decorative. Let me use what I can do."

"It's dangerous—"

"Everything is dangerous." My hands cut through the air, sharp with frustration. *"You brought me here to help,"* I added. *"Let me actually help."*

His conflict—the desire to protect me—warred with the knowledge that I was right. Finally, he sat up beside me and nodded.

"We set a trap," he said. "At the next Court function. You read the room, see what you can find. But—" His hand caught mine, squeezing. "You stay close. And if anything feels wrong, you tell me immediately."

"Through the bond?"

"However works fastest. Though I have to admit"—His mouth quirked—"having you in my head is going to make things much easier."

"And more distracting," I teased, then sobered. *"What if I find something? What do we do?"*

"We identify the threat, and we eliminate it." His voice went cold with ruthless calculation. "No more playing games. No more mercy."

A knock at the door interrupted us, quick and urgent. Kieran was already moving, pulling on trousers while I grabbed one of his shirts and held it against my chest.

"Your Highness?" The voice was familiar—Elias.

Kieran shot me a look, eyebrow raised in question. I nodded, already pulling on his shirt. It fell to my thighs, large enough to be decent if barely. He opened the door only wide enough to block the view of the room's interior.

"What is it?"

"I need to speak with you. And..." Elias' voice dropped. "With your companion. It's urgent."

His tone set my teeth on edge. *"Something feels off,"* I projected to Kieran.

His wariness spiked. "Give us a moment," he said, closing the door.

I emerged from behind the privacy screen, tying the robe securely. Kieran's eyes met mine, a silent question passing between us.

"Ready?" he asked quietly.

I nodded, squaring my shoulders despite the unease coiling in my chest.

His jaw tightened, but he didn't argue. Instead, he opened the door. Elias stepped in, and immediately I tried to read him.

His thoughts were... wrong. Fragmented. Like listening to a conversation through a wall—I could hear the words but not make sense of them. Confusion, urgency, fear—but underneath it all, something else. Something that didn't quite fit.

"His mind is fractured," I projected to Kieran while keeping my face neutral. *"I can barely read him."*

"Well?" Kieran prompted aloud.

Elias' eyes flicked to me, then back to Kieran. "There's been another attempt. On the southern gate. The guards managed to stop it, but..." He swallowed. "One of the attackers was wearing your personal sigil, Your Highness. A forgery, but a good one."

The bond between us went taut as a piano wire. Kieran's fury bled through, sharp and hot.

"Who?" The word was barely more than a growl.

"They're dead. Took poison before we could question them." Elias' jaw tightened. "But I think—I think someone's trying to make it look like you're behind the attacks. To turn your own people against you."

I watched him carefully, trying to push past the strange static in his mind. His fear felt genuine. His urgency, real. But that underlying note, that thing I couldn't quite identify...

"Thank you for bringing this to my attention," Kieran said, voice controlled but laced with steel. "I'll need to see the body. And the sigil."

"Of course, Your Highness." Elias bowed, but his eyes found mine again. "My lady, I... I apologize for the interruption."

His thoughts brushed against mine—fragments, jumbled, wrong—and for just a heartbeat, I caught something that felt like him, the real him, before it snapped away like a door slamming shut.

My breath caught. *"Kieran,"* I projected urgently. *"He knows something's wrong with him."*

Kieran's hand immediately found the small of my back, steadying, while his face remained impassive. "That will be all, Elias," he said dismissively.

When the door closed behind him, Kieran turned to me. "Tell me everything."

My hands shook as I signed, reinforcing with the bond so he'd understand the full scope. "His thoughts are confused. Fragmented. Like someone's been in his head." I paused, dread settling in my stomach. *"But for just a moment, something broke through. Fear. Desperation. Like he's fighting something he doesn't understand."*

Kieran's expression went cold, calculating. His mind was working, piecing things together.

"If someone can control him," he said slowly, "they can use him to get close to us. To you."

"We need to find out who's doing it. Before they use him to strike."

He nodded, already moving toward his wardrobe. "Then we spring our trap sooner than planned. Tonight, there's a formal dinner. Half the Court will be there."

"Including whoever's controlling Elias?"

"Let's hope so." He turned back to me. His determination, his fear for me, and underneath it all, that fierce protectiveness that made my chest ache spiked through him. "Because if they are, you're going to find them."

"What if I can't?" Fear slipped through before I could stop it. *"What if my abilities aren't enough?"*

He crossed to me in three strides, tilting my chin up until I had no choice but to meet his gaze. "Then we'll find another way. Together." His thumb brushed my lower lip. "You're not alone in this anymore, Merrit. Whatever happens, we face it together."

The bond thrummed with his certainty, his absolute faith in me. It should have been terrifying—someone believing in me that completely. Instead, it felt like armor.

"Together," I agreed.

I dressed in silence, choosing practical clothes from the wardrobe—dark trousers, a simple tunic, boots that wouldn't slow me down if I needed to run. The weight of the dagger at my thigh was a comfort, a reminder that I wasn't helpless. That I'd survived far worse than this.

When I emerged, Kieran was already waiting, fully dressed in his princely regalia. But his eyes found mine immediately.

"Are you ready for this?"

I squared my shoulders, lifting my chin. My hands moved with conviction as I signed: "Let's catch a traitor."

"And save Elias while we're at it," I added. *"He doesn't deserve to be a pawn, even if he is a pompous asshole."*

His smile was sharp as a blade, proud and fierce and dangerous. "That's my girl."

The words should have rankled—I wasn't anyone's girl, wasn't anyone's anything. But through the bond, I knew what he meant: partnership, not possession. Trust, not ownership.

And saints help me, I was starting to like it.

We left the chambers side by side, ready to walk into the vipers' nest. Together.

The bond hummed between us, a secret thread connecting us in ways the Court would never understand. My shield. My weapon. My salvation.

Each other's ruin, the old stories said.

But as Kieran's hand found mine, warm and steady, I couldn't help but think that maybe we'd be each other's salvation instead.

CHAPTER 20

KIERAN

The war room smelled of old leather and even older blood—iron ground into the wood from centuries of royal councils held over maps, stained with the evidence of past campaigns. Morning light filtered through the tall windows in sharp angles, illuminating dust motes that danced like restless spirits.

Solis stood at the far end of the table, arms crossed, jaw tight enough to crack teeth. He stared at the map of Morathen spread out before us, as though he could burn holes through it with his gaze alone.

Something was wrong.

Solis joked. Always. Even in the worst situations—hell, *especially* in the worst situations—he had some quip or dark humor ready to ease the tension. We'd fought side by side for centuries—through wars, betrayals, the kind of bloodshed that bound men together or broke them apart. But today? Nothing. Just that rigid posture with shoulders bunched so tight I could see the strain through his shirt.

"The southern gate," I said, tapping the location on the map. "Elias said the attacker wore my sigil. A forgery."

"A good one," Solis muttered, not looking up. "Good enough to fool the guards until they got close."

"Which means it's someone with access. Someone who's seen the real thing enough times to try to replicate it." I traced the path from the gate to the castle proper. "They're getting bolder. More brazen."

"Or more desperate." Solis' hands flexed against his biceps, the only tell that he was holding something back.

The door opened, and Merrit slipped inside. She'd insisted on being present for these meetings, and I'd agreed—she needed to understand what we were up against. Her eyes found mine immediately, and the bond carried her determination threaded with uncertainty.

"You don't have to be here," I projected.

"Yes, I do," she replied, moving to stand beside me.

Solis' attention jerked toward her, and for a heartbeat, something raw flickered across his face. Not attraction—nothing like that. It seemed almost like... grief. Guilt. His shoulders went rigid, and he looked away quickly, but not before I caught it.

Strange. In all our centuries together, I'd never seen Solis look at anyone like that. Professional respect, yes. Camaraderie with fellow soldiers. But this seemed different. Personal.

Merrit's confusion echoed through our connection, mirroring my own. She'd noticed it, too.

"The attackers are dead," Solis said, pulling my attention back. "Both took poison before we could question them. Fast-acting, probably carried in a false tooth."

"Professional, then." I studied the map, looking for patterns. "Not random malcontents."

"No." He pushed off the table, pacing to the window. "This is organized. Funded. Someone's been planning this for months, maybe longer."

His hand went to the back of his neck, rubbing at tension that wouldn't ease. When he returned his focus to Merrit, there was another flash of that same haunted expression before he shuttered it.

"We need to tighten security," he said. "Double the watch rotations. Search everyone entering the castle grounds, no exceptions."

"Agreed. And I don't give a fuck what the barons say. They'll be searched, too." I moved around the table to pour wine from the decanter, needing something to do with my hands. "But that's defensive. We need to draw them out."

"The Exhibition," Solis said quietly.

I nodded. "It's in three days. Perfect opportunity. Everyone who matters will be there."

"How many events do you all have here? And what's the Exhibition?"

Merrit's thought brushed mine, curious and irritated at the pomp and circumstance of royal life. I couldn't say I blamed her.

"A display of power," I explained. *"Combat demonstrations, trials of strength and magic. The nobility showing off for each other."*

I felt her understanding, then her resolve hardening like steel. *"I'm reading that crowd."*

"If you're willing."

Her spine straightened, chin lifting. *"I didn't survive the Divide by being delicate. I can handle this."*

"She shouldn't be there," Solis said, voice tight. His attention stayed on Merrit, that guilt-grief expression back and stronger. "It's too dangerous. Too many weapons, too much chaos. If someone wanted to strike—"

"Then they'll find out what happens when they try." I set my glass down harder than necessary. "She's not some courtier who faints at the sight of blood. She killed a man with a fucking paring knife to save my life. She can handle the Exhibition."

Merrit's grim satisfaction at the reminder trickled through me, pulling at the corner of my mouth.

Solis' lips compressed into a thin line, and for a

moment, I thought he'd argue. But he just nodded once and looked away. Whatever was eating at him, he wasn't ready to share it.

Merrit's unease spiked. *"What's wrong with him?"*

"I don't know," I admitted. *"But I intend to find out."*

A knock at the door interrupted us before I could press the issue. One of my pages entered, bowing low. "Your Highness. Your brothers have answered your summons."

"Already?" Solis' eyebrows rose. "That was fast."

"Bring in the mirror," I ordered.

The page nodded and backed out. Moments later, two guards carried in an ornate full-length mirror, its frame carved with runes that pulsed faintly with magic. They set it against the far wall, and I moved toward it, pulling the small crystal from my pocket—identical to the ones each of my brothers carried.

I pressed it to the mirror's surface, and the glass rippled like water.

The first face that appeared made my teeth grind together.

Lorenzo.

My eldest brother stared out from the mirror, his expression carved from the same stone as his province's mountains. Everything about him was sharp—his cheekbones, his jaw, his eyes that missed nothing. His dark hair was pulled back severely, revealing the rigid line of his mouth and the golden, hazel eyes he shared with our mother when she was still alive.

"Kieran." My name wasn't a greeting. It was an accusation.

"Lorenzo." I matched his tone, ice for ice. "Thank you for responding so quickly."

"You summoned. I answered." His gaze flicked past me, taking in the room, cataloging Solis and Merrit in a single sweep. "Though I see you've acquired some new... additions to your household."

Merrit stiffened at the dismissive tone. Her hands moved, precise and deliberate. "Merrit Locke. A pleasure."

Lorenzo's eyebrows rose fractionally—the only sign of surprise that she'd signed rather than remained silent. "You know the hand language. How... quaint."

"Most of the Court does," Merrit signed, her movements precise. "Evara's temples demand it. Though I suppose military provinces have less use for subtlety. Or manners."

A ghost of emotion—Respect? Amusement?—flickered across Lorenzo's face before it hardened again. "Indeed."

Every conversation with Lorenzo felt like walking through a field of knives—one wrong step and you'd bleed. And now Merrit was dancing through them— with him.

"There have been attempts on my life," I said,

steering us back to the point. "Coordinated attacks. I'm calling in resources."

"Resources." His lip curled. "Is that what we are now? Not brothers. Resources."

Here we fucking go. "You swore fealty to the Crown," I said, voice flat. "That makes you exactly that."

The mirror flickered with Lorenzo's barely contained rage. Even through the magical interface, the temperature in the room seemed to drop.

"The crown you were handed."

There it was. The wound that never healed, the resentment that colored every interaction between us. He was the eldest. By every tradition, every law of succession, the Crown Province should have been his. But Father had chosen me instead—the second son, the one who could smile while sliding a knife between your ribs. The one who could play the political games Father excelled at.

I hadn't wanted it. Still didn't. The Crown Province was a gilded cage, beautiful and suffocating in equal measure. But refusing would have been seen as weakness, and weakness in our family was death.

At least now, with Merrit at my side, the weight felt... lighter. Like maybe I could actually build a province worth keeping instead of just maintaining what Father had created.

"We've had this conversation," I said quietly. "A thousand times. Father made his choice. I didn't ask for it, and you've made your feelings abundantly clear. Can we move past it long enough to address the actual threat?"

Lorenzo's expression didn't change, but something in his gaze shifted. "Fine. What do you need?"

"Eyes on your province. Any unusual activity, strangers asking questions, anything that feels wrong. Someone is funding these attacks, and the money has to be coming from somewhere."

"You think I'm harboring traitors in Tharros?" His voice went dangerously soft.

"I think someone with resources is moving against me, and I need to know if any of those resources are flowing through your territory." I held his stare. "Unless you'd prefer I ask Father to investigate instead?"

The threat landed. Lorenzo's jaw flexed, but he nodded once. "I'll send word if anything occurs in Tharros. But don't mistake this for approval of how you've chosen to rule, Kieran."

Before I could respond, another face appeared in the mirror, shoving Lorenzo aside with casual grace.

Nikolai.

My brother grinned, all white teeth and golden charm. His hair fell in artful waves around a face that belonged on sculptures, and even through the mirror, I could see the glint of jeweled rings on his fingers.

"Oh, good, family drama before noon. My favorite." He winked at me. "Hello, darling brother. Lovely to be summoned like a common servant. Really makes one feel valued."

"Nikolai—"

"And who is this vision?" His gaze locked on Merrit, interest sparking. "Don't tell me. Let me guess. The latest conquest? No, wait—she's got that look about her. The one that says she'd rather gut you than kiss you. Which means either you're paying her very well, or..." His grin widened. "Oh. Oh, this is delicious."

Merrit's hands moved before I could stop her. "Merrit Locke. And you must be the brother who thinks charm can substitute for substance."

Nikolai's laugh seemed delighted. "Oh, I like her. She's got teeth." He leaned closer to the mirror. "Tell me, gorgeous, what's a woman with your obvious intelligence doing with my tragically serious brother?"

"Keeping him alive," she signed. "Someone has to."

"Keeping him—" Nikolai's eyes widened, then his grin turned positively wicked. "Oh, you're not just decoration. You're actually useful. Kieran, you've outdone yourself. Where did you find her?"

"The Divide," Merrit answered before I could. "Where people don't waste time with pretty words when a knife will do."

Through the bond, I felt her satisfaction at Nikolai's surprised respect.

"Enough," I snapped. "Both of you."

A third face appeared, shoving both Lorenzo and

Nikolai to the edges of the mirror. Henrick's pale features swam into view, his eyes too wide, too knowing. Dark circles shadowed them, and his skin had that translucent quality of someone who spent too much time with magic and not enough replenishing himself with blood.

"The currents are disturbed," he said without preamble. His voice was soft, almost whispered, but it carried an edge that made the hair on my neck stand up. "Something is moving through the magical weave. Something old. Hungry."

"Henrick," I said carefully. My brother unnerved me at the best of times. "What are you sensing?"

"Blood magic. Death magic. Threads that shouldn't exist, being pulled by hands that shouldn't touch them." He focused on me with unsettling intensity. "You've brought something into your house, brother. Something that draws the darkness."

My hand found Merrit's immediately, protective instinct overriding caution. Her alarm spiked through me.

Merrit's hands moved, steady despite the tension. "I'm not the darkness you're sensing. But I'll help find what is."

Henrick's gaze shifted to her, and for a moment, those pale eyes seemed to look through her rather than at her. "Perhaps. Or perhaps you're the key that opens the door." His attention snapped back to me. "Be careful,

Kieran. The threads are tangling. Soon they'll choke everything they touch."

Then he was gone, and the mirror was just glass again.

Tension bled from my shoulders. "Well. That went about as well as expected."

"Your family is delightful," Solis said dryly. Some of his usual humor had returned, though the tension in his shoulders remained. "Really makes you understand why you're so well-adjusted."

"They're always like this?" Merrit asked, her question streaking across my already-frayed nerves.

"This was them being cooperative," I replied. *"You should see holiday gatherings."*

Her amusement, mixed with her wariness, rattled inside my chest.

Another knock. This time, Elias entered without waiting for permission.

He looked... off. Not obviously wrong, but the way he moved, the slight delay in his reactions, made me take notice. Like a puppet whose strings were being pulled by someone still learning the motions.

"Your Highness." He bowed, deeper than necessary. "I wanted to offer my services."

"Services?" I kept my voice neutral, watching him carefully.

"For the Exhibition. I could coordinate additional security measures." His attention slid to Merrit, and something in his expression made my hackles rise. Too focused. Too intent. "And I assume your companion will be attending?"

It wasn't really a question. More an assumption he was testing, waiting to see if I'd confirm or deny.

"That's thoughtful of you," I said slowly.

Merrit's warning filtered through my thoughts. *"His mind is still fractured. Worse than before."*

"I insist," Elias continued, taking a step closer to Merrit. "A woman of her... *unique position*... would need proper protection. Especially at such a volatile event."

Every protective instinct in me screamed to refuse, to put distance between Elias and Merrit. But if someone was controlling him, keeping him close might help us identify who.

"Very well," I said, hating the words even as I spoke them. "You'll coordinate with Solis on security arrangements. And you'll stay close to Merrit during the Exhibition."

"Kieran—" Her alarm shot through me.

"Trust me," I projected back. *"I have a plan."*

Elias' smile was too bright, too eager. "Excellent. I won't let anything happen to her, Your Highness. You have my word."

The words should have been reassuring. Instead, they landed like a threat.

"If you'll excuse me, I should begin preparations."

He bowed again and left, his steps slightly too measured, too careful.

The moment the door closed, Solis swore. "You can't seriously be considering—"

"I'm not," I said flatly. "Not without insurance."

As if summoned by my thoughts, shadows in the corner of the room deepened, thickened, and Nadia stepped through them like she'd been there all along.

Merrit's hands moved immediately, signing a greeting. "You have the worst timing."

"It's more fun this way." Nadia flashed a predatory grin as she leaned against the wall. "Heard you've got a puppet problem."

"Elias," I confirmed. "Someone's controlling him. I need to know who, and I need Merrit protected while we figure it out."

"So you're using her as bait." Nadia pushed off the wall, moving closer to Merrit. "Ballsy. Stupid. But I respect it."

Something unexpected filtered through—Merrit's ease around Nadia. Recognition, almost. Like seeing a familiar face in a foreign land.

Merrit's hands moved, quicker now. "I can handle myself. I've survived worse than Court politics."

"Have you, though?" Nadia tilted her head. "Because Court politics here means poison in your wine, a blade between your ribs, and a charming smile to distract you while it happens."

"You mean a regular Tuesday in the Divide?" Merrit signed. "Just with less silk and more honesty about the knives."

Nadia's grin widened. "Oh, I like you. Most court ladies would be clutching their pearls right now."

"I'm not a court lady."

"No shit." Nadia circled her once, assessing. "All right, Divide-girl. I'll watch your back. But if things go sideways, I'm getting you out. Even if I have to drag you through the shadows kicking and screaming."

Merrit signed something that made Nadia laugh. I caught the edge of it: a Divide phrase about shadows being safer than sunlight, anyway.

"It's settled then." I moved toward the door, needing air, needing space from the weight of too many factors I couldn't control. "Solis, coordinate with Elias but keep eyes on him at all times. Nadia, shadow Merrit. And Merrit—"

I stopped, turning back to find her watching me with those sharp green eyes that saw too much. In three strides I was beside her, my hand cupping her face, thumb brushing her cheekbone.

"Be careful," I projected. *"Please."*

Her hand came up to cover mine. *"Together, remember?"*

"Together."

I pressed a kiss to her forehead, lingering there for a heartbeat, breathing her in. When I pulled back, Solis was studiously examining the map like he hadn't seen anything, while Nadia's grin had turned knowing.

I didn't care. Let them see. Let them know she mattered.

I left before the fear could root any deeper, before I could second-guess the decision to use her as bait. The corridor outside was mercifully empty, giving me space to breathe.

Until it wasn't.

Tobias materialized from a side passage, his footsteps too quiet for someone who wasn't trying to sneak. "Your Highness. Might I have a word?"

Every instinct screamed to refuse. To walk away. But Tobias had been my father's advisor for decades, had served the Crown longer than I'd been alive. Dismissing him without cause would raise questions I couldn't afford.

"Make it quick."

"The Exhibition," he said, falling into step beside me. "A bold move, bringing your companion to such a volatile event. I ran into Elias in the corridor—he mentioned you'd be attending together."

Of course he had. Elias' fractured mind probably couldn't keep anything contained anymore.

"She's under my protection."

"Of course, of course." His voice was honey-smooth, concerned. "I merely wonder if... well, forgive me for overstepping, but have you considered all the variables?"

I stopped walking, turning to face him fully. "What variables?"

"Your brothers, for instance." He clasped his hands behind his back, the picture of a troubled advisor. "Lorenzo in particular. I know there's... history between you."

"Lorenzo swore fealty. He wouldn't break that vow."

"Wouldn't he?" Tobias' eyebrows rose delicately. "I'm not suggesting treason, Your Highness. Merely pointing out that Tharros has been... quiet lately. Too quiet. And Lorenzo's province has one of the largest military forces in the kingdom."

The words settled like lead in my gut, even as I rejected them. "Lorenzo lives and breathes duty. Rules are sacred to him. He'd sooner cut off his own hand than break his vow."

"Perhaps." Tobias spread his hands, the picture of innocence. "But even the most dutiful can be pushed too far. And the crown that should have been his by birthright..." He let the sentence hang, unfinished but heavy with implication.

"Lorenzo and I have been over this a thousand times," I said flatly. "Yes, he resents me. Yes, he thinks Father made the wrong choice. But he's no traitor."

"Of course not." Tobias smiled, but it didn't reach his eyes. "Forgive an old man his paranoid musings. It's just that with everything happening—the attacks, the unrest —one can't help but wonder who benefits from destabilizing your rule."

He didn't wait for a response, just bowed and continued down the corridor, leaving me alone with doubts I didn't want.

I knew Lorenzo. We'd fought, bled together, survived our father's brutal training side by side. He was rigid, disciplined, furious about being passed over for the Crown—but a traitor?

No. Lorenzo would never break the rules. They were the only things that made sense to him in a world that constantly disappointed.

But Tobias' words wormed into my thoughts anyway, planting seeds of suspicion I couldn't quite uproot.

I needed air. Space. Merrit.

Mentally, I reached for her, found her still in the war room with Solis and Nadia. *"Meet me in the eastern corridor. Please."*

Her response was immediate. *"On my way."*

I headed toward our meeting spot, a quiet stretch of hallway with windows overlooking the training yards. By the time I arrived, she was already there, silhouetted against the light.

The bond thrummed between us as I closed the distance, and when I reached her, I couldn't help myself

—I cupped her face, tilting it up to study those defiant green eyes.

"You don't have to do this," I said aloud, even as I projected the same thought. "We can find another way."

Her hands came up, signing even as her thoughts brushed mine. "There is no other way. And I'm not backing down."

"I'm terrified," I admitted, the words too raw to speak aloud. *"Of losing you. Of making the wrong choice. Of using you as bait and watching you pay the price."*

Her hand covered mine where it rested against her cheek. *"Then don't lose me. Keep me close, and we'll face it together."*

The simplicity of it—the absolute certainty in her mental voice—should have steadied me. Instead, it only made the fear sharper. Because she didn't understand yet. Didn't know what it meant to rule, to carry the weight of a province on your shoulders while your father watched and judged every move.

But with her here, that weight felt... bearable. Like maybe I could actually build something worth keeping instead of just maintaining what Father had created. Like maybe the Crown Province didn't have to be a cage.

"Three days," I murmured, pressing my forehead to hers. "Then we spring the trap. And we end this."

"Together."

"Together," I repeated.

I kissed her then, brief and fierce, tasting the promise on her lips. When I pulled back, she was watching me with something that looked almost like hope.

Then her gaze shifted past my shoulder, and her expression changed. Her alarm spiked, piercing and sudden.

I turned.

At the far end of the corridor, Tobias stood frozen. But he wasn't looking at me.

He was staring at Merrit.

Not the casual assessment of a courtier observing the prince's companion. This was focused. Intent. The kind of stare a hunter gave prey when recognizing something it had lost.

His expression was carefully neutral, but his eyes—saints, they burned with an emotion I couldn't name. Recognition? Calculation? Hunger?

The moment stretched too long. Then Tobias seemed to realize he'd been caught staring. His expression smoothed into practiced courtesy, and he inclined his head in a shallow bow before turning and walking away.

But the image of his face remained burned into my mind.

Merrit's fear tasted like copper on my tongue. *"Did you see—"*

"I saw." My hands curled into fists at my sides. *"And*

we're going to find out exactly what the hell that was about."

She turned back to me, signing with shaking hands. "He looked at me like he knew me."

"Impossible. You've never met before coming to Court."

"Unless..."

The thought trailed off, but I caught the edge of it. Her missing memories. The years before the orphanage. The blank space where her childhood should have been.

"We'll figure it out," I promised, though cold dread settled in my gut. "After the Exhibition. After we catch whoever's pulling the strings."

She nodded, but her uncertainty, her fear that we were missing something crucial, rang through me. Something that would come back to destroy us both.

I pulled her close, wrapping her in my arms, and felt her heartbeat steady against mine. The bond hummed between us, a thread of connection that felt both fragile and unbreakable.

Three days until the Exhibition.

Three days to identify the threat.

Three days before everything came crashing down.

I just hoped we'd both survive to see what came after.

CHAPTER 21

MERRIT

Three days seemed like three hours and three years all at once.

Kieran had thrown himself into preparations with the single-minded focus of a man going to war. I'd watched him through the bond—felt his exhaustion, his determination, the way fear threaded through every decision. He was terrified of losing me. I was terrified of being the reason he fell.

We'd stolen moments between strategy meetings and security briefings. A kiss in a shadowed alcove. His hand finding mine under the table during dinner. The bond thrumming between us like a lifeline, keeping us tethered when the weight of what was coming threatened to pull us under.

But now, standing in his chambers with Serenya,

circling me like a hawk assessing prey, those three days were gone.

Serenya had figured out I could hear within days of my arrival. She was too observant, too sharp—she'd caught me reacting to things I shouldn't have been able to hear. When she'd confronted me, I'd admitted the truth: not deaf, just mute. And I wanted the Court to keep believing the lie because it made them careless with their words around me.

"Oh, I like you even more now. Half this Court deserves to have their secrets spilled." She'd grinned like I'd just handed her a weapon.

"Stop fidgeting," she grumbled. "You look like you're about to bolt."

"I am about to bolt," I projected to Kieran, wherever he was in the castle.

His response came immediately, warm with amusement. *"Don't. Serenya will hunt you down, and I'd rather not have to rescue you from my cousin before the Exhibition even starts."*

"Some partner you are."

"I'm delegating. It's a leadership skill."

Despite everything, I almost smiled.

"There," Serenya said on a sigh, stepping back to admire her work. "Now you look like you belong here instead of like you're about to murder someone."

"I can do both," I signed.

"Oh, I know." Her grin was wicked. "That's what makes you perfect for him."

The gown she'd chosen was blood-wine velvet, darker than rubies, rich as sin. Long sleeves of black lace climbed to my wrists, while the bodice plunged into a deep V that exposed more skin than I'd shown in years. The skirt was a masterpiece of dramatic layers—a high-low hem that would let me move while the train pooled behind me like spilled wine.

It was stunning. It was bold. And I hated how exposed it made me feel.

My hands moved before I could stop them. "The neckline is too low."

"It's perfect for Court," Serenya said, already moving toward a velvet case on the table. "Besides, that's what this is for."

She opened the case, and my breath caught.

Diamonds. Layers upon layers of them, cascading like frozen waterfalls, each strand catching the light until the whole thing seemed to glow. The choker was a work of art—delicate and heavy all at once, clearly worth more than everything I'd ever owned combined.

"These were his mother's," Serenya said softly, her hands gentle for once. "Kieran wanted you to have them."

My throat tightened. *"Kieran."*

His attention sharpened, his focus zeroing in on me,

even though he was somewhere else in the castle. *"Do you like them?"*

"They're... they're too much."

"They're yours." His mental voice was firm, absolute. *"My mother would have wanted you to have them. And I want the Court to know exactly how I feel about you."*

Heat crawled up my neck. *"And how do you feel about me?"*

"Like you're mine. Like I'd burn the kingdom down before I let anyone hurt you. Like—" He stopped, the emotion too big to fit into words. *"Just wear them. Please."*

Serenya was watching me with knowing eyes, a small smile playing at her lips. "He's talking to you right now, isn't he?" Her grin turned sly. "I walked in on you two the morning after the Hunt. Saw the way you were looking at each other—the way you both went still at the exact same moment, like you'd heard the same thought. The whispered legends aren't as dead as people think."

I stiffened, but she waved a hand dismissively. "Relax. Your secret's safe with me. I think it's romantic as hell, actually. Terrifying, but romantic." She moved behind me, gathering my hair to expose my throat. "And since he can probably feel how much you're panicking, maybe he'll remember to breathe."

The choker settled against my skin, cold and heavy. Serenya's fingers worked the clasp, and with each strand that locked into place, the scar disappeared beneath diamonds and white gold. The weight pressed against the puckered flesh, hiding what I'd always hidden, turning vulnerability into armor.

When she finished, I barely recognized myself in the mirror.

The woman staring back looked like she belonged in Kieran's world. Polished. Elegant. Dangerous in a way that had nothing to do with knives and everything to do with the way the gown clung to curves I usually hid, the way the diamonds caught the light, the way my copper hair had been swept up to expose my neck—now protected by a queen's jewels.

"There," Serenya said, satisfaction clear in her voice. "Now you look like a prince's consort instead of a bartender playing dress-up."

"She's mean," I projected to Kieran.

"She's right," he replied, his hunger pulsing. *"Saints, Merrit. I can feel how beautiful you are through this thing, and I'm not even there yet."*

"You're biased."

"I'm bound to you. I'm allowed to be biased."

The bond hummed with his want, his pride, his fear all tangled together until I couldn't tell which emotions were his and which were mine.

A knock at the door made us both turn. One of Kieran's guards stood at attention, his thoughts a disciplined blank—trained to keep his mind quiet. "Prince Kieran is waiting in the courtyard, my lady. The Exhibition is about to begin."

"Stay close to Elias and Nadia," Kieran reminded me. *"And keep your shields up. If anything feels wrong—"*

"I'll tell you immediately," I finished. *"We've been over this."*

"I know. I just—" His mental voice cracked. *"I can't lose you."*

"You won't." I touched the choker at my throat, feeling the weight of his mother's diamonds. *"We're in this together, remember?"*

"Together."

The courtyard had been transformed into something between a festival and a battlefield.

Banquet tables lined the perimeter, groaning under the weight of spelled food and bloodwine that shimmered in crystal decanters. Torches burned in iron braziers, their flames dancing blue and green from whatever magic fueled them. The air smelled of smoke and expensive perfume, of magic and anticipation.

But it was the center that drew the eye.

A massive arena had been constructed, the ground covered in sand that had been raked into perfect patterns. Viewing boxes ringed the space, each one draped with house colors—crimson and gold, silver and black, green and bronze. The nobility clustered in their designated areas, already drinking, already watching, already judging.

And in the royal box, elevated above the rest, Kieran waited.

He looked every inch the Crown Prince—dark coat embroidered with silver thread, his crown a subtle circlet that caught the torchlight. But his eyes found mine the moment I stepped into the courtyard, and through the bond, I felt his reaction like a physical blow.

"Gods, you're fucking exquisite."

"Serenya's work," I deflected, suddenly self-conscious under his stare.

"No." His mental voice was rough, almost reverent. *"It's you. It's all you."*

I climbed the steps to the royal box, hyperaware of every eye tracking my movement. The whispers started immediately, and I didn't need telepathy to know what they were saying. The diamonds at my throat, the queen's diamonds, had just made a statement louder than any words ever could.

A collective intake of breath rippled through the nearest nobles as the torchlight caught the jewels. Fans snapped open, providing cover for urgent whispers. I caught fragments of thoughts—shock, speculation, outrage from some of the older courtiers who remembered the queen wearing these very diamonds.

The queen's choker—

He's claiming her publicly—

Does the king know?

Bold move, even for him—

Kieran rose as I approached, offering his hand. I took it, and the bond flared hot and bright between us.

"You're stunning," he said aloud, his voice pitched for the nearby nobles to hear. But mentally, he added: *"And terrified. I can feel it."*

"I'm fine."

"Liar." His thumb brushed over my knuckles. *"But a beautiful one. And they're talking about you exactly the way I wanted them to."*

"By questioning your judgment?"

"By realizing I'm serious about you." His mental voice was fierce, possessive. *"Let them talk."*

He guided me to the seat beside his, the chair clearly meant for someone important. Not a mistress tucked away in shadows. A consort. An equal.

The weight of it pressed down on my shoulders, heavier than the diamonds at my throat.

Elias stood behind us, rigid and perfect, his fractured mind still a mess of static and broken thoughts. But Nadia was there, too, melting out of shadows near the back of the box, her presence a comfort, even if Elias made my skin crawl.

She caught my eye from the shadows and signed, quick and fierce: "Anyone gets stupid, I'll gut them before they finish."

I signed back, "Thanks."

Her grin was razor-sharp as she signed: "Don't thank me yet. Night's still young."

The Exhibition began with a flourish: horns blaring, announcements shouted in magically amplified voices. The first demonstration was pure spectacle: a pair of vampires dancing through a weapons display, their movements so fast they blurred, blades singing as they clashed and parted.

The crowd roared their approval.

I should have been watching the arena. Should have been scanning the nobles, reading thoughts, looking for threats.

But I couldn't shake the feeling of being watched.

Not by the Court—I expected that. This was different. Focused. Intent.

My gaze swept the viewing boxes, searching for the source.

And found Tobias.

He stood in one of the lower boxes, surrounded by other advisors and courtiers. But his attention wasn't on the demonstration. It was on me.

Not the casual observation of a courtier noting the prince's companion. This was something else entirely: sharp, assessing, almost hungry.

Our eyes met across the distance, and his expression smoothed into practiced courtesy. He inclined his head in a shallow bow, the picture of respect.

But I'd seen his face before the mask fell. And Kieran had felt my spike of alarm.

"What is it?"

"Tobias. He's watching me."

"He's been watching you since you arrived." Kieran's mental voice was tight with barely suppressed fury. *"I've been watching him watch you."*

The demonstration ended with thunderous applause. Servants moved through the crowd, refilling drinks, offering delicacies. The nobles mingled, forming alliances and breaking them with every conversation.

And through it all, Tobias' attention felt like a weight pressing against my skull.

The next demonstration was magic—two Fae, spinning illusions that made the crowd gasp. Dragons made of light swooped through the air. Flowers bloomed and withered in seconds. Stars fell from an artificial sky and shattered into glittering dust.

It was beautiful. It was distracting.

And Tobias was moving closer.

I tracked him through the crowd, watched him navigate the social landscape with practiced ease. A word here, a smile there. He was working his way toward the royal box, casual enough that it wouldn't raise alarm.

But I knew. Somehow, I knew he was coming for me.

"Kieran."

"I see him." His hand found mine under the armrest,

squeezing once. *"Stay calm. Elias is right behind you. Nadia's in the shadows. He won't try anything here."*

"Then why do I feel like prey?"

He didn't have an answer for that.

The Fae finished their display, and the crowd erupted. Kieran rose, the movement drawing every eye in the courtyard. He was expected to speak, to thank the performers, to play his role.

"Magnificent," he said, his voice carrying with easy authority. "A demonstration worthy of the old legends."

The crowd murmured its agreement. Kieran smiled, charming and distant, every inch the prince they expected.

But through the bond, his tension ratcheted higher.

"The next demonstration will feature combat trials," he continued. "Our finest warriors testing their skills against worthy opponents."

More applause. The arena cleared, sand raked smooth again by servants in house colors.

And Tobias reached the steps to the royal box.

"Your Highness," he said, bowing low. "Might I have a moment?"

Kieran's jaw tightened, but he nodded. "Of course, Tobias."

The old advisor climbed the steps with the ease of someone who'd done it a thousand times. His attention slid to me, lingered just long enough to be noticeable, then shifted back to Kieran.

"I wanted to commend you on the Exhibition thus far," Tobias said smoothly. "The displays have been exceptional."

"Thank you." Kieran's tone was polite but cool. "Was there something specific you needed?"

"Not at all. I simply wanted to pay my respects." His gaze shifted to me again, and this time, it stayed. "And to compliment your companion. The queen's jewels suit you, my lady."

I couldn't respond verbally, couldn't tell him to fuck off the way I wanted to. My hands stayed still on my lap, but I knew Kieran felt my revulsion like acid.

"They do," Kieran said, his voice carrying a warning. "My mother had excellent taste."

"Indeed, she did." Tobias' smile didn't reach his eyes. "Such a tragedy, her passing. She would have been pleased to see them worn again."

The words were innocuous. The tone was perfect. But something in the way he looked at the diamonds, at my throat beneath them, made my skin crawl.

Kieran's fury burned white-hot. *"He's done. I'm getting him away from you."*

But before Kieran could dismiss him, the horn blared again. The combat demonstration was beginning.

Two fighters entered the arena: a vampire and a shifter, both armed with practice weapons that would still hurt like hell. The crowd's attention shifted, drawn to the promise of violence.

Tobias bowed again, descending the steps. "Enjoy the demonstration, Your Highness."

He melted back into the crowd, but I could still feel his attention on me like a brand.

"Something's wrong," I projected. *"The way he looked at the necklace—"*

"I know." Kieran's hand found mine again. *"After this demonstration, we're moving you somewhere more secure."*

"No." My spine stiffened. *"That's not the plan."*

"The plan just changed."

"I came here to read the crowd, to find the threats." My frustration bled through the bond. *"If you lock me away every time something feels dangerous, what's the point of me being here at all?"*

His jaw tightened, muscle jumping. *"The point is keeping you alive."*

"The point," I shot back, *"is catching whoever's trying to kill you. And I can't do that from your chambers."*

I felt his war—the need to protect me versus the knowledge that I was right. That pulling me out now would waste the trap we'd set, would show our hand before we'd identified all the players.

"Stay close to me," he finally conceded, though his grip on my hand tightened. *"If anything—and I mean anything—feels wrong, you tell me immediately."*

"That was always the plan."

"Merrit—"

"Together, remember?" I squeezed his hand back. *"We face this together, or we don't face it at all."*

The combat trial began before he could argue further.

The fighters circled each other, weapons raised. The vampire struck first—a blur of motion that would have been too fast for mortal eyes to track. The shifter blocked, barely, and the crowd roared its approval.

They were good. Skilled. The kind of warriors who made demonstrations look like art.

But something felt off.

The vampire's strikes were getting closer to the viewing boxes. The shifter kept driving him back, pushing toward the royal box, toward us.

Elias shifted behind me, his hand going to his sword. Kieran's alarm spiked through me.

Then the vampire's blade caught the light wrong—not practice steel, but real, sharp, deadly.

"Kieran—"

The warning came too late.

The vampire lunged, not at the shifter, but at the royal box. His blade arced through the air, impossibly fast, aimed not at Kieran but at the space between us— at me.

Elias moved, pulling me back. The blade missed my throat by inches, but the momentum of Elias' pull sent me stumbling forward instead of back.

Straight toward the railing.

My hip hit the carved wood, and for one horrible moment, I teetered on the edge. The diamonds at my throat swung forward, catching on something—a decorative finial, maybe, or the edge of a banner pole mounted to the railing.

The clasp gave way.

The weight of the queen's jewels slid forward.

Cold air hit my throat where diamonds had once been.

No—

I caught the choker before it fell, my other hand flying up to cover my throat. But it was too late. The scar had been visible for a heartbeat, maybe two.

Long enough.

The crowd's attention was on the arena, on the guards now subduing the vampire whose demonstration had "accidentally" gone wrong. Nobles shouted, scandalized, as the fighter was dragged away.

But one person wasn't watching the chaos.

Tobias stood at the base of the royal box, and his eyes were locked on my throat. On the hand I'd pressed there to hide what I'd spent a lifetime concealing.

His expression went through a series of changes too fast to catalog—shock flickering to something I couldn't name, before smoothing into careful neutrality.

I tried to push into his mind, desperate to know what he was thinking. But his thoughts were a wall of static, impenetrable as always. Except for flashes—fragments that made no sense:

A small room. Blood on wooden floors. A woman's scream cut short.

The images vanished as quickly as they'd come, leaving only the sick certainty that whatever Tobias was remembering, I was at the center of it.

His mouth moved, but I couldn't hear what he said over the chaos. Then he bowed—smooth, practiced, perfect—and turned away, disappearing into the crowd.

But the way he'd stared at my throat, at the scar I'd kept hidden for so long...

Kieran's alarm crashed into mine. *"What did you see?"*

"I don't know." My hand trembled as I clutched the broken choker. *"Fragments. Blood. Screaming. I couldn't piece it together."*

"But he recognized the scar."

"Yes." The certainty settled in my gut like lead. *"He knows what it means. Even if I don't."*

CHAPTER 22
KIERAN

The blade had been real.

That single thought kept circling my mind as I stood in the interrogation chamber, Merrit at my side. Practice weapons didn't draw blood. They didn't slice through air with that lethal whisper. And they sure as fuck didn't come within inches of severing her godsdamned neck.

Someone had switched the weapons. Someone had orchestrated the entire "accident."

And judging by the purple foam bubbling from the vampire's lips, someone wanted to make damn sure he couldn't tell us who.

"Poison," Solis said flatly, crouching beside the dying fighter. "Fast-acting. He took it the moment the guards grabbed him."

"Or someone gave it to him." I kept my voice level, cold, even as fury burned through my veins.

"Can you read him?" I projected to Merrit. *"Before he dies?"*

Her immediate agreement carried through our connection, but also her caution. We'd been careful to hide what she truly was—even from Solis. Her cover as a seer and the Whisperbound connection gave us a plausible explanation for some of her insights. Visions, intuitions, the kind of thing that happened with magical bonds.

But admitting she was a full telepath? That would be a death sentence in any other province. And while I trusted Solis with my life, there were some secrets too dangerous to share. Not because I didn't trust him—but because knowing it would put him in danger, too.

"She might be able to see something," I said aloud, carefully casual. "Her ability sometimes gives her... impressions. Especially in moments of strong emotion."

Solis glanced at Merrit, then back to me. If he suspected I was downplaying her abilities, he didn't show it. "It's worth trying."

Merrit moved closer to the dying vampire, her expression focused. To anyone watching, she looked like she was concentrating, trying to catch some vision or impression through our bond.

But through our actual connection, I felt her dive deep into his fractured mind.

Her face went pale almost immediately. I caught fragments of what she was seeing: gold promised, orders given, a voice he couldn't quite remember, static where clear thoughts should be.

"Someone controlled him," she projected, her mental voice strained. *"Like Elias. His mind is broken in the same way—"*

The vampire's eyes rolled back, his body arching in a final spasm.

And then blood began streaming from Merrit's nose.

"Saints!" Solis was on his feet in an instant.

I lunged forward, catching Merrit as she stumbled. A spike of pain lanced through her skull, the nauseating disorientation of a mind snapping away from hers mid-connection.

"What happened?" Solis demanded, concern etched across his face.

"Sometimes when she pushes too hard—" I kept my voice steady, even as panic clawed at my chest. "She's done this before. She'll be fine."

I felt useless as I shoved my handkerchief into her hand.

"Liar," Merrit projected weakly. *"I've never bled from this before."*

"I know. Which is why you're not doing it again."

"I'm fine," she signed with one hand, the other pressing my handkerchief to her nose. "I got something. Just give me a—"

But she swayed, and I tightened my grip on her.

"What did you see?" Solis asked, his tone careful. He'd accepted my explanation about the bond, but I could see the questions in his eyes. Questions he was too loyal to voice.

Merrit's gaze went unfocused as she signed, "A vision. Fragments. Someone promised him gold. But it wasn't..."

"What do you mean?"

Before she could answer, the vampire gasped—one final, desperate breath. "Elias... promised..."

Then he went still.

Silence crashed over the room.

Merrit's certainty flooded our connection. *"His dying words don't match what I saw. Someone old. But the name was buried, and it sure as fuck wasn't Elias."*

"You're sure?"

"Yes. Someone put those words in his mouth. Or made him believe Elias was the one who gave the orders when it was actually someone else."

Aloud, I said, "She saw confusion. Like he didn't really know who gave him the orders."

It was close enough to the truth to be believable. And vague enough not to reveal exactly how much Merrit had seen.

Solis looked between us, and I knew he suspected there was more to the story. But he just nodded. "The mind control we've been seeing. It makes sense the memories would be fractured. If it's compulsion and not a spell, it would have to be a vampire with some years under his belt. Elias is old, but not that old."

"Search Elias' quarters, anyway," I said, the order tasting like ash. "If this vampire believed it was Elias, there might be evidence planted to support that belief."

"And the lady?" Solis gestured to Merrit, who was still bleeding sluggishly.

"I'll take care of her." I kept my arm around her, feeling her exhaustion and pain. "Start the search. Bring me whatever you find."

He hesitated, clearly wanting to say something. Then he just nodded and left, taking the guards with him.

The moment we were alone, Merrit sagged against me.

"That was..." Her fingers moved weakly. "I've never felt anything like that. His mind was dying, tearing itself apart, and I was in it—"

"You're not doing that again." I tilted her face up, checking her eyes. The bleeding had slowed, but her pupils were slightly dilated, her skull pounding. "Ever."

"We might not have a choice."

"We always have a choice. And I'm not watching you bleed out because someone needs their thoughts read."

Her hand came up to touch my face, her fear mixing with frustration. *"I'm the only advantage we have. The only one who can see through the lies."*

"Not if it kills you."

"It won't kill me," she signed, then swayed again.

I caught her, scooping her up before she could protest. "We're going to my chambers. You're resting. And we're figuring this out without you diving into dying minds."

She wanted to argue, but the pain was too much, the exhaustion too deep.

She signed against my chest as I carried her: "Solis suspects something."

"I know."

"Will you tell him?"

"No." The answer was immediate. "The fewer people who know what you really are, the safer you are. Even Solis. Especially Solis."

She looked up at me, questioning.

"Because if the wrong person finds out what you can do, they'll kill you. Or worse—try to use you." I pressed a kiss to her forehead. "Solis is loyal, but loyalty won't protect him if someone decides to dig through his mind the way they did Elias'. What he doesn't know, he can't reveal."

"You'd lie for me?"

The answer was as clear as day, and she fucking well knew it. *"I'd burn the kingdom down for you. Lying is easy."*

I carried her through the corridors, past guards who straightened at attention but knew better than to question their prince carrying his bleeding companion. By the time we reached my chambers, the handkerchief was soaked through, and Merrit's skin had taken on a grayish cast that made my chest tighten with fear.

I laid her on the bed, fetching clean cloths and water. The bleeding had nearly stopped, but the damage was done—she looked wrung out, hollowed by pain.

"Rest," I ordered, pressing a damp cloth to her forehead. "I'll be back soon."

"Don't leave." Her mental voice was small, vulnerable in a way she rarely let herself be. *"Please."*

The "Please" broke me.

"I'm not going anywhere." I settled beside her on the bed, pulling her close. "Solis can handle the search. You're more important."

"The evidence—"

"Can wait." I kissed her temple, careful of her pain. *"You can't."*

I felt her giving in. The exhaustion was too much to fight, the headache still pounding behind her eyes. She curled into me, and within minutes, her breathing had evened into sleep.

I held her, feeling her heartbeat against my chest, and tried not to think about how close that blade had come. How her blood had looked streaming from her nose. How fragile she suddenly seemed despite all her strength.

A knock at the door pulled me from my thoughts.

"Enter," I called softly, not wanting to wake Merrit.

Solis stepped inside, his expression grim. He took in Merrit asleep in my arms, then held up a cloth sack. "You're not going to like this."

"Show me."

He laid items on my desk one by one, each more damning than the last.

A purse of gold. Heavy, clinking, far more than a diplomatic advisor's salary would explain.

The forged sigil from the southern gate attack. The one that had gotten an assassin close enough to try for my life.

Coded correspondence in Elias' handwriting— vague enough to be innocuous or treasonous depending on interpretation.

A map of the castle and grounds with locations marked. The southern gate. The Exhibition arena. My private chambers.

And a small vial of something dark and viscous that made my skin crawl just looking at it.

"Blood magic," Solis said quietly. "Or poison. Maybe both. We'd need to test it to be sure."

I stared at the collection, my mind refusing to accept what my eyes were seeing. "This is too much. Too convenient."

"That's exactly what I thought." Solis crossed his arms. "Everything we'd need to convict him, all in one place. Like someone wanted us to find it."

"Or like he's been sloppy because his mind is break-ing." I picked up one of the coded letters, scanned the contents. *The bird flies at dawn. The rose blooms red. The crown weighs heavy.*

Nonsense. Or code. Impossible to tell without context.

"We need to question him," I said. "Now. But care-fully—I want Merrit there when she wakes. Her impres-sions might tell us if he's lying."

It was the safest way to phrase it. "Impressions" from the bond, not outright mind reading. Plausible. Deniable.

Solis nodded. "I'll have him brought to your study. Give the lady time to recover first."

When he left, I returned to the bed, sliding back in beside Merrit. She was still sleeping, copper hair spread across my pillow, one hand curled near her face.

Weeks ago, I'd had Nadia follow her. The odd Divide bartender who knew people's orders before they spoke. I'd thought she was a seer, maybe useful for rooting out the traitor in my Court. A tool. A means to an end.

Now, watching her chest rise and fall, seeing the dried blood still crusting her upper lip from pushing too hard to save me—

Now, the thought of losing her made my chest tighten with a fear I couldn't name.

I should have let her rest longer. Should have waited until the headache faded completely.

But we were running out of time. And Elias—loyal, confused, possibly innocent Elias—was sitting in his quarters with damning evidence stacked against him.

"Merrit," I projected gently. *"I need you to wake up."*

Her consciousness stirred. Reluctant. Still hurting.

"How long was I asleep?"

"An hour. Maybe less." I brushed hair away from her face. *"Solis found evidence in Elias' quarters. We need to question him, and I need your... impressions."*

Understanding rippled through her. She knew what I was really asking—*Read his mind, tell me if he's guilty, but do it carefully enough that Solis doesn't realize the full extent of what she can do.*

"Give me a few minutes."

I held her while she woke fully, feeling the headache still throbbing but manageable now. The bleeding had stopped completely, leaving only dried traces on her upper lip that I gently cleaned away. Then, I helped her out of the ruined Exhibition gown and into something more practical—a simple dress that wouldn't remind us both of how close she'd come to dying.

"Better?" I asked aloud.

She nodded, signing: "Functional."

"That's not the same as better."

"It'll have to do." She sat up slowly, testing her balance. Her determination overrode her pain. "Let's talk to Elias."

CHAPTER 23
KIERAN

They brought Elias to my private study—not the throne room, not the interrogation chamber. Somewhere quieter. More personal.

If this were truly betrayal, I wanted to see it in his eyes.

He looked worse than when I'd last seen him. His hair was disheveled, his clothes rumpled, and there was a tremor in his hands that hadn't been there a week ago. The fractured quality of his mind had gotten worse—I could see it in the way his gaze couldn't quite focus, the way he flinched at sounds that weren't there.

But when he saw me, something cleared in his expression. Recognition. And fear.

"Your Highness." His voice cracked. "What's happened? The guards wouldn't tell me—"

"Sit." I gestured to the chair across from my desk.

He sat, and I watched him take in the evidence laid out before him. The gold. The sigil. The letters. The map.

The color drained from his face.

"I don't..." He reached for the purse of gold, then pulled his hand back like it had burned him. "I've never seen this before."

"It was in your quarters. Hidden beneath a loose floorboard in your chambers."

"That's not—I didn't—" He looked up at me, and the confusion in his eyes was genuine. I'd known this man for decades. I knew when he was lying.

This wasn't lying. This was bewilderment.

"The vampire who tried to kill Merrit," I said, keeping my voice level. "His last words were your name. He said you promised him something."

"What?" Elias' voice pitched higher. "No. No, I would never—Your Highness, you have to believe me. I would never betray you. Never."

Merrit stood beside me, her focus on Elias. To Solis, it would look like she was concentrating, trying to catch impressions, but through our connection, I felt her diving into his thoughts.

"Then explain the evidence," I said.

"I can't!" His hands shook as he gestured at the items. "I don't know where any of this came from. The gold, the letters—saints, that's my handwriting, but I don't remember writing those words. I don't remember—"

He stopped, his breath coming faster. "There are gaps. Days I can't account for. Times when I wake up somewhere and don't remember how I got there. I thought I was just tired, stressed, but—"

Merrit's certainty surged into me. *"He's telling the truth. His mind is fractured, controlled. Someone's been giving him orders he can't remember, making him do things and then wiping the memory."*

"You're sure?"

"Yes. The pattern is the same as the vampire. But Elias has been controlled for longer. Months, maybe."

I kept my expression neutral, but inside, relief and fury warred. Relief that Elias hadn't betrayed me. Fury that someone had violated his mind, turned him into a weapon against me.

"Merrit," I said aloud. "What are you getting?"

She signed carefully, each movement deliberate: "Confusion. Genuine fear. Like he truly doesn't remember. The bond is showing me... gaps. Empty spaces where memories should be."

It was close enough to the truth. And vague enough not to reveal too much.

Solis frowned. "Mind control. Like we suspected."

"Someone's been using you," I told Elias. "Planting evidence. Setting you up to take a fall."

"I'm so sorry." His voice broke. "I didn't know. I swear I didn't know."

"It's not your fault." The words came automatically, even as my mind raced through implications. "Someone's been in your head. Making you do things, then erasing your memory of it."

"Then drink my blood." Elias offered his wrist immediately, desperate. "See for yourself. See that I'm telling the truth."

I wanted to. Saints, I wanted the certainty that would come from tasting his blood, seeing his memories, knowing without doubt whether he was innocent or guilty.

But Solis stepped forward, alarm on his face. "Kieran, no. His mind is compromised. What if his blood is tainted? Poisoned? What if drinking it transfers whatever's controlling him to you?"

The words hit like cold water. He was right. If someone had been manipulating Elias' mind, his blood could be toxic. Magically poisoned. Or worse—it could be the vector for the control itself.

Drinking it could kill me. Or turn me into another puppet.

"Fuck." I dropped my hand, looking at Elias. "He's right. I can't risk it."

Merrit's fear spiked. She hadn't thought of that possibility either, and now the realization terrified her.

"Then what do we do?" Elias asked quietly.

"We confine you." The words tasted like betrayal even as I spoke them. "Not in the dungeons. Comfortable quarters, under guard. Protective custody—for your safety and ours."

"I understand." He slumped in the chair, looking smaller somehow. "I'd do the same in your position."

"We'll find who's controlling you," I promised. "And when we do, I'll clear your name."

"If I'm truly innocent," he said softly, tears of shame welling in his eyes. "What if I'm not?"

"You are." Merrit's hands moved with absolute certainty, her conviction filtering through me. "I can feel it."

He looked at her with something like gratitude. "Thank you, my lady."

The guards took him away—gently, respectfully, to a secure room in the residential wing. Somewhere comfortable but contained.

When he was gone, I sagged against my desk, exhaustion crashing over me. "This is a fucking nightmare."

"It's a setup," Solis said. "Someone's playing us. Framing Elias, staging attacks, staying three steps ahead."

"But who?" I looked at the evidence still spread across my desk. "Who has the access, the knowledge, the skill to do all this?"

Solis straightened, glancing toward the door. "I

should check on Elias. Make sure he's settled in his quarters, and the guards understand he's not to be treated as a criminal."

"Good idea. And Solis?" I waited until he met my gaze. "No one hears about what Merrit saw in that vampire's mind. Not even the other guards."

He nodded, understanding in his expression. "The lady has a gift for impressions. That's all anyone needs to know."

When he left, silence settled over the room. Merrit moved to the window, staring out at the courtyard where the Exhibition had been, her thoughts carefully shielded even from me.

A knock at the door made us both turn.

"Enter."

Tobias stepped into the room, his expression grave with concern. "Your Highness. What happened at the Exhibition was..." He trailed off, shaking his head. "I've never seen such a breach of protocol. A real blade in a demonstration? Unthinkable."

His gaze swept the evidence on my desk, lingering on the forged sigil. "And now I hear Elias has been confined. Surely there must be some mistake?"

Every instinct in me screamed that something was wrong. The timing of his arrival, the convenient observations, the way his eyes kept finding Merrit—it all seemed calculated.

But Tobias had been my father's advisor for

centuries. Had served the Crown longer than I'd been alive. That kind of loyalty wasn't easily faked.

Was it?

"We're investigating," I said carefully.

"Of course." He clasped his hands behind his back, the picture of a concerned advisor. "I hate to add to your burdens, but I thought you should know—I've seen Elias in strange places recently. Speaking with people I didn't recognize. At odd hours. I thought nothing of it at the time, but now..." He let the sentence hang, heavy with implication.

Merrit's attention sharpened with suspicion.

"What kind of people?" I asked, pressing him.

"Foreign. Well-dressed but not nobility. The kind who slip in and out without being noticed." Tobias' expression was troubled. "And once, I could have sworn I saw him near the armory where the Exhibition weapons were stored. But when I approached, he was gone."

The detail seemed too perfect. Too convenient.

But it also fit with everything else we'd found.

"I should have said something sooner," Tobias continued. "I just didn't want to believe—"

"It's not your fault," I said, though the words felt hollow. "You couldn't have known."

"Still." He moved closer, studying the evidence. "If there's anything I can do to help with the investigation, I'm at your service. I've served this Crown for six centuries. I won't let some traitor tear down what we've built."

"I'll keep that in mind."

He bowed and left, and the moment the door closed, Merrit's hands moved in quick, agitated signs.

"I don't trust him."

"I don't, either," I admitted, surprising myself with the honesty. "Something about this feels wrong."

"His face when he looked at the evidence," she signed. "He wasn't surprised. And all those convenient observations about Elias?"

"Too perfect," I agreed. "But that doesn't mean—"

"Someone controlled Elias." She cut me off, her hands moving faster. "Someone old enough and skilled enough to fracture minds and hide their tracks. Someone with access to everything."

The implication hung between us.

Tobias had both. Age and access.

"It's not proof," I said, even as my mind turned over the possibility. "Suspicion isn't evidence."

"Then we get evidence." Her hands stilled. "We watch him. We find proof."

Through the bond, I caught the flicker of her thought—searching his chambers herself, finding concrete evidence—and shut it down immediately.

"We watch him," I agreed. "Nadia can shadow him. But you—" She stiffened, knowing what I was about to say. "You stay away from him."

Merrit nodded, but her dissatisfaction bled through our connection. She wanted more. Needed proof. And despite my warning, the thought kept surfacing, persistent as a tide.

"Don't even think about it," I said aloud.

She looked at me, feigning innocence.

"I felt that. You're not searching anyone's chambers. Especially not alone." I pulled her closer, needing the physical contact. "Someone tried to kill you today. Whether through Elias or someone else, they got close. Too close. And I'm not giving them another chance."

Her fear echoed mine. "The necklace..."

"I know." My thumb brushed over where the queen's diamonds had been, now replaced by a simple velvet ribbon she'd tied around her throat. "The way Tobias looked at your scar—"

"He recognized it," she signed, her hands trembling slightly. "I saw his face. Just for a moment before he controlled it. He knew what it meant."

"How could he recognize a scar?"

"I don't know." Her frustration bled through me. "But he knows something about my past. About the attack that left that mark. And if he knows that, then he either witnessed it or—"

"Or he was part of it." The words settled cold and heavy in my gut.

I felt her certainty, her conviction that Tobias was

the key to everything—the attacks, Elias' control, her missing past.

But conviction wasn't proof. And without proof, all we had was suspicion.

"We'll figure it out," I promised, though I had no idea how. "Together."

She leaned into me, her exhaustion worsening. The headache had faded but not disappeared. The strain of reading the dying vampire, then Elias, had taken its toll.

"Come on." I kept my arm around her as I guided her back toward my private chambers. "You need rest. Real rest, not just an hour between interrogations."

"I can't just rest while—"

"Yes, you can." I cut her off gently. "Because if you collapse from exhaustion, you're no good to anyone. And I need you sharp, Merrit. I need your... impressions. But I can't use them if you're running on fumes and bleeding from your nose."

Her reluctant agreement hit me square in the chest. She was exhausted. Still hurting from pushing too hard earlier.

My chambers were quiet when we returned, the sun setting outside the windows and casting everything in shades of amber and shadow. I locked the door. Spelled it for extra measure. Then turned to find Merrit standing in the middle of the room, looking lost.

"I almost lost you today." The words came out

rougher than I'd intended. "That blade—if it had been an inch closer—"

"But it wasn't." She moved toward me, hands reaching up to cup my face. "I'm here. I'm alive."

"This time." I pulled her closer, needing to feel her solid and real against me. "But next time..."

"There won't be a next time. We'll figure this out before—"

I kissed her, cutting off the reassurance we both knew might be a lie. Because whoever was hunting us had gotten closer today than ever before. Had orchestrated an attack in broad daylight, in front of the entire Court, and nearly succeeded.

The kiss turned brutal fast. Her hands fisted in my shirt hard enough to tear fabric, pulling me closer. Her need matched mine—raw, desperate, the kind that had nothing to do with softness and everything to do with survival.

I walked her backward until her legs hit the bed, and she yanked me down with her, nails scraping down my back hard enough to sting.

"Don't be gentle," she whispered into my mind before her hands went to my buttons, ripping them open. *"I don't want gentle right now."*

"Good." I caught her wrists, pinned them above her head with one hand while the other worked at the laces of her dress. "Because I don't have gentle in me tonight."

She arched into me, fighting my grip not to escape

but to get closer, and I released her wrists to tear at her clothing properly. The dress came off in a tangle of fabric and frustration, her hands just as rough on my clothes, both of us moving with the graceless urgency of people who'd almost died.

When we were finally skin to skin, I didn't take my time. Didn't worship her gently. My hands mapped her body like I was checking for injuries I knew weren't there—rough, possessive, needing to confirm she was whole.

She matched me, nails dragging down my ribs, teeth finding my shoulder hard enough to leave marks.

"You're so fucking brave," I growled against her throat, one hand fisting in her hair. "You shouldn't have to be. But you are, and I—" I stopped, the words catching.

Through the bond, her love flared bright and warm —and it fucking terrified me.

Not because I didn't feel it back. I did. That was the problem.

I loved her. Completely. Impossibly. After barely a week of knowing her, after blackmailing her into this life, after putting her in danger over and over.

The bond wasn't my fault—that had been fate, magic, something neither of us controlled. But everything else? That was on me. I'd taken her from her home, used her abilities, put her life at risk, fucked her, and then tried to push her away like I could undo what we'd started.

And now she loved me, anyway.

I pulled back enough to meet her eyes, my hand still tangled in her copper hair. "I blackmailed you."

"I know." Her hips rolled against mine. *"Keep going."*

"I took you from your home. Used you. Put your life at risk—"

"I know." Her mental voice was steady, fierce. *"And I'm still here. Still choosing this. Still choosing you."*

"That doesn't make it right."

"No." She wrapped her legs around my hips, pulling me closer. *"But it makes it ours."*

I kissed her then—brutal and claiming and tasting like hunger. This wasn't the love of fairy tales or ballads. This was the love forged in fire and blood, built on raw need and the absolute certainty that losing each other would destroy us both.

When I finally pushed into her, the bond exploded between us. Her pleasure was mine, mine was hers, and the intensity of it was almost violent. We moved together without grace or tenderness—all teeth and nails and the kind of rough urgency that came from almost dying.

I felt everything. Her fear mixing with pleasure. Her anger at being put in danger tangled with her need for me. Her resentment of the situation wrapped around her choice to stay, anyway.

And underneath it all, her love. Messy and complicated and real.

"The bond wasn't your fault," she projected as I drove into her harder, both of us chasing something we couldn't name. *"But the rest? Yeah, you were an asshole."*

"I know."

"And I love you, anyway." Her nails raked down my back. *"Deal with it."*

The honesty of it, the absolute acceptance, broke something in me. I let my own feelings flood our connection—my love just as messy, just as unearned, wrapped in guilt and need and the terror of losing her.

"This is fucked up," I projected.

"I know." She bit my shoulder hard enough to draw blood. *"Say it anyway."*

"I love you." The words tore out of me, rough and desperate and completely inadequate for the tangle of emotions behind them. "Saints help me, I love you."

Her answering surge of emotion was triumph and relief and love so fierce it hurt. She pulled me closer, deeper, her body demanding everything I had to give.

We fell over the edge together, the bond flaring so bright it whited out everything else. For one perfect, terrible moment, there was only us—two souls bound together by magic and blood and a love that had no business existing but refused to die, anyway.

When we came back to ourselves, we were tangled

together, both breathing hard, sweat-slicked and marked by each other's hands and teeth.

"That was..." I started.

"Messy," she finished, signing against my chest with a tired hand.

"Yeah."

"But ours."

"Yeah." I pressed a kiss to her forehead, gentler now in the aftermath. "Ours."

She traced a finger over the bite mark she'd left on my shoulder, her satisfaction at marking me filtered through my chest. *"No taking it back now."*

"Wouldn't if I could." I caught her hand, pressing a kiss to her palm. *"We're fucked up together."*

"Better than being fucked up alone."

Her exhaustion finally caught up with her. The adrenaline crash, the headache that had never fully faded, the bone-deep weariness of almost dying and choosing to love, anyway.

Her fingers traced lazy patterns on my chest, and I began to drift off, too, sleep pulling me under like a tide.

But underneath the exhaustion, underneath the satisfaction and the love, something nagged at me. A flicker of thought from her. Not quite hidden, but not quite shared, either.

Determination. Purpose. Planning.

I tried to focus on it, to ask, but sleep was already dragging me under. The warmth of her body, the safety of locked doors and spelled wards, the bone-deep exhaustion of the day—it all conspired to pull me into darkness.

My last conscious thought was a question I didn't have the energy to voice: *What are you planning?*

But then I was asleep, Merrit safe in my arms, and the world narrowed to just her heartbeat and mine, beating in sync.

Tomorrow. I'd ask tomorrow.

If only I'd stayed awake.

If only I'd pushed past the exhaustion to read that flicker of determination in her thoughts.

If only I'd known what she was planning to do.

But I didn't. And by the time I woke, it would be too late.

CHAPTER 24
MERRIT

I waited.

Kieran's breathing had evened out minutes ago, his chest rising and falling in the steady rhythm of sleep. Through the bond, his exhaustion pulled him deeper, his mind finally quiet after the chaos of the day.

I should have felt guilty. Should have hated myself for what I was about to do.

But all I felt was determination.

The past three days waiting for the Exhibition, I'd spent every spare moment memorizing the castle. Servant passages, guard rotations, the layout of the advisors' wing. Kieran thought I was resting, recovering, but I'd been preparing.

And now, lying in his arms while he slept, I was going to use everything I'd learned.

"I'm sorry," I projected into the bond, knowing he was too deep in sleep to hear it. *"But I have to know."*

Carefully, so carefully, I began to extract myself from his embrace. His arm tightened reflexively, and I froze, my heart hammering. I kept my emotions muted—sleepy, content, nothing to wake him.

After a moment, his grip loosened.

I slid out of bed inch by inch, my bare feet silent on the cold stone floor. Kieran shifted, rolling onto his back, one arm sprawled across the space I'd just vacated.

He looked peaceful. Younger, somehow, without the weight of the Crown and Court pressing down on him. The moonlight through the window cast shadows across his face, softening the hard edges.

I loved him. Saints help me, I loved him.

And I was about to break every promise I'd made to stay safe.

But Tobias had recognized my scar. Those fragments I'd caught from his thoughts—blood, screaming, a small room—they'd been haunting me. And if he knew something about my past, about the family I couldn't remember, I needed to know what.

I needed proof to free Elias.

And I needed answers for myself.

Moving quickly now, I dressed in the darkest clothes I could find—practical things from my Divide days that Serenya had insisted I keep "for sentimental value."

Black trousers, a dark shirt, soft-soled boots that wouldn't echo on stone.

I strapped a knife to my thigh. Small, sharp, the kind I'd carried for years when working late nights at the bar.

One last look at Kieran, sleeping peacefully, trusting me to be beside him when he woke.

"I'm sorry," I projected again. *"I love you. But I can't let this go."*

Then I slipped out the door and into the darkened corridor.

The castle at night was a different beast entirely.

Shadows pooled in corners, thick and menacing. Torches burned low in their sconces, casting more darkness than light. Every creak of settling stone made my heart jump, every distant footstep sent me pressing against the wall.

But I'd planned for this.

The servant passages I'd memorized were mostly empty this late—the staff had retired hours ago, leaving only the night watch to patrol the main corridors. I moved through the narrow spaces like a ghost, counting doorways, remembering turns.

Left at the third junction. Down the stairs. Past the kitchens where the banked fires still glowed.

A guard's voice echoed from somewhere ahead, and I ducked into an alcove, holding my breath. Two of them passed by the main corridor just beyond my hiding spot, their conversation low and bored.

"—heard Elias is locked up in the residential wing—"

"—about time someone dealt with the traitor—"

"—Prince seemed pretty torn up about it, though—"

Their voices faded as they continued their patrol.

I waited a full minute before moving again.

The advisors' wing was quieter than I'd expected. No guards posted outside the doors—why would there be? They were trusted members of the Court, not prisoners. The hallway stretched before me, lined with identical doors bearing brass nameplates.

I counted them as I walked, my heart pounding so loud I was sure someone would hear it.

Three doors down. There. **Tobias Serrant, Royal Advisor**

The nameplate gleamed in the low torchlight, polished and pristine. Just like everything else about him.

I pulled my lockpicks from my pocket—thin metal tools I'd learned to use in the Divide, when getting into locked storage rooms meant the difference between eating and starving.

The lock was better than I'd expected. Complex, well-made, likely spelled with minor protections. My hands shook as I worked, the picks scraping softly against the mechanism.

Come on, come on—

A sound down the hallway made me freeze. Footsteps. Getting closer.

I worked faster, my fingers clumsy with panic. The lock resisted, fighting me, and I wanted to scream with frustration.

The footsteps were almost at the corner—

Click.

I shoved the door open, slipped inside, and eased it closed behind me, just as light from a lantern spilled into the hallway. I pressed my back against the door, not breathing, as whoever it was walked past.

Their footsteps faded.

I let out a shaky breath and turned to face the room.

Moonlight streamed through tall windows, casting everything in silver and shadow. The chamber was exactly what I'd expected from Tobias—neat, orderly, almost obsessively so. Books lined the shelves in perfect rows. Papers on the desk were stacked with military precision. Not a single item out of place.

It smelled like old parchment and something else. Something metallic and faintly sweet that made my stomach turn.

Blood magic.

I moved to the desk first, careful not to disturb anything. Letters, reports, schedules—all innocuous. All exactly what a royal advisor should have.

The bookshelves were next. Histories, political treatises, books on governance and law. Nothing suspicious.

I checked the wardrobe. Clothes, all dark and expensive. A few cloaks. Nothing hidden in the pockets or lining.

Growing frustrated, I returned to the desk, running my hands along the drawers, checking for false bottoms or hidden compartments. This was taking too long. Kieran could wake at any moment, reach for me through the bond, realize I was gone—

My fingers caught on something. A slight inconsistency in the wood of the bottom drawer.

I pulled the drawer out completely, set it aside, and there—a false bottom, expertly crafted but just slightly off if you knew to look.

My hands shook as I pried it open.

Inside: files, old ones, some of the paper yellowed with age.

I pulled them out, spreading them across the desk, and my breath caught.

Names. Descriptions. Locations.

All mind readers.

All marked **ELIMINATED** in blood-red ink.

Oh, gods.

This wasn't just evidence of framing Elias. This was a list of murders spanning *decades*. Maybe longer.

I forced myself to read, even as my stomach churned.

Subject: Marcus Lark, Age 34, Shifter (wolf), Telepathic
Location: Southern Morathen
Threat Level: Moderate
Status: ELIMINATED
Method: Arranged accident. Cliff fall during hunt. Body recovered.

Subject: Lyra Moonwhisper, Age 156, Fae, Telepathic
Location: Eastern Morathen
Threat Level: High
Status: ELIMINATED
Method: Poison. Slow-acting. Subject expired over three days. Screaming minimal.

The clinical language. The casual notation of suffering. My hands were shaking so badly I could barely hold the pages.

There were dozens of them. Fifty, maybe more.

Subject: Helena Darkwater, Age 12, Vampire (turned young), Telepathic
Location: Capital City
Threat Level: Extreme - child vampire with mental abilities
Status: ELIMINATED

Method: Staking. Quick. Child cried for mother. Ignored.

A child. He'd killed a *child.*

I wanted to be sick. But I kept reading, because I had to know. Had to see if—

There. At the bottom of the stack. The file was thicker than the others, dated more recently. Twenty years ago. My hands trembled as I opened it.

Assignment Record Date: 18th day of Autumn
Location: Ashford Village, Northern Morathen
Subjects: Aldric Vaerin, Fae, Age 167, Scholar, Telepathic
Elara Vaerin, Witch, Age 134, Healer, Telepathic
Child (female), Fae/Witch Hybrid, Age 10, Telepathic (emerging)
Threat Level: EXTREME

My vision blurred. The words swam on the page.

Vaerin. My name was Vaerin. Not Locke. That name had been... what? A lie? A protection? Something the orphanage made up?

I had a real name. *They* had names. Aldric. Elara. My parents.

I forced myself to keep reading through the tears.

Threat Assessment: *Telepaths immune to mental*

compulsion. Family unit of three represents uncontrollable element in vampire-ruled province. Hybrid offspring power level unknown. Fae/Witch combination untested in records - potential for abilities beyond either parent species. Cannot permit immunity to royal authority.

Method of Elimination: *Subjects 1 & 2: Direct physical elimination. Neither could be compelled to compliance. Subject 1 (Aldric) resisted. Fae strength considerable. Required sustained force. Eventually subdued. Subject 2 (Elara) fought to protect offspring. Begged for child's life. Emotional manipulation ignored. Throat wound during struggle proved fatal. Subject 3 (Child): Small, weak. Eliminated with mother. Structure burned. Evidence destroyed. Apprentice Solis confirmed: three bodies recovered from ruins. Assignment complete.*

The words blurred completely now. I couldn't see through the tears.

My mother had fought for me. Had *begged* for my life. And Tobias had killed her, anyway. Killed all of us. Except—

I was alive.

Which meant Solis had lied in his report.

Which meant Solis had saved me.

Which meant he'd known all along who I was, what I was, and he'd been carrying that secret for twenty years.

I shoved the thought aside. I could deal with Solis later. Right now—

There was a portrait tucked into the back of the file. Small, painted on aged parchment, the kind of magical image that captured a moment in time.

A man with kind eyes and sharp Fae features, his dark hair shot through with silver. Scholarly, gentle, with a half-smile, like he was thinking of something amusing.

A woman with copper hair like mine, bright green eyes, her hands glowing faintly with healing magic as she laughed at something beyond the frame.

And between them, a girl. Maybe nine or ten, all wild red waves and gangly limbs, holding a book nearly as big as she was. She had her mother's eyes, her father's pointed chin, and a defiant tilt to her shoulders that looked achingly familiar.

Me. That was me.

I had been loved. I had been *wanted*. My parents had been good people—a scholar and a healer, living quietly, hurting no one. And Tobias had murdered them.

Not because they were threats. Not because they'd done anything wrong.

But because they couldn't be controlled. Because *I* couldn't be controlled.

Anger unlike anything I'd ever felt before hit me like a physical blow.

I stared at the files, hands shaking—not with grief, but with *fury*.

My parents had kept to themselves, and used their gifts carefully, without offense or harm. And Tobias had butchered them for what they *might* become. What *I* might become.

"Unacceptable risk."

"Preventive measure."

Polite words for murdering a family.

I wanted to scream. Wanted to tear the files to shreds, burn them like he'd burned my home. Wanted to march back to Kieran's chambers, wake him up, and demand they drag Tobias to the dungeons *now*.

But that wouldn't help Elias. Wouldn't prove anything except that I'd disobeyed Kieran and broken into an advisor's chambers.

I needed to take the files. Needed proof.

My hands were trembling as I shoved the portrait and key documents into my shirt. Evidence. Finally, I had—

Footsteps sounded in the corridor.

I froze, my heart stuttering in my chest.

No. No no no—

The footsteps stopped outside the door.

A key scraped in the lock.

I looked around desperately. The window—too high, no escape. The wardrobe—too obvious. Under the desk—

The door opened.

Tobias stood in the doorway, his expression completely unsurprised.

"I wondered when you'd come looking," he said calmly.

For a heartbeat, we just stared at each other. Me with the files still clutched in my hands, him blocking the only exit.

Then I bolted.

I didn't think. Didn't plan. Just *moved*, trying to get past him, to the door, to—

He was faster.

His hand caught my wrist, yanking me back with vampiric strength, sending pain shooting up my arm. I tried to scream, reaching desperately for the bond—

"Kieran!"

But Tobias pulled a small vial from his coat, crushing it against the floor between us.

Purple smoke erupted, thick and choking. It filled my lungs, burned my throat, and the bond—

The bond went *silent*.

Not muffled. Not distant. *Silent.*

Like someone had severed the connection completely.

I tried to reach for Kieran again, screaming through the mental void, but there was nothing. Just static. Just emptiness.

My legs gave out.

The world tilted sideways, and I hit the floor hard, the files scattering around me. I tried to get up, to crawl, to do *anything*, but my body wouldn't respond. The smoke had paralyzed me, leaving me conscious but helpless.

Tobias crouched beside me, his face coming into view. Calm. Almost gentle.

"You should have stayed dead, little girl," he said softly.

I tried to spit at him, to curse, but my jaw wouldn't work.

He picked up one of the scattered files—my family's file—and studied the portrait with something like nostalgia. "You have your mother's eyes," he mused. "I remember them. She looked at me just like this when I —" He stopped himself and smiled. "Well. You'll learn all about it soon enough."

No. *No.*

I tried to move, to fight, but the paralysis held firm. Tears leaked from the corners of my eyes, the only part of me I could still control.

Tobias set the file aside and lifted me easily, my paralyzed body limp in his arms.

"Don't worry," he said, carrying me toward the door. "I have so many questions for you. Like how you survived? Who helped you? What you remember."

He paused in the doorway, looking down at me with cold curiosity.

"And once I have my answers, I'll finish what I started twenty years ago."

He carried me out into the corridor. Cold air hit my face—we were moving outside, away from the castle. I tried to scream through the bond again, desperate, terrified—

"Kieran, please. Please!"

Nothing. Just that terrible, empty silence.

Voices sounded somewhere nearby. Others were helping him. And a carriage waited in the shadows.

"Carefully," Tobias instructed someone. "She's valuable. For now."

They loaded me into the carriage like cargo. I couldn't move, couldn't fight, couldn't do anything but lie there and feel the vehicle start to move.

Taking me away from the castle. Away from Kieran. Away from any hope of rescue.

My last conscious thought before the darkness took me completely:

"I'm sorry. I'm so sorry. I love you."

But the bond stayed silent.

And the carriage rolled on into the night.

CHAPTER 25
KIERAN

Something was wrong.

I knew it before I opened my eyes, before I reached across the bed to find cold sheets and an empty space where Merrit should have been.

Through the bond, I reached for her—

Nothing.

I sat up, heart suddenly pounding. Not the comfortable quiet of her sleeping beside me. Not the distant hum of her being in another room.

Nothing.

Complete and utter silence, like the bond had been cut with a knife.

"Merrit?"

My voice echoed in the empty chamber. No answer from the bathing room. No sound of her moving about. I threw off the covers, checking the room with growing panic. Her clothes—the practical ones from the Divide —were gone. The knife she kept strapped to her thigh. Her soft-soled boots.

She'd dressed for stealth. For breaking in somewhere she shouldn't be.

No. Please, no.

I reached for the bond again, desperate, and found the same terrible emptiness.

She was gone. And I couldn't feel her.

The bond had never been silent. Not since the moment it formed. Even when she slept, even when she shielded her thoughts, there was always a *presence*. A warmth. A connection that hummed between us like a heartbeat.

Now there was nothing. Either the bond had been severed—

Or she was dead.

No.

I refused to believe it. Refused to accept that she could be gone, just gone, with no warning, no chance of saving her. Which meant someone had blocked it. Which meant she was alive. Which meant someone had *taken* her.

Or worse—she'd gone somewhere dangerous on her own.

Tobias.

The realization hit like a fist to the gut.

She'd promised to stay away from him. Promised to

let me handle the investigation. But I'd felt her determination last night, that flicker of thought she couldn't quite hide.

She'd planned this. Waited for me to fall asleep. Snuck out to search his chambers for proof.

That stubborn, brave, reckless—

I was already moving, throwing on clothes without bothering to fully dress. Shirt, trousers, boots. Good enough.

I ran.

Servants scattered as I tore through the corridors, my footsteps echoing off stone. Guards straightened, alarmed.

"Your Highness—"

I didn't stop to explain. Just ran, following the path I knew she would have taken. The advisors' wing. Tobias' chambers.

Please let me be wrong. Please let her have stayed safe in bed and I'm just paranoid—

But I knew. The silent bond, her missing clothes, the way she'd looked at me last night with that terrible determination. She'd gone after Tobias alone.

The advisors' wing was quiet, still dark in the pre-dawn gloom. I counted doors as I ran, my heart hammering.

There. **Tobias Serrant, Royal Advisor.**

The door was closed but unlocked.

That was wrong. Tobias locked everything. The man was paranoid about security, always had been.

Unless he'd left in a hurry.

Unless he'd had a reason to abandon his chambers.

I shoved the door open.

The room was pristine—exactly as Tobias kept it. Books in perfect rows, papers stacked with meticulous attention. Everything neat, orderly, obsessively controlled.

Except—

A drawer pulled out from the desk and set aside on the floor. The false bottom exposed, empty. Files scattered across the desk surface; some spilled onto the floor like someone had dropped them in a hurry.

And the scent. Gods, the scent.

Merrit's scent—determination and fear—mixed with something else. Something metallic and sickly sweet that made my stomach turn.

Blood magic.

I crossed to the desk, hands shaking as I picked up the files.

Names. Dates. Descriptions.

ELIMINATED stamped across them in blood-red ink.

Subject: Marcus Lark, Age 34, Shifter (wolf), Telepathic
Status: ELIMINATED

Method: Arranged accident. Cliff fall during hunt.
Subject: Lyra Moonwhisper, Age 156, Fae,
Telepathic
Status: ELIMINATED
Method: Poison. Slow-acting. Subject expired over
three days.

I flipped through them with growing horror. Dozens of them. *Dozens.* All telepaths. All murdered.

All by Tobias.

My father's most trusted advisor. The man who'd served the Crown for six centuries. A monster hiding in plain sight.

And I'd never suspected. Never questioned. Never *looked*.

I reached for the bond again, desperate—

Still nothing.

One file lay separate from the rest, on the floor like it had been dropped. Thicker than the others, the folder more recent.

I picked it up, and a portrait slipped out immediately, landing face-up on the desk.

The Fae looked scholarly, compassion softening his features, his hair peppered with silver threads. His companion—a witch with bright emerald eyes and copper-colored hair—laughed freely, her hands radiating the gentle glow of healing magic. Between them: a girl of about ten summers, red curls rioting around her face, shoulders squared in defiance as she gripped an enormous book.

My heart stuttered in my chest.

That face. Those eyes. That stubborn tilt to her chin.

Merrit.

That was Merrit.

Younger, smaller, but unmistakably her. The same copper hair, the same green eyes, the same fierce determination in every line of her small body.

I forced myself to look at the file.

Assignment Record Date: 18th day of Autumn
Location: Ashford Village, Northern Morathen
Subjects:
Aldric Vaerin, Fae, Age 167, Scholar, Telepathic
Elara Vaerin, Witch, Age 134, Healer, Telepathic
Child (female), Fae/Witch Hybrid, Age 10, Telepathic (emerging)

Vaerin. Not Locke. That was a false name, given to her for protection.

Her real name was Vaerin.

The scholar in the portrait. The healer. Her *parents*.

I forced myself to keep reading, even as rage built in my chest.

Method of Elimination: *Subject 1 (Aldric) resisted. Fae strength considerable. Required sustained force. Eventu-*

ally subdued. Subject 2 (Elara) fought to protect offspring. Begged for child's life. Throat wound during struggle proved fatal. Subject 3 (Child): Small, weak. Eliminated with mother. Structure burned. Evidence destroyed. Apprentice Solis confirmed: three bodies recovered from ruins. Assignment complete.

Solis.

Solis had been there.

My eyes went back to the portrait. To the smiling woman with Merrit's copper hair. To the gentle Fae man with kind eyes. To the ten-year-old girl who didn't know she had minutes left to live.

Tobias had murdered them. Had tried to murder *her*.

And somehow, she'd survived, hidden in the Divide for twenty years under a false name.

Until he'd seen her scar at the Exhibition.

Until he'd *recognized* her.

And now he had her.

Rage flared slowly at first. A cold, soul-deep, creeping fury that started in my chest and spread like ice through my veins.

Then it exploded.

I didn't remember moving. Didn't remember making the decision. One moment, I was staring at the portrait of Merrit's murdered family, and the next, I was destroying everything.

The desk overturned with a crash. Books flew from

shelves, spines cracking against the walls. Papers scattered like leaves. I tore through Tobias' perfect, pristine chambers with my bare hands, roaring with a fury I'd never felt before.

He'd *murdered* them. Murdered dozens of innocent people for the crime of being born with abilities they couldn't control.

And then he'd taken Merrit. My Merrit. The woman I'd just told I loved, who'd smiled at me with such trust and hope—

Footsteps thundered in the corridor. Guards burst through the door, weapons drawn. "Your Highness—"

"Get out," I snarled.

They backed away, eyes wide. Smart.

I stood in the ruins of Tobias' chambers, breathing hard, files clutched in my hands. The portrait of Merrit's family stared up at me from the floor.

More footsteps *dared* to enter the corridor. Slower this time. Measured.

Solis appeared in the doorway, took one look at the destruction, and went pale.

His eyes landed on the files in my hands. The portrait on the floor. "Kieran—"

I moved.

Didn't think. Didn't plan. Just *moved*.

One moment, I was across the room, the next, I had Solis by the throat, slamming him against the wall hard enough to crack the stone. His head hit with a sickening *thud*.

"You *knew*." The words came out in a snarl, barely human. "You've known all along."

He didn't fight back. Didn't try to defend himself. Just stood there with my hand around his throat, guilt written all over his face.

"Kieran—" he choked out.

"Twenty. Years." I tightened my grip, watching his face go red. "She's been here for a *week,* and you never said a fucking word. You watched her. Watched me with her. Knew what she was, who she was, and you said *nothing*."

"I was—" He gasped for air. "I was protecting her—"

"By lying?" I slammed him against the wall again. "By letting Tobias get close to her? By keeping her in the dark about her own fucking family?"

"Let me—explain—"

Part of me wanted to keep squeezing. Wanted to watch the life drain from his eyes for letting this happen. For twenty years of lies. For every moment Merrit had spent not knowing who she was, where she came from, that her family had been *murdered*.

But I needed answers more than I needed revenge.

I released him. He slumped against the wall, gasping, hand going to his throat.

"Talk," I ordered, my voice deadly. "And if I don't like what I hear, I'm ripping your fucking head off."

He coughed, breathing hard, taking a moment to compose himself.

"I was two hundred and thirty years old," he finally said, voice raw. "Tobias was the king's enforcer. Respected. Feared. I was his apprentice, trying to prove myself worthy of serving the Crown."

"Get to the part where you helped murder her family."

His face went gray. "He took me on an assignment. Said we were eliminating threats to the throne. Made it sound official, necessary. I'd helped with others before —didn't ask questions, just followed orders like a good little soldier."

"And?"

"And he posted me as lookout, far from the house. Told me to watch for witnesses, keep the perimeter secure." Solis' hands clenched into fists. "I didn't know what he was doing. Not until I saw the smoke. Not until a child stumbled out of the burning house with her throat cut, dying, and I realized—"

He stopped, breathing hard.

"He'd murdered a family. A *child*. And he expected me to confirm the bodies and move on like it was just another job."

"So you lied."

"I lied." His voice dropped to barely a whisper. "Healed her as much as I could with my blood. Told him three bodies were in the rubble, all dead. Took her to the Divide, gave her to the orphanage, told them her name was Merrit Locke. Changed it from Vaerin. To hide her."

I stared at him, trying to reconcile this with the man I'd known for centuries. My friend. My most trusted guard.

The man who'd been lying to me for twenty fucking years.

"And you never told me."

"I was complicit." Solis met my eyes, and I saw the guilt there. The shame. "I'd helped him cover up murders before that night—didn't know what I was helping with, but ignorance isn't innocence. If I'd exposed him, I'd have exposed myself. Been imprisoned for murder or staked for treason. And I told myself I was protecting her by keeping quiet. Watching him, making sure he never found out she'd survived."

"For twenty years."

"For twenty years." His voice cracked. "And now he has her anyway. Because I wasn't brave enough to stop him when it mattered."

The rage threatened to consume me. I wanted to hit him. Wanted to throw him through the fucking window. Wanted to make him hurt the way Merrit's family had hurt.

But I didn't have time for that.

I needed her back. And for that, I needed his help.

I grabbed him by the front of his shirt, yanking him

close. "You're going to help me find her. You're going to use everything you know about Tobias—every secret, every hiding place, every fucking habit—to get her back. And when this is over, you're going to get on your knees and beg her forgiveness."

"I will." His voice was steady, despite the fear in his eyes. "Whatever it takes."

"And if she dies because you weren't brave enough to tell the truth?" I leaned in close, letting him see the cold fury in my eyes. "I will make sure you spend the rest of your very long life wishing you'd died with her family."

I released him with a shove.

He caught himself against the wall, still breathing hard.

"We're moving to my study—more room to plan." I started gathering the scattered documents, shoving them back into some semblance of order. "And get Nadia. I need her to bring my brothers."

"Your brothers?" Solis' voice was hoarse. "Not the king?"

"My father kept Tobias as his advisor for six centuries. Either he knew what Tobias was doing and didn't care, or he was willfully blind." I picked up the portrait carefully, tucking it in my pocket along with Merrit's family file. "Either way, I'm not risking it. And I'm not exposing what Merrit is to him. Not until I know if he was in on this."

Understanding dawned in Solis' eyes. "Your brothers have armies. Resources. No royal oversight."

"Exactly." I gathered the rest of the files. "My study. Now."

We moved quickly through the corridors, Solis leading the way while I carried the damning evidence. Guards who saw us coming stepped aside without question—one look at my face and they knew better than to ask.

My study was larger than Tobias' chambers, with space for maps and planning. More importantly, it was warded. Private. Secure.

I spread the files across my desk while Solis brought maps of the northern territories, marking locations with quick, efficient movements.

"Get Nadia," I ordered again. " I need her to—"

"Already here." Nadia stepped through the shadows in the corner, materializing from the darkness. "You look like someone ripped your soul out. What happened?"

"He has Merrit."

"Shit." She moved closer, expression grim. "Blood magic can sever a Whisperbound temporarily. Old magic, powerful. It'll wear off eventually, but—"

"How long?"

"Hours. Maybe a day."

Not good enough. Not even close.

"I need you to get my brothers. All of them. As fast as possible."

Nadia's eyes widened. "Shadow-walking that far, with passengers—Kieran, that's—"

"I know what I'm asking. Will you do it?"

She studied me for a long moment, then nodded. "Which brothers?"

"Lorenzo, Nikolai, Henrick. The others can send resources, but I need those three *here*. Now."

"Shadow-walking with passengers hurts like hell." Nadia's grin was sharp, feral. "Good thing I like her."

Shadows pooled around her feet, darkness rising like water.

"Nadia—" Solis started.

"I know the cost." She cut him off. "Worth it."

Then she was gone, vanishing into the void between spaces.

I turned to Solis. "Get me a map. All of Tobias' known properties, every nook and cranny he might hide in."

"On it." He hesitated at the door. "Kieran. I'm sorry. For all of it. For not being brave enough to—"

"Save it. You can apologize to *her* when we get her back." I met his gaze. "And you're coming with us. You owe her that much."

He nodded once, and disappeared.

I stood alone in my study, surrounded by evidence of decades of murder. The files scattered across my desk, each one a life stolen. A family destroyed.

Merrit's family.

I reached for the bond again, knowing it was useless, and doing it anyway.

"I'm coming. Hold on. I'm coming for you."

Nothing. Just that terrible silence.

I closed my eyes, centering myself. I couldn't fall apart. Couldn't let the rage and terror consume me. Merrit needed me functional, not destroyed.

So I locked it down. Buried the fear deep. Let the cold fury settle over me like armor.

Tobias had made a mistake. He'd taken something that belonged to me. Something I loved more than the Crown, more than the kingdom, more than my own life.

And I was going to make him regret it.

Ten minutes later, shadows exploded in the corner of my study.

Lorenzo stumbled out, hit his knees, and vomited violently. His face was gray, hands shaking, eyes wide with something that looked like terror.

"What—the *fuck*—was that?" he gasped between heaves.

"Shadow-walking." Solis appeared with water and helped Lorenzo to a chair. "It gets worse each time."

Nadia swayed against the wall, paler than I'd ever seen her. Blood trickled from her nose, thin and dark.

"Two more," she whispered, and vanished again before I could stop her.

Lorenzo wiped his mouth with a shaking hand, still gray. "What happened?"

"Wait for the others. I'm only explaining this once."

Fifteen minutes later, shadows spat Nikolai into the room.

He *screamed*. Actually screamed, collapsing in a heap, curling into a ball like a child.

"Never again," he wheezed. "I'll walk. I'll fucking *crawl* before I—"

Nadia hit the floor beside him, barely conscious. More blood dribbled from her nose, her eyes unfocused.

"Nadia—" I started toward her.

"One more." Her voice was thread-thin. "I-I can do one more."

Regret speared through me. "You're killing yourself—"

"She killed someone for you." Nadia's eyes found mine, fierce despite the pain. "With a *paring knife*. I can bring one more brother through the shadows."

Then she was gone again.

I crouched beside Nikolai, who was still curled up and shaking. "Can you stand?"

"Give me a minute to remember how my body works," he gasped. "What—oh, gods, I think I'm going to be sick—"

Solis shoved a waste bin in front of Nikolai's face right before he threw up.

Lorenzo handed him water with a grim look. "It doesn't get better, I'm afraid."

Twenty minutes later—the longest twenty minutes of my life—shadows erupted for the third time.

Henrick fell through first, his pale face somehow even more ghostly. He lay there gasping, eyes wide and staring at nothing.

"The void," he whispered. "I saw... things in the void..."

Nadia collapsed beside him.

This time, she didn't move.

Solis was there instantly, checking her pulse. "She's alive. Barely. That much shadow-walking with passengers—she'll be unconscious for days. Maybe longer."

"Get her to the healers," I ordered. "Now."

Two guards lifted Nadia carefully, carrying her out. She looked small, fragile. Nothing like the fierce warrior who'd just torn herself apart to help me.

I'd owe her for this. For the rest of my life.

Solis was back within moments, his expression grim as he moved to my desk. Whatever he'd seen in the healer's wing hadn't eased the tension in his shoulders.

I turned to my brothers, all three of them still recovering on the floor of my study.

When they could finally sit upright, I closed the door. Spelled it for privacy.

"Before we go any further, you need to know what you're risking by helping me." I met each of their gazes in turn. "Merrit and I are Whisperbound."

Silence. Then Nikolai whistled low. "Well. That explains the panic."

"It explains more than that," I continued. "She's a telepath. A mind reader. Which makes her existence *illegal* in all provinces of Veyntheir and a death sentence if the wrong people find out."

Lorenzo's expression didn't change, but I saw the calculation in his eyes. "Father—"

"Doesn't know. Can't know. Not until I'm sure whether he was complicit in Tobias' killings." I let the threat settle into my voice. "If any of you breathe a word of what she is to *anyone*—Father, the Court, your own people—I will take your head myself. Blood or not."

"Dramatic," Nikolai muttered. But he nodded. "Your secret's safe."

"Mine too," Lorenzo said quietly. "Whisperbound trumps everything else. She's family now, whether she wants to be or not."

Henrick just stared at me with those unsettling pale eyes. "The threads recognized her from the beginning. I told you something was drawn to your house. I didn't realize it was Fate itself."

"Good." I turned to the maps Solis had spread across my desk. "Now here's what we know. Tobias has been murdering telepaths for decades." I gestured to the files. "Dozens of them. All killed because they couldn't be controlled by vampiric compulsion."

I picked up Merrit's family file and showed them the portrait.

"Twenty years ago, he murdered her family. Parents and a ten-year-old child. Except the child survived. Solis found her, lied to Tobias, hid her in the Divide under a false name."

Lorenzo studied the portrait. "She was ten when this happened?"

"Yes. Doesn't remember any of it. The trauma wiped her memory." I set the portrait down carefully. "Last night, she went to Tobias' chambers looking for proof. He was waiting. Took her. Used blood magic to sever our bond."

"Where?" Lorenzo was all business now, the soldier taking over.

"North. Probably heading for the border, out of our jurisdiction." Solis pointed to several marked locations on the map. "These are properties Tobias has access to. Remote. Defensible. Places he can disappear."

"Then we don't let him get there." Lorenzo studied

the map. "I'll mobilize my forces. We can cover the northern routes, set up checkpoints."

"Good." I turned to Nikolai. "I need your information network. Anyone who's seen him, heard anything, knows anything."

"Already on it." Nikolai pulled out a spelled mirror. "I've got contacts everywhere. If he bought supplies, hired help, crossed a border—I'll know."

"And I can track the magical disturbance," Henrick added, his pale eyes distant. "Blood magic that powerful leaves traces. Tears in the fabric of things. I can follow them."

"Do it." I looked at each of them in turn. "We leave within the hour. Lorenzo, how many of your men can ride fast?"

"Twenty. Veterans. They can keep up."

"Bring them." I directed my gaze to Nikolai. "Before we go, I need you to send word to the Divide. There's a bar called Locke & Key—Merrit's bar. The bartender is Rhett, bouncer is Jex. They need to know what's happened."

"You want them involved?" Nikolai's fingers traced symbols on the mirror's surface. "What are they, friends?"

"They are her people. And they know the Divide better than any of us. If Tobias has connections there, safe houses, places to hide—they'll know."

"Smart." The mirror began to glow. "What do you want me to tell them?"

"That Merrit's been taken. That we're hunting north but the Divide is on the route. That if they hear *anything*—any strangers, anyone asking about her or her past, anyone buying supplies for a long stay somewhere remote—they report it immediately."

"And if they want to help?"

"Tell them to be ready. We might need local knowledge."

Nikolai nodded, speaking into the mirror. His voice echoed strangely as the spell carried his words across the distance.

A moment later, a gravelly voice came back through: "This is Rhett. Who the fuck is this and why are you using Merrit's emergency contact?"

"Prince Nikolai of Silvarin. Merrit's been kidnapped. Prince Kieran is mobilizing to get her back."

Silence. Then: "Where." Not a question. A demand.

"We don't know yet. Heading north. But the Divide might be involved—the man who took her has operated there before."

"We'll ask around. Quietly." Rhett's voice was cold, deadly. "Anyone comes through here looking suspicious, we'll know. Jex!"

A deeper voice sounded in the background. "Already gearing up. Someone took our girl, they're gonna regret it."

"Anything you find, report back through this channel," Nikolai instructed. "And be careful. The man who took her has killed dozens. He's dangerous."

"So are we." Rhett's voice was lethal. "Bring her home, Your Highness. We'll do what we can from here."

The connection ended.

I met Nikolai's eyes. "Good?"

"They're loyal. And pissed." He pocketed the mirror. "If Tobias is anywhere near the Divide, they'll find him."

We spent the next hour planning. Lorenzo's forces mobilizing. Nikolai's network spreading across the kingdom. Henrick preparing tracking spells.

Solis brought weapons. Real ones, not the decorative court shit. Armor that had seen battle. Supplies for days of hard riding.

I armed myself carefully. The sword that had killed before. The one I'd use to end Tobias.

"Ready?" Solis asked quietly.

"No." I checked the blade one more time. "But we're going anyway."

Dawn was breaking as we gathered in the courtyard. Me, Solis, my three brothers. Lorenzo's best warriors waited in his northern province at a prepared portal circle. Once we located Merrit and Tobias, the court mage could pull them through—twenty veterans who'd seen real combat, not decorative court guards. We just had to find them first.

But pulling that many soldiers across such distance would drain even a powerful mage. It would take time.

Time we didn't have.

The horses stamped and snorted, sensing our urgency.

I swung onto the saddle, every muscle tense.

One last time, I reached for the bond—

And felt something.

Faint. So faint I almost missed it. A flutter, like a dying heartbeat trying to restart.

She was alive.

The blood magic was wearing off.

Relief crashed over me so hard I nearly fell from the saddle. She was alive. Terrified, in pain, gods knew what else—but *alive*.

I closed my eyes, sending everything I had through that fragile connection.

"I'm coming. Hold on. I'm coming for you."

I didn't know if she could hear it. The bond was too weak, too damaged.

But I sent it anyway.

Over and over as we rode out of the castle and into the dawn.

"Hold on. I'm coming."

"Don't give up."

"I love you."

"Hold on."

CHAPTER 26

MERRIT

Rope burned against my wrists.

That was the first thing I noticed as I woke—rough hemp rending skin, my bound wrists. Then the cold. Then the pain radiating through my skull. I tried to move and couldn't.

My hands were bound behind me, rope cutting deeper as I tested it. My legs were tied at the ankles. I was sitting—no, slumped against something hard. A wall, maybe?

I forced my eyes open.

Darkness. Then shapes emerging from shadow. Stone walls, rough-hewn and damp. A single candle flickered on a table across the room, flame guttering in some unfelt draft. No windows. One door—heavy wood reinforced with iron bands.

A basement. A cell. Somewhere underground where no one would hear.

The bond.

I reached for it desperately, searching for Kieran's presence.

"Kieran!"

Nothing.

Not the comfortable silence of him sleeping. Not the distant hum of him in another room. Just that terrible emptiness, like the bond had been severed completely.

No—wait. Not severed. There, so faint I almost missed it: a flicker. Like a candle flame about to go out, struggling to stay lit.

The blood magic was wearing off. Slowly. But the bond was still there, buried under whatever spell Tobias had used.

Which meant Kieran was alive. And probably losing his mind trying to reach me.

"I'm here," I projected into the void, knowing he couldn't hear. *"I'm alive."*

My throat ached. I tried to swallow, and pain lanced through my neck. The paralysis had worn off completely, leaving me with just rope burns and whatever damage the blood magic had done.

I cataloged my body: head pounding, throat sore, wrists bleeding from the rope, but nothing broken. No new injuries beyond what the fall and the magic had caused.

Where was I?

I surveyed my surroundings more carefully, and something tugged at the edges of my awareness. Not quite memory—more like familiarity my body recognized before my mind did.

The table held more than just the candle. Shapes in the dim light—metal blades—that made my stomach turn.

The room was small. Ten feet across. Old stone walls with that particular texture—

Wait.

My breath caught.

I knew this texture. These walls. Not from seeing them, but from touching them as a child. Running my hands along rough stone while learning to navigate by feel when Samona turned out the lights for "stealth training."

The orphanage.

Not these rooms—I'd never been in the basement. But above me, up those stairs I couldn't see but knew were there, was the building where Samona had taught me everything. How to sign. How to fight. How to read people's faces for the emotions they tried to hide.

Where she'd told me about Whisperbound on cold nights when I couldn't sleep. Stories I'd thought were fairy tales until Kieran appeared in my bar with that pull I couldn't explain.

Tobias had brought me back to the only home I remembered. And he was turning it into my grave.

The violation of it—using this place, *this* place—made rage flare hot beneath the fear.

The walls were stained dark in places. Old blood, probably. The floor beneath me was stone worn smooth by time and gods knew what else.

How long had Tobias been using this basement? How many others had died down here while I lived upstairs, safe and ignorant?

The cruelty of it settled cold and sharp in my bones.

I tested the ropes. Tight, professionally done. My lockpicking skills were useless here. I needed my hands free to work a lock, and there was no lock to pick anyway. The door was barred from outside; I could see the shadow of the beam across the crack.

My knife was gone. Of course it was gone.

Think. *Think.*

I'd found the files. Seen my parents' portraits, their names, the clinical description of their murders. The portrait of me as a child, wild red hair, and a book bigger than I was.

Vaerin. My name was Vaerin.

Had I dropped the files? Had Kieran found them?

Gods, I hoped so. I hoped he knew everything. Hoped he'd put the pieces together and was coming for me.

If the bond would just *work*—

Footsteps echoed outside, and I froze, every muscle tensing despite the pain. The bar scraped across the door. The lock clicked. The hinges groaned as the door swung open.

Tobias stepped through, carrying a second candle. The light threw his shadow long and monstrous across the stone. He closed the door behind him, setting the candle on the table next to the first.

Then he turned to look at me.

His expression was calm. Pleasant, even. Like he was visiting an old friend rather than the woman he'd kidnapped and planned to torture.

"You're awake," he said, voice mild. "Good. I was starting to worry I'd used too much of the paralytic. It's a delicate balance—too little and you fight back, too much and you die before we can even begin. I'd hate for this to be over too quickly."

I stared at him, rage building in my chest.

He crossed to me, crouched down so we were eye level, studying my face with calculating interest.

"You look so much like her. Your mother. Same eyes, same stubborn set to the jaw." He reached out, and I jerked my head away. He smiled. "Same defiance. She fought, too. Begged for your life. Offered me anything—knowledge, service, her own death in your place."

I tried to spit at him, but my mouth was too dry.

"I told her no." His voice stayed conversational. "Because it was never about what she could offer. It was about what you *were*. A telepath. A hybrid. Immune to compulsion. Capable of powers we couldn't predict or control."

He stood and walked back to the table.

"Your father tried to fight. Fae strength is considerable—I had to use sustained force to subdue him. He kept trying to get to you. Even when he was dying, he was trying to protect you."

My vision blurred with tears. I blinked them away furiously. I wouldn't cry. Wouldn't give him the satisfaction.

"And you." He picked up something from the table—a blade, iron, glinting in the candlelight. "Small. Weak. Just ten years old and already showing signs of telepathic ability. Your mother died with you in her arms. I gave her that mercy at least—she didn't have to watch you die first."

I tried to sign something—anything—and felt the rope carve deeper into my wrists. Right. My hands were bound.

I was mute. And he'd tied my hands.

I couldn't communicate at all.

The realization must have shown on my face because Tobias smiled.

"I know you can't speak," he said pleasantly. "And I know you need your hands to sign. That's intentional. You see, I'm not here for conversation, Merrit. Or should I say—" He tilted his head. "Merrit *Vaerin*. That *is* your real family name, isn't it? The one someone changed to Locke to hide you."

My family name. Spoken for the first time in twenty years by the man who'd murdered them.

In the basement of the building where I'd been hidden. Where I'd been safe.

Where I'd learned my name was Merrit Locke and that my past was gone.

"I'm here to tell you a story," Tobias continued, setting the blade back on the table and selecting another, testing the edge. "About why you're going to die. About why your prince is going to die. About why everything your parents tried to protect died the moment I set your house on fire."

He pulled a stool from the shadows, sat facing me. Comfortable. Like we had all the time in the world.

"Do you know what telepaths represent?" he asked. "Not to you, obviously. To people like me. To the kingdom. To the structures of power that have kept this realm stable for millennia."

I just stared at him.

"Chaos," he answered his own question. "The end of order. For thousands of years, vampire nobility ruled through compulsion. We kept the peace. Maintained structure. Your kind can't be compelled. Can't be controlled. One telepath in the right place could topple kingdoms. Read the thoughts of kings, expose secrets, manipulate from the shadows."

He leaned forward.

"I've spent six hundred years preventing that. Quietly. Efficiently. Eliminating threats before they could grow into problems. The king knew some of it—enough to turn a blind eye. But the details?" He shrugged. "He didn't need to know everything. Just that the threats were handled."

My parents weren't threats, I wanted to scream at him. *They were scholars. Healers. They hurt no one.*

"Your parents?" He read my face. "Threat number three hundred and twelve and three hundred and thirteen. Living too close to the border, too close to power. Their hybrid child? Unacceptable risk. Better to eliminate the problem early than wait for it to grow."

He stood, pacing slowly around the room.

"But I had a different reason for being so... thorough. So dedicated to this particular duty."

He stopped, back to me, staring at the candle flame, like he could see something in it I couldn't.

"I had a Whisperbound once." His voice softened, almost reverent. "A seer. The most beautiful mind I'd ever touched. When she looked at the world, she didn't see what *was*—she saw what *could be*. Threads of Fate, possibilities, futures branching like tree roots in every direction. Infinite and luminous and utterly breathtaking."

He was quiet for a moment, lost in memory.

"The king used her. Oh, he was polite about it at

first. Respectful. But then he started demanding more. One more vision. Just one more glimpse of the future. 'For the kingdom,' he'd say. 'For the realm's safety.' She tried to refuse—told him her sight was failing, that pushing further would break something inside her that couldn't be repaired."

He turned slowly, meeting my gaze.

"He ordered her to try anyway. Not requested. *Ordered.* 'One more vision. For the kingdom.' And she..." His jaw tightened. "She was loyal. Obedient. So she tried."

The silence stretched between us, heavy and suffocating.

"Do you know what it's like to feel a Whisperbound die?" His voice dropped to barely above a whisper. "Not the slow fade of illness, or the shock of violence. But to feel their mind *fracture*. To watch them bleed from their eyes while their consciousness tears itself apart, trying to see too far, too deep. To feel the bond—that perfect, impossible connection—shatter like glass."

He looked down at the blade in his hands.

"She died in my arms. I felt every second of it. Felt her slip away while I begged her to hold on, to stop, to let the vision go. But she was trying to obey. Trying to serve her king until the very end."

His expression stayed flat, but something cold and broken radiated from him like winter wind.

"The king came to see her body afterward. Expressed

his *regret*. Gave me a title—some meaningless honor that was supposed to make her death worth something. Then he moved on. Attended a feast that same evening. Smiled and laughed while I sat in empty chambers where her presence used to fill every corner."

He set the blade down carefully, then selected another.

"He expected me to move on, too. To accept that she died in service to the realm. That her sacrifice was *noble*."

He selected the iron blade again. Inspected it.

"I've spent three hundred and fifty years pretending to be loyal. Eliminating 'threats' to the throne. Seers, telepaths, mind readers—anyone with gifts the king might use and destroy the way he destroyed her." He walked toward me slowly, savoring each step. "At first, I told myself I was protecting them. Giving them quick deaths before the king could wring them dry. A mercy, really."

He crouched in front of me again.

"But that was a lie. I was angry. Broken. And I wanted him to feel what I felt—loss, helplessness, the exquisite agony of watching everything you love die while you stand there, powerless to stop it."

He studied my face, looking for a reaction.

"I started with his wife. Fifty years ago." His voice took on an almost dreamy quality, like he was remembering something pleasant. "A slow-acting poison.

Elegant, really. Six months of watching her fade—losing weight, losing color, losing strength. The healers couldn't figure out what was wrong. I brought her medicine every day. Held her hand. Offered comfort."

A cold smile crept across his face.

"The medicine was what was killing her, of course. Tiny doses, carefully measured. Not enough to raise suspicion, just enough to ensure she'd never recover."

My stomach turned. Kieran's mother. He'd killed Kieran's mother while pretending to help her.

"I thought..." He paused, and for the first time, something genuine flickered across his face. Pain, maybe. Or disappointment. "I thought he would understand then. That watching his wife die slowly, inevitably, would make him feel what I felt. The loss. The helplessness. The way time stretches out endlessly when you know someone you love is slipping away and there's nothing —*nothing*—you can do to save them."

His jaw tightened.

"But she wasn't his Whisperbound. Just a political marriage. Duty, alliance, convenience. He mourned, yes. He was appropriately solemn at the funeral. But two months later, I saw him laughing at some courtier's joke. Six months later, he'd moved on completely."

The blade pressed against my cheek, cold and sharp.

"That's when I understood. One death—even a slow, cruel death—isn't enough. One loss won't make him understand what it's like to have your *soul* ripped out while your body keeps breathing. To have the bond shatter and still be expected to wake up every morning and pretend to be whole."

He stood and began to pace.

"So I changed tactics. His kingdom. His legacy. His sons. If I couldn't make him feel my pain through one death, I'd make him feel it through a thousand cuts." The blade traced down my throat, stopping at my scar with delicate precision. "The southern gate attack? Mine. I hired the assassin, forged the sigil, planned the route. Wanted to test Prince Kieran's security, yes, but also to plant seeds of doubt. The king gave his favorite son Morathen—the Crown Province, the capital itself. If I could make even *that* unsafe, what would it say about the kingdom's stability?"

He moved around behind me, blade trailing across my shoulder like a caress.

"The poisoning attempts in the kitchen? Also mine. Nothing fatal—not yet. Just enough to weaken the guard, create paranoia. Slow-acting toxins that made people doubt their own food, their own servants. Made everyone suspect everyone else."

My heart was pounding so hard I could hear it.

"Framing Elias was particularly satisfying." I could hear the smile in his voice. "Prince Kieran's loyal advisor, his most trusted guard. I've been in his mind for months—such a tedious process, compulsion is so much cleaner—planting suggestions, making him do things he'd never remember. Watching him fracture under the weight of lost time and inexplicable evidence."

He came back around to face me.

"Each piece carefully placed. Each domino positioned. The southern gate, the poisonings, Elias' fall from grace—all building toward destabilizing Morathen, weakening the king's precious Crown Province."

He laughed, and it was the first genuine emotion I'd heard from him besides the grief when he spoke of his mate.

"And then you and the prince went and became Whisperbound. I couldn't have *planned* something so perfect. A telepath—bonded to the king's favorite son. The future heir with a mind reader who can't be compelled, can't be controlled."

His smile widened.

"It was a gift. A beautiful, terrible gift."

He walked back to the table, selecting another blade. A smaller one. Studied it.

"The Exhibition was supposed to end you. Real blade, perfect accident in front of the entire Court. Tragic." He glanced at me. "But you survived. Again."

He tilted his head, surveying me with that clinical interest.

"Do you know how frustrating that is? I gave you that scar twenty years ago." His finger traced the line across my throat. I flinched before I could stop myself.

"You should have bled out in seconds. Died in the fire with your parents. For twenty years, I believed you had."

He leaned closer, staring at the scar with something like fascination.

"Then I saw it at the Exhibition. That scar. And I knew—someone saved you. Someone lied to me. Someone's been hiding you for two decades."

I kept my face blank. Didn't react. Didn't think about Solis.

"I'll find out who," he said softly. "Eventually."

He picked up a torch from the corner, lit it, then used it to heat an iron brand.

"But first, I'm going to finish what I started. And when I do, your Whisperbound prince will feel every moment of your death through that bond." The iron began to glow red. "Your prince was there, you know, when his mother died. Over three hundred years old and still begged her to fight. Held her hand. Promised her she'd be fine."

He tested the brand's heat.

"He'll do the same for you. Hold your hand through the bond while you die screaming. And the king—finally, *finally*—will understand what it's like to watch his favorite son destroyed by loss. To watch him become as hollow and broken as I am."

He lifted the brand.

"If killing his wife didn't work, maybe watching his son's soul shatter will."

He turned, carrying the blade and the brand.

"You want to know why I'm telling you all this?" He crouched in front of me again. "Because I want you to understand what's coming. Why it's necessary. Why your death—and his—will finally make the king feel what I felt when I lost her."

He set the brand aside to cool slightly, then held up the iron blade.

"Iron. Fascinating metal. Burns Fae blood on contact. Your father screamed quite beautifully when I used this on him."

Nausea rose in my throat. I'd always reacted badly to iron—burns that hurt worse than they should, scars that took too long to heal. I'd never known why.

Now I did. My father was Fae. Half my blood carried that weakness.

And Tobias knew exactly how to exploit it.

"I've never tortured a mute before," he said, voice casual, curious. "I wonder what noises you'll make."

The blade touched my arm.

Pain exploded as he drew the blade across my skin— shallow, precise, just deep enough to hurt without being fatal.

I couldn't scream. My throat worked, trying, but nothing came out. Just a choked, broken sound—air forced through a damaged windpipe.

He watched like a specimen he was preparing to dissect.

"Interesting. Not silent after all."

The blade cut again. My other arm this time. The same shallow, burning cut. Tears streamed down my face, and I hated it, hated that he could see me cry, but I couldn't stop. A rough keening sound escaped me, breathy and jagged.

"Your mother made similar sounds," he said conversationally, making another cut. "Though hers were more... articulate. Begging. Bargaining. Threatening. You can't do any of that, can you?"

I tried to glare at him through the tears. Tried to put every ounce of hate and rage into my eyes since I couldn't put it into words.

He smiled. "There's the defiance. Good. I was worried you'd break too quickly."

The blade traced across my collarbone. Cut. Burn. Pain.

Again. And again. Methodical. Precise. Each cut exactly as deep as the one before. Not fatal. Not even close. Just pain, building and building until I couldn't think past it.

My throat kept trying to scream. Kept making those choked sounds, those broken cries that hurt almost as much as the cuts. Small whimpers escaped between hitched breaths.

He paused, examining his work. Blood ran down my arms, soaking into my shirt. The iron burned in the wounds, worse than regular cuts, making my Fae blood react with fire that spread under my skin.

"Let's try something else," he said, setting down the blade and picking up the brand.

It had cooled to a dull red. Still hot enough to burn, but not hot enough to kill instantly.

He pressed it against my shoulder.

The smell hit first—burning flesh, my flesh—and then the pain. White-hot and all-consuming. My body convulsed, trying to get away, but the ropes held. That horrible sound tore from my throat—harsh, strained, a broken cry that rattled in my chest.

He held the brand there for three seconds. Four. Five. Then lifted it.

I sagged against the wall, gasping, tears and snot streaming down my face. Every breath came in broken, shaky gasps. Every heartbeat sent fresh pain radiating from the brand on my shoulder.

"Your mother fought until the very end," Tobias said, setting the brand aside. "Kept trying to reach you even when she was dying. Love makes people do irrational things. Sacrifice themselves for those who can't be saved anyway."

He selected another blade. Smaller. Sharper.

"Tomorrow, we'll continue this. I have so much more to show you. Different blades, different techniques. I've had six hundred years to perfect my craft."

The small blade cut across my side. Shallow. Precise.

"But tonight..." Another cut. "Tonight, I just wanted you to understand. This isn't personal. This is necessary. Your death serves a greater purpose."

Cut. Burn. Pain.

"You're going to help me destroy a king."

He worked for what seemed like hours but might have been minutes. Time stopped meaning anything past the pain. Cut after cut, each one measured, controlled. Never deep enough to be fatal. Never in a place that would kill quickly.

Just pain. Endless, building pain that made the world narrow to nothing but fire beneath my skin and the sound of my own choked, strangled gasps.

Finally, he stopped, setting the blade down, and stepping back to admire his work.

"That's enough for tonight. Don't want you dying before we've really begun."

He walked to the door, paused with his hand on the latch.

"The bond will heal eventually. The blood magic wears off in a day or so. Then your prince will feel you again." He smiled. "He'll feel every bit of pain I cause tomorrow. Every cut, every burn. And he'll be helpless to stop it."

He gestured around the room. "Do you know where you are? I thought about telling you, but..." He glanced up toward the ceiling. "I think you've already figured it out. This building—your childhood home. Where you learned to survive. Where someone kept you safe."

His smile turned cold.

"I've been using this basement for decades. Long before you came here. Long after you left. This place that meant safety to you?" He looked around at the bloodstains, the torture implements. "It's where dozens died screaming."

The violation of it hit me like a physical blow.

And Tobias had been here the whole time. Using it. Killing people in the basement while children slept upstairs. While I slept upstairs. While Samona told us bedtime stories, people were dying beneath our feet.

"Sleep well, Merrit Vaerin."

The door closed. The lock clicked. The bar scraped back into place. Then I was alone in the dark.

In the basement of the orphanage where Samona had taught me to be strong. Where I'd learned I wasn't broken. Where I'd heard stories about Whisperbound and thought they were fairy tales.

This isn't home, I thought fiercely. *Home was upstairs. Where Samona cared for me. This basement— this place he's using—has nothing to do with what that building meant to me.*

Blood ran down my arms, my side, soaking through my clothes. The brand on my shoulder throbbed with every heartbeat. The iron burns felt like they were still cutting, fire spreading under my skin.

I couldn't move. Couldn't reach the bond. Couldn't do anything but sit there and hurt.

Time passed. I didn't know how much. The candles burned lower. The pain settled into something constant, all-consuming. And then—

A flicker in the bond. So faint I thought I imagined it. Like a candle flame struggling to catch. Then stronger. Just barely. Still distant, still muffled by the blood magic, but *there*.

"Hold on. I'm coming."

Kieran's voice. Desperate. Determined. Distant but real.

I tried to respond, tried to send something back through that fragile connection.

"Hurry."

Did he hear it? I couldn't tell. The bond flickered and faded again, like the magic was fighting to keep us separated.

But he was there. He was coming.

I just had to survive until he got here.

I focused on that. On the bond, weak but present. On Kieran's voice, desperate and full of love. On the fact that I was still alive, still breathing, still capable of fighting back if I could just get free.

The ropes around my wrists were tight, but not impossible. The knots were behind me, out of reach, but the rough stone wall might work. If I could find an edge, start fraying the rope...

I shifted, pain screaming through every cut and burn, and found an outcropping in the stone behind me. Sharp enough. Maybe.

I started working the rope against it. Slowly. Carefully. Every movement sent fire through my injuries, but I kept going.

Fraying. One fiber at a time.

I'm not fucking dying here, I told myself. Told Kieran through the bond, even though I didn't know if he could hear. *Not after surviving this once already.*

"You're coming. I just have to hold on."

The rope frayed. Just a little. Just enough to give me hope.

Samona had taught me to survive. To fight. To never give up, even when everything seemed hopeless.

I wasn't going to let her down.

I wasn't going to let Kieran down.

"Hold on."

CHAPTER 27

KIERAN

The bond pulsed stronger with every mile.

Not the comfortable warmth I was used to —this was pain. Fear. Exhaustion. Each flicker through our connection made my chest tighten, made the horse beneath me push harder, even though we'd been riding for hours.

She was alive. Hurt, terrified, but alive.

I clung to that.

"We're getting close," Henrick said from my left, his pale eyes distant. "The magical disturbance is stronger here. Blood magic, old and powerful. It's like a stain on the world."

Lorenzo rode on my right, silent and deadly, checking his weapons with mechanical precision. He hadn't said a word since we'd left the castle at dawn, but I could feel the cold fury radiating from him. Someone had threatened his future sister-in-law. That made it personal.

"How much farther?" My voice came out rough. I hadn't stopped to rest, hadn't eaten, had barely spoken since we left. The sun was climbing now, painting the Divide in shades of gold and shadow.

"Minutes. Maybe less." Henrick's hands moved in the air, following threads only he could see. "The magic is... anchored. Not moving. She's stationary."

Good. That meant we could reach her. That Tobias hadn't taken her farther away.

Through the bond, I sent everything I had: *"Hold on. I'm coming. Hold on."*

Did she hear it? I couldn't tell. The connection was too weak, too damaged by whatever spell he'd used. But I kept sending it anyway, over and over, like a prayer.

Behind us, Nikolai and Solis rode in grim silence. Solis' guilt was a palpable thing—he'd been there twenty years ago, had saved her from Tobias once. Now she was in danger again because of secrets he'd kept.

We'd deal with that later. Right now, we were getting her back.

Nikolai's spelled mirror chimed. He pulled it from his coat, and Rhett's gravelly voice came through.

"We found something."

"Talk," I ordered, leaning closer.

"Old orphanage on the northern edge of the Divide. Decommissioned about twelve years ago. No one's been near it in a decade." Rhett paused. "Except last night. Local saw lights in the basement. Said it looked like torches or candles."

My blood ran cold.

An orphanage. In the Divide.

Where Merrit had grown up.

Tobias hadn't just taken her. He'd taken her *home*. Back to the one place she'd felt safe, and he was using it to destroy her.

"We're watching the building now," Rhett continued. "No movement in or out since last night. But there's definitely someone inside. Jex can feel it—says there's death magic in the air."

"We're close," I said. "Hold position. Don't engage until we arrive."

"Wouldn't dream of it," Rhett said. "That's our girl in there. We're not letting her down."

The connection ended.

"An orphanage," Solis said quietly. His voice carried guilt, grief, knowledge. "I took her there. After I found her. After Tobias—"

"I know." I didn't look at him. Couldn't. "We'll deal with that later. Right now, we get her back."

Lorenzo's hand found my shoulder and squeezed once. Solidarity. Support. Then he pulled out his own spelled mirror, spoke quickly into its surface. "We have the location. Bring my warriors through."

A voice crackled back—the court mage confirming

the order.

Lorenzo tucked the mirror away and met my eyes. We'd face whatever was coming together—with reinforcements on the way.

We rode harder.

THE BUILDING APPEARED THROUGH THE morning mist like a ghost.

Three stories of gray stone, windows dark and empty, the kind of institutional architecture built for function rather than beauty. The front door hung slightly open, weeds growing through cracks in the steps.

Abandoned. Forgotten.

Perfect for what Tobias needed.

Rhett and Jex emerged from the shadows as we dismounted. Rhett looked like he always did—compact, wiry, sharp-eyed, with intricate braids falling past his shoulders and glass vials strapped across his chest like a bandolier. But there was steel in his expression now, none of his usual easy charm.

And Jex...

Jex was seven feet of pure demonic fury.

Gray skin, horns that curved back from his forehead,

adding another foot to his height, eyes like molten gold, and an expression that promised violence. He wore minimal armor—didn't need it when his skin was that thick—and carried a massive war hammer that would have required three normal men to lift.

"They have Merrit." Jex's voice rumbled like distant thunder. Not a greeting. Not a courtesy. Just the only fact that mattered.

Not "the lady" or "Miss Locke." Merrit. Our girl.

The accusation in his gold eyes was clear: *This is your fault. You brought her into this.*

"I know," I said, meeting his stare. I wouldn't look away. Wouldn't make excuses. "And we're getting her back."

"Damn right we are." Rhett's voice was hard. "Six to eight hostiles in the basement. Multiple heartbeats. Jex can feel death magic saturating the place."

Jex's massive hand tightened on his war hammer. "If she's dead when we get down there, Prince or not, you and I are going to have words." His grim mouth curved into a cruel smile. "And by words, I mean I'll smash your fucking head in with my hammer. Are we clear?"

It wasn't a threat. It was a promise.

"She's alive," I said. Through the bond, I could feel her—hurt, terrified, but alive. "I can feel her."

"Then let's move," Jex growled. "Before that changes."

Lorenzo dismounted with fluid grace, already

assessing the building with a military commander's eye. "Multiple entry points, but they'll be watching all of them. We go in fast and hard—no time for stealth after we breach."

"Agreed," I said.

Through the bond, I felt her. Closer now. So close I could almost—

Pain. Sharp and sudden, like a knife dragging across skin. I sucked in a harsh breath, hand going to my chest.

"Kieran?" Lorenzo was beside me immediately, steadying me.

"He's hurting her." My voice shook with barely controlled fury. "Right now. We need to move. Now."

"My men—" Lorenzo started.

"We can't wait." I was already moving toward the building. "Every second we delay is another second he has her. They'll follow when the mage brings them through."

We entered the building as quietly as seven armed warriors could.

The main floor was exactly as I'd imagined—dust-covered furniture, faded paintings on walls, the sad remnants of a place that had once housed children. Merrit had lived here. Learned to sign here. Heard stories about Whisperbound and thought they were fairy tales.

Now it was a tomb.

Footprints in the dust led toward the back of the building. Recent. Multiple sets.

We followed them to a door, reinforced with iron bands. A basement entrance, locked and barred from our side.

"Stand back," Jex rumbled.

He didn't wait for agreement. Just raised his war hammer and brought it down.

The door exploded inward with a crash that echoed through the empty building. So much for stealth.

"If they didn't know we were here before," Nikolai muttered, "they sure as fuck do now."

"Good," Lorenzo said, drawing his sword. "Let them know."

We descended.

The stairs were narrow, forcing us into single file. Jex went first—his massive frame filled the stairwell, making him a living shield. I followed, then Lorenzo, Solis, Nikolai, Henrick, and Rhett taking up the rear.

At the bottom, the stairs opened into a corridor. Doors lined both sides, all closed. Torches burned in sconces, casting flickering shadows. And two figures waited for us.

They stood at attention, weapons drawn, but their eyes were wrong. Glazed. Empty. Moving with the eerie unison of puppets.

"They're compelled," Solis said immediately, his voice tight. "Like Elias. Their minds are broken."

The first guard—a vampire, maybe a century old—raised his sword. "None may pass. Lord Tobias' orders."

"Lord Tobias is a traitor and a murderer," I said. "Stand aside."

"None may pass." The same flat tone. No recognition. No choice.

They attacked.

Jex met the first one head-on, hammer against sword. The clash of metal rang through the corridor. The second guard came for me, and I had no choice but to fight.

He was skilled—trained, professional—but his movements were predictable. Compulsion made fighters efficient but not creative. I parried, dodged, looked for an opening to disarm rather than kill.

Lorenzo moved in beside me, helping drive the guard back without delivering fatal blows.

"Henrick!" I called out. "Can you break it?"

"Working on it!" Henrick's hands moved in complex patterns, following invisible threads. "The compulsion is strong. Give me *time*."

Time we didn't have.

The vampire guard pressed harder, and I could see the desperation behind his empty eyes. He didn't want this. Didn't want to fight. But he had no choice.

Lorenzo and I worked in sync—years of training together paying off. He swept the guard's legs while I disarmed him, putting him on the ground.

"Sleep," Henrick commanded, threads snapping into place.

The guard's eyes rolled back. He collapsed, unconscious but alive.

Jex had pinned his opponent against the wall, hammer pressed to his chest. "Any time now, threadweaver."

"Working on it," Henrick gritted out, threads straining against the compulsion.

"Done." His fingers twisted one final time. "He's free. Barely."

The second guard blinked, confusion replacing the empty stare. "What... where..."

"Run," Solis told him. "Get out of here. Get help."

They scrambled up the stairs, fleeing.

"They'll warn Tobias we're here," Nikolai said.

"He already knows." I could feel it in the bond—Merrit's terror had shifted. Changed. She knew I was close. "Move."

We advanced down the corridor.

The next attack came from multiple directions at once.

A blade whistled past my head—fast, professional, deadly. I spun, catching a glimpse of the assassin—twin daggers, dark clothing, moving with supernatural speed. A vampire. Young, but skilled beyond his years. His brother—identical, same weapons, same deadly grace—came from the opposite direction, targeting Solis.

Twins. Fighting in perfect coordination, like they'd trained together their entire lives.

From a doorway ahead stepped a figure in formal military dress, a vampire who moved with the confidence of centuries.

"Commander Raleth," Solis breathed. "You served with Tobias."

"I *serve* the true future," Raleth corrected. His voice carried the crisp authority of a lifetime soldier. "Not this weak, progressive mockery of a Crown. Your reign ends tonight, Prince Kieran."

And from the room behind him emerged more figures. Lady Morana—I recognized her from Court— vampire nobility who'd always resented my father. Behind her, a shifter mercenary with a massive axe and a demon nearly Jex's size.

Seven enemies. Seven of us.

But they were fresh. Waiting. Prepared.

"Formation!" Lorenzo's command cut through the chaos. Years of military training took over—we shifted into combat positions automatically.

Raleth attacked first, coming straight for me and Lorenzo.

He was good. Better than good. Centuries of combat experience flowed through every movement—efficient, precise, deadly. He came at us with sword and dagger, and even with Lorenzo beside me, I realized with cold clarity that this wasn't just a guard.

This was a coup.

"How many?" Lorenzo demanded, his blade meeting Raleth's with a clash of steel.

"Enough." Raleth smiled. "We've been preparing for three centuries. Every piece in place. Your father's reign ends. The old ways return."

Behind him, chaos erupted.

Jex roared and charged the enemy demon—demon against demon. The corridor shook with their impact, both massive, brutal, built for destruction. The vampire twins split up. One went for Solis, moving with terrible speed. The other came at Nikolai, daggers flashing in perfect coordination.

Lady Morana's eyes fixed on Henrick. I felt the pull of her charm magic, even from here, and saw Henrick stagger as compulsion hit him full force. Nikolai shouted, breaking away from the second twin to help, his magic flaring to counter hers. The shifter mercenary charged with his axe raised, targeting whoever was closest. Rhett.

Rhett threw a vial—paralysis potion, from the color —and the shifter stumbled but didn't stop. Too determined. Too strong.

And Raleth pressed harder, driving Lorenzo and me back.

"You're good," he said conversationally, blade scoring

across my shoulder. "Both of you. Lorenzo's military precision, Kieran's speed. But I've been fighting since before your parents were born."

He was right. Even together, we were struggling.

Lorenzo fought with textbook perfection—every strike measured, every defense calculated. But Raleth was faster, more experienced, and he knew every trick we'd try before we tried it.

A cut across my arm. Another across Lorenzo's side.

We were losing ground.

Down the corridor, Jex and the demon traded devastating blows. Jex's hammer cracked against the demon's ribs. The enemy demon's claws raked across Jex's chest, drawing blood even through demon-thick skin.

The twins were everywhere at once. Solis was bleeding from half a dozen cuts, barely keeping up with the first twin's speed. The second twin had forced Nikolai back, away from Henrick.

And Henrick—saints, Henrick was on his knees, fighting Morana's compulsion with everything he had. His threads lashed out weakly, trying to break her concentration, but she was too strong.

Rhett threw another potion—this one shattered at the shifter's feet. Acid splashed, making the shifter roar and stumble.

"That's for Merrit," Rhett shouted, already reaching for another vial.

But he was running low. I could see it in the way he hesitated before each throw, calculating what he had left.

Raleth's blade found my ribs. Shallow, but it hurt, slowing me.

Lorenzo intercepted the follow-up strike that would have taken my heart, but it cost him. Raleth's dagger opened a line across Lorenzo's shoulder.

"Your brother bleeds," Raleth said. "Your demon falls. Your guards die."

He wasn't wrong. Jex was holding his own against the demon, but barely. Both of them were wounded, both refusing to yield.

Solis managed to get inside the first twin's guard—one perfect thrust. The young vampire's eyes widened in shock, then dimmed.

One down.

The surviving twin screamed—actual grief, not compulsion—and threw himself at Solis with reckless fury. The distraction cost Solis. The surviving twin's blade found his side, sinking deep.

"No!" I started toward him.

Raleth's blade cut across my back. Pain exploded through me and drove me to one knee.

Lorenzo stood over me, blocking the killing blow, but he was bleeding, too. We both were.

"Mistake," Raleth said calmly.

I forced myself up and threw my dagger. It took him in the shoulder. Not fatal, but it made him hesitate.

The moment's pause let Lorenzo press an attack—a combination I'd seen him drill a thousand times. Fast, brutal, efficient. Raleth blocked most of it, but one strike got through, opening his side.

Now he was bleeding, too.

Behind us, Nikolai finally broke through to Henrick. Together, their combined magic shattered Morana's compulsion.

Henrick gasped, threads snapping back under his control. They lashed out, wrapping around Morana, binding her.

"Irritating," she hissed, fighting the threads with charm magic, trying to compel them to release her.

It was working. Slowly.

Rhett threw something that shattered at her feet—not a potion, but a vial of pure silver dust. She screamed as it touched her skin, her concentration breaking.

Nikolai didn't hesitate. A spell crackled from his hands, hitting her square in the chest, and she fell.

Two down.

But Nikolai swayed, pale, magically exhausted. And Henrick wasn't much better, maintaining those threads against her compulsion had cost him.

Solis and the surviving twin were locked in desperate combat. Both wounded, both determined. But

Solis was older, more experienced, fighting with guilt-driven fury. His blade found the last twin's heart.

Three down.

But Solis didn't get up. He collapsed against the wall, bleeding from too many wounds, conscious, but barely.

"Solis!" I broke away from Raleth, starting toward him.

Raleth's blade cut across my thigh. I stumbled and nearly fell.

Lorenzo caught me, pulling me back. "Stay focused!"

He was right. We couldn't help Solis if we were dead.

Jex roared in pain, not fury. The demon had gotten past his guard, claws raking across Jex's already-wounded chest. Jex staggered, and the demon pressed the advantage.

But the shifter—bleeding from Rhett's acid, furious—charged in from the side. His axe caught Jex in the shoulder, biting deep. Even Jex went down from that.

"Jex!" Rhett's voice cracked.

He threw his last explosive potion—something that detonated on impact, fire and concussion. It caught the shifter full in the chest, sending him flying back.

But now Rhett was running low. Maybe one or two offensive potions left. The rest were healing draughts.

The demon stood over Jex's fallen form, breathing hard, wounded but victorious. Until Jex's hand shot out, grabbing his ankle.

"Not. Done. Yet." Jex's voice was gravel and pain.

He yanked, bringing the demon down. They grappled on the floor, both too injured for finesse, just raw strength and determination. Jex got on top, his hands around the demon's throat—and squeezed.

The demon struggled, clawed, but Jex held on. Demon strength against demon strength, and Jex's fury was stronger.

A brutal snap rent the air, and the demon under Jex stopped moving.

Four down.

Jex rolled off him, gasping, bleeding, and not getting up.

The shifter was down, too, badly burned from Rhett's explosive. Still breathing, but out of the fight.

Five down.

That left Raleth against Lorenzo and me. Both wounded, both exhausted, both determined.

"Impressive," Raleth said. "But you're running on nothing but will now, and will isn't enough."

He attacked with renewed fury, and he was right. We were exhausted: every wound slowing us, every blocked strike taking more effort. Lorenzo's blade work was still perfect—textbook, precise—but he was slowing. A cut across his arm. Another across his ribs.

I tried to cover him, but Raleth was too fast. Too experienced. He got past my guard, blade slicing across my side. Deep this time, and I went down.

"Kieran!" Lorenzo called out.

He stood over me, blocking Raleth's killing blow, but he was bleeding from a dozen wounds. He couldn't hold alone.

Raleth knew it, too. His battle-hardened face twisted into a victorious grin. Then a bottle shattered against his face—Rhett's last offensive potion.

Smoke billowed, thick and choking as he screamed in agony.

"Go!" Rhett shouted at me. "Get to her! We'll hold him!"

Lorenzo hauled me to my feet. "Go, brother. We've got this."

I looked at him—wounded, exhausted, facing Raleth alone in the smoke.

"That's an order, little brother," he said, managing a bloodied smile. "Now go. Get to her."

I didn't think, I just moved, sprinting down the corridor while Raleth was blind, while my brothers were still fighting, while I still could.

It seemed to take a year before I reached the door at the end. It was barred from the outside, but I ripped the bar away with strength I didn't know I had left, shoving the door open.

The room beyond was small. Stone walls stained dark. A table with blades and tools that made my stomach turn. Two candles burning low.

And Merrit.

Slumped against the far wall, hands bound behind her, covered in blood. Cuts on her arms. A brand on her shoulder. Her clothes soaked through with red.

But alive. Conscious. Her green eyes met mine, and through the bond—

Relief. Love. Terror.

"You came."

"I will always come for you."

I started toward her.

"I wondered how long it would take."

The voice came from the shadows beside the door.

Tobias stepped into the candlelight.

He looked exactly as he always had. Neat. Composed. Not a hair out of place. Like he'd been waiting patiently for us to arrive rather than orchestrating a coup.

"Your Highness." He inclined his head in mock courtesy. "Thank you for coming. I was growing bored."

Behind me, I heard the others still fighting. Lorenzo and Raleth. The sound of desperate struggle.

My brothers were out there, bleeding and exhausted, holding the line so I could reach her.

And Tobias was here. Fresh. Rested. Ready.

"Let her go," I said. My voice came out steady despite the pain, the fear, the bleeding wounds across my body.

"Oh, I don't think so." Tobias moved with casual grace, positioning himself between me and Merrit.

"She's the key to everything. The leverage that brings you here. The bait that works every time."

He drew his sword. Old, well-maintained, a blade that had killed many times before.

"You think this is about her? About telepaths?" He smiled. "This is about a kingdom built on weakness. About a king who let his most loyal servant's Whisper-bound die and offered a meaningless title in return. About three centuries of watching that same king rule with soft hands while the realm fractures."

He moved fast—faster than I'd expected—and his blade sliced across my already-wounded shoulder.

I fell back, barely parrying the next strike.

"This is about a coup, Prince Kieran. About ending your father's reign and restoring the old ways. Vampire supremacy. Rule through compulsion. Order through strength."

Another strike. I blocked it, but the impact jarred my injured arm.

"You and your progressive ideas. Treating other species as equals. Keeping a telepath as your Whisper-bound." He pressed harder. "You represent everything weak about the current reign."

Behind me, I heard a crash. Shouting. Lorenzo was still fighting, but he sounded desperate.

"Your brothers exhaust themselves," Tobias said, reading my thoughts. "Your demon falls. Your guards bleed out. And you..." Another cut, across my ribs. "You die here. Tonight. The first domino in the kingdom's destruction."

I fought back, but he was right. I was wounded, exhausted, had been fighting since the stairs. And he was fresh, skilled, six hundred years of combat experience flowing through every movement.

The door behind him burst open.

Lorenzo stumbled in, barely standing, bleeding from a dozen new wounds. "Kieran—"

Tobias didn't even look. Just turned and thrust.

His blade took Lorenzo through the chest. Not the heart—thank the saints, not the heart—but close enough that Lorenzo staggered to his knees, struggling to stay upright. His gaze found mine, and the fear there was unmistakable.

"No!" I lunged forward.

Tobias pulled the blade free, letting Lorenzo hit the floor. "Your brother. The military commander. Did he tell you how many battles he's won? How many enemies he's killed?"

Blood spread beneath Lorenzo, his hand reaching toward me, falling short.

"None of it matters now," Tobias said.

Rage exploded through me. I attacked with everything I had left. But it wasn't enough. Tobias was better. Older. Stronger.

He disarmed me with a twist of his wrist, sending

my sword skittering across the floor. I reached for my dagger, but his boot caught my hand, crushing it against the stone. I heard bones snap and crack.

"Your mother, by the way?" Tobias said conversationally, forcing me to my knees with a hand on my shoulder. "That wasting illness she succumbed to?"

His blade pressed against my throat.

"I poisoned her. Slowly. Methodically. Brought her medicine every day—medicine that was killing her. Watched her fade for six months while your father mourned."

My vision blurred. Pain. Exhaustion. Shock.

Merrit's terror was palpable in the bond. She was trying to get free, to help, but she was too injured, too weak.

"I'm sorry," I sent to her. *"I love you. I'm sorry."*

"I've been dismantling your family for decades," Tobias continued. "Building my network. Placing my people. Eliminating threats. All leading to this moment."

He pressed the blade harder, and blood trickled down my throat.

"This is where the real coup begins." His voice carried satisfaction. "Where your father finally understands what he took from me."

Behind him, I saw Merrit, still struggling with the ropes. Still fighting, even though she could barely move.

Lorenzo was on the floor, not moving. Solis somewhere in the corridor, wounded. My brothers outside, maybe dying. Rhett. Jex.

And I was on my knees with a blade at my throat.

"I love you," I sent to Merrit one more time.

Tobias raised his blade for the killing blow.

"This is where you die, Prince. And she watches."

The rope had been fraying for hours.

One fiber at a time, working it against the sharp edge of stone behind me while pain screamed through every movement. My wrists were raw, bleeding, the hemp cutting deeper with each twist. But I kept going.

Because I could feel them getting closer.

Through the bond—weak, flickering, damaged by whatever blood magic Tobias had used—I felt Kieran. Determination. Fury. Love. It grew stronger with every passing minute as the distance between us shrank.

He was coming.

And I could hear them fighting now.

Out there, beyond this door. Shouting. Metal on metal. The crash of bodies hitting walls. Rhett's voice raised in something between a war cry and a curse. Jex's roar—pain, not fury.

Through the bond: Kieran's spike of alarm. His rage as someone fell. His desperation bleeding through the damaged connection.

They were dying for me, and I was tied up like a fucking sacrifice, helpless while Tobias waited for Kieran to reach me so he could kill him in front of me.

No.

I worked the rope harder, ignoring the way my shoulders screamed, the way the brand on my shoulder sent fire through my nerves with every movement. The iron cuts burned like they were still being made, my Fae blood reacting to the metal even now.

Through the bond: pain. Fierce and sudden. Kieran was hit. Wounded. Still fighting but hurt.

"Hold on," I sent, even though I didn't know if he could hear me through the damaged connection. *"I'm here. Hold on."*

Almost there. Just a few more fibers.

The door burst open, and Kieran stepped through. Our eyes met across the room—his wild with desperation and fury, mine likely showing every bit of terror and relief I felt.

The relief hit me, even as his desperation became clear. He was wounded. Badly. And the fight wasn't over yet. *"You came,"* I pushed through our connection that was slowly knitting back together.

"I will always come for you."

He started toward me.

"I wondered how long it would take."

Tobias stepped from the shadows beside the door, blocking Kieran's path. Neat. Composed. Like he'd been waiting patiently instead of orchestrating a massacre.

"Your Highness. Thank you for coming. I was growing bored."

Kieran stopped, instinctively positioning himself between Tobias and me. His hand went to his sword—already drawn, already bloody.

They began to fight.

I'd never seen Kieran truly fight before. Not like this. He moved with desperate precision, every strike calculated, but Tobias was faster. Older. Six hundred years of experience against three hundred and fifty.

And Kieran was already wounded. Already exhausted from fighting through Tobias' conspirators to reach me.

Through the bond: his pain. His determination. His fear—not for himself, for *me*.

Steel clashed against steel. Kieran was good, but Tobias was better. A cut across Kieran's shoulder. Another across his ribs. But Kieran held, continuing to fight as if he hadn't just been wounded further, his rage tangible through our connection.

Then the door burst open again, and Lorenzo stumbled through, barely standing, bleeding from a dozen wounds. His eyes found Kieran first, then me.

"Kieran—"

Tobias didn't even look. Just turned mid-strike and thrust.

So fast I barely saw it. Just a blur of motion, the wet sound of steel punching through flesh.

Lorenzo went down.

No.

Through the bond—the bond that had been flickering weakly for hours, damaged by whatever blood magic Tobias had used—I felt Kieran's horror. His rage. His desperation.

He attacked with everything he had left.

But Tobias was faster. Centuries of experience against exhaustion and grief.

I watched Kieran fight. *Really* fight. Not the controlled sparring I'd glimpsed in training, but desperate, brutal combat. Every strike was blocked, every opening closed. Tobias was toying with him, wearing him down.

A cut across Kieran's arm. Another across his side, deep enough to make him stagger.

He was losing.

I could see it in the way his movements slowed, the way he favored his left side, the blood soaking through his clothes. Could feel it through the bond—pain, exhaustion, determination fraying at the edges.

Tobias disarmed him with a casual twist of his wrist. Kieran's sword clattered across the floor, and he reached for his dagger.

Tobias' boot caught his hand, crushing it against the stone. The sound of bones breaking was sickeningly clear.

Kieran dropped to his knees, Tobias' hand forcing him down, blade pressing against his throat.

No. No, no, no—

The rope snapped.

My hands were free.

I brought them around—saints, everything hurt, my shoulders on fire from being bound for so long, my wrists slick with blood—and fumbled with the knots at my ankles.

Come on. Come on.

My fingers were numb and clumsy. The knots were tight, professional, and I couldn't get them—

Tobias' voice cut through the room. Calm. Conversational. Like he was discussing the weather rather than preparing to execute someone.

"Your mother, by the way? That wasting illness she succumbed to?"

I looked up, finding him standing over Kieran: blade at his throat, Kieran on his knees, and blood trickling down his neck.

My fingers found the edge of the knot, and I pulled desperately.

"I poisoned her. Slowly. Methodically. Brought her medicine every day—medicine that was killing her."

The knot loosened. Just a little.

"Watched her fade for six months while your father mourned."

Faster.

Through the bond—clarity rang, suddenly, terribly clear—Kieran's shock slammed into me. His grief. The way that revelation hit him like a physical blow.

Tobias raised his blade.

And underneath Kieran's grief: acceptance. Resignation.

He thought he was going to die.

No.

The ankle binding came free.

I tried to stand, and my legs gave out immediately, crashing to my knees, biting back the sound trying to escape my ruined throat. Everything hurt: the cuts, the burns, the exhaustion, the blood loss.

I forced myself up, anyway.

Used the wall for support, every muscle shaking, and took one step toward them. Then another.

Kieran on his knees, and Tobias stood over him, raising the blade for the killing blow. Lorenzo lay motionless on the floor beyond them, chest rising and falling shallowly, but alive. Barely.

"This is where you die, Prince. And she watches."

Through the bond, Kieran sent everything he had left. Love. Grief. Apology.

"I love you."

Not a declaration. A goodbye.

Fuck. That.

I didn't think. Didn't plan. Just reached for the one weapon I had left.

My mind.

I'd been gentle before. With Kieran, in the castle, learning the shape of his thoughts. Careful. Controlled. Asking permission with every tentative probe.

This wasn't that.

This was invasion. Violation. The same thing Tobias had done to my body with his blades, I did to his mind with my power. I found his consciousness—six hundred years old, layered with shields and walls and carefully constructed defenses—and I *slammed* into it.

His mental shields were strong. Ancient. Built over centuries of practice. I ripped through them anyway.

Desperation made me strong. Terror made me vicious. But underneath both was something stronger: *rage.*

For my parents. For Kieran's mother. For his mate. For every person he'd killed over six centuries of systematic genocide. I tore through his defenses like they were paper. Found his mind—cold, calculating, broken—and invaded every corner of it.

His memories were there. Organized. Clinical. Three

hundred twelve kills, each one cataloged. Each threat eliminated. Each telepath, seer, mind reader erased from existence. And buried beneath them all, locked away where he thought no one could reach was *her*.

The seer. His Whisperbound. The most beautiful mind he'd ever touched.

I saw her through his eyes. Small, dark-haired, with eyes that saw futures branching like tree roots. Luminous. Breathtaking. The other half of his soul. I saw the king demanding one more vision. Her bleeding from her eyes, consciousness tearing itself apart trying to see too far. Tobias begging her to stop, to let it go, to hold on.

I saw her die in his arms. Felt the bond shatter like glass. Felt him break.

And I grabbed that memory—that perfect, terrible, devastating memory—and I *shoved* it to the front of his mind. Made him relive it. Feel it. Experience it again like it was happening *now*.

Every second.

Every moment.

The sound she made when her mind fractured. The way her hand went slack in his. The emptiness where the bond used to be. The king's empty condolences. The feast that same evening while Tobias sat alone in chambers that would always be too empty.

I unleashed three hundred and fifty years of grief all at once.

Tobias screamed—a raw, broken sound that had nothing to do with physical pain and everything to do with a wound that had never healed. His blade clattered to the floor. He staggered back, hands going to his head, trying to block out the memory, the pain, the bond that had shattered and left him hollow.

My knees buckled. The psychic attack had taken everything. I felt it immediately—the backlash, the cost. My vision blurred. Blood poured from my nose. I caught myself against the wall, barely, everything spinning.

Too much. I'd pushed too hard, burned too bright, used power I didn't have.

But Kieran was moving.

Through the haze, I saw him grab the fallen blade with his off-hand. Drive himself up off his knees through sheer force of will.

Our eyes met across the room. Through the bond—fully open now, the blood magic finally burned away—I felt everything. His love. His fury. His determination. His understanding.

"Together."

I nodded, even though the room was spinning, even though I could barely stand. Took one step toward him, then another, using the wall for support.

My legs were shaking. The world kept tilting. But I kept moving.

Tobias was still reeling, still lost in the memory I'd

forced on him, still experiencing his mate's death over and over as he crumpled to the ground.

Kieran met me in the middle.

Up close, he looked like death: blood soaking through his clothes, cuts across his face and arms and chest. His sword hand hung useless, bones shattered. But his eyes were clear.

He looked down at the blade in his hand—not his sword, something he'd grabbed from the floor—and then at me.

Held it out.

I took it with shaking hands. The weight was wrong, unfamiliar, but I gripped it tight anyway. Had to. This was ending. Now.

Kieran's good hand closed over mine.

His fingers wrapped around my knuckles, steadying me, lending me strength I didn't have left. Holding me up as much as guiding the blade.

He reached for me through the bond. *"For your parents. For my mother. For everyone he killed."*

"For them all," I agreed.

Tobias was recovering. The psychic assault was fading, his shields reconstructing, his consciousness fighting back toward control.

His eyes focused on us. Saw the blade. Understood.

"Do it," he said. His voice was raw, broken. "End it."

We moved together.

Kieran's hand guided mine, my hand holding the

blade, both of us driving it forward with everything we had left.

The blade punched through Tobias' chest.

Through cloth and skin and muscle and bone, straight into his heart.

He gasped, looking down at the blade buried in his chest, at our palms still wrapped around the hilt. Our hands fell away, leaving the blade where it was.

Blood bubbled at his lips, and he looked at Kieran first. "You think..." He coughed, red spattering his neat clothes. "You think this changes anything?"

His eyes moved to me. "The king... killed her..." Another cough. "He'll kill you, too..."

Then back to Kieran. "Duty... always comes first..." His voice was fading. "You'll see... you'll become... just like him..."

His gaze found me one last time. "You should've... stayed dead..."

Then there was nothing. His eyes went empty. His body went slack. Tobias—King's enforcer, coup conspirator, murderer of hundreds—was dead.

I stared at him. At the blood spreading across stone.

He was dead. It was over.

And the last of my strength went with him.

My legs gave out. I didn't feel myself falling. Just suddenly the world tilted, gravity became wrong, and the floor rushed up to meet me.

Kieran caught me before I hit the ground.

His arms—saints, even injured he was so *strong*—wrapped around me, pulled me against his chest, held me like I might disappear if he let go.

I tried to say something. Tried to tell him I was okay, that we'd won, that it was finally over.

Nothing came out, and I was so *tired*. The psychic attack had taken everything I had left: every reserve of strength, every last bit of will. I'd burned myself out completely just to save him.

Worth it—worth all the pain, worth everything—because we were together, safe.

Through our connection—so clear now, so *loud* after being muffled for hours—his emotions crashed over me.

Relief. Love. Terror. Gratitude. Horror at my injuries. Rage at what had been done to me. Joy that I was alive. Fear that I was too hurt, that he'd been too late, that—

"I'm okay," I sent, even though it wasn't quite true. *"You came. You saved me."*

"You saved yourself." His hand was in my hair, cradling my head against his chest. *"You saved me. Again."*

I tried to laugh. It came out as a choked, breathy sound.

"We saved each other."

His other arm tightened around me. I could feel him

shaking—exhaustion, adrenaline crash, relief, all of it hitting at once.

"You're safe now," he said out loud, voice rough. "It's over. You're safe."

I wanted to stay awake. Wanted to make sure he was okay, check on Lorenzo, see if the others had survived.

But darkness was pulling at the edges of my vision, exhaustion dragging me down.

The last thing I felt before everything went black was Kieran's arms tighten around me and his voice through the bond:

I've got you. I'll always have you.

Then blackness took me.

KIERAN

She went limp in my arms.

For one terrible, heart-stopping moment, I thought—

But no. I felt her. Distant, quiet, but *there*. Not gone. Just... spent. Completely and utterly exhausted. Her chest rose and fell in shallow breaths. Blood from her nose had dried on her face. The cuts on her arms were still bleeding sluggishly. The brand on her shoulder—

I forced myself to look away from the damage. To focus on what mattered.

She was alive.

We'd won.

Tobias' body lay a few feet away, the blade still buried in his chest. Dead. Finally, permanently dead. I had half a mind to burn him to ash or string him up on a pole in front of the whole Court so everyone could see what happened to traitors.

But it would have to wait. My family came first.

Lorenzo was sitting up now, one hand pressed to the wound in his chest. Not the heart—thank the saints, not the heart—but close enough that he'd nearly died. His face was pale, but vampire healing was already working. He'd live.

The door burst open.

I moved instinctively and shifted to cover Merrit with my body, my good hand going to where my sword should be and found nothing. I'd lost it in the fight.

Luckily, it was just my brothers.

Nikolai stumbled through first, pale and magically drained but walking. Then Henrick, barely standing, used the doorframe for support. Solis was last, bleeding from too many wounds, moving like every step cost him.

"Kieran." Nikolai's eyes found me, then dropped to Merrit in my arms. "Is she—"

I relaxed slightly but didn't move away from her. "Alive. Unconscious."

"Everyone?" I asked.

"Alive," Henrick confirmed, sagging against the wall. "Barely. Raleth's dead. The conspirators are all down."

Footsteps thundered through the corridor, heavier, accompanied by the sound of breaking glass.

Rhett and Jex appeared in the doorway.

Jex looked like he'd been through a meat grinder—deep gouges across his chest where the other demon's claws had raked him, one shoulder hanging wrong where the shifter's axe had bitten deep. But he was standing. Moving.

Rhett limped in behind him, most of his vials shattered, blood soaking through his shirt from half a dozen cuts. But his eyes were sharp, assessing.

"Everyone still breathing?" His gravelly voice cut through the room.

"Barely," Nikolai said, sliding down the wall to sit.

"Good thing I brought the entire fucking pharmacy." Rhett pulled out the remaining intact vials from his bandolier—maybe seven or eight, glowing faintly with different colors. "Healing draughts. They won't fix everything, but they should keep you lot from dying in the next hour."

Rhett moved through the room with practiced efficiency, distributing healing draughts, each tailored to the injury—Lorenzo first for his chest wound, then Solis, Jex, Henrick, and Nikolai.

When he handed one to me, I tried to refuse. "Give it to her."

"Already planned on it," Rhett said, pulling out another. "Take yours or you'll pass out before we get her home. You're bleeding from about fifteen different places."

I hadn't noticed. Adrenaline, probably. But looking

down, I saw he was right—blood soaked through my clothes. I took the vial with my good hand and drank it. Warmth spread immediately, dulling the worst of the pain. Not healing, but helping.

Rhett crouched beside me, pulling out a glowing amber vial. "Make her drink this. All of it."

I shifted her carefully, tipping the potion against her lips. She was unconscious but swallowed reflexively, instinctively. The liquid disappeared, and warmth spread through her—not just physical, but through the bond, too. Like the potion was reaching the damage inside as well as out.

Color returned to her face, just slightly. Her breathing evened out, deepening with each inhale.

"She'll be okay," Rhett said, watching her with the eye of someone who'd seen too many injuries. "Burned herself out with that psychic attack. Telepaths always push too fucking hard."

I went still. "You know?"

"That she's a telepath?" Rhett snorted. "Yeah. Jex and I have known for years. The way she'd know things she shouldn't, react to thoughts instead of words." He shrugged. "Wasn't our secret to tell."

Jex rumbled his agreement from where he sat against the wall, one massive hand pressed to his wounded shoulder. "Family keeps secrets."

"Family," Rhett agreed simply. He met my gaze.

"Which means if anyone comes for her because of what she can do, they go through us first."

Something tight in my chest eased. They'd known for *years*. Protected her. Kept her secret without question or hesitation.

"Thank you," I said quietly.

Rhett waved it off. "Nothing to thank. She's our family. Has been since the day she gave us a chance." He stood, wincing. "Just keep her safe. She's been through enough."

"She will be," I promised. "Whatever it takes."

Rhett nodded, satisfied, and moved to check on the others.

Lorenzo was already looking better—color returning, breathing easier. The healing potion combined with vampire physiology was knitting the worst of the damage. He'd have a scar, but he'd live.

"We need to secure the area," he said, voice still rough but functional. "Make sure there aren't more conspirators waiting."

"I'll check." Nikolai pushed himself to his feet with visible effort. "Henrick?"

"Right behind you."

Nikolai and Henrick disappeared into the corridor. I heard footsteps, voices, then the methodical sound of blades meeting flesh—beheadings, the way we'd been trained. Better to be certain.

They returned minutes later, Nikolai's sword bloodied. "All clear. All down. Permanently."

"The compelled guards?"

"Gone. Fled when Henrick broke the compulsion." Henrick sagged against the wall again. "They won't remember much. The trauma of forced compulsion usually fragments memories."

"Good." I didn't want innocent people punished for what Tobias had forced them to do.

Nikolai approached Tobias' body, crouched down carefully, and started searching his pockets.

"What are you looking for?" Lorenzo asked.

"Evidence. Proof." Nikolai's hands found something in an inner pocket. "Ah. There."

He pulled out a folded stack of papers, opened them, scanned quickly, his expression darkening.

"What is it?" I asked.

"Names. A list of conspirators in other provinces." He looked up. "Correspondence about the coup. Timeline of attacks—the southern gate, the poisonings, everything. And..." He pulled out another document. "Orders. Signed and sealed."

"Let me see."

He brought them over. I read through them with growing cold fury.

It was all there. Every attack. Every assassination attempt. Every part of the coup laid out in meticulous detail. Tobias had documented everything, probably as insurance, or maybe just because six hundred years of being the king's enforcer had made him compulsively thorough.

"There are more," I said, reading the list of names. "Other conspirators. In Lorenzo's province, in the eastern territories, even in the capital itself."

"We'll root them out," Lorenzo said grimly. "Now that we know who they are."

"This cell is eliminated," Henrick added. "The immediate threat to Morathen is over. The rest... we can handle."

Solis pushed himself off the wall, wincing. Blood still seeped through the bandages Rhett had wrapped, but vampire healing was already knitting the worst of it.

"There's one more thing," he said quietly. "Something I didn't tell you before."

I looked up from where I sat holding Merrit.

"When I saved her... I didn't just save her life." He met my gaze. "I took her memories. The fire, her parents, all of it. Suppressed them completely."

The words hit like a physical blow. "You *what*?"

"She was ten years old and just watched her parents get murdered. I couldn't..." He stopped, steadying himself. "I made a choice. To spare her that trauma."

"Without asking."

"There was no time." His voice was flat. "I can give them back. When she's ready. If she wants them. But it has to be her choice."

I looked down at Merrit, unconscious and finally peaceful after so much pain. Another choice made for her. Another piece of her stolen, even if it was meant as mercy.

"When she wakes," I said, "you'll tell her. And then she can decide."

Solis nodded. "I will."

I looked down at Merrit again. The immediate threat was over. She was safe. That was what mattered most.

"We need to move," Lorenzo said, pushing himself to his feet. He swayed slightly but stayed upright. "But first—"

He didn't finish the sentence. Just drew his sword, moved to Tobias' body, and with one clean strike, severed his head from his shoulders.

Better to be certain. Especially with someone as old as he was.

"Now we can go," he said, cleaning his blade.

"Agreed." I shifted, trying to stand while holding Merrit.

Jex was there immediately, despite his own injuries. "I'll carry her."

I hesitated, not wanting to let her go. I didn't want her out of my arms for even a second.

"You're injured," Jex said, voice gentle despite the gravelly rumble. "Exhausted. Let me. You know I've got her."

I did know. Jex had protected her for years, would

die before letting harm come to her. And I was injured, exhausted, barely able to stand myself.

Reluctantly, I nodded, carefully transferring her to Jex's massive arms. He held her like she weighed nothing, cradling her against his chest with surprising gentleness for someone so large.

"Let's move," Lorenzo ordered.

We made our way out of that terrible room. I didn't look back as we passed Tobias' body. Didn't linger on the table with its torture implements.

Bodies lined the hallway. The conspirators who'd tried to stop us. Raleth. The twins. Morana. The demon. The shifter. All dead.

We'd fought through all of them, and barely survived.

But we *had* survived.

We headed up the stairs, out of that basement, through the orphanage main floor—dust and abandoned furniture and the ghosts of children who'd once lived here. Who'd learned and played and grown in this building, never knowing what horrors existed in the basement below.

Merrit had been one of them, had walked these floors, touched these walls. Samona had taught her here. This had been her home, her refuge.

And Tobias had violated it with his torture chamber.

Now we were leaving it behind. Forever.

Outside, dawn had fully broken. The sun painted

everything in shades of gold and pink, almost obscenely beautiful after the darkness below.

Horses waited where we'd left them. And beyond them—Lorenzo's men, finally arrived. Too late for the fight, but here now to help with cleanup and transport.

"Your Highness." The captain saluted, eyes widening as he took in our condition. "Saints, what—"

"Secure the building," Lorenzo ordered, his voice brooking no argument despite his injuries. "The basement is a crime scene—torture chamber, evidence of the coup, bodies of the conspirators. Document everything. Catalog every piece of evidence. The bodies need to be transported back to the castle for identification and records."

He paused, then added grimly, "And search the surrounding area. Make sure no one fled before we arrived. Check the roads, the nearby buildings. Anyone suspicious, bring them in for questioning."

"Yes, my lord. Immediately."

Wagons were being prepared, and someone had thought to bring medical supplies, blankets.

Jex placed Merrit gently in the most cushioned wagon, arranging blankets around her. I climbed in immediately, pulled her against my chest, positioning myself so she was supported and comfortable.

Through the bond: *"Safe. You're safe now."*

No response. She was too deep, too exhausted. But I kept sending it, anyway.

My brothers mounted horses as Rhett and Jex took another wagon—Jex's injuries were bad enough that even demon healing needed rest. Solis rode alone, quiet and guilty.

The wagons began to roll, slow and steady.

I held Merrit as we traveled through the Divide, watching the orphanage disappear behind us. That gray stone building grew smaller until it vanished into the morning mist—no longer a safe haven, but a nightmare.

She stirred once, awareness flickering through the bond—confused, frightened—and I sent immediately: *"I'm here. You're safe. Just sleep."*

She settled, consciousness sinking back down.

"How is she?" Lorenzo rode alongside the wagon, looking better with every mile, as vampire healing continued its work.

"Alive. Exhausted. But stable." I looked at my brother. "How's your chest?"

"Healing. I'll have a scar, but..." He shrugged. "Small price."

"He nearly killed you."

"Nearly." Lorenzo's expression was grim. "But he didn't. We're all still here. That's what matters."

Nikolai joined us on the other side. "The documents. We need to show them to Father."

"I know."

"There are conspirators in other provinces. This isn't over."

"It is for us," I said firmly. "For Morathen. The imme-diate threat is eliminated. The rest..." I looked down at Merrit. "The rest can wait until she's healed."

"Kieran—"

"It can wait." My voice left no room for argument. "Father can handle the political fallout. We've done our part."

Nikolai studied me for a moment, then nodded. "All right. But he'll want to see you. Immediately."

"He can wait, too."

Behind us, I heard Rhett and Jex talking quietly.

"Think she'll be all right?" Jex asked, voice deep and solemn.

"Yeah. She's survived worse." He paused. "She's got us. And she's got him now."

"Better be enough."

"It will be."

Silence settled between them, comfortable and certain.

I tightened my arms around Merrit slightly, careful not to disturb her rest.

It *would* be enough. I'd make sure of it.

THE SUN CLIMBED HIGHER AS WE TRAVELED. THE Divide gave way to better roads, then to farmland, then to the outskirts of the capital city.

People stopped to stare as we passed. The prince and his bloodied companions, returning from gods knew what battle. Word would spread quickly.

Let it spread. Let everyone know Tobias was dead. Let the remaining conspirators know their leader had fallen and their coup had failed.

Morathen was secure.

The castle appeared on the horizon: blackened stone and high towers, the runes flashing in the morning light. *Home.*

As we rolled through the gates, guards snapped to attention, eyes widening at our condition. Someone ran ahead, likely to alert the healers and staff.

The courtyard filled quickly: servants, guards, healers with their supplies ready.

And standing at the top of the steps, like he'd been waiting—my father.

The king had come. Someone must have sent word ahead, or perhaps he'd felt the disturbance through whatever channels kings used to know when their realms were threatened. Either way, he was here now, watching with those cold, calculating eyes as we pulled in.

I hadn't seen him in months. He looked the same as always—ancient, powerful, untouchable.

I didn't go to him. Didn't dismount to give him a report or explanation.

Instead, I gathered Merrit carefully and lifted her from the wagon. She was so light that she seemed so fragile in my arms. The healers approached immediately, hands reaching for Merrit.

"Your Highness, let us take her—"

I pulled her closer to my chest, instinctively protective. "Show me to a private room. The best you have. Now."

The head healer—an older woman whose name I should know but couldn't recall—hesitated. "Of course, Your Highness, but it would be easier if we could examine her while—"

"*Now.*"

The word came out harsher than I intended, but I didn't apologize. Couldn't. Not when every instinct screamed to keep her close, to not let her out of my sight for even a moment.

They scrambled to obey, the head healer gesturing quickly to her assistants. I followed them toward the healing wing, adjusting my hold on Merrit so her head rested more securely against my shoulder. She was so light, felt so fragile. Blood had seeped through the makeshift bandages Rhett had applied, staining my shirt, but I didn't care.

"Kieran."

My father's voice cut through the courtyard bustle.

Not a greeting. A summons. The tone that had made princes and generals snap to attention for a thousand years.

I didn't stop. Didn't even slow my pace toward the healing wing entrance.

"Later, Father. She comes first."

I heard him start to speak again, but I was already through the doors, already moving down the corridor toward the healing wing. Whatever he wanted could wait.

She came first. Now and always.

The healers led me to a private room—large, well-appointed, with a soft bed and clean linens. Herbs hung from the ceiling, filling the air with the scent of lavender and something medicinal I didn't recognize.

I placed her on the bed as carefully as I could, smoothing her hair away from her face.

The head healer approached immediately, bringing supplies. "Let me examine her, Your Highness."

Reluctantly I stepped back, standing by the bed and holding Merrit's hand while she worked.

"Multiple lacerations," she murmured, cutting away bloodied clothing to reveal the damage beneath. "Iron burns—these will take longer to heal. A brand here, recent. Severe bruising around the wrists and ankles. Signs of..." She paused, looking up at me with understanding in her eyes. "Torture."

"Yes."

"And magical exhaustion. I can feel it—there's a... hollowness where her spark should be. She pushed too hard, burned herself out completely."

"Will she recover?"

"Yes. With time and rest." She began cleaning wounds with gentle efficiency. "The physical injuries will heal. The magical exhaustion will take longer—that kind of depletion requires deep rest, sometimes days of unconsciousness while the magic repairs itself. But she's strong. She'll recover."

I watched her work. Each wound revealed made my rage flare again—evidence of what Tobias had done, the hours of torture she'd endured.

But Tobias was dead. He couldn't ever hurt her again.

The healer applied salves, wrapped bandages, and used gentle healing magic on the worst of the burns. All the while, I held Merrit's hand, sending constant reassurance through the bond, even though I didn't know if she could feel it.

"I'm here. Right here. Not leaving."

The door opened quietly, and I looked up, ready to tell whoever it was to leave.

Lorenzo stood in the doorway, and I barely recognized him. The chest wound that had nearly killed him hours ago had clearly healed completely—he stood straight and strong, moving without pain or hesitation. His fresh shirt showed no blood, no sign of injury.

Vampire healing combined with what was clearly a recent feeding had worked its usual magic.

He looked like he'd never been stabbed at all.

Meanwhile, I was still covered in blood—most of it mine—exhausted beyond measure, and couldn't bring myself to give a shit about any of it.

"How is she?" Lorenzo asked quietly, his gaze moving from me to Merrit on the bed.

"She'll recover. It'll take time, but she'll be okay."

"Good." He stepped into the room and leaned against the doorframe with deceptive casualness. But I knew that stance—he had something to say I wouldn't want to hear. "Father wants to see you."

"He can wait."

"Kieran—"

"I'm not leaving her." I met his gaze, letting him see exactly how serious I was. "Not until she wakes up. Not until I know she's truly okay. Father's demands can wait."

Lorenzo studied me for a long moment. I watched him weigh options, calculate responses, probably running through a dozen arguments about duty and protocol and the king's displeasure.

Then he just nodded. "I'll tell him. He won't like it."

"I don't give a fuck."

Something shifted in Lorenzo's expression—not quite a smile, but close. "I know." He pushed off the doorframe, started to leave, then paused. "You've changed, little brother. It's good to see."

"Changed how?"

"You used to care what Father thought. Used to try to balance everyone's expectations." He glanced at Merrit, then back to me. "Now you know exactly where your priorities are. That's... rare. Especially for princes."

He didn't wait for a response. Just gave me a small nod of approval and left, closing the door quietly behind him.

I looked down at Merrit, still unconscious, still so pale despite the healer's work.

Lorenzo was right. I had changed. A month ago, I would have gone to my father immediately, left Merrit in the healers' care, and done my duty as Crown Prince.

Now?

Now she came first. Before duty, before protocol, before my father's expectations.

And I didn't regret it for a second.

The door opened, and Nikolai and Henrick entered together, both looking drained but functional.

"The documents are secure," Nikolai said, sinking onto a chair. "Twenty, thirty conspirators in other provinces. Manageable." He glanced at Merrit. "Father's been asking to see you every hour."

"I don't care."

Nikolai's lips twitched. "Message received. I'll handle the debriefing."

Henrick leaned against the wall, smiling despite his exhaustion. "The blood magic on your bond is completely gone. She didn't just break the spell—she purified it. You're more closely bonded now than before."

"She saved my life."

"She saved all of us," Henrick said quietly. "She's remarkable."

Nikolai stood. "She's worth it. What you're doing... I hope I find something like that someday."

They left together, and I was grateful for brothers who understood.

Time passed in a blur. The healer finished her work, declaring Merrit stable, leaving to attend to the others.

I stayed by the bed, refusing to move, even when my legs cramped and my back ached from sitting in the same position too long.

The door opened again, and I looked up.

Rhett and Jex stood in the doorway, and like Lorenzo, they looked significantly better than they had any right to. Rhett's arm was in a sling—the only visible sign of injury—and his face had more color than before. Jex still moved carefully, favoring his wounded shoulder, but the deep gouges across his chest had closed—demon healing working its magic.

They'd both cleaned up, changed clothes, and had likely been forced to sit still while healers worked on them.

And now they were here.

"Can we—?" Rhett started.

"Come in."

They didn't need to be told twice. Rhett and Jex moved into the room and positioned themselves on either side of the door, her guards, even here in the castle's healing wing. Even now, when the threat was eliminated and she was as safe as she could possibly be.

"She okay?" Jex asked quietly, his gold eyes fixed on Merrit's sleeping form.

"She will be. The healer said she just needs rest."

"Good." Jex settled against the wall, clearly planning to stay. His massive frame made the corner seem small, but he looked comfortable. Settled. "We'll wait."

"You don't have to—"

"We're staying." Rhett interrupted, his tone brooking no argument. "Until she wakes up. Until we see with our own eyes that she's okay."

I shifted my gaze between them. These two who'd protected her for years, had kept her secrets, considered her family long before I'd ever walked into her bar.

"Thank you," I said quietly.

"Nothing to thank." Rhett leaned back, getting comfortable. "She's ours. Been ours for a long time. We're not going anywhere."

Jex rumbled his agreement.

Family. They'd called her family, and they meant it with every fiber of their being.

I turned back to Merrit, their presence somehow making the vigil less lonely. We were all waiting together. All watching over her.

All making sure she'd be safe when she woke.

More time passed—hours, though, I'd honestly lost track. Healers came and went, checking on her, adjusting bandages, and monitoring her condition.

And I stayed, holding her hand and watching her breathe, sending constant reassurance through our connection.

The sun moved across the sky, visible through the high window, as afternoon faded toward evening.

And then—

Her eyes fluttered.

I was on my feet immediately, leaning over her. "Merrit?"

Her eyes opened slowly, struggling to focus—confusion first, then fear, and then recognition.

She saw me, the room, and finally realized where she was.

The relief was so intense through our connection, it nearly knocked me over.

"Hey." I kept my voice gentle. "You're safe. You're in the castle. In the healing wing."

Her presence flickered against my consciousness—weak, exhausted, but unmistakably *her*. *"How long?"*

"About eight hours. We brought you back from the orphanage. You've been unconscious the whole time."

"The others?"

"Everyone made it. Lorenzo, Solis, Nikolai, Henrick, Rhett, Jex—all alive, thanks to Rhett's potions and sheer stubbornness."

Her eyes moved past me, finding Rhett and Jex by the door.

Her hand lifted slowly—bandaged, shaking with exhaustion—but she managed a simple sign: *"Thank you."*

Jex gave her his version of a smile—more of a showing of teeth, but the meaning was clear. "Told you you're tough."

Rhett grinned. "Can't get rid of us that easily."

She managed a weak smile, then her attention returned to me.

Her next thought came sharper, more focused—fear and desperate hope tangled together. *"Tobias?"*

"Dead. You killed him. We killed him. Together." I took her hand and held it carefully. "It's really over."

Relief flooded through the bond, so intense she sagged back against the pillows. *"Really?"*

"It's really over."

She closed her eyes for a moment, breathing deeply. When she opened them again, they were wet with tears she didn't try to hide. *"I was so scared."*

"I know. I felt it." I brushed a tear away gently. "But you were so brave. What you did—that psychic attack— you saved my life."

"You came for me."

"And I always will. No matter what. No matter where. I will always come for you."

Her hand squeezed mine weakly.

The bond flooded with emotion—hers crashing into mine like a tsunami. Love, gratitude, bone-deep exhaustion, relief so intense it hurt, and underneath it all, the warm certainty of safety.

I answered with my own surge: love that went soul-deep, pride in her strength, protectiveness that bordered on possessive, overwhelming joy that she was alive, and a promise—silent but absolute—that she'd never face danger alone again.

"We saved each other," she sent, and the thought carried such warmth, such wonder, that it made my throat tight.

"We did."

She looked like she wanted to say more—I could feel thoughts forming at the edges of her consciousness, trying to take shape—but exhaustion was pulling at her again, relentless as a tide. The brief waking had cost her what little strength remained.

"Sleep," I said gently, brushing my thumb across her knuckles. "I'll be here when you wake up. And every day after that."

Her presence flickered against mine, clinging like she was afraid to let go. *"Promise?"*

The vulnerability in that single word nearly broke me.

"I promise." My voice roughened despite my best efforts. "You're safe now. We both are."

Something in her loosened—relief, trust, peace settled into place like the final piece of a puzzle. Her eyes drifted closed, and her breathing evened out, deepening into sleep.

But it wasn't the unconsciousness of before, that terrible emptiness where I could barely feel her through the bond. This was natural, healing sleep. Her body and mind were finally able to rest now that the danger had passed, now that she could truly believe she was safe.

I stayed beside her, holding her hand, watching the gentle rise and fall of her chest. Each breath a gift, each moment proof that we'd survived.

Rhett and Jex remained by the door, silent guardians who'd proven their loyalty in blood and battle. Family in every way that mattered.

Outside, the castle buzzed with activity. I could hear it even through the thick door—footsteps in corridors, voices raised in discussion, the organized chaos of a crisis being managed. My father wanted reports. There were conspirators to root out in other provinces, political consequences to manage, a coup attempt to explain to the nobility and the realm at large.

But none of that mattered right now.

What mattered was here. In this room. This moment. Her hand in mine, warm and real and alive.

We'd survived.

Against everything—against Tobias and his vendetta, against a carefully orchestrated coup three centuries in the making, against systematic genocide, and blood magic and torture and despair.

And now we had something I'd barely dared to hope for: time.

Time to heal the wounds—physical and otherwise. Time to figure out what came next, what our life would look like now that we weren't running, weren't hiding, weren't fighting for our lives. Time to build something real and lasting from the ashes of what we'd been through.

She was Whisperbound to me. My mate, my other half, the person my soul had been searching for across three and a half centuries of existence.

She was also a telepath: immune to compulsion, capable of powers that had kept her hidden and hunted for twenty years.

The healers had been discreet, calling what she'd done "her magic" rather than naming it specifically. My brothers knew the truth, as did Rhett and Jex and Solis. But the wider Court? The nobility? They didn't know yet. Might never know, if we chose to keep it hidden.

But that was the thing, wasn't it? *We* couldn't choose. *I* couldn't choose.

It had to be her decision. Whether to hide or reveal, to keep living in careful secrecy or to finally step into the light—that choice belonged to her alone. She'd had too many choices stolen already. I wouldn't take this one, too.

When she woke, when she was healed and strong and ready—we'd talk about it. About what she wanted. About what came next.

If she chose to keep it secret, I'd guard that secret with my life. If she chose to reveal it, I'd stand beside her through whatever storms might come.

Either way, she wouldn't face it alone.

The Court would have opinions regardless—about her, about us, about a Crown Prince Whisperbound to someone from the Divide with no title or family name they recognized. There would be challenges ahead, even without the telepath revelation.

But I'd face them all. Whatever it took to keep her safe, to give her the life she deserved after a lifetime of hiding and surviving and being hunted.

Whatever she chose, whatever she needed—I'd be there.

Whatever it took—no matter the consequences, I'd stand at her side—she was strong and brave, and she needed to be reminded. Not of what she went through, but what she *survived*.

"Together, always," I projected, and I hoped like hell

she could hear me through our connection, even through the haze of sleep. It was unlikely, but I projected my thoughts even harder. She needed to know how much I loved her, how much I cared. How I'd do anything to protect her—raze the whole damn kingdom if necessary.

I looked down at her, sleeping peacefully for the first time in days. Her face was bruised, bandaged, marked by everything she'd withstood. The cuts would heal. The burns would fade. The brand on her shoulder would scar, but even scars told a story—and hers was one of survival, of strength, of refusing to break, even when everything tried to shatter her.

She was beautiful, not despite the damage, but because of what it represented. She'd endured. She'd fought. She'd won.

She was alive. She was here.

She was mine.

And I was hers.

Through our bond, I felt her consciousness like a distant star—peaceful in a way I'd never felt before. No fear. No pain. No desperate vigilance waiting for the next threat.

Just peace, safety, and the deep, certain knowledge that she could rest now. That someone was watching over her. That she wasn't alone anymore.

"I love you," I sent into that peaceful darkness, knowing she probably couldn't hear in the depths of

healing sleep but needing to say it anyway. *"We're going to be okay. Both of us. I promise."*

The bond hummed contentedly between us, that invisible thread that tied soul to soul, life to life. Unbreakable now, purified by what she'd done to save me, strengthened by everything we'd survived together.

Whisperbound.

Forever.

Outside, evening faded toward night. The sun set beyond the window, painting the room in shades of amber and gold before giving way to silver moonlight. The castle settled into its nighttime rhythms. The immediate crisis passed, managed by my brothers and the household staff, who'd seen a thousand emergencies and knew how to handle them.

And I stayed exactly where I was, holding her hand, keeping watch over her sleep.

Not leaving—not for my father's summons, not for political necessities, not for anything.

Not ever.

She was safe. We were safe.

And that, I realized as exhaustion finally began to pull at me, too, was all that mattered.

Everything else—the politics, the conspirators, the questions and challenges and complications—could wait.

This moment was ours.

And I intended to hold onto it for as long as I possibly could.

CHAPTER 30
MERRIT

I woke to sunlight and safety in Kieran's chambers. And beside me in bed right there where he belonged—Kieran slept.

One arm was draped across my waist, our fingers still loosely linked. His face was turned toward me, relaxed in sleep but still showing the exhaustion of the last few days. Dark circles shadowed his eyes. Thick stubble darkened his jaw.

How many nights had he stayed awake watching over me? How long had he refused to really rest, terrified I wouldn't wake up?

Through the bond—clear and strong now with no blood magic muffling it—I felt him. Deep sleep, finally. But even unconscious, there was that constant awareness checking that I was still *there*. Still breathing. Still safe.

I gently prodded connection. *"Good morning."*

His eyes flashed open immediately. Not the slow blink of someone waking naturally, but instant alertness. Those icy-blue eyes focused on me with such intensity it took my breath away.

"Merrit." My name came out rough, sleep-thick and full of emotion. His hand tightened on mine. "You're awake. Really awake."

I smiled. *"Really awake. How long was I out?"*

"Three days since we got back." He shifted closer, touching my face gently like he needed to confirm I was real. "You've surfaced a few times, but never fully conscious. Never like this."

"I'm here. I'm okay."

"You're okay." He said it like he was trying to convince himself. Like he'd been terrified I'd slip away.

I reached up and cupped his jaw, felt the rasp of stubble under my palm, the cool of his skin. He leaned into the touch, eyes closing briefly as overwhelming relief and love flooded our connection, making my chest tight.

When he opened his eyes again, there was a question in them. Hesitant. Hopeful.

"Kiss me?"

He didn't need to be asked twice. I leaned down carefully and pressed my lips to his. Gentle. Reverent. Like I was something precious that might break.

I kissed him back, ignoring any twinge from healing

cuts, the lingering ache in my ribs. None of that mattered. What mattered was this—*him, us,* alive and together and safe.

When he pulled back, there were tears on his cheeks.

"Don't cry," I urged, brushing them away with my thumb.

"I thought I'd lost you," he whispered. "When you went limp in my arms, when the bond went so quiet I could barely feel you—"

"I'm here. You came for me. You saved me."

"*We* saved each other." His hand covered mine, pressed it more firmly against his face. "You killed him. That psychic attack—Merrit, you shouldn't have survived that. The backlash alone should have—"

"But I did survive," I sent through the bond what I couldn't say with words: *"Because of you. Because I had something worth surviving for."*

He caught his breath, feeling the depth of what I meant.

We stayed like that for a long moment. Touching, breathing, letting the reality of being *alive, safe, together* sink in.

The moment was broken when my stomach roared to life.

He laughed—the first real laugh I'd heard from him in what seemed like forever. "Of course you're hungry.

You haven't eaten in days. I'll get something brought up." He started to rise.

I caught his hand. *"Stay. Just another minute."*

He settled back immediately, brought my hand to his lips. "As long as you need."

But my stomach betrayed me with another audible growl. *"Fine. Food first."*

Breakfast arrived quickly—real food, not invalid broth. Bread and cheese and fruit and meat that actually smelled appealing rather than medicinal.

I ate carefully at first, then with increasing enthusiasm as my body remembered what hunger was. The healers had done incredible work—days of magical healing meant I was recovered. Not weak or fragile. Just... healed. Some lingering soreness, the brand on my shoulder still tender, but functional. Whole.

Kieran watched me eat with such open relief that it would have been embarrassing if I wasn't doing the same—cataloging him, checking that he was really here, really whole.

Except... he wasn't. Not quite.

I set down the bread I'd been reaching for, really *looking* at him for the first time since waking.

Too pale. Even for a vampire, he was too pale. The skin around his eyes looked thin, almost bruised. And when he reached for the water pitcher, his hand trembled slightly before he caught himself, steadied it.

I signed slowly, deliberately, "When did you last feed?"

He went very still. "I'm fine."

"Kieran. When?"

His jaw tightened. "Before." He spoke aloud since I couldn't see his hands. "Before everything. With you."

So the last time we'd made love. Before I'd been kidnapped, tortured, nearly killed. Before everything had gone to hell.

"That was almost two weeks ago."

"I wasn't leaving you to—"

I cut him off with a gesture, signed firmly, "You haven't fed from anyone else."

Not a question. I could see it in the way he held himself too carefully. The exhaustion that went deeper than simple lack of sleep. The slight tremor he was trying to hide.

"There wasn't time. Between the fight and watching over you—"

"Three days while I was unconscious. You could have."

"I wasn't leaving you." His voice was flat, absolute. "Not for an hour. Not for minutes. And I wasn't..." He stopped, averting his gaze. "I wasn't feeding from anyone else."

Through the bond, I felt why. It wasn't just about time or convenience. Feeding had become something that belonged to us, to our bond. Taking blood from anyone else felt wrong on a level he couldn't articulate.

My chest tightened with love and exasperation in equal measure.

I tilted my head to the side, exposing my throat. Pushed through our connection, *"Take what you need."*

He went completely still. Stared at the line of my neck, at the pulse beating visibly beneath my skin. "Merrit—"

"I'm healed. Strong enough. You've been taking care of me for days." I kept my head tilted, offering. *"Let me take care of you."*

"I can wait. Feed from—"

He was pissing me off, proof positive we were both on the mend. "From who?" I signed sharply with one hand while keeping my neck exposed. "A random donor? Servant? Or your willing Whisperbound?"

His hunger twisted through me, hot and demanding. Not just the physical need for blood—though that was there—but the deeper desire. For connection. For intimacy. For me.

That hunger crossed his features, his eyes bleeding to scarlet as his fangs lengthened. His gaze was locked on my throat, on the vulnerable line of my neck that I was offering him.

"You're sure?"

"Very sure."

He moved closer, slowly, giving me every opportunity to change my mind, to pull back. But I didn't. I tilted my head further, a clear invitation.

His hand came up to cup the side of my neck, cool fingers gentle against my skin. His thumb brushed along my jaw as his breath ghosted across the sensitive skin of my throat.

"Tell me if it's too much," he said quietly, lips so close to my skin I could almost feel them. "If you need me to stop."

I nodded slightly, careful not to move my throat from its exposed position. *"I will. But I won't need to."*

He hesitated one moment more, searching my face for any sign of uncertainty.

"Trust me. Like I trust you."

Then he struck. The sting was sharp but brief as his fangs sank into the side of my neck, fading almost immediately into warmth. Heat. Connection. The bond between us flaring bright and clear as my blood flowed into him, feeding not just his body but the tie that linked our souls.

His relief as the hunger eased filtered through me. His gratitude, so deep it almost hurt. The way I tasted to him—not just blood, but life. Strength. Home. Love.

And I felt myself through his senses. How precious I was to him. How the fear of losing me had been like a blade against his throat for days. How having me here, alive, offering the most intimate feeding position freely —it meant everything.

His arm wrapped around my waist, pulling me closer as he drank. His other hand cradled the back of my head, fingers threading through my hair. Holding me. Protecting me even as he fed from me.

One minute. Two. I felt the pull, felt my strength flowing into him, but it didn't hurt. Didn't weaken me. If anything, the bond carried strength back—his gratitude becoming my own sense of peace, his growing vitality feeding into my confidence that this was right, this was good, this was us taking care of each other.

The intimacy of it stole my breath. His mouth on my throat, his body pressed against mine, the bond singing between us with every pull of blood. It was more than feeding. It was trust. Vulnerability. Love made tangible.

My nipples tightened against his chest as my sex pulsed in time with his swallows. All too soon, he pulled back carefully, slowly, his tongue sweeping across the wounds to seal them.

Color had already returned to his face. The exhaustion in his eyes had eased, replaced by alertness and strength. He looked whole again. Powerful. The Crown Prince rather than an exhausted man running on stubbornness alone.

"Better?"

"Better." His voice was deeper now, stronger. He brought my wrist to his lips, pressed a kiss to my pulse point. But something flickered through him, not just gratitude and relief. Something sharper. Hotter.

I touched his face. *"What's wrong?"*

"Wrong?" His jaw tightened under my palm. "You're asking me what's wrong?"

I blinked, surprised by the edge in his voice.

"You left." The words came out quiet but intense. "While I was sleeping. Snuck out of our bed in the middle of the night and went after him alone."

"Kieran—"

"Do you have any idea—" He stopped, closed his eyes, took a breath. When he opened them again, they were blazing. "I woke up and you were gone. Just gone. And I knew something was wrong, that you were in danger, and I—"

His hand came up to cup my face, grip almost too tight. Fury and terror and overwhelming relief all tangled together through our connection.

"I thought you were dead," he said, voice raw. "When I got there and saw you on that floor, saw what he'd done to you—" His thumb brushed across my cheekbone, trembling slightly. "You could have died. You nearly did die. And if you had—"

"I'm sorry." I covered his hand with mine. *"I didn't want you to try to stop me. I had to—"*

"I know." He leaned his forehead against mine, breathing hard. "I know why you did it. I understand. But that doesn't make it okay. It doesn't make it less terrifying to wake up and find you gone."

The full weight of what he'd experienced—the gut-wrenching fear, the desperate ride to reach me, the horror of seeing me bleeding—filtered through me. Three days of watching me unconscious, terrified I'd never wake up.

And underneath it all: fury that I'd taken such a risk. That I'd left him. That I'd nearly taken myself away from him permanently.

"I'm sorry," I sent again, meaning it completely. *"I should have told you. Should have let you come with me."*

"Yes, you should have." His eyes met mine, still burning with emotion. "We're partners, Merrit. Equals. That means you don't get to make decisions like that alone. You don't get to protect me by risking yourself."

"You're right."

"I know I'm right." He kissed me, hard and almost angry. "Don't ever do that again. Don't ever—"

I kissed him back, pouring every piece of my heart into him. *"I won't. I promise."*

He pulled back just enough to study my face, searching for the truth. What he found there must have satisfied him because some of the fury eased, though the intensity remained.

"I love you," he said, voice still rough. "So much it terrifies me. And when I thought I'd lost you, when I thought you'd died without knowing how much you mean to me—"

"I know." I touched his face gently. *"I felt it. Even*

unconscious, I felt you there. Watching over me. Refusing to leave."

"Of course I didn't leave." His hand slid into my hair, grip possessive. "You're mine. My Whisperbound. My partner. My everything. And you scared me half to death."

The bond pulsed between us—relief and anger and love all tangled together in a way that made my chest tight.

"I want to be pissed at you," he murmured, lips brushing mine. "I want to yell at you for being so reckless. For leaving me."

"But?"

"But you're awake. You're alive. You're here." He kissed me again, slower this time but no less intense. "And I can't think about anything except how grateful I am that you're okay. That I didn't lose you."

"You didn't lose me." I wrapped my arms around his neck. *"I'm here. I'm whole."*

Something shifted in his expression—the anger bleeding into desire. Desperation. "I need you," he said roughly. "Need to feel you. Need to know you're really here, really alive, really mine."

"I'm yours." I pulled him down for another kiss. *"Show me."*

He groaned against my mouth, the sound vibrating through both of us. "Three days," he murmured between kisses, hands already pulling at my shirt. "Three days of watching you sleep and being terrified. Three days of needing to touch you and not being able to. Three days of thinking about how you left me—"

"I'm sorry."

"I know." He pulled the shirt—his shirt—off in one smooth motion. "We'll talk more about it later. About not making decisions alone. About being partners in everything."

"Everything," I agreed.

"But right now—" His gaze raked over me, hot and possessive. "Right now, I need you too much to be angry. Need to feel you too much to think about anything except this."

"Yes." I reached for his pants, tugging them down. *"I need you, too."*

He stripped them off, and then we were skin to skin. His hands moved over me with a desperation that had nothing to do with gentleness and everything to do with confirmation—alive, whole, his.

"Mine," he growled against my throat. "You're mine and you don't get to leave me like that again."

"Yours. Always yours."

He kissed me hard, claiming, the full force of his emotions—the fury and fear and desperate relief—all channeling into raw need. I matched him, kiss for kiss, touch for touch. Showing him through action what I couldn't adequately express in words or signs—that I was here, I was whole, I was his.

The bond blazed between us, carrying sensation and emotion in equal measure. His hands explored without hesitation, touching and claiming and confirming. Every kiss was deeper than the last, every touch more desperate.

"I'm here. I'm alive. I'm yours."

"Mine," he agreed roughly, moving against me. "And I'm yours. We belong to each other."

We moved together, finding our rhythm, and the bond between us blazed so bright it was almost blinding. Every touch carried the weight of what we'd almost lost. Every kiss was a confirmation that we'd survived.

The pleasure peaked between us, carried through our connection in waves that left us both shaking. For a moment, the bond was pure light—relief and love and the confirmation that we were both alive, both here, both whole.

Then slowly we came back to ourselves, still tangled together, still connected. Kieran gathered me close, pressed his face into my hair. His arms were tight around me, almost too tight. Overwhelming relief and residual fear and so much love it made my chest ache, filtered through our connection.

"Okay?" I sent tentatively.

He let out a shaky breath. "I will be. Now that you're awake. Now that I know you're really okay."

"I scared you."

"Terrified me." He pulled back just enough to look at me, and his eyes were bright. "Don't do it again."

"I won't. Partners, remember?"

"Partners," he agreed. "In everything. Which means we make decisions together. Even the dangerous ones. Especially the dangerous ones."

"Especially those," I promised.

He kissed me again, softer this time. Gentle. "Sleep now. Rest. You gave me a lot of blood, and you need to recover."

"Not tired."

He raised an eyebrow. "Liar. I can feel your exhaustion."

He was right. The energy I'd given him through feeding, combined with everything else, was pulling me toward sleep.

"Fine. But you stay."

"Until the day I die." His arms tightened around me. "I'm not letting you out of my sight for a while. You're stuck with me."

"Good." I pressed closer, feeling his heartbeat under my ear. *"That's exactly where I want to be."*

I closed my eyes, feeling his arms around me, his love surrounding me.

Safe. Loved. His. Home.

WHEN I WOKE AGAIN, THE LIGHT HAD SHIFTED—afternoon rather than morning. I felt better. Clearer. The exhaustion from feeding him had lifted, leaving me rested and ready.

Kieran was awake, watching me with those icy-blue eyes.

"Hi." He smiled, soft and genuine. *"How do you feel?"*

"Good. Better." I stretched, testing my body. Everything worked. The magical healing had done its job. *"What did I miss?"*

"Other than several near heart attacks on my part?" His tone was light, but the truth of it filtered through the bond. He'd been terrified. "My father officially cleared Elias of all charges yesterday. Reinstated him with full honors."

"Thank the gods." Relief crashed through me. *"He deserves that."*

"He'll need time to heal his mind after what Tobias put him through, but I know he'll want to thank you for clearing his name." Kieran's expression shifted slightly. "But there are other things we need to talk about first. Decisions to make."

Something in his face made me go still. Not bad

news—I would have felt that through the bond—but serious. Important.

"What kind of decisions?"

"Yours." He sat up, helped me do the same, arranged pillows behind me so I was comfortable. "Completely yours. I'll support whatever you choose, but these have to be your choices."

I studied him, as my fingers moved carefully. "You're being very careful about this."

"Because you've had too many choices stolen from you. By Tobias. By circumstance." His hand found mine, squeezing gently. "By me. I won't take another one. Even if I think I know what's best. Even if I have opinions."

He meant every word.

"Okay. What do I need to choose?"

"First—your memories." His expression tightened with something between anger and understanding. "Solis told me something while you were unconscious. When he saved you twenty years ago, he didn't just heal your body. He took your memories. The fire, your parents dying, Tobias cutting your throat—all of it. Suppressed completely."

I went very still. I'd always assumed my memory loss was trauma, or time, or just the way the brain worked when you were that young. Never thought someone had actively *taken* them.

"He wanted to give them back. Offered to restore

them when you were ready." He paused. "But I don't think he can. Not anymore."

The loss of them hit like a blow. *"Why not?"*

"You dared me to compel you when we first met, because you knew as a telepath, you couldn't be compelled. When he took your memories, you were dying. Your mind was broken, vulnerable. He could reach in, suppress what was destroying you. But now?" He touched my face gently. "Now you're strong. Healthy. Your mind has its own defenses. The memories are locked away so deep even he can't reach them. Your own power protects you from reliving that trauma."

Relief and disappointment tangled together in my chest as tears stung my nose.

"So I'll never remember them? My parents?"

"The deaths? No. But there's someone—your father's best friend. A Fae scholar who knew your parents well. He's been in hiding since their deaths, afraid Tobias would find him, too. But Solis located him recently. He's willing to meet you. To tell you about who they were. What they loved. What they were like." His thumb brushed across my knuckles. "You can know them without remembering how they died."

The trauma staying buried felt like... protection. My own mind keeping me safe. A gift, even if it hadn't been my choice initially. But learning about them from someone who loved them? Someone who had real memories, real stories?

"Yes. When I'm ready."

"Whenever you want. No rush. He'll wait."

"Thank you."

"Nothing to thank." He squeezed my hand. "Now—the second choice."

I waited.

"The Court doesn't know what you are, not specifically." He watched my face carefully. "The healers were discreet. Called it 'magic' rather than naming it. My brothers know. Rhett and Jex. Solis. But the wider Court? The nobility? They just know you're my Whisperbound. That you helped stop the coup."

He took a breath, his hand tightening over mine. *"We can keep it that way. Or reveal it with full backing from the Crown. Entirely your choice."*

Twenty years. Twenty years of hiding what I was, terrified of being discovered, of being hunted, of being killed for the crime of existing.

And now I had a choice. To keep hiding—but this time it would be *my* choice, not survival. Or to step into the light. To let people know. To risk everything I'd spent my life protecting.

"If you were in my shoes, what would you do?"

"I think..." He paused, choosing his words carefully. "I think you deserve to live without fear. Without hiding. But I also think revealing it will paint a target on your back. There will be nobles who fear you. Who see you as a threat. Who think telepaths can't be trusted."

"Your father thought that. Made it law."

"He did." Something flickered across his face. "But we'll talk about that later. The point is, I'll support whatever you choose."

I thought about it. Really thought.

Part of me wanted to shout it from the towers. *"I'm a telepath and I'm not a monster. I saved you all. I can be trusted."*

But the smarter part—the part that had survived twenty years through caution and careful secrets—knew better.

"But I still think we should keep it quiet. For now. Let the Court adjust to me first. Let them see I'm not a threat before they know what I can do."

"And later?"

"Later... maybe gradually. Start with the Court. Then the realm. Show them telepaths aren't what they think." I met his gaze. *"But not yet. I need time. To be strong. To be ready."*

"You'll have it." He pressed his forehead to mine. *"Whatever you need. However long it takes."*

There was no disappointment that I'd chosen caution. No impatience. Just understanding.

We stayed like that, breathing together, until I pulled back and signed, "You said we'd talk about your father later. Is 'later' now?"

His expression shifted—something complicated. Nervous? Hopeful?

"He wants to meet you. Today, if you're well enough."

My stomach dropped. *"Today?"*

"Only if you're ready. We can wait—"

"No," I signed firmly. "I'm ready. Let's do this."

THE KING'S STUDY WAS IN A PRIVATE WING, guarded by two massive warriors who nodded to Kieran and opened the doors without question.

Inside was... not what I expected.

Books. Everywhere. Lining walls, stacked on tables, piled on the floor in organized chaos. Maps covered one entire wall, marked with pins and notes in cramped handwriting. A large desk dominated the center, cluttered with papers and inkwells and half-drunk tea.

It looked like a scholar's study. Not a throne room. And behind the desk sat the king.

Old. Older than ancient. Silver hair pulled back, face lined with age that vampires usually didn't show. Eyes that were silver rather than the icy blue of his son. Sharp. Calculating. Like he could see through you to the truth underneath.

He studied me in silence. I stood still, letting him look, trying not to fidget or show nerves.

"Lady Vaerin," he said finally. His voice was dry, academic. Not warm, but not unkind. "Sit."

I froze. Signed quickly, "I'm not—"

"You are." He gestured to the chair across from his desk. "The Vaerin family held land near the Divide border for three centuries. Minor nobility, but nobility, nonetheless. Your father was Lord Aldric Vaerin." His eyes fixed on me. "Did you truly not know?"

I shook my head, still standing. Kieran's hand squeezed my shoulder gently.

"Then allow me to be the first to acknowledge it properly. You have a rightful claim to the title and the lands—abandoned though they are." He paused. "Lady Merrit Vaerin, please sit."

It wasn't a request this time. It was an acknowledgment. Recognition.

I sat, hands shaking slightly as I signed, "Your Majesty."

"You're Whisperbound to my son."

I nodded.

"You killed Tobias. Stopped his coup."

I shook my head, signing, "We killed him. Together."

Those silver eyes studied me for a long moment. "Interesting. Most people would claim full credit. Especially when facing a king." He gave a slight smile. "You're either remarkably honest or remarkably foolish."

"Just honest, Your Majesty."

The smile lasted longer this time. "Indeed."

Silence stretched. I waited, refusing to fill it with nervous gestures.

"My kingdom is stagnant," the king said abruptly, leaning back in his chair. "Inbred nobility clinging to old power. Old ways. Old prejudices. We need new blood. Fresh perspective." His eyes fixed on me. "You're Vaerin by birth. That gives you standing. But more importantly—you saved my son's life. Stopped a coup that would have destroyed this realm."

He stood, walked around the desk, and looked down at me with those ancient, calculating eyes.

"That earns you more than tolerance, Lady Vaerin." He glanced at Kieran.

The king returned to his desk. "The Court will have opinions about you. About your origins. About a Crown Prince taking a Whisperbound from the Divide with no voice." He paused deliberately. "Let them have their opinions. They bore me."

I couldn't help it—I smiled slightly.

His expression shifted, almost amused. "You find that funny?"

"I find it reassuring," I signed. "I was afraid you'd care what they thought."

I couldn't prove it, but I could have sworn Kieran's father almost rolled his eyes.

"I'm a thousand years old. If I cared what those foolish fucks thought, I'd have gone mad centuries ago."

He picked up a paper from his desk and scanned it. "Besides, half of them are vipers. The other half are incompetent idiots. You'll be running this outfit better than your bar in less than a month."

Behind me, Kieran's surprise shot through the bond. His father was... joking? Complimenting me?

The king set the paper down, fixing me with that sharp gaze again. "You should know... I know what you are."

My breath stopped. Every muscle in my body went rigid. Kieran tensed behind me, but the king raised a hand.

"Peace. I'm not here to threaten." He leaned back. "And don't insult my intelligence by pretending otherwise. I've lived a thousand years. I know a telepath when I see one."

I signed slowly, carefully, "How?"

"I examined Tobias' body myself. Cause of death was listed as a blade through the chest, but that's not what degraded his brain." He walked to his desk, pulled out a folder. "His mind was destroyed. Shattered. The kind of catastrophic psychic trauma that only comes from one source—a telepathic assault powerful enough to destroy a six-hundred-year-old vampire from the inside out."

He set the folder down. "The backlash from an attack like that should have killed whoever did it. Yet my son's Whisperbound—who was present when Tobias died—is alive and recovering." His eyes fixed on mine.

"Which tells me you're not just any telepath—you're exceptionally powerful."

"Your Majesty—"

"You could have used your power for anything. Compelled my son. Manipulated the Court. Seized control through the minds of others. You had days to do it while he was vulnerable." His gaze didn't waver. "Instead, you killed the man trying to destroy us. Protected my son. Saved my kingdom."

He returned to his chair. "You proved me wrong, Lady Vaerin. That's rare."

"I would never use my power to hurt people," I signed, almost offended.

His smile was slight, but there. "I know. That's why I'm going to change the law."

Kieran's hand tightened on my shoulder as he sat forward in his chair. "You'll change the decree?"

"Keep it quiet for now. Let the Court adjust to you first, Lady Vaerin. Learn to trust you. See you as my son's Whisperbound, as a hero who stopped a coup." He steepled his fingers. "But when you're ready—when the time is right—we'll reveal the truth. And I'll publicly change the decree. Show the realm that telepaths can be trusted. That my law was based on fear rather than fact."

I wanted to melt into the floor with relief. "Why would you do that for me?"

"Because I'm old enough to admit when I'm wrong. And because my kingdom needs to evolve or it will die."

He looked at Kieran, then back to me. "And because what I see between you two isn't just a Whisperbound bond. That's real."

His expression softened almost imperceptibly. "Love like that is rare. I won't let outdated laws destroy something genuine."

"Thank you, Your Majesty."

"Don't thank me yet. The Court will be insufferable." His mouth curved into a slight smile. "But you survived Tobias. You can survive Court politics."

He stood—dismissal. "Welcome to the family, Lady Vaerin."

I stood, signed, "Your Majesty."

Kieran guided me toward the door. We were almost there when the king spoke again:

"Lady Vaerin?"

I turned.

"Try not to read my ministers' minds," he signed in perfect, if antiquated, movements. "Even when they're thinking stupid things. It would be too tempting to act on what you learn."

Despite everything, I smiled. "I'll try, Your Majesty."

His expression was almost fond. Almost.

Then we were through the door, in the corridor, and I started shaking.

CHAPTER 31
MERRIT

Evening found us in the Divide.

We'd taken a carriage with two guards who stayed outside—discreet but present. I was healed, but Kieran wasn't taking chances. Not after everything.

My bar was busier than usual. Warm light spilled through windows, voices and laughter louder than normal. As we approached, I realized why—someone had spread the word. All my people were here.

Kieran squeezed my hand. "Ready for this?"

I hesitated. A crowded bar meant dozens of minds. Thoughts bleeding together into noise I'd need Sable's elixirs to dampen. Except, I didn't have any elixirs with me. Hadn't taken one in days and the bond had burned through what had been in my system.

Kieran felt my anxiety. *"What's wrong?"*

"Crowds. Too many minds. I didn't bring—"

"You don't need them anymore." His presence wrapped around me through our connection, steady and calm. *"When it gets too loud, retreat here. To me. I'll anchor you."*

I tested it. Reached out with my awareness toward the bar, felt the wash of thoughts and emotions from inside—

—glad she's alive—

—Prince actually came—

—heard she killed—

Too much. Too fast. The familiar pressure building behind my eyes.

But then Kieran's presence surged through the bond. Not blocking the thoughts, but giving me something else to focus on. A quiet space within the noise. His mind, clear and calm and *there*.

The pressure eased. The voices didn't disappear, but they became manageable. Background noise instead of overwhelming static.

"Better?" he sent.

"Better." I looked up at him, amazed. *"I don't need the elixirs anymore."*

"The bond gives you what you need." He smiled. *"Including silence when the world gets too loud."*

I squeezed his hand and pushed open the door.

The familiar space washed over me—but it was *full*. Scarred tables packed with locals, the bar crowded, but I'd already found my silence in Kieran, my refuge.

Rhett saw me first. His face split into a genuine grin. "Well, look who's not dead! Everyone, the boss has finally left her castle!"

A cheer went up. Actual cheering. My face heated, and the surge of emotions from the crowd—*relief, joy, pride, welcome*—threatened to overwhelm me again.

I pressed closer to Kieran, used the bond to steady myself. His calm flowed through our connection, giving me the space I needed to breathe. To process.

This was new. Having an anchor that wasn't a potion or an elixir, but a person. A connection. Someone who could give me silence when I needed it, simply by being *there*.

"He's been insufferable waiting for you," Jex rumbled from his corner, though his golden eyes were warm. "Cleaned this place three times."

"I have not—" Rhett stopped, grinning. "Okay, maybe twice."

"Three," Sable said from a barstool, Trouble curled in her lap. The little fox familiar's ears perked when he saw me, and he yipped once—sharp and accusing, like *where have you been?*

When I reached Sable, she stood, set Trouble on the bar, and pulled me into a brief hug that smelled of smoke and herbs.

"You look better than last time." Her dark eyes cataloged me—healer's instinct and witch's intuition combined. Then she paused. "You're not using my elixirs anymore."

"Don't think I'll be needing them anymore," I signed, giving her a tentative smile.

"The bond?" I didn't know how she knew, but she didn't need me to confirm. She simply nodded, accepting. "Good. My supplies were running low anyway."

That was a bold-faced lie from a witch who could taste them. Sable always had supplies. But she wasn't going to pry, and I wasn't going to explain.

Trouble hopped across the bar to sniff at my hand, whiskers twitching. I scratched behind his ears, and he chittered contentedly.

"Missed you," Sable said. "So did this one. Kept stealing things from my workbench."

Trouble's tail swished, unrepentant.

The door opened, letting in a blast of cool night air —and Nadia.

The shadow Fae looked rough. Exhausted. Her dark clothes were travel-worn, and I could see the faint tremor in her hands she was trying to hide. Transporting Kieran's brothers through her shadows had nearly killed her.

She moved through the crowd with the efficiency of someone who didn't want to be here long.

"You're alive." Nadia's voice was clipped, matter-of-fact. "Good. Would've been a waste otherwise."

"Thank you," I signed, knowing that wasn't big enough for what she'd done. "For bringing them."

"Did my job." She glanced at Kieran, then back to me. "Lorenzo's outside with the horses. We leave at dawn for Tharros. Rooting out the rest of Tobias' people."

"Horses?" I signed, surprised. "Can't you just—"

"Shadow-walk? Sure. *Alone.*" Her expression was sour. "But your brother-in-law needs to get to Tharros, too, and I can't bring passengers yet. Not after..." She gestured vaguely at herself. "Nearly killed me bringing three vampires through the shadows. Need time to recover before I can do that again."

"How long?" Kieran asked quietly.

"Months. Maybe half a year." Nadia's jaw was tight. "Transporting living beings through shadow takes more than just power—it takes precision. One mistake and they're scattered across the realm in pieces. I'm not risking that until I'm fully healed."

"So you're stuck on horseback," I signed, eyes wide. I'd only met Lorenzo once, and I had a feeling he'd met his match with the surly shadow Fae.

"For two weeks with your uptight bastard of a brother. Yes." She looked at Kieran. "I offered to go ahead, scout everything out, meet him there. But apparently, he needs to 'personally oversee the operation' and 'maintain proper chain of command.'" The air quotes were sharp. "So. Horses. For two weeks."

Kieran's mouth twitched. "That sounds like Lorenzo."

"He's infuriating." But there was something in her tone—grudging respect, maybe. "Competent, though. I'll give him that."

"He usually is," Kieran said.

"Makes him worse." Nadia clasped my shoulder once—brief, firm. "Be safe. And don't get kidnapped again. I'm not shadow-walking passengers for at least a few months."

"You take care, too," I signed, barely containing my grin.

"I'll survive. Even if Lorenzo bores me to death with proper procedures and strategic planning." She headed for the door, then paused. "He's waiting outside with the horses."

"Try calling him Enzo," Kieran suggested, his smile turning wicked. "He hates it."

Nadia's lips curled—the first real smile I'd seen from her. "Does he now?"

"Loathes it. Our father used it when he was in trouble as a child. He'll probably threaten you."

"Perfect." Nadia's smile widened into something wicked. "Two weeks of 'Enzo' it is. Thanks for the tip."

Then she was gone, the door swinging shut behind her.

"That was cruel," I signed to Kieran, but I was smiling.

"He'll survive. Besides"—Kieran's grin was unrepentant—"she needs something to make the trip bearable. And watching Lorenzo try to maintain his dignity while being called Enzo for two weeks? That'll do it."

"You're terrible to your brother."

"I'm helpful. I just gave her a way to cope with his strategic planning lectures." He pulled me closer. "That's basically a gift. I almost feel sorry for him. Almost."

A commotion at the door announced another arrival. Serenya swept in like she owned the place, took one look around, and beamed.

"This is wonderful! Merrit, why didn't you tell me your bar was so perfectly *gritty*?"

"Because you'd never leave," Kieran muttered.

Serenya ignored him, making a beeline for the bar where Rhett was mixing drinks. "You. Bartender. Make me something that'll scandalize my mother."

"Everything scandalizes your mother," Kieran said.

"Exactly. So make it strong." Serenya leaned on the bar, studying Rhett with open appreciation. "You're the alchemist, aren't you? The one who makes the potions in this place?"

"That's me." Rhett's eyes were wary but amused. "And you're the prince's cousin who's going to be trouble."

"Oh, I'm definitely trouble." She grinned. "But the fun kind."

Jex moved closer—protective instinct—and Serenya's attention shifted to him. Her eyes went wide.

"You're enormous. Do you fight?"

"When necessary," he growled, but there was a distinct darkening at his cheeks that could be a blush.

"Fascinating. I bet you're magnificent when you're violent." She said it as if she were discussing weather. "We should spar sometime. I'd love to see how you move."

Jex looked at Rhett. Rhett looked at Kieran. Kieran looked at me.

"They are going to have their hands full," I signed, my eyebrows hitting my hairline.

"Unfortunately," he muttered.

Serenya had already launched into an animated discussion with Rhett about alchemy, asking sharp questions that proved she knew more than expected. She was also shamelessly flirting, which left Rhett looking distinctly off-balance.

"Is she always like this?" Sable asked.

"Worse, usually," Kieran said.

"Gods help us," Jex grumbled.

But I caught the hint of amusement in the pull of his lips. And Rhett, for all his wariness, was engaged in the conversation—debating reagent ratios and extraction methods while Serenya leaned closer than strictly necessary.

The evening settled into comfortable chaos. Serenya continued to fascinate and scandalize in equal measure. Sable stayed nearby with Trouble, adding dry commentary. Locals came over to welcome me back, to tell me they were glad I was safe.

This was my place. My bar. My people. And they were here celebrating that I'd survived.

At one point, Rhett pulled me aside. "You good? Really good?"

"Really good."

"The prince treating you right?"

I looked at Kieran, who was patiently suffering through another of Serenya's stories. "Better than right. Perfect."

"Good. You deserve perfect." Rhett's expression shifted—something between awe and discomfort. "Speaking of royalty... the *king* took care of something while you were unconscious."

I went still. "What?"

"The tithe. The pack tithe for the land." Rhett's voice was quiet, like he still couldn't quite believe it. "The king himself came to the Divide. Personally delivered payment to the pack alpha. Full tithe for the next twenty years. In gold."

My hands froze mid-sign. "The king? Not Kieran?"

"Not Kieran. His father. The actual king walked into pack territory and paid your debt himself." Rhett shook his head. "Alpha nearly shit himself. You don't refuse a king, especially not one who's lived a thousand years and could probably kill everyone in the Divide if he wanted to."

The floor seemed to tilt under me. "Why would he—"

"He said"—Rhett's smile was wry—"and I'm quoting here because I asked around, wanted to make sure this was real—he said 'The Crown pays its debts. Consider this matter settled.'"

The Crown pays its debts. The king had stepped in and cleared everything.

"Twenty years, Merrit. You don't owe them shit. The bar's secure. You're free."

I looked across the bar to where Kieran stood. I felt his surprise—he hadn't known, either. His father had done this without telling him.

Kieran's attention snapped to me, feeling my shock through our connection. He moved through the crowd toward us.

"What's wrong?" he asked when he reached us.

"Your father paid my tithe. To the pack. Twenty years."

Kieran went absolutely still. "What?"

"Came himself," Rhett confirmed. "Walked right into pack territory like he owned it—which, I guess technically he does own the whole realm, but still. Paid the full tithe."

Kieran looked stunned. "He didn't tell me."

"Didn't tell her either, apparently." Rhett's gaze darted between us. "But it's done. Signed, sealed, delivered. The pack's not going to argue with the king."

"No," Kieran said slowly. "They wouldn't dare."

"Why would he do that?" I signed, the disbelief hitting me square in the chest.

Kieran's features softened—something between surprise and understanding. "Because you're family now. And my father... he protects what's his." He touched my face gently. "You're under the Crown's protection. He made that clear to the pack. They won't touch you. Won't demand anything from you. Not now."

My throat felt tight. The king—who'd met me once, who'd questioned me, who'd acknowledged my title— had gone into pack territory personally and eliminated the debt that had controlled my life for years.

"It also means something else," Rhett said quietly. "Politically, I mean. King paying your tithe personally? That's a statement. He's telling the whole realm you're under royal protection. Anyone who comes after you is coming after the Crown."

Tears stung my eyes. Not just freedom from debt, but *safety*. Real safety backed by the most powerful vampire in the realm.

"Hey." Rhett's voice was gentle. "The bar's yours. Secure. No strings. Well—except your prince, but that seems like a string you want."

"It is," I signed, trying to get myself together.

"I should thank him," I sent to Kieran, not knowing how I could possibly repay a debt that big.

"He won't want thanks. This is just..." Kieran shook his head, something like pride in his expression. "This is him saying you're family. In the only way he knows how."

Kieran's surprise gave way to warmth. His father had accepted me. Truly accepted me. Not just tolerated his son's choice but actively protected it.

"Your father is..."

"Surprising?" Kieran offered with a slight smile.

"Yes."

"He does that sometimes." Kieran pulled me close. "But he's right. You shouldn't have been in debt in the first place."

"The king said basically the same thing," Rhett added. "Told the alpha it was a matter of honor."

I leaned against Kieran, still processing. Free. Truly free. The bar secure. No debt hanging over me. No fear of the pack coming to collect.

And Kieran's father—the ancient, calculating king—had done it himself. Had made a political statement so clear that no one could miss it: *she's ours now.*

"So yeah," Rhett said, his smile warm. "You're good. We're good. Bar's good. And apparently, you've got the most powerful vampire in the realm as your father-in-law. How's that for protection?"

"It's fucking terrifying," I signed, but I did it with a smile on my face.

Kieran laughed. "Fair."

Rhett's eyes softened. "But don't forget—this is your bar. Your home. Doesn't matter how many castles you've got access to now. This place is yours."

"I won't forget."

"And we're running it fine, but you're still the boss. You say the word, we step aside."

I shook my head firmly. "You're family. You run it. I trust you."

"Yeah, well. Trust goes both ways." He squeezed my shoulder. "We've got your back. Always."

LATER, WHEN EXHAUSTION PULLED AT ME, Kieran appeared at my side. "Ready to go home?"

Which one? I answered with a slight smile.

"Ours. The one with the bed I plan to keep you in for at least twelve hours."

Heat rose to my face, but I nodded.

Saying goodbye took time. Sable made me promise to visit properly—"for tea, not just emergencies." Trouble yipped agreement.

"Stay safe," Jex rumbled. "Come back soon."

Rhett hugged me hard. "You're family. Remember that. No matter what happens up at that castle, you're ours."

"Always."

Serenya had somehow convinced Rhett to explain his entire alchemical process and was taking notes. She waved absently as we left. "Don't do anything I wouldn't do! Which gives you lots of options!"

Then we were outside, in the cool night air, the sounds of my bar fading behind us.

"That was..." Kieran started.

"Perfect. Chaotic and loud and perfect."

"Your family's as exhausting as mine."

"That's why they'll get along."

We climbed into the carriage. I leaned against him as we started moving, watching the Divide fade into the distance.

Two homes. Two families. Two worlds becoming one.

"Tired?" Kieran asked.

"Very. But good tired."

"Let's get you home. Our home."

I looked up at him. *"I am home. Wherever you are."*

His arms tightened around me. *"Forever."*

"Forever."

*Thank you so much for reading **A Silence of Shadows**. I*

can't express just how much I love Merrit & Kieran along with their ragtag bunch of friends.

If you would love to see a special extended epilogue, turn the page! I hope you enjoy it!

BONUS SCENE

Dear Reader,

I hope you enjoyed ***A Silence of Shadows***. Merrit & Kieran have a very special place in my heart, and I am absolutely ecstatic for you to read more about them.

I have an extra special extended epilogue for you as a thank you for reading. All you have to do is follow the link below, sign up for my newsletter, and you'll get an email giving you access!

SIGN UP HERE:
https://geni.us/asos-bonus

BOOKS BY ANNIE ANDERSON

WHISPERBOUND

A Silence of Shadows

SEVERED FLAMES

Ruined Wings

Stolen Embers

Broken Fates

IMMORTAL VICES & VIRTUES

HER MONSTROUS MATES

Bury Me

SHADOW SHIFTER BONDS

Shadow Me

ALL HALLOWS' EVE

Heal Me

THE ARCANE SOULS WORLD

GRAVE TALKER SERIES

Dead to Me

Dead & Gone

Dead Calm

Dead Shift

Dead Ahead

Dead Wrong

Dead & Buried

SOUL READER SERIES

Night Watch

Death Watch

Grave Watch

THE WRONG WITCH SERIES

Spells & Slip-ups

Magic & Mayhem

Errors & Exorcisms

THE LOST WITCH SERIES

Curses & Chaos

Hexes & Hijinx

THE ETHEREAL WORLD

ROGUE ETHEREAL SERIES

Woman of Blood & Bone

Daughter of Souls & Silence

Lady of Madness & Moonlight

Sister of Embers & Echoes

Priestess of Storms & Stone

Queen of Fate & Fire

PHOENIX RISING SERIES

(Formerly the Ashes to Ashes Series)

Flame Kissed

Death Kissed

Fate Kissed

Shade Kissed

Sight Kissed

To stay up to date on all things Annie Anderson, get exclusive access to ARCs and giveaways, and be a member of a fun, positive, drama-free space, join The Legion!

facebook.com/groups/ThePhoenixLegion

Acknowledgments

A huge, honking thank you to Shawn, Barb, Jade, and Angela. Thanks for the late-night calls, the endurance of my whining, the incessant plotting sessions, the food runs... (*looking at you, Shawn.*)

Every single one of you rock and I couldn't have done it without you.

ABOUT THE AUTHOR

 Annie Anderson is the author of the international best-selling Rogue Ethereal series. A United States Air Force veteran, Annie pens fast-paced Paranormal Romance & Romantasy novels filled with strong, snarky heroines and a boatload of magic. When she takes a break from writing, she can be found binge-watching The Magicians, flirting with her husband, wrangling children, or bribing her cantankerous dog to go on a walk.

To find out more about Annie and her books, visit www.annieande.com

facebook.com/AuthorAnnieAnderson

instagram.com/AnnieAnde

amazon.com/author/annieande

bookbub.com/authors/annie-anderson

goodreads.com/AnnieAnde

pinterest.com/annieande

tiktok.com/@authorannieanderson

www.ingramcontent.com/pod-product-compliance
Lightning Source LLC
Chambersburg PA
CBHW021329310726
48971CB00001B/41